Catch Me
If You Can

Catch Me
If You Can

Donna
Kauffman

BRAVA

KENSINGTON PUBLISHING CORP.
http://www.kensingtonbooks.com

BRAVA BOOKS are published by

Kensington Publishing Corp.
850 Third Avenue
New York, NY 10022

ISBN 0-7582-0587-2

First Kensington Trade Paperback Printing: July 2004
10 9 8 7 6 5 4 3 2 1

Printed in the United States of America

*This book is dedicated to everyone who asked
for another Scotland story.
It was my pleasure!*

*And to Mark,
Forever and always,
the quest continues . . .*

Acknowledgments

It takes a village to write a book, and I would like to take a moment to thank my own villagers for being so generous with their help and support. To the Ramsay family of Bamff Castle, your kind hospitality and historic home fascinated me. And although I was researching a different project at the time, I knew Bamff would someday inspire a new story. (Something about sleeping in a four-hundred-year-old bed, perhaps!) Thank you for your patience and taking the time to answer my endless questions.

And to the residents of Huntly, you all are the most friendly and welcoming group of people I've had the pleasure of meeting. It was an unscheduled visit that turned out to be a highlight of that journey. My undying gratitude for making me feel so at home and for also being an inspiration. I only wish I could have stayed longer.

To my Celtic Connection, thank you for the wealth of information on pagan religions. Though oftentimes conflicting and confusing, the history of the Druids and Picts is a fascinating one, and I beg forgiveness now for any mistakes made or artistic license taken.

And while I'm at it, my apologies to the Sinclair, Ramsay, and Morgan clan members, as I've definitely taken artistic license with your history. But I was having so much fun! I hope the enjoyment of the story outweighs any outrage for the liberties I've taken.

Chapter 1

When he looked around the room, what he remembered most were the beatings. Maybe it was the fatigue. Maybe it was the confusion still messing with his head.

Taggart Morgan II leaned back in the well-worn leather chair and rubbed his tired eyes, closing them against the view of his father's home office. The floor-to-ceiling shelves stocked with leather-bound law books, the thick, polished oak desk with its always precisely arranged blotter, letter opener and Cross pen set. The hard wooden chair he'd been made to sit in while he received the daily lecture that always preceded the sound of his father's thin leather belt, slipping through the loops of his pants. He could hear his voice as clearly now as he had seventeen years before.

I went to law school, passed the bar, fought my way up. I showed this town what a Morgan is made of! Just because we're descended from trash doesn't mean we have to be trash. You'll show them, too, if I have to beat the smart into you.

CRACK!

When a Morgan wants something, he grabs it. That's the mark I'm making here. And that's the mark I'll make on you, if I have to whip it into you. I'll accept nothing less from you. You come home with that class election won and your head held high for all to see, or you'll pray to God you'd listened for once in your godforsaken, pansy-ass life. Ands if the belt doesn't do the trick, perhaps this will leave an impression.

Tag flinched away from the memory of his father's palm, connecting so hard to the side of his head, he'd gone sprawling to the floor. But by letting one memory slip through, it was as though he'd unleashed the demons of hell. His father's violent tirades echoed inside his head, and around the room itself, as clearly as if the man himself were here and striding up and down in front of this very desk. One after the other, the memories assaulted him, moments of his life he'd long since packed away, suffocated by sheer will and determination. And yet it took only the breath of a single memory to resuscitate each and every one to their full, fire-breathing glory.

How many judges are there in Marshall County? Two. And your old man is one of them. And now my oldest son is telling me he wants to make a living digging in the goddamn dirt? I'm paying for your college education and I'll decide where you go and what you major in.

SMACK!

Obviously you're more of a fucking idiot than I thought if this is the best life plan you can muster.

Tag absently lifted his hand to his face, as if he could still feel the imprint of the back of his father's hand, the blood trickling down where the heavy school ring he always wore had split open his cheek.

Jesus fucking Christ, you can't even manage to be half the man I am! If I hadn't walked you through life, you'd be an even bigger pussy than you already are. But fine. Embarrass me, embarrass the town, embarrass the family. Your mother is probably looking down from the heavens right now, crying over the waste of space you're taking up. So you want to forge your own path, well today is the day you're going to begin it. When you walk out that office door, you'd better damn sight keep on walking. Don't pass go, don't collect your things, and don't let the door hit your sorry ass on the way out.

Tag could still see the veins bulging in his father's forehead, the alarming red flush that enflamed his face and neck, as he ordered his firstborn to leave home with nothing but the clothes on his back. As if he were the one making the bigger sacrifice.

And you better damn well never look back. From this moment forward, I have only three sons. You are dead to me.

Eyes squeezed shut, Tag's heart pounded just as it had back then. His hands shook as he fisted them, humiliation and blinding fury pulsing through him as cleanly as if it had just happened all over again. And he hated himself for the weakness, for allowing his past to punish him all over again. He fought back instinctively, much as he had back then and for years afterward. With rigid and unswerving diligence, he'd buried his reaction, his emotions. Back then, it was because he'd known that any reaction, any at all, would only make his father go harder on him. And now . . . because there was no one left to lash out at but himself.

He abruptly shoved himself away from the desk. Breathing heavily, it took every last shred of his control to keep from sweeping his arm across the desk, sending every perfectly placed article flying onto the carefully chosen antique woven rug. Just as it had taken every ounce of the man he was becoming to walk calmly through that door seventeen years ago, shoulders square, gaze firmly forward.

Because from the moment he'd claimed his emancipation, terrified, relieved, exhilarated, and heartbroken, his father had been dead to him, too.

Tag braced his hands on the edge of the desk, dipping his chin, willing his heart rate to slow as he shut out the words, shut out the past, going instead to that place deeper inside himself, a place no one ever penetrated. The physical scars had healed many years ago. And until this moment, he'd have sworn the emotional ones had, too. Out of sight, out of mind. That had been his motto when he'd left Rogues Hollow. And, until he'd been summoned back upon learning of his father's death, it had worked quite well for him.

Dead to me.

"Yeah, well, now it's just official," he muttered. "For both of us." He straightened slowly, grunting at the muscles that had stiffened from sitting hunched over the desk. Midnight had long since come and gone. He'd lost track of time, as he often did when something of interest caught his attention. His single-minded focus and tenacity were a boon in his chosen field of anthropology. Tonight? He wasn't so sure. He stared down at the sheaf of material his father's close friend, Mick Templeton, had dropped off earlier today in a surprising visit.

Mick had been a newly minted councilman the last time Tag had seen him. But he'd risen through the ranks since then to become mayor, a position he'd held close to ten years now. Along with that position had come a friendship with Justice Taggart Morgan Sr. And given the nature of the bombshell Mick had dropped on him today, it was a friendship that was a great deal closer than the surface social contacts his father lived to cultivate and loved to parade in front of everyone.

According to Mick, no one else in Highland Springs, or all of Marshall County for that matter, had known about this. Not Taggart's lawyers, not his associates, or his other acquaintances. He'd even hidden the funds he'd used to finance the thing under a dummy corporation so Frances York, his longtime accountant and reigning town busybody, didn't know. That alone was a feat he could hardly believe. But even more surprising, given the nature of the news, was that the Ramsay and Sinclair families, who, along with the Morgans, owned the valley property known as Rogues Hollow, were also unaware of Taggart's late-in-life acquisition.

He'd only confided in Mick.

And now, by his father's specific request, his oldest son, Tag.

Who still could not fathom what sort of bizarre mind-fuck his father hoped to achieve with the final arrangements he'd made. And now this bullshit. It had been almost a month ago, just a few days past Christmas, since the formal reading of the will. The day their father's lawyer had very calmly announced that Taggart James Morgan, Sr. had left the entire Morgan share of Rogues Hollow, and every scrap of the estate that went with it, to his oldest son and heir. Tag could recall with stunning clarity how the news had literally sucked the breath out of everyone in the room.

He didn't know exactly what he'd been expecting, but probably something along the lines of a blistering lecture, followed by the grand announcement that their father had left the entire family heritage to the Sinclairs or Ramsays. A final harsh reality check that was supposed to teach them all something. Taggart Sr. would love nothing more than delivering a final set down. But Tag had known his father would never let the Morgan land escape Morgan ownership. He supposed he'd expected that the property would have gone to all four of them.

Not that any of them had wanted the burden. All three of his brothers had left under somewhat similar circumstances. None had had any contact with their father since leaving this house. He'd told himself the day of the reading that if there was one positive in all this, it was that his younger brothers, Austin, Burke, and Jace, wouldn't have to deal with any of it. They wouldn't have to worry about what to do with their father's personal effects, how to handle matters pertaining to the estate. Nor would they bear the burden of deciding what to do with a legacy that had been in Morgan hands for almost three hundred years. A legacy that should instill pride and a strong sense of stewardship in the last remaining Morgans, but because of one man, instead held only heartache and the echoes of memories better left forgotten.

Nope. That thrill belonged to him and him alone.

And to think that day he'd assumed it couldn't get any worse.

Apparently time away from the old man had dulled his instinct for self-preservation. Years spent living on dig sites, subsisting off of dried beef, overripe fruit, and water that most people wouldn't bathe in, much less drink, hadn't honed those skills a tenth of the percentage that one hour sitting in this well-appointed room would have. He could picture the look on his father's face, that combination of smug disgust he so often wore, as he pointed out that very fact to his eldest son.

Tag blocked that mental image as he stretched and shook the stiffness from his arms and legs. He carefully avoided looking down at the last piece of evidence that had come with this latest bombshell. The polished cherrywood box Mick had dropped off, complete with tarnished skeleton key sticking out of the lock. Taunting him, begging him to turn it, to open the Pandora's box that was his father's secret other life. One quick twist, and he could have the answers to the fresh raft of questions that had haunted him since Mick had left hours before. Or, worse perhaps, he'd only end up with more questions.

He had opened the accompanying leather-bound portfolio that held all the legal papers pertaining to his father's startling late-in-life acquisition. A certain piece of property. In Scotland. But not just any property. His father owned a piece of Morgan heritage. The very heritage he'd spent his whole life trying to live down. The castle Ballantrae, and all that went with it. Including, apparently, a land manager, farm tenants, a slew of assorted sheep, and a huge pile of debt.

What the papers didn't explain was why in the hell his father would purchase, much less own and manage, the very castle and surrounding tenant-leased land that his much-scourged ancestor, Teague Morgan, along with his thieving cohorts, Dougal Ramsay and Iain Sinclair, had run from in the dark of the night three centuries earlier. Their ill-gotten gains strapped to their mounts as they headed hell bent for the coast and a neck-saving passage to the colonies.

Mick said all the business details were in the leather portfolio. But all the personal details of his relationship with the tenants and villagers in general, and apparently one woman in particular, lay inside the cherrywood box. No one on this side of the ocean had been privy to that part of his life. Not even Mick.

Well, as far as Tag was concerned, it could stay private. Turning his back on the box, and the questionable treasure it held, he paced the length of the carpet, then turned suddenly and kicked the wooden chair across the room, where it clattered against the bookshelf, knocking loose several carefully shelved tomes. *Fuck.* He didn't want to know. Didn't want to give a shit. What he wanted was to be on the next plane headed south of the border. Back to the current dig, and the life he'd made for himself. Far, far away from the one he'd been born to.

And yet the curiosity was eating him alive. Blame it on his nature, on his training, his very occupation. Had it been related to anyone other than his father, he'd have been inside that box within minutes of learning of its existence. But it *was* his father. And therefore nothing could be as it seemed. Nothing was ever that simple with Taggart Sr.

And he refused to be drawn in.

All he had to do to make it go away was sign one of the sets of papers on the desk. He could either sign away his rights to the property, or set up a trust with his father's estate that would keep funneling money overseas. The lawyers, accountants, and land agents could take it from there. He would never have to give the matter another thought. Why his father hadn't made this decision, he had no idea. He'd certainly had the time. He'd known he was dying. Which meant he'd very specifically put this decision in Tag's hands. Another reason not to open that box.

He stared at the portfolio. A few quick scratches with his father's beloved Cross pen and he could be one giant step closer to leaving this legal nightmare behind. Escaping for good the bucolic winter wonderland that was Rogues Hollow, all tucked up against the Blue Ridge mountains, smugly out of step with the ebb and flow of urban life.

A few signatures on the dotted line, and he could be booking passage back to a distant land even more out of pace with the world. Back to the sweaty, torpid, bug-infested rainforests of the Yucatan. Back to mosquito netting and questionable drinking water. Back to piecing together the lives of families who had existed thousands of years ago.

And mercifully escaping piecing together any more of his own.

He heard the door from the garage open and had crossed the room and opened the office door before he realized his brother Jace wasn't alone. The couple tumbled in the door, all pink cheeks and dusted with snow. Although he imagined with the heat sparking between the two, they could have rolled naked in the stuff and been perfectly comfortable. Given what he'd witnessed the past couple of weeks, he wouldn't be surprised if they already had.

Jace tugged Suzanna up against him, all stupid grin and oversized libido, not caring in the least who noticed. "Hey, T.J.," he said, when he noticed his brother standing there.

Tag wished he could remember a time in his life when he'd felt like that. "Sorry," he said, moving to duck back into the study and leave them their privacy.

"No problem. What in the hell are you still doing up anyway?" Jace looked at the grandfather clock that graced the long hallway connecting garage and office to the main rooms of the house. "It's almost two."

"I could ask the same of you," Tag said, trying to match a smile to the wry tone. He tipped his chin. "Evening, Zanna."

The pink in her cheeks deepened a bit, but her eyes flashed with fun. "Morning is more like it. And please forgive your baby brother. We had a flat tire about down past Ramsay's pond. The snow was blowing around too much to see to fix it. So we pushed it off the road and hiked our way back in."

Tag frowned. Zan and Jace had both grown up in the Hollow, so they both well knew the dangers of the winters here. "You should have called. I'd have come to get you."

"I guess we thought you'd be sleeping," Jace said, brushing off Zanna's coat, then his own.

"So wake me up. It's not like I have to be in the office at nine."

"Hey," Jace shot back good-naturedly. "If that's a dig at me, my meeting with Mr. Wayne and the athletic director isn't until eleven." He peeled his coat off. "Not all of us have the luxury of crawling around in the jungle for a living, Tarzan."

"Jace," Zan gently scolded. "He's just worried about you." She turned to Tag. "We're sorry if we kept you up waiting, or worrying."

To be honest, he'd forgotten all about Jace being out. But then he wasn't used to having to keep track of anyone but himself. Nor did he intend to start now. "I wasn't. I was just . . . looking over some things."

Jace glanced up at his brother as he started helping Zan off with her coat. Tag must not have been as adept at masking his feelings as he'd thought, because Jace frowned and said, "What's up? Frances said something about Templeton paying a visit out here today, but she didn't know what it was about." He glanced at Zan and grinned. "Which I know comes as a shock to us all."

She just laughed. "Yeah, Mom's status as Grand Poobah of the Grapevine is in definite jeopardy."

If they only knew, Tag couldn't help but think, wondering what Zan's mom, aka the town busybody, would think when she found out the man whose books she'd been doing for the past quarter century had kept such a major investment from her.

Jace laughed with Zan, then turned back to Tag. "Seeing

as Mack is the mayor and a friend of Dad's, I figured it was just a formal visit to pay his respects or something." His smile faded as he caught Tag's expression. "I'm guessing I was wrong."

Zanna tugged her coat back on. "Listen, I should head home. You two obviously need to talk. Or sleep and then talk. I can just take the old pickup and bring it back over tomorrow if that's okay."

Zanna's mother had been the accountant for all three Hollow families over the years, but most recently for Taggart Sr. and Mack Ramsay, as the elder Sinclairs now spent most of their time in Florida. She'd moved herself and her infant daughter to a small cabin on Ramsay property after her husband died, had raised Zan there, staying on alone after her daughter went off to college. Zan had only recently moved back to Marshall County, reuniting with her high school flame, Jace, on her way in, in fact.

Frances had moved closer to town when old man Ramsay had retired and moved south, leaving his share of the Hollow to his only son, Mack, the current town sheriff. And now mother and daughter were joining forces and opening up an accounting firm in town, hoping to cater to the small but steady influx of new business as the county took baby steps toward new growth. Zan was staying at her mother's for the time being, but Tag had an idea that she and Jace might be looking at some joint property before too long.

Which brought him back to some decisions he'd made in the wee midnight hours. "Don't head out in this mess, Zan," he told her. "I do need to talk to you," he said to Jace, "but it can wait until morning. Or later this morning at any rate. Can you give me say, thirty minutes before heading in to meet with Wayne?"

"No problem. You sure you don't want to talk now?"

"Positive." The dull throb behind his eyes had grown more insistent. He needed sleep and a clear head before broaching Jace with his proposal. "'Night."

" 'Night," they both echoed.

Tag pulled the office door shut as he walked past, not bothering to lock it, much less tuck away the cherrywood box that still sat on his desk. Jace was going to be rolling in the sheets with Zan for what was left of the night. It was high season for yachting in the tropics, so Burke had already headed back to crew his next island charter tour. And Austin was on a cover shoot in Milan, showing his favorite haunts to his new love, Delilah Hudson.

Tag's mouth quirked. Jace going all moony-eyed was one thing. He'd always had a soft spot for Zanna York and it was no big surprise to anyone that the two of them had picked up where they left off, despite their long separation. But he still couldn't get over Austin plunging headlong off the love pier right after him. Tag had already decided to make a point of meeting up with them somewhere so he could get a look at the woman who'd brought down the man who made his living taking pictures of half-naked cover models.

But even if all three of his brothers had still been there, he needn't have worried they'd go nosing about. Not in the office. Never there.

Surprisingly, it hadn't been as uncomfortable being home again. In general, anyway. It was rare they were all under the same roof, but they'd never once been together under this one since he'd left. In fact, all of them had been gone the moment they were of age too, and in some cases before. Not one of them had ever looked back. They kept in touch with each other, but not with their past.

There had been a tacit, unspoken agreement the moment they'd all finally made it in a month ago, to not discuss the harsher aspects of their childhood. None of them wanted to revisit that horror. But it had been a welcome surprise when they'd all sat around the kitchen table and dredged up any number of good times they'd spent, growing up in the Hollow. Memories of times shared as brothers, not as the sons of Taggart Morgan, Sr. Laughter had been rare under the Morgan roof, but it hadn't been nonexistent. Tag remembered wondering how long it had been since that sound had echoed inside these walls.

They'd talked fondly of swimming, fishing, and ice-skating on old man Ramsay's pond, once the center of their social universe. Sighed in post-adolescent harmony about parking up on Black Willow Ridge with the girl of the moment. Pointed fingers of blame over who had stolen the most eggs from Mrs. Sinclair's chicken house when they'd camped out. And laughed over the pranks they'd pulled on each other, and their Hollow "cousin" Mack.

They didn't talk about the lectures. The whippings. The whispers in town when they showed up at school with another unexplained bruise or welt. Of what it had felt like, being constantly berated for never measuring up to their father's rigid expectations. Being told time and again what a disappointment they were. And never once having their dreams listened to, much less respected or treated as worthy goals.

No, Tag didn't have to worry about locking the office door. No Morgan son went into that room unless it was absolutely necessary. He'd done so tonight, sat at that desk, propped his feet up on the polished surface, as a final act of defiance. It was his office now, after all.

Yet he knew all he'd get for it would be a sleepless night, filled with memories that were a lot fresher than he'd believed possible. Some scars, he realized as he climbed the wide wooden stairs to his bedroom, never did heal.

Chapter 2

Sleep hadn't come easy, when it had come at all. Something Jace and Zan didn't seem to have any problem doing. Coming, that is.

Grumpy and feeling surprisingly resentful, Tag washed down three aspirin with his morning coffee. Sex had been the last thing on his mind of late. But it had been rather hard to ignore the contrast between Jace's rather active sex life and the wasteland that was his own social life.

Ordinarily this didn't bother him. He liked sex as much as the next guy, but he'd gotten used to putting his needs aside. Which was handy considering his prospects for sex were usually limited to college coeds volunteering on a dig, or women from whatever neighboring village was nearby. And considering the locales of most of his recent digs, this was generally not a teeming metropolis. Or even a one-mule town. Tribal came closest to describing the usual local social scene.

And, as he was too old for the coed crowd, that left the occasional seasoned colleague who was up for a no-strings roll in the hammock. And even then he had to be careful. Passions generally heated up and cooled way down long before the dig was over. Which could make life uncomfortable for everyone. Tag preferred things to go as smoothly as possible. Day-to-day life generally being enough of a challenge for him.

He massaged his closed eyes, hoping the headache he'd woken up with would fade quickly. Normally he dropped off to sleep the instant his head hit the pillow and woke up refreshed and ready, whether he'd slept for one hour or ten. Apparently dig survival training didn't hold up under his childhood roof. At least his father had long since converted their old bedrooms to guest rooms, he thought. It could have been worse. He could have had to stare at the remnants of his childhood as he lay, gritty-eyed and awake, listening to the muffled giggles and long, satisfied groans coming from across the hall.

Actually, he should thank his baby brother for the diversion. Thinking about sex, even the sore lack of it, had kept his thoughts from veering back to this most recent surprise. Taking another sip of the bitter coffee, Tag reminded himself, as he had most every morning since Austin had taken off, taking his mad coffee-making skills with him, that though he wasn't any better making a decent pot with a top-of-the-line machine rather than the tin pot they used in camp, he didn't have to drink it black.

He was pouring in milk and adding way too much sugar, wondering how to broach his discussion with Jace, when the object of his ruminations trudged into the kitchen, bleary-eyed and tumble-haired, scratching his bare chest.

"Morning," Jace grunted, reaching blindly into the cupboard over the sink.

"Coffee's strong, but hot," Tag told him.

"Bless you and everyone that looks like you."

Tag smiled a little. "You get no sympathy from me. I didn't get any sleep either, only I didn't get the side benefits."

Jace pulled a mug down, smiling now despite the dark circles beneath his eyes. "Well, you have me there."

Though the bedrooms had changed and some of the furnishings in the main rooms had been updated, the kitchen was still pretty much the same as it had been when they were young. Same woodblock countertops, same glass-front cabinets. The dishwasher was new, as was the fridge, but the old gas stove was the same one Tag had warmed soup on every day after school. And the round pedestal table was the same one he and his brothers had sat at every evening doing homework. Praying none of them would be summoned.

Some kids were afraid of being sent to the principal's office. Not the Morgan boys. They knew the long walk of dread down the school hallway was nothing compared to the terror a person could feel in the few short steps it took to get from the kitchen to their father's office.

"So," Tag said, gladly shoving those memories away as Jace took a seat and reached for the sugar, "you and Zanna are getting serious pretty quickly."

Jace shrugged. "I guess it looks that way. Doesn't feel that way."

Tag raised his eyebrows in surprise. "Meaning?"

Jace snatched Tag's spoon and used it to stir his sugar. "I don't know if I can explain it. It is serious. But it doesn't feel rushed or too quick. It's not like we could just pick up where we left off after high school or anything. A lot has happened over the intervening years. To both of us. But it wasn't time wasted. And now this feels perfectly right for us. I guess we don't want to waste any more time. It took us this long to figure things out." He shrugged again. "So why wait, you know?"

Tag understood what his brother was saying, even though he couldn't fathom feeling that way himself. "Have you made any long-range plans?"

"You mean like marriage plans?" Jace smiled, laughed a little. "Nothing specific. Not yet. We're in no rush. Although, we, uh, we are going to look for a place in town. Together," he added unnecessarily.

Tag glanced up now, his mouth quirking. "My baby brother, shacking up? And you being the good Morgan boy. What will the townfolk say?"

"I haven't been back that long, but the town doesn't seem

like it's exactly remained stuck in a time warp all these years."

"Wouldn't have surprised me," Tag said dryly. "How's Frances feel about this?"

"You know Zan's mom. Hopeless romantic. She's very happy we're together. Pushing for a wedding, of course. And it's likely that's where we'll end up, but not right yet. We might raise a few eyebrows around town, but it won't cost me the teaching position, if that's what you're worried about." He took a sip, noted Tag's expression and smiled. "What's so funny? Hell, if Austin can get all moony-faced over a woman, me thinking about getting married shouldn't shock anybody. Now, *you* going ass over heartstrings? *That* would be headline news."

Tag took the teasing in stride. Jace was right after all. He'd dated some through school—okay, a lot—but he'd kept his heart to himself, and that pattern hadn't changed much over the years. Austin was the one who provoked and taunted, always looking for trouble. Girls were drawn to his bad-boy image. Burke was blessed with a glib tongue and quick wit. He could smooth talk his way out of any scrape . . . and into any girl's pants. Jace had been the quiet one, the perfect student with perfect grades, perfect kid, careful to draw only positive attention. Tag hadn't been any of those things.

Well, he'd gotten into his fair share of scrapes, but mostly he had just tried to be normal, because he'd felt anything but. He'd just turned eight when his mother died, old enough to be excruciatingly aware that being motherless was not normal. He remembered her as being soft and reserved, bowing to her husband in most things. She'd been sick as far back as Tag could remember, so it was hard to tell how she might have been if she'd been healthy. But that hadn't lessened the grief that had walloped her sons when she'd passed away. If Taggart Sr. had grieved, he'd done it in private, sending an unmistakable signal to his young sons that they, too, were to deal with their loss privately. And that included not involving their father. Which left Tag to help his younger brothers through a task he'd been woefully unprepared to take on.

Tag had dealt with his own grief by not getting too close to anyone outside his siblings, lest they find out the normal kid with the normal looks, normal grades, and normal friends felt anything but normal on the inside. Or that his home life was anything other than the picture of success and stability their father worked so very hard to portray. It was hard enough living up to his father's endless expectations without inviting new ones from outside influences.

"I guess you have a point there," Tag said, not particularly upset by it. He enjoyed companionship, but he'd generally been so busy that he'd never dwelled on the lack of it in any sort of continuing fashion in his life. He supposed he'd gotten good at being alone. He'd started young enough. "I was just trying to imagine what Dad's reaction would have been to your coed housing plan," Tag teased.

"Jesus, I know," Jace said, still turning a bit pale, despite knowing it was a battle he'd never have to wage. "I thank God every day I don't have to deal with that. Although, truth be told, I'm not sure I would have considered the offer here if he were still alive."

"I know," Tag said. In public, around townspeople, they'd been respectful of their father's passing, accepting the stream of condolences with sincere thanks. But here, alone with each other, they didn't have to pretend. It had been a profound relief to them all.

"I've wanted to come back to the rest of it, though. I feel like I'd run long enough. Like it was time to come back." Jace looked across the table at Tag, his expression earnest. "You know, I was never sure how I'd feel with him gone. If I'd regret . . . I don't know, not trying to get to know him. As an adult."

Tag knew that none of his brothers had made contact with their father since leaving home. Nor had their father ever contacted any of them. "Do you?"

Jace shook his head. "I keep waiting to feel guilty about it. Hasn't happened yet. What about you?"

Tag shook his head. His emotions might be a raw jumble, but he knew better than to dwell on things he couldn't change.

They both sipped their coffee in silence for a few moments, then Jace said, "You know, Frances says Dad changed a lot, toward the end."

So, Tag thought, *Jace was wrestling with it a bit more than he'd let on.* "Knowing you're dying can make a person rethink a few things I guess," Tag said, with no particular inflection to his tone. "Nine months gives a person a long time to sort things out."

Jace nodded. "Yeah, I suppose it would. Although, I don't know, the man I remember . . . well, I figured he'd stare even death in the face without flinching. Berating it for daring to take him before he was ready."

Tag studied his younger brother. "Does it bother you? That he might have, I don't know, mellowed or something?"

Jace held his gaze easily. "No. Although I have to admit I'm curious about it. I try to picture it, imagine him more . . . laid back, if you want to call it that." His mouth curved at one corner. "Can't seem to picture it."

Tag had wondered about that, too, during those long hours in the office last night. Zan's mother wasn't the only one talking about how Taggart Sr. had been a changed man. Mick had mentioned it, too, though briefly. Tag knew his father's friend had wanted, maybe even needed, to talk about it. Stunned by Mick's initial news, Tag hadn't exactly been open to that kind of conversation. Apparently whatever changes his father had made didn't include reaching out to his only family before he died. Tag supposed he shouldn't care, seeing as that indifference had always gone both ways. Mercifully, after a few awkward attempts, Mick had let the conversation drop and taken off. And Tag had left the cherrywood chest unopened.

"But I think this change, or maybe the start of it, goes back farther than the cancer diagnosis," Jace was saying, pulling Tag from his thoughts. "Something happened a few years ago, though I'm not sure what. Zan's mom didn't know." He smiled a little. "Which means no one knows."

A few years ago. That would have been right around the time the land in Scotland had been deeded to him. If what Jace said was true, Tag doubted it was a coincidence. And he hated to admit it, but the puzzle provoked him. After all, that's what he made his living doing, solving the puzzles of the past. His job was to put the pieces together from the clues people left behind after they'd gone. He figured out how people lived, why they'd chosen to live where they did, the way they did, how they'd died, what they'd left behind. And why. That he had a deep-seated need to solve these puzzles didn't surprise him. He hardly needed a degree in psychology to figure that one out.

But his desire was based on the need to solve these puzzles for others, for the sake of a greater understanding of humanity in general. Yes, his childhood had sucked, and yes, his father hadn't been a very nice man. But Tag had never felt compelled to dig any deeper than that. His father was who he was. Tag counted himself fortunate he'd gone on to discover something in life that was both rewarding and enjoyable. Despite flirting briefly with a major in Celtic history, his ancestral past, much less his father's recent one, had never been a puzzle begging to be solved. And Tag didn't want it to become one now.

And, if it was possible, he resented his father that much more for even momentarily making him feel otherwise.

"I have a proposition for you," Tag said abruptly. Time to move forward. "And Zanna, too, I suppose, since it will affect her as well."

Other than leaning his chair back on two legs, Jace didn't react to the sudden change in topic. They'd all become adept at rolling with the punches at a very early age, with nary an outward sign of reaction. "Is this what you wanted to talk to me about last night?"

Tag nodded. "I've been going over all of the papers, trying to figure out the best way to settle the estate." He rested his weight on his elbows, cradling his mug. "You're just starting out here in town, teaching P.E., coaching the high school basketball team."

"We hope. Remember, the meeting isn't till later today."

Tag waved his hand. "Formality. They're lucky to have you and they know it. With your college playing history and the fact that you're a hometown boy? You're a shoo-in."

Jace didn't bother to argue the point. "Go on."

"Zan is also starting up the business with her mom, so you two have a lot going on, but it's all just beginning." Tag took a steadying breath, not realizing until just then how much he hoped Jace would agree with this plan he'd worked out. He might not have a personal desire to stay connected to this place, but he did respect the history attached to it. And he'd like to think that the four young men who'd had a place in it, no matter how brief, had to count for something, too. "So, I happen to own this big old house with absolutely no intentions of living in it." He rubbed his thumbs on the mug, uncomfortable with the flash of sentimentality, unwilling to label it as such. He was merely being practical.

Jace's eyes widened. "You want me and Zan to move in? Here?" He blew out a sigh, then rocked his chair forward so the legs hit the floor with a loud thump. "I don't know, T.J.," he said, using the nickname Tag heard so rarely, as only his brothers and those in Highland Springs used it. Kept things less confusing growing up, with him and his father having the same name. Still, it felt kind of nice hearing it again.

Jace looked around the room, and Tag wondered what memories it held for him. He'd already been gone by the time Jace was a teenager.

"It's been hard enough bunking out here the past couple of weeks. I'm not sure—"

"The thing is," Tag broke in, wanting—no, needing—to get this said. "I don't want to sell it. Not because I'm attached to it, but because our ancestors are. This house, well, this land anyway, along with our third of the Hollow property, is a legacy to all the Morgans before us."

"Such as they were," Jace said with a wry smile.

Tag matched his brother's expression. "Yes, well, wastrels and bastards though some of them may have been, it's the unbroken chain I'm most interested in keeping intact." He leaned forward. "I dig up history for a living. And while I'm in no hurry to relive my own, I'm not in any rush to sell it off, either." He pushed on, not letting Jace speak. "I could give a shit about the house. Raze it to the ground if you want, build a new one, for the two of you. In fact, maybe that's exactly what you should do. Say what you will about the old man, but he knew how to make money. And as I have no need for it, you might as well use it to start over here." He thought briefly about the documents waiting for his signature, the ones that could continue funneling some of that private stash overseas. If he were so inclined. He didn't want to think about that at the moment. Family came first. The Hollow came second. Everything else was a distant third. A castle and caretaker an ocean away felt pretty distant to him at the moment.

"I don't know, man." Jace gripped his mug, then shoved it away, once again looking around the room. "It's not just the house. The whole property has history. Some of it mine."

"Not all of it bad," Tag pointed out.

He nodded, agreeing. "True. I just . . ."

"You came back home for a reason. Of the four of us, you're the one who wants to make your mark here."

"Nothing is going to change our father's history here," Jace reminded him. "Not in my lifetime anyway. Or the impact he's had on the town, good and bad. I can't wipe that memory clean, from my mind or theirs."

"I didn't expect you to. But maybe you'll set the standard

for the Rogues Hollow Morgans of our generation, and hopefully the next."

"What about you? What do you want?"

"Hell, I don't know. I only know I don't want to be the Morgan that dissolves what three hundred years of previous Morgans fought to preserve." He sighed, shoved his chair back. "I could lease the place, the land, like the Sinclairs have done. But I don't want to do that, either. I don't need that hassle. Neither do you. And somehow it seems worse to let the place sit here and rot. Like we're giving in to the festering wounds of the last thirty-odd years, letting him kill whatever's left, with no hope of resurrection."

Jace looked at him, then suddenly his somber expression split into a bark of laughter. "Jesus, T. Talk about dark despair. I bet you're a howl at parties, too." He downed his coffee, then got up and rinsed his mug out in the sink before turning it upside down on the drain rack. He stayed there, though, hands braced on the counter, his back to his oldest brother. The silence spun out, then he took a deep breath, blew it out in one huff. "I'll need to talk to Zan," he said.

Even with his impassioned plea, the instant punch in the gut, of relief, surprised him. Why did he care so damn much? "Okay. That's good. Great, actually. Thanks." He said it calmly, matter-of-factly. When, in truth, his insides were a jangle of nerves and he was at a loss to explain why.

Jace turned. "When do you need to know?"

"What? Oh. I—I don't know. I guess we'd need to sign some papers over. Talk to a lawyer." He looked at Jace. "This isn't a caretaker offer. If you do this, it will be your name on the deed. If nothing else, it will give you leverage with the bank for a loan if you ever need one, or if Zan does for her business. Dad's pockets were flush, but not bottomless." He didn't glance around the room as Jace had. He didn't have to. Fifty years could pass, a hundred, and he'd be able to picture every last inch of this house. Some more sharply defined than others. "In fact, the more I think about it, the more I think you should rebuild here, from the ground up." He smiled at his youngest brother. "Hell, by the time the two of you get done arguing over wallpaper and carpeting, you'll know for sure if you're meant to stick it out together."

"Very funny." Then Jace shook his head. "But as far as the deed goes, we'll all own it. You can put my name on the power of attorney papers, or whatever the hell, I don't care. But I want the deed in all of our names. It's our heritage, not just mine." He looked up. "Or yours."

Tag held his baby brother's direct gaze with new respect. They were all men now, and despite, or maybe because of their childhood, none of them were afraid to make their voices heard. He stood, stuck out his hand across the table. "Deal. Although we'll have to hunt down Burke and Austin to get their signatures. I'm sure they'll go for it, though."

Jace smiled. "I imagine they have fax machines in Milan. Tracking down Burke will be the harder part of the deal." He rounded the table. "I guess I should break the news to Zan."

"If she doesn't want—"

Jace waved him silent. "She loves the Hollow as much as I do. Growing up on Ramsay's plot makes her, in a way, as much a part of history here as any of us. That's why we both came back here." He grew serious. "You're right, you know. Maybe part of that journey is to right some old wrongs. Put our own stamp on this place." This time when he looked around, it was with an expression of interest, curiosity, a little anticipation . . . and a lot of responsibility.

"You'll do a great job of it," Tag told him, not wanting him to feel it as a burden, knowing he would anyway. "God knows, anything you two do will be an improvement." He pulled Jace into a one-arm hug. "Thanks." He knew he should say more. Wished he could.

"Don't thank me yet," Jace joked. But he hugged him back. "It's the right thing to do. We'll make it right." Then, as neither of them were comfortable with prolonged displays of sentimentality, Jace pushed past his brother into the hall.

He tossed a smile over his shoulder as he headed toward the stairs. "I'm thinking I know just the way to warm Zan up to this idea."

"You might consider starting by bringing her a cup of coffee."

Jace's smile spread to a grin. "We won't be needing any artificial stimulants, thanks. Perfect way to start a Sunday morning if you ask me."

"Heathen."

"Pagan," Jace shot back with an affectionate laugh.

Whereas Jace was every bit the tall, lanky, close-cropped jock he'd always been, Tag knew he was anything but. From the shaggy head of curly hair, to the permanent tan, to the string of teeth and bones he wore woven around his neck, and the tribal tattoos that dotted his body, Tag no more fit in with the fine folks of Marshall County than a Papuan aborigine would. But here, in Rogues Hollow, *he* was the aborigine. Directly descended from highwaymen and thieves, wanderers and settlers. And long before that, the Celts and the Druids. Even sixty-plus years of his father's attempts to force a new history onto the Morgan name couldn't stamp out the core genetics passed down through the ages.

He'd always taken some comfort in that.

Jace took the stairs two at a time, and Tag took additional comfort in the fact that the Morgan future was, for now, in good hands.

His bemused smile faded as he turned back and looked the opposite way down the main hall, to the office door. And, he supposed, that left him to be the keeper of the Morgan past.

Chapter 3

Tag poured himself another cup of coffee, then headed into the office and flipped the key on the cherrywood box before he could think too long on it. This wasn't about digging up the artifacts of his father's life. That would happen as a by-product, he knew. Just as he knew that any attempt to categorize whatever he uncovered in the same careful, deliberate way he would any other excavation would be woefully unsuccessful. He'd simply have to deal with that.

He flipped open the lid and lifted out a small card that lay on top of stacks of letters and other items that were obscured from immediate view. His gaze fell on the handwritten words scrawled across the card, in what he still recognized as his father's hand. With the first words, his body went rigid. This note was intended for him.

You claim you were born to dig. That your mark is to be made uncovering past truths rather than adjudicating new ones. So be it. Here is your chance to uncover a few of your own. Are you man enough for it?

Tag's fingers tightened on the small card, curling the edges in. A taunt from beyond the grave. Now this was more like the man he'd known and lived to forget. *Man enough.* "You mean like leaving cryptic messages to be found after your death? When no one can question them? Or judge you?" *You bastard,* he thought, *so what the hell kind of man does that make you, huh?*

Tag crushed the card in his palm, then tossed it toward the waste can, not bothering to note if it went in or landed on the floor. His hands were on the lid of the box now, and he had every intention of slamming it shut. Serve his father right if he burned the whole damn thing, contents and all. "Man enough, my ass."

So many years later and worlds apart, netherworlds now, his father could still tweak him to instant fury with one carefully worded note. But instead of heaving the trunk, Tag's grip merely tightened on the open lid, as did the bands slowly constricting around his heart. It didn't matter that they hadn't communicated once in all this time. The asshole knew he wouldn't react well to that taunt, would likely do exactly what he was currently contemplating, trash the trunk and its contents, unread.

Which begged the question: what did his father hope to gain by this? Because there was always a morality play, a lesson to be learned, a new reality to be embraced, where his father was concerned. Did he want his son to walk away from whatever this ridiculous clan land baron thing was all about, sight unseen? Hoping to lay one last eternal guilt trip on him? If so, he was going to be sorely disappointed. If Tag hadn't felt guilty once since he'd walked out of here the last time, he wasn't about to start now.

And if he wanted this property to continue getting his financial aid, well, he could have certainly entrusted his friend Mick to handle that for him. Which meant his father wanted him to take on handling this property personally, as he'd done. Of course, Tag could take care of that little bit of business in about two seconds if he wanted to. His gaze drifted to the folder containing the documents. All he had to do was sign on the dotted line, and one Maura Sinclair could claim continued stewardship, using his father's monthly stipend however she saw fit.

Or, she could be out on her ass, the property put up for auction, or whatever the hell one did with a castle he wanted to sell.

On the surface, it would appear his father would want him to do the former, but for all he knew, Taggart Sr. simply hadn't wanted to be the bad guy in this particular business arrangement. Not all that shocking, really. For all that his father had been a son of a bitch to his sons, to the townsfolk and those he was trying to impress, Taggart Morgan, Sr. could be quite the charming statesman. At least, his father had believed that of himself, perhaps had needed to believe it. After all, gaining the respect of everyone who had for so long cast a dark eye on the Morgans preceding him was what he'd spent his whole life chasing after.

Tag and his brothers knew those same people who bowed and scraped before the local judge, privately suspected what really went on back home, where no one was watching. He'd heard the whispers, seen the looks.

He shut that track down, looked down at the box. "So, what was Ballantrae," he murmured. The sentimental purchase of a lonely man, aging alone and suddenly wanting to connect with his roots, or a monstrosity of a white elephant investment that he'd get the last laugh over pawning off on his unsuspecting son?

There was one way to find out.

He fingered the stack of letters, debating on how much more of Pandora's box he wanted revealed. Just sign over the damn money, set up a trust, whatever the hell it took and be done with it. The who, what, where, when, and most especially why of it didn't matter. His conscience would be clear. No one would be out of a job and the castle would remain in Morgan hands. That should satisfy everyone, right? And the hell with whether it was what his father wanted, or if it thwarted his final power play.

Which did nothing to explain why he sat in the chair, and, rather than pick up a pen and slide the folder containing the documents in front of him, he untied the band that held the letters together. They were sorted in order, with the newest being on top. He looked at the postmark, but had already deduced from the postage stamps that the letters had come from Scotland. The handwriting on the envelope was cramped, more a chicken scratch really, so it was with some surprise that he noted the name above the return address. Maura Sinclair. The caretaker. He wondered at that last name. Coincidence? Of course, Scotland was riddled with Sinclairs and Ramsays, and probably a fair share of Morgans. It could very well mean nothing. The top letter was postmarked this past October. Less than three months ago. About six weeks before his father had passed away.

The letter had been opened, so he surmised his father's health had still been decent enough at that point to allow him to read. He didn't want to think about that, hadn't in fact, until now. He didn't want to imagine his father as he must have looked, toward the end. Drawn, pale, wasted away to some degree, as he would have been from the months of chemo he'd gone through. The lawyers had referred to their father's illness and passing in compassionate, sparing, but specific terms. Not one of his sons had asked them to elaborate.

He put that envelope aside, and flipped through the others. There were a dozen or so here, with another packet or two still in the box. On cursory glance through the rest, they appeared to have been sent on an average of once a month, the first one dating back about three years. About a month or two after Mick said he'd bought the property. All of them bore the same cramped script on the outside. It made him wonder about this Maura Sinclair. What the actual involvement was between her and his father. The writing was cramped, but not what he'd term spidery. So . . . was she young? Old? Married, widowed? That sparked another thought. Had this been some kind of long-distance love affair?

He glanced at the handsomely made box. It might explain the elaborate manner in which his father had preserved the letters. Or why he'd saved them at all. As an adult, Tag could understand, if he were given to wanting to, why his father had chosen to grieve his young wife's death in private. It didn't explain why he'd shunted his children's pain onto others, allowing family members from the Ramsays and Sinclairs to cook, clean, even take in the Morgan boys on this night or that, during the months immediately after her death.

One thing Tag had never questioned, however, was his father's devotion to his late wife. In all the years after, his father had never so much as dated seriously, much less remarried. On the one hand, the cynical side of him said his father could simply have enjoyed the added emotional sway that being a widower brought with it. A man so devoted to his long-dead wife definitely played well with the locals. But Tag had been gone a long time, and they'd certainly never spoken of it before that. So what did he really know of it?

Did it bother him, thinking his father had been involved in some kind of grand passion with a woman in another country? No. He didn't care what his father did, or with whom. In general, he didn't believe in pining for things that could never be recovered, but rather living for today, for what treasure might be just around the corner.

His lips quirked. An odd sentiment, he supposed, for a man who immersed himself in the past as a matter of due course. Still, it was a tangible past he studied. That wasn't the same as longing for what could never be.

He fingered the envelopes, and intended to put them aside, look through the remaining items in the box first. Maybe he wouldn't read them at all. Okay, who was he kidding? He was going to skim one or two, at the very least. His curiosity had been officially unleashed. If not about his father's side of this secret life, then about the woman on the other side of it. The one who was still alive and well and living somewhere in Scotland. Was she pining? Had she merely lost her employer, or the love of her life? Did she know about his plans, to leave this burden to his son to decide upon? It had been several months. How was she managing without the money coming in every month?

Jesus. Tag scrubbed a hand over his face, cursing his father to hell. Though he hoped that was now a redundant wish.

Well, there was no turning back now, he might as well admit that much. Screwing his father over was one thing, but on the other hand, he wasn't going to blithely sign away a chunk of money that could be better spent here, by Jace and Zan and their future offspring for all he knew. He needed to understand the bigger picture first. Then he'd sign the papers one way or the other, maybe even send the box and its contents to this Maura Sinclair if he still felt, after going through everything, that she was best served by that decision. If not, he'd leave it to Jace, or toss it away.

His attention returned to the letters. He noted how the earliest letter had been addressed to Mr. Taggart J. Morgan, Sr. As one would to a business associate. The next few had been addressed the same way. But after that, it had been simply Taggart Morgan on the envelopes. And M. Sinclair in the upper left corner. Glancing at the other packets, he noted that held true until the last few letters, when her full name had appeared again. Had she known he was dying? That someone else might be reading her letters?

Tag lifted the oldest packet of letters and leaned back, absently wincing at the creaking sound of the leather chair, a sound he'd always hated. In defense he propped his feet up on the pristine white blotter, crossed his ankles, and turned the stack over, so the first letter she'd written, or the first one he'd kept at any rate, was now on top.

Flipping open the neatly tucked flap, he slid out several sheets of folded writing paper. They bore the same cramped scrawl he'd noted on the envelope. He smoothed out the creases, ignoring the fact that his heart had begun to kick into gear, just like it did on the first day of a new dig. The anticipation of possible discovery, of unearthing the unknown. He was feeling all those things. Only this time another emotion threaded amongst the more familiar ones. Dread.

"Too late now," he murmured, and began to read.

He had no idea how much time passed while he sat in that chair. Hadn't heard Jace or Zan leave, though surely they both had by now. He was completely, irrevocably immersed in the story unfolding in his hands. Or the half of the story that was unfolding. Maura's half.

Maura. She of the quick wit and charming self-deprecation, tossing out bold declarations with unabashed honesty, while exhibiting clear and obvious concern for a man she'd met only via correspondence, but who, according to her, had changed her life. Tag read every word she'd written. And, dozens of letters later, he felt as if he knew her. Like he would definitely recognize her if their paths were ever to cross.

And yet he still couldn't answer any of his previous questions. Her age, her marital status, or even what she looked like. One thing he had learned was that she'd grown up in the castle, apparently raised by her uncle, meaning her last name was apparently no coincidence. But he was unclear on exactly what her role there had been, or what it really was now. She still lived there, obviously, and it was evident that she had a deep and abiding connection to the place, as he supposed someone would who'd lived there all her life and had a family history tied to it as well. But was she a paid caretaker, or was there something more to it, he had no idea. Hell, he still wasn't entirely sure how his father had come to own the castle in the first place.

There had obviously been other correspondence between them before the more personal letters had begun. He'd glanced through the accompanying legal files, but other than what appeared to be progress reports on work being done to the castle, and the contracts themselves, which he hadn't gone over in detail, he really didn't know who had contacted whom initially.

But one thing was clear, and that was that she considered his father to be a savior of sorts and was quite happy with their arrangement. She did talk about the castle itself, but mostly her letters weren't about that, or even herself, so much as her observations of life. Life in Ballantrae. A hard and demanding life for most, that, according to her letters, had been made better by his father's grand beneficence.

Though, for all that, she didn't exactly defer to him. She accorded him respect, but there was clearly a camaraderie between them that went beyond a mere business arrangement. Not a romance, however, at least not that he could discern, but certainly a close friendship of sorts. And as that friendship had blossomed, she'd written with an increasing confidence that surprised him. She spoke quite freely, and felt at ease enough to scold, argue, even tease. This last part flabbergasted him.

Perhaps it was the distance, and the power of the pen, so to speak, that had emboldened her. After all, it was quite a different matter to put your thoughts to paper than it was to speak face-to-face. And, without seeing his father's replies to her letters, he had no idea how he'd reacted. And yet, the relationship had continued, the letters had come in a steady stream. Indicating that his father had, at the very least, not discouraged her.

He smiled a little then, thinking Maura Sinclair was not a woman easily discouraged. Then shook his head at his own deduction. As if reading a handful of letters was really enough to feel he knew her that well. And yet, he felt he did. The curiosity that had sparked him to open the chest, to look at contents, read the letters, had caught and flamed fully to life with every passing sentence he read. And with each ensuing letter, that flame had burned brighter, the need to know more about her, about Ballantrae, about this place that was part of his heritage, had built up inside him until he could no longer deny that a handful of letters, no matter how skillfully and colorfully written, wouldn't be enough.

He wanted to meet her. To see Ballantrae with his own eyes, instead of only through hers. The very place Teague Morgan and his band of rowdies had fled, escaping the hangman's noose, in pursuit of a better life in the colonies.

He was still able to deny that this had anything to do with his father. He didn't much care about the whats or whys of his father's association with her, or his feelings about the place, or what he hoped came of his investment there. For the first time since entering college, Tag wanted to explore his own heritage, only now it had nothing to do with his father's impact on it.

Back then it had been a knee-jerk reaction to his father's insistence that they stamp out their collective past, whitewash over it. He'd thought to prove to him the value of the past and what it said about those who came after. But he'd barely begun his first dig when he'd done an almost immediate one-eighty, realizing he'd never gain his father's approval. And had spent a bit of time castigating himself for being foolish enough to want to try. So he'd gone in a completely opposite direction, studied an ancient culture that was nothing like his own.

Now his father was gone and Tag was free to feel however he wanted about his ancestry, to do whatever he felt like doing about it. Which, at the moment, he was still undecided about. But one thing he knew for certain was that anything he did now would be for himself, and only himself. His gaze fell to the crumpled note card that had landed next to the trash can. His father's words came back to him.

Are you man enough for it?

Tag downed what was left of the whiskey he'd poured some hours back. "Yes, by damn, I am," he swore, wincing as it burned the back of his throat. "More a man than you ever were."

Then he carefully folded the last letter, before tucking them all back in the box, closing the lid, and carrying the whole thing with him from the office room. Like that day, long ago, he left without looking back.

And when the sun rose the following morning, and Tag was on the phone booking a flight to Glasgow, he wasn't thinking about his father, or the taunt from beyond the grave. He was thinking of Ballantrae. And Maura Sinclair. And wondering if her voice was anywhere near close to the one he'd come to imagine in his mind, while reading her vividly descriptive letters. It wouldn't be long before he found out.

Chapter 4

"**R**uddy bastard!" Maura dropped the damp bath towel she'd found laying by the front door, and let fly with the first hard thing she could grab. Her mobile phone flew like a silver bullet toward the down-filled double bed—*her* down-filled double bed—and the two people presently occupying it.

"Now, Mo, wait just a—Ouch!" Jory MacTavish flinched as Maura followed up with her key ring, which bounced off his fine, muscled bum.

The very same fine muscled bum she'd just caught clenching in all its well-defined glory as he gave that other fine part of himself to a slender brunette. Maura had no idea who she was, but then she hadn't gotten a look at the woman's face. Mostly because she'd been on all fours at the time. Oddly enough, what pissed her off most was that, after six months with the guy, how come she didn't know he liked to do it doggy style?

"Jesus, Mo, careful with yer aim."

"Aye," she agreed readily. "I was off by about, oh seven inches with that last shot. I won't be with my next one."

"Now, now, hold off. See, Mo, I can explain," Jory began, scrambling off the woman, who quickly tried to slither from the bed on her stomach.

Appropriate, Mo thought, considering she was a snake in

the grass. Or ass, as the case may be. She'd deal with her in a minute. She faced Jory, who remained unconcernedly naked. "I've seen quite enough, thanks. And the only thing you're going to see is a swirl of stars twinkling about your head if you don't get your lying, two-timing ass off my bed and out of my home. *My home,* Jory! Jesus and Mary."

"Home? Don't ye mean the elephant on yer back? The very same one you've been a slave to for as long as I've known you," he shot back.

Her eyes narrowed. "I don't think you're going to be wanting to mince words with me at the moment. Say what you will about the rest of the place, aye it's a burden and one ye should thank yer lucky stars your laze arse isn't in charge of maintaining. But this?" She gestured at the room, the whole of it. "This tower is mine. And yes, it's my home as much as your rent-free little apartment over yer father's pub is yours."

"And we could hardly go there, could we now?" he said, completely missing her point. "The whole town would know."

Incredulous, she grabbed the small crystal vase that sat on the small table beneath the mirror, and unceremoniously dumped both water and flowers from it onto the wooden floor. She'd be sure to regret it later when she had to buff out the water marks, but at the moment, it was far down on her list of things she'd wished she'd thought twice about before doing. She swung the heavy crystal up, the neck tight in her fist. "So, you brought her here for some *privacy?*"

"I didn't bring her anywhere, I was already here. You should know that, you just left here an hour ago."

Her eyes threatened to bulge from her head. "Yes," she all but shrieked. "I did. What, since you were already in a nice warm bed, you figured you'd just ring her up and see if she could join you?"

"It wasn't like that, it—"

"I mean, Christ Jory, if you can't keep your goddamn dick in your pants for more than an hour at a time, there's eleven other bedrooms in the main house of this 'white elephant' you could have used. You didn't have to screw her in mine!"

"But it's the only one with electric heat and—"

"Jesus and Mary, Jory, shut your trap," the other woman grumbled beneath her breath.

Maura turned her steely glare on the woman presently grabbing around the floor for her clothes. And got her second shock of the afternoon. Her anger wheezed out of her, along with her breath. "Priss?"

Her best—former best—friend paused in mid-panty retrieval and attempted an apologetic smile. Her thick brown hair was a rat's nest, probably from Jory grabbing the back of it in his fist, and her neck—and her thighs, bitch—were red and splotchy from razor burn. Topping it off was the flushed glow and glassy-eyed satisfaction, both oh so familiar to Maura. Somehow the apologetic smile didn't go a long way toward easing the tension screaming between them. Or even a short way. Because, in truth, this betrayal was far harder to take than Jory's.

"How could you do it to me?" she asked, her voice choked with hurt and stunned disbelief. It was harsh enough discovering how cavalierly the bond of a trusted friendship could be broken and tossed aside. She'd be damned if she'd give either one of them an inch of her pride. Anger made a welcome and strong resurgence.

Priss lifted one softly rounded shoulder. Everything about Priss was softly rounded. And petite. In direct contrast with Maura, who was a wee bit taller than average, with long, wiry limbs and a narrow frame. It had never really been a sore point for her before. Funny how things change.

"I'm so sorry," she said quietly, remorse clear in her eyes.

"I trusted you," Maura said. "With . . . everything. I've bared my soul to you. And this is how you honor that? By baring yours to the guy I'm sleeping with?"

"Hey, now—" Jory began, only to be waved silent by both women.

Priss gathered herself, her mouth pursing, as a hint of steel came into her own blue-eyed gaze. "I said I'm sorry, okay? I didn't exactly plan this. I have no excuse. Well, an explanation maybe, but you're not in any frame of mind to hear it now. And nothing excuses this," she gestured to the bed, to a still-naked Jory. "I know. But, Mo, honestly, it's not like you two were any great love match. I know that better than anyone. Besides, we both know your track record at long-term relationships, and, well, it's been six months. That's a record for you. You two wouldn't have lasted the winter and you know it." She didn't so much speak with defiance, as with, well, pity. As if this was all the result of Maura being somehow lacking, and therefore should have expected something like this to happen.

Maura felt like she'd been slapped twice.

It didn't matter that, for the most part, what Priss said was true. Sure, six months pretty much matched her personal best for relationship longevity, and yes, she'd been questioning whether she was keeping Jory around because she honestly saw their relationship going somewhere, or because she'd been going through a tough time lately and winters in Ballantrae were cold and lonely enough as it was. But that didn't give Priss the right to make that decision for her. "So what, you thought you'd help me out?" She struggled to decide how she should feel, how to act. Anger and hurt and confusion were all twisted up inside her. "You couldn't have waited? You didn't even tell me you were interested in him."

Priss began pulling on enough clothing to be decent. Which, of course, was all a matter of opinion. Maura was of a mind that while Priss's little black skirt and skimpy white stretch top might have covered her former best friend's bits and pieces, it could hardly be called decent. "I wanted to," she said at last, and with surprising emotion, "many times. But what was I going to say? 'If you're not going to get serious, could I have a go at him?' " She sighed heavily, and if

Maura wasn't mistaken, Priss was just as twisted up emotionally at the moment as she was.

Of course, Maura wasn't feeling particularly sympathetic about that.

"I was going to wait," Priss said. "I didn't come up here to see him, I came up here to see you. And, well, Jory answered the door in a bath towel and—" She glanced at Jory and her cheeks flushed. She tried to look repentant when she glanced back at Maura, but didn't even come close. So she did the shoulder lift again.

Typically Maura was the kind of person who would do whatever it took to make things work. Life was tough enough, and being a hard-ass every time she encountered another stumbling block was only going to make it harder on her. Having trusted only a handful of people in her life, she well understood the value of friendship. In her heart, she knew she didn't want to lose the one she had with Priss. She knew she should make some kind of last-ditch effort to salvage at least one relationship from the ashes of this fiasco.

As it turned out, she wasn't feeling that generous.

"Funny, I didn't think you were the type for sloppy seconds," she said, apparently more pissed off than she'd realized. And once she'd given in to the anger and pain, the hurt of it all, it just kept flowing. She might not be proud of herself tomorrow, but at the moment, it felt pretty damn good. "I suppose it's a good thing he'd already showered me off of him before giving you a go, eh?" She didn't enjoy the little punch of hurt that opened Priss's eyes wide, but she was a bit too wounded at the moment to feel particularly bad about it either. Instead she glanced dismissively at Jory. "He's certainly all yours now." She tucked the vase under her arm and clapped her hands. "Well done, both of you. Really." She looked at Priss. "Of course, I don't suppose I need to tell you how good he is in bed, seeing as you took the details I shared in private as a ringing endorsement. Perhaps I should think

twice about broadcasting such an explicit advert next time."
She blinked back the sudden burning sensation crowding at
the corners of her eyes. Clinging to her wounded pride was
the only thing keeping the tears at bay. "I only hope he was
worth it." She stepped back to clear the path to the door.

"Mo, come on, we can talk this out," Priss began, clutching her black leather boots to her chest. She took a step back
when Maura glared at her. "Not now, of course, but later. I
want to explain it all to you. Will you at least promise me
you'll hear me out? It wasn't just sex."

Since being shushed, Jory had wisely stayed out of it. He'd
remained sitting on the bed, still quite naked and making no
attempt whatsoever to cover himself up. Of course, it had
been his absolute comfort in his own skin, and his ability to
make her feel the same, that had drawn her to the charming
bastard in the first place.

But his ego—which was just as healthy as his appetite for
sex, and justly so she'd always thought, up until now anyway—couldn't let that last comment pass. "What d'ya mean,
'just sex,' " he demanded of Priss, all male affront and stung
pride. "Sure, I had you coming less than a minute after I slid
my hand in your panties, but it was you who put my hand
there in the first place. Otherwise, I'd have—"

"Otherwise you'd have *what*?" Priss exclaimed, rounding
on him. "It's not like I jumped you. You answered the door
wearing a goddamn towel, which you conveniently let drop.
You know damn well we've been less than a heartbeat away
from going at each other for weeks. What in the hell did you
think was going to happen?"

Jory looked confused, which Maura realized wasn't unusual for him. What was unusual was the honest hurt she
thought she saw in his eyes. Which confused her now as well.

"So then that's it?" he said. "That's all you were after?"

"No!" Priss huffed. "For Christ's sake, I said it *wasn't* just
sex. *Wasn't.*"

"Then why did you just say—"

"Shut up, both of you!" Maura exclaimed, momentarily clamping her hands over her ears. "And get dressed while you're at it. I want you out of here in the next five minutes or I'm ringing up Constable Stiles." She glared at Jory. "And wouldn't your dear, sweet uncle be quite interested in hearing how you've spent your morning?"

"Mo, come now, no need for threats," Jory said, his voice quickly turning all cajoling and reasonable. Although they both knew his uncle had a fondness for Jory that would likely preclude him doing anything worse than giving him a stern lecture. He would also likely tell his brother Gavin, Jory's dad, who wouldn't go so easy on him. Although who knew for sure, Jory was a master of talking his way out of— and into—things.

Being the baby in a family of eight certainly had its benefits, she thought morosely. Being an only child herself, she was technically oldest, youngest, and everything in between. Unfortunately, the only benefit she'd received from that arrangement was not having to wear hand-me-downs or wait in line for the loo.

Jory quickly climbed from the bed and pulled on his pants, then stepped between the two women, his back to Priss as she finished dressing. "Don't be mad at her, Mo. I should have told you myself, but . . . well, you know how my father goes on about you and about how being with you was the smartest thing I've ever done and well, I—"

Maura held up her hand. "Please, if you think telling me you didn't end things because you didn't want to hurt your dad is going to make me feel better—"

"No, I was just tryin' to explain." He had the gall to reach for her hands.

Not only wasn't Maura soft and rounded, she wasn't short or petite either. And Jory still had a good four inches on her in height. Imposing and all male, she'd never gotten past that little rush of arousal every time she had to look up to look into his eyes. He had a body that had surely been chiseled by the gods. And the face of a fallen angel. She felt a little pang when she realized she'd never again have those shamelessly soft lips kissing every inch of her skin, from the back of her neck, all the way down to the instep of her foot. Never again would she get the chance to run her hands over those broad, keg-hauling shoulders, down that muscled back.

He must have seen something in her eyes, because he gentled his voice, making it all deep and drowsy. She could almost forget Priss was still in the room with them. Almost. "I didn't mean to hurt you. Honest. It just . . . we'd been flirting a little and somehow it got a wee bit out of hand." His mouth pulled down at the corners in a way that made him look remorseful and adorable at the same time. Like a little boy who'd gotten his hand caught in the cookie jar. The same little boy who knew he was mama's favorite and could likely talk his way out of a spanking.

Of course, for all Maura knew, given the scene she'd walked in on and those knee-high black leather boots Priss was clutching, he might just enjoy a good whipping. Which was image enough to snap her out of her foolish little reverie. She'd known him to be a charming scoundrel even before she'd gone to bed with him, so she really had no one to blame but herself, she supposed. But if he thought he could sweet talk his way out of this, he was about to learn otherwise. She stepped back, out of his reach. "A wee bit out of hand?" she repeated. "Is that what you'd call this? Well, you'd best be following Priss out that door in the next minute," she said, teeth clenched. "Or I'll be taking your wee bit in my hand and yanking it off."

When Jory flinched and covered himself, she smiled for the first time since entering the room. Then sighed a little as her gaze was naturally drawn downward. A shame she couldn't find a way to keep that bit for herself. A parting gift, as it were. Ah well. She'd known it was going to end at some point. Probably much like this, with her kicking him out of her bed. She just hadn't expected to be kicking someone else

out along with him. And even if she had, she'd never imagined it would be her best friend.

"Maura," Jory began, but swallowed whatever else he'd
been about to say when she made a *snip, snip* motion with
her fingers. He finished getting dressed without saying anything else.

She supposed she should feel grateful that he'd at least
hadn't tried the always unoriginal tactic of turning it all back
on her, claiming she was awful in bed and had driven him
into the arms of another. Because given what they'd been
doing all last night and up until daybreak this morning, they
both knew that would have been a bunch of rubbish. Jory
definitely had the goods and knew how to deliver them. But
Maura knew she'd more than compensated him in return.
She glanced at Priss and her smile returned.

The two women had shared every intimate detail of their
lives since they'd begun having sex, Maura having shared for
a somewhat longer period of time than Priss. Whose given
name was Patrice, and hadn't earned that nickname unwar-
ranted. Jory might be the one getting the short end of the
stick after all, she thought a bit smugly.

Speaking of which, she made a mental note to add batter-
ies to her next shopping list. Just because Jory wasn't going
to be having multiple orgasms anytime soon, didn't mean she
had to deprive herself of them.

"Come on, Priss," Jory said, holding the bedroom door
open.

He was trying to look like the wounded party, all beautiful
pouty lips and wounded puppy-dog eyes. But Maura didn't
have enough temper left to call him on it. She just wanted
them both gone.

Priss zipped up her boots and snagged her coat, looking at
Maura as if she wanted to make one last attempt to explain
away her duplicity. In the end, she wisely opted to remain
silent. Instead she delivered a cool look at Jory, then left the
room with her chin up, in a way only Priss could manage,

considering she'd just been caught buck naked in her friend's bed, with her friend's lover.

"Come on, now, Priss," Jory cajoled, quickly heading out behind her without so much as another glance at Maura.

She sighed, listening as he began a running dialogue, all the way down the curving stone stairs to the main floor. When she heard the ground-floor door shut, she wandered across her room and stepped out onto the small balcony that wrapped around the top of the spire. She looked directly down into the main courtyard of the crumbling ruin she always had, grumbling aside, called home.

She'd known Jory hadn't really understood her connection to this big pile of stone, but she hadn't realized he was resentful of it. Which is sure what it had sounded like. Of course, working for his parents at the pub and still living off of them at twenty-eight, he didn't exactly have a clear appreciation of responsibility, much less a dedication to doing anything more with his life. And God knows her life was a master class in dedication.

The sky was gray and bleak, matching her mood, with the promised winter storm growing ever closer. The wind had an even sharper bite to it than usual, snatching at her auburn curls and tossing them whiplike about her face. She yanked them back in a knot, as she dispassionately watched Jory talk his way into getting Priss to give him a lift into town. Jesus and Mary, she thought, had she really fancied herself building a life with that one? She hadn't, of course. Not really. Which, strangely enough, was more depressing. He'd just been the one who happened to be in her life when, at thirty, she'd finally began wondering if this was all there was ever going to be to it. Was it to be just one long string of days that began and ended with her worrying about Ballantrae and how to keep it going? There should be more, she'd thought, and still believed. Just not with Jory.

Priss's small Renault rolled through the main gates and edged down the pitted gravel drive, before disappearing amongst the towering pines crowded along the entrance road. Only then did Maura feel a pang of true pain. She could find another lover. It was going to be a lot harder to find another best friend.

She turned her attention to the west, away from betrayal and pain.

"Toward burden and responsibility, instead," she said on a weary sigh, looking out over the land that stretched on as far as the eye could see. Though it was winter in the surrounding Cairngorms, green grass grew atop fallow soil here in the valley. The countryside rolled out before her like so much carpet, on and on in gentle swells, dotted occasionally with black-faced sheep and shaggy brown cows. Low, stone walls separated one tenant plot from the next. Small crofts marked each plot, their stone walls and thatched roofs looking a bit haggard and worn in the dull winter light. Smoke wisped from far too few of the stacked chimneys. However, the faint smell of burning peat mixed with the mist that rose off the loch, making the air feel even more dank than usual. She shifted her gaze out over the choppy gray waters of Loch Ulish, which formed the eastern boundary of her property. *Her property.*

Her shoulders hunched a little. More from the weight of responsibility than as a shield against the cold. She didn't know which was heavier, the air . . . or her heart, but for reasons far more complex than this most recent betrayal. With another sigh, this one deeper, longer, and—only because she was alone, tinged with an edge of despair she didn't bother trying to stifle—she turned away from the view of the land she both loved, and on occasion, loathed. Instead she leaned back on the railing and tugged the crumpled letter from the pocket she'd angrily shoved it into what now seemed like a lifetime ago.

She hadn't bothered to open it then, nor did she now. The sorrowful look on Argus Danders' face as he'd handed it over to her had been all the answer she'd needed. She'd known the bank wouldn't extend her loan, but she'd held out for the miracle. Tearing the white packet slowly in two, she let the halves drift heedlessly to the ground, then tipped her head back and looked up at the sky. "I guess I only get one of those in a lifetime, eh, Taggart?"

Grief pulled at her and she fought off the fresh threat of tears. She wasn't much for weepy theatrics, but she supposed if anyone deserved to indulge herself in a brief fit of them at the moment, it was probably her. Of course she'd known she was going to lose Taggart, had known for months now. But it hadn't made the reality any easier to deal with when the time had finally come.

Her first clue had been the monthly letter that had never shown up. Then had come the official word. A single sheet of paper from his friend Mick Templeton, offering a brief line of condolence on her loss, followed by an even briefer notification that as soon as Taggart's will was properly read to his heirs, he would fulfill Taggart's final wishes regarding the Scotland property. He'd ended by promising that someone from the family would be in touch with her regarding the future of her financial arrangement.

She'd crumpled the letter, hating that she'd been reduced to a "financial arrangement" in the final picture of Taggart's life, and at the same time, knowing she was doomed if that arrangement didn't survive his death.

That had been over three months ago. And there had been nary a word nor any form of contact since. Much less a bank draft. At the time she'd signed the papers with Taggart, she'd been so grateful to him, still was, that she'd agreed to the hundred-and-twenty-day window. Which meant his heirs still had another couple of weeks to make their decision on maintaining their investment agreement, before the property reverted back to her by default. For all the good that would do her. Of course, she'd had no way of knowing cancer would claim Taggart a few short years after their agreement had been signed. Nor did she know, at the time, that his heirs weren't likely to be in any great hurry to jump in and pick up where their father had left off. Not that it would have mattered. She'd have accepted his offer if he'd written every clause he could think of into the contract. She hadn't much of a choice.

It was hard enough losing the friendship she'd forged with Taggart Morgan, no matter how odd the circumstances that had initially founded it. What had begun as a business relationship had, over time, become a much stronger bond. He'd not only offered guidance and wisdom, but he'd felt as strongly as she did about preserving the last remaining stronghold of their families' oft-joined clan. Losing the promised funding, which had only barely kept Ballantrae from complete ruin in the first place, had only made the blow that much worse.

And, she admitted, there was a small part of her that was a bit hurt that he hadn't done more to safeguard their arrangement. He'd been well aware of her meager income here. What she earned from her own job writing articles and short stories for an Edinburgh magazine, plus the income from the crofters, hardly put a dent in the monthly maintenance alone on a place of this size. He'd mentioned more times than she could count how proud he was of her determination and dedication. It had certainly been in his power to make permanent arrangements, as he'd known for some time he wasn't going to beat the disease.

But then, she'd remind herself that she really knew nothing about the situation between him and his sons, other than that it was severely strained. She had no idea what he'd felt obligated to do on their behalf, as the final chapter of his life, of their life together, was winding to a close.

Once again she contemplated reaching out to Taggart's sons, much as she'd reached out to their father years ago. He'd been a complete stranger to her then, a name she'd stumbled across after much research and digging into the Ballantrae ancestry. Through a quite lengthy lineage, she'd discovered that he was The Morgan, the oldest living direct descendant of the last chief of Clan Morganach and therefore, technically current clan chief. As she was of her clan, being the most direct descendant of The Sinclair. The two clans had had a long and entwined history and ownership of Ballantrae. She saw no reason that history couldn't be resurrected, and that relationship perhaps renewed.

She'd traced the last Morgan chief, Teague Morgan, to the colonies, and had discovered Rogues Hollow, astonished, given American history, to find it still existed. Further astonished to find it was still populated by Morgans, Ramsays and Sinclairs. The American Sinclairs were descended from Iain, the younger brother of her direct ancestor, the clan chief during that time, Calum Sinclair. But if the stories she'd read in her vast collection were to be believed, Morgan held a more direct claim. And, seeing as the American Sinclairs didn't even live in the Hollow but a few months of the year, she'd eagerly contacted Taggart instead.

That initial letter to him had resulted in a surprising relationship that had provided far more than the financial backing she'd been so desperate to secure. But she was reluctant to strike again.

She'd known from her research that Taggart had four sons, but he'd never spoken of them. Even after they'd established a rapport that had her quite comfortably giving him her opinion on any number of subjects, she'd been reluctant to push him about the estrangement between him and his children. After all, it was none of her business and had no bearing on their relationship, personal or business. Had he brought them up himself, perhaps she would have pushed more. She'd been quite curious about it. But his complete silence on the matter had left her feeling she had no option but to tacitly agree to leave them unmentioned.

So far as she knew, they had no idea of her existence, much less that of Ballantrae. Mr. Templeton had only said he'd follow Taggart's wishes. And despite Taggart's promise that she and the tumbledown castle would be taken care of after his death, she had no way of knowing if he'd put it in writing, or simply made it a verbal request to his close friend to take it up with his sons.

Even if Taggart had put it in writing, it was quite likely that without her presence, his sons could easily initiate some sort of legal maneuver to get out of the obligation entirely. After all, none of them still lived in the Hollow, and if they had no emotional tie to their only parent, it was doubtful they'd feel strongly about those ancestors who had come before him, much less the land they'd built their heritage on. On American or Scot soil.

Which left her with very few options.

A cold gust of wind blew in off the loch, making her tuck her arms more tightly around her waist. She hoped the storm held off a bit longer. She had an article that needed polishing and printing, so she could leave first thing in the morning for the three-hour drive to Durnish, to keep the appointment she'd made earlier, on the chance the bank didn't come through. Her meeting was with Doug Wentworth, a land agent. Not that she was going to sell so much as a tuft of Sinclair soil, but she had to be realistic. If it got to the point where the bank was going to come and take it all away, she might have to reconsider that stance. Of course, she had no idea if there would be a buyer, or what the property would even be worth, as it was mostly farmland and she had a hard enough time leasing it to crofters as it was. But a smart girl understood her options. She looked across the loch at the gloom that was quickly deepening the gray skies, and wished she felt wiser.

Ducking back inside, she took one look at the bed and the tousle of linens piled on it, and kept on walking. Maybe Wentworth would see her early, she thought, snagging her keys from the bed and her mobile from the floor before shoving both into her pockets. She'd make Durnish by nightfall, and see him first thing in the morning and be back in time to still get the article done and make her deadline.

She pulled her mobile back out and punched up the number of a friend of hers from university who lived just outside Durnish. If she was lucky, Val wouldn't mind her bunking out on her sofa for the night. It was the perfect plan, really, since she certainly didn't fancy being alone in her own bed tonight. She and Valerie didn't keep in touch often, but her former dorm mate was always good for a few ales and some laughs at the local pub.

With the ringing phone pressed to her ear, she threw a few things together and grabbed her files. Pleased with her plan, she headed out. This way she'd be back before the storm hit. Which was a good thing, because she had a busy agenda planned for tomorrow.

She'd finish her article, go over her notes for the next one and get the proposal out for the one after that. Then spend the remainder of her day figuring out her options for Ballantrae, maybe formulating a letter to Taggart's sons depending on how her meeting with Doug went. After which she'd settle in for a nice cozy evening while the storm raged outside. A bottle of wine, maybe some cheese, a good book. And there would be a nice fire to keep her warm.

After all, she had plenty of bed linens that needed burning.

Chapter 5

Tag downshifted and switched the windshield wipers to a faster speed as he began pushing the little rental uphill again. He'd landed in Glasgow just after eleven A.M. local time, which was the wee hours of the morning by his internal clock. By all rights he should have been bleary-eyed and exhausted. Any hope he'd had of sleeping his way across the Atlantic had been abandoned pretty early on. He'd tried, but as the other passengers around him had dozed, he'd been fidgety and edgy and unable to settle down. So he'd pulled out Maura Sinclair's letters and read them over again.

Jace had ribbed him about developing some masochistic crush on his dad's pen pal. Tag had taken it in stride, but privately he thought Jace might not be that far off. He was undeniably curious. What kind of woman signs her heritage over to a complete stranger? A desperate one, of course. In rereading the letters, reading between the lines, he could only surmise that it had been Maura who'd come to his father for help. How else could he have known about the place? No matter how much the man had changed in his later years, Tag simply could not see him tracing back his much-reviled ancestry and hunting up this place. Of course, he couldn't imagine him buying it either, so who the hell knew what was going on.

But though Tag might not know much about Ballantrae,

he knew enough from her letters to understand that it was directly connected to the origins of Rogues Hollow, and the three men who had founded it: Teague Morgan, Iain Sinclair, and Dougal Ramsay. He could only gather she was somehow tied to Iain. Which meant this was every bit as much her heritage, however loosely, as it was his.

And somehow, some way, she managed to con Taggart Morgan into single-handedly saving the rundown remains of their entwined family history, complete with dwindling tenant farms and a village struggling to stay alive. The cynic in him said that she'd just been looking for a patsy, a sugar daddy of sorts. Her correspondence painted a different picture, of course. Her dedication to preserving this part of her heritage appeared absolute, but she made it clear she wasn't just looking for a handout. She wanted Taggart to feel the same bond to the place she did, even at the expense of giving up whatever legal right she might have had to it.

Of course, that might have been a ploy to make sure he didn't renege on the deal and sell it off to someone else. Someone who might not be as keen on letting her stick around. After all, she had a pretty sweet deal going. She'd figured out a way to keep the roof over her head she'd lived under all her life, without being responsible for the financial obligation of maintaining it. All she had to do, basically, was house sit and oversee the occasional work crew.

Not that he had any right to judge, seeing as his father had barely been cold in the ground before he'd just signed over his share of his own heritage, thereby freeing him from any responsibility whatsoever to its upkeeping and maintenance. Hell, he didn't even have to house sit.

But as cynical an edge as he'd tried to maintain while reading her letters, he'd still ended up feeling as if he'd formed an odd sort of personal attachment to her. The way she related the stories about life in Ballantrae, from the difficulties leasing out the land to farmers, to the struggles of the villagers

trying to keep their businesses afloat despite the steady dwindling of the local population, had given him a different sort
of insight. A portrait that was quite intimate in a different
way.

As his plane had circled the airport, he'd found himself
wondering as he had that first night, why they'd chosen
posted letters versus the more commonly accepted e-mails.
His father had a computer, but, curious, he'd checked, and
there was no correspondence to or from Maura there.
Perhaps she didn't have access to e-mail. So why not call?
International calls weren't so expensive these days. But a
glance at the last few phone bills hadn't turned up any overseas phone charges either. The cherrywood box and file from
Mick were the sum total of his father's connection to his
Scotland property. And Maura.

The sun had long since set as Tag climbed further up the
next mountain. The thrumming sound on the roof of the car
softened, then disappeared completely as the rain that fell in
the valleys changed over to the snow that capped the Grampian
peaks. He slowed on the curves, and tightened his grip on the
wheel as he renewed his focus on the road ahead. He probably should have stayed in the city for the day, acclimated
himself to the time change and headed out in the morning.
But he'd still been edgy and restless upon arriving, and had
decided to just get in the car, buy a map, and head out, figuring he'd stop when he got too tired to keep driving.

Which, he realized now, he should have done a while back
when he'd passed through Durnish, the last town he'd passed
through that could actually be called such. But it was too far
back to turn around now. He'd managed his way out of
Glasgow well enough, and by the time he'd hit the more
rural, single-track roads, he was comfortable enough driving
on the left, going through the occasional roundabout. But
now, hours later, climbing into the mountains, his shoulders
and neck were tightening up from the strain of peering

through the fogged windshield; he was still struggling to master using a stick shift with his left hand rather than his right. And the weather was growing worse by the minute.

To top it off, he hadn't passed by so much as a barn, much less a town, in over an hour. There were dots and town names on the map he'd bought in the airport, but he'd quickly learned that just because a town had a name, that didn't necessarily correspond to there being any visible signs of actual civilization there.

Unless of course you counted the sheep.

Initially, despite the bleak weather, he'd enjoyed his view of the countryside as he'd left Glasgow and Stirling behind. If he weren't so distracted by what lay ahead, he might have stopped and done some wandering. He'd only worked briefly on that first dig, which had been in Wales, but he'd been so confused then, about what he really wanted, why he was really there, that he hadn't done much more than show up on site before the opening had come on the dig in Peru. He'd jumped on it, and never looked back.

He knew the countryside was rife with the detritus of its heritage, from the small cairns that dotted the roadside, to the occasional sign directing tourists to this battlefield or that castle. Under different circumstances, he'd have been immediately captivated by the possibilities of what lay out there, waiting to be discovered. Once upon a time, he had been fascinated by the history surrounding the beginnings of this country. Specifically the Picts, with their mystical beliefs, rife with mixed interpretations and controversy. His mind would have been spinning, lost in imagining those who had walked this very land before him, wondering about their beliefs, their rites and rituals. What they had done, who they had loved, how they had died, what mark they'd left behind.

He didn't need a shrink to explain to him why he'd fled that dig site in Wales, or why he'd focused his skills and talents half a globe away. He knew that coming here would unearth a wealth of memories he'd just as soon leave buried.

But maybe it was time to do exactly that, to deal with his own demons once and for all, put his father's legacy to rest, and maybe allow himself to look beyond the immediate past of the Morgan clan to that of their distant ancestors. Who knows, he might even enjoy it.

If he could ever find a place to get out of this damn cold weather.

He cranked up the heater and flexed his shoulders, working the kink out of his neck. He supposed he had Maura to thank for this epiphany, or at least the actions he'd taken because of it. He smiled briefly, wondering how she would feel if she knew about the impact she was having on the life of a man she'd never met. And since he'd alerted no one on this side of the pond of his impending arrival, she couldn't possibly know that was about to change.

He rounded the peak bend and downshifted, gently riding the brakes as he began the winding crawl downhill. The snow was coming down so hard now, and the air so thick with damp fog and swirling flakes, his meager headlights barely penetrated the gloom enough to see the road. It was only a little after six in the evening, but days were short here in the winter. It had been fully dark for some time now, made darker still by the storm. He squinted, looking for the marker. He should only be a few kilometers from the next dot on the map, which had been slightly bigger than the others, so he was holding out hope there was an actual town attached to it.

Calyth, he thought, recalling the sign some clicks back. He didn't care what kind of accommodations were available. His usual digs included a heavy tarpaulin, a woven hammock, and some mosquito netting. So he wasn't exactly picky. He just wanted to get some sleep, and if he was lucky, put some food in his belly. Hopefully by the time he got down off this mountain and into town, the current blizzard would change to rain again. Ballantrae looked to be only an hour or two beyond Calyth, so he could sleep in and still be there by noon.

And now that he'd committed himself to this course of action, a part of him wanted to see Ballantrae for the first time by daylight anyway. Plus he had no idea what kind of welcome he'd receive, in town or at the castle. Maybe it was just as well he found lodging outside Ballantrae altogether. For all he knew, he wouldn't be staying on at the castle itself, despite the fact that he technically owned it now. A lot of that would depend on Ms. Sinclair. And what he might find out about the castle itself.

He was still undecided on exactly what he wanted to do about any of it. Whether he wanted to maintain the financial arrangement with her, or hire someone else, or for that matter get rid of the property altogether. He'd need to know a lot more before he made any final decisions. He'd read her letters and let himself get swept up in the emotion of it, the passion of discovery, which wasn't unusual in his line of work. A vivid imagination was mandatory, an ability to see the people he was studying, visualize how they looked, walked, talked, interacted.

But that didn't mean he wasn't a scientist as well, careful to find out the facts, piece together the truths that he could prove. He shouldn't have been so quick to head out, he knew that. He should have done some research first, on Ballantrae, and maybe Maura Sinclair herself. He should have even talked to Mick, find out what else he knew about the story behind this deal his father had struck with her. But he hadn't wanted to do that. Mostly, he acknowledged, because he hadn't wanted to risk giving himself enough time to talk himself out of doing this. Or question what might really be at the root of his curiosity.

He had no idea if they'd both feel comfortable staying under the same roof. No matter how big that roof might be. And he didn't see himself striding in and kicking her out until further notice, either.

He didn't know how long he expected to stay, but there was no denying his curiosity was growing the farther into the country he traveled. He recognized that steady thrum, stirring his blood. The one that generally meant digging would soon follow. Literally or figuratively. He still wasn't sure how he felt about that, but before leaving Virginia, he'd extended his leave from the dig in Chacchoben by another week or two. Just in case.

His mind drifted to tomorrow, to just how he'd approach Ballantrae. Best to go directly to the castle, rather than poke around town. Rural townships the world over had at least one commonality: they all had a well-established form of communication. The Internet had nothing on a small village when it came to spreading the latest news. And it would be best if Maura heard about his arrival directly from him.

He tried to imagine how she'd react to his surprise visit, which was tricky given he had no idea what she looked like. His predictions had ranged from young, vibrant, with curly black hair and milkmaid skin, to older, with white hair cut in some no-nonsense fashion, matched with blue eyes that shone with the wisdom she'd gained from years of responsibility to the castle and dependent villagers. Perhaps a bit stooped in posture, but square of shoulder. It was probably somewhere in between.

He was jerked from his reverie when a dark object suddenly loomed large and unmoving through the swirl of snow, right in front of him.

"Shit!" He spun the steering wheel hard and swerved, barely avoiding a head-on collision with whatever the hell was currently blocking almost the entire narrow track. The back end of his car fishtailed dangerously. He fought hard to straighten it out, but traction was minimal and as soon as the rear tires slid off the pavement, the entire back end of the car was swallowed trunk deep into a snowbank.

He knew from the angle of the car that, even with a stick shift, he wasn't driving out of this. Which meant getting out in this freezing blizzard to push, pull, or otherwise dig himself out. With what, he had no idea. It hadn't occurred to him to buy a shovel before leaving the city. And if the car came with an emergency kit or flares, it was buried in the trunk, under a ton of snow. Not that there would likely be another traveler on the road this late at night, during a storm.

No, he was the only idiot trying that particular maneuver, he thought, smacking the steering wheel with open palms. Which also meant that if he didn't dig his way out, his sleeping quarters had just gotten a hell of a lot more cramped for the night. Compared to the small compact, a hammock would have been roomy.

It was only after he'd zipped up the flannel-lined, heavy canvas jacket he'd bummed off of Jace before leaving, and tugged on the gloves he'd tossed aside a few hours back, that he thought to look back at what had sent him off the road in the first place. Visibility was poor bordering on nonexistent with his headlights aiming in the wrong direction. But he could distinctly make out . . . something.

Swearing under his breath, he shut off the engine and got out of the car. If he couldn't dig out, he had to at least clear out a small area around the tailpipe if he wanted to be able to run the engine periodically for heat. He shivered hard and tucked his hands beneath his armpits as he began trekking back the thirty or so yards to the shadow blocking the road. He had to duck his chin to keep the snowflakes from stinging his eyes. He had on leather boots that had seen better days and his toes quickly began to feel the chill. He'd packed his winter boots in his duffel. Which was also in the trunk.

The call of the rain forest grew stronger with every step.

But, even freezing his ass off and stranded miles from the nearest town, he couldn't quite convince himself that he'd made a mistake coming here. Not yet, anyway.

About five yards out, he realized that the dark lump was actually a vehicle, half covered with snow. It was a small pickup of sorts, white, which is why he hadn't seen it clearly. The back end was sticking up at an odd angle, jutting directly into the path of traffic. Had it been clear weather, he could have easily avoided it, but coming around a corner like that, with the dark and reduced visibility, it had looked as if it were right in front of him. On closer examination, the front end of the truck was pitched at a downward angle beyond the edge of the road. The wheel he could see was half off the edge of the road, which meant the passenger-side wheel on the opposite side was probably no longer in contact with the ground. All he could see beyond the road's edge was a swirl of gloom and blowing snowflakes.

It was impossible to see how far down the mountainside the truck would have plunged, but if the skid had continued a few inches farther the driver would have found out. The engine wasn't running, no lights were on. And there were no flares stuck on the roadway. Though, judging from the amount of snow already accumulated in the open truck bed, the accident might have happened some time back. For all he knew, the flares or danger signs had long since been swallowed in the snow. Which, on the side of the road, was piling up over his calves and edging kneeward.

"Hello?" he called out, but with the wind and weather, even a shout didn't travel very far. He carefully drew closer, not wanting to slip and slide his way over the edge. But he wanted to make sure no one was hurt inside the vehicle. "Although what good that will do either of us, I have no idea," he grumbled. Gingerly, he scuffed forward, making sure the soles of his boots stayed in as direct a contact with hard ground as possible. He swiped a sleeve very carefully over the driver-side window and tapped on the glass. "Hello?" He bent down to peer inside, not realizing how much he was dreading what he'd find until he spied the driver seat and sighed deeply when he saw it was empty. There was no one on the passenger side either, and no backseat to worry about. He glanced in the open truck bed, but the lumpy shapes beneath the snow weren't the right size for a human body.

Good Samaritan deed done, he resolutely turned himself

back to the other immediate problem: digging himself out. As he trudged back to his half-buried car, he wondered where the occupant of the truck had gone. Hopefully it had still been daylight, and not snowing yet. Maybe a rain-slick road was cause for the accident. The driver had probably hiked down into town or caught a ride in.

Which left him with the fun task of finding something suitable for digging out the rear tires. Or, barring that, at least clearing out the tailpipe so he could stay warm through the night. Digging with his hands, clad in nothing more than his meager leather driving gloves, was not much of an option. Partly because his fingers were already numb. But mostly because it would be pretty much like trying to hand scoop water from a quickly flooding boat.

A quick rummage in the glove box yielded nothing of help. The oversized map book was briefly considered and rejected. The floor mat proved too unwieldy. He was contemplating trying to liberate the skinny license plate from the front bumper, when it occurred to him to go back and hunt around the bed of the truck. One of those lumps might actually be something useful.

The snow was beginning to accumulate rapidly on the road now as the storm seemed to be settling in for a good night's run. If he didn't dig out soon, it wouldn't matter much. The Escort he'd rented had proven to be a tough little car on the steep inclines and winding roads in the mountains, but it didn't have much in the way of ground clearance, nor did it come with four-wheel drive. He wished now he'd pushed a bit harder on having them locate a truck, but the look on the rental clerk's face when he'd inquired about one had quickly disabused him of that idea. SUV's weren't too popular on this side of the pond as it turned out.

He dug around in the pile of snow in the rear of the truck, going by touch, sighing in relief when his fingers bumped up against a long wooden handle. "Please be a shovel," he muttered. Unfortunately, it turned out to be a heavy garden rake. He struck out twice more with a post hole digger and an old straw broom. "Great, I'll just sweep my way clear." He kept the broom out, though, thinking he could at least clear his windshield during the night to keep a lookout for oncoming vehicles. And the handle might prove helpful in clearing a tailpipe tunnel.

He went back to the hunt, careful not to lean on the truck or rock it in any way. The last thing he wanted to do was send it over the edge of the road. He wanted to meet the locals at some point, but that was not exactly the kind of welcome he was hoping for.

He ended up using the broomstick to gently probe the far side of the truck bed, but between the dark and the snow, he had no idea what he was poking at. His hands, toes and nose were numb as he took the broom and turned back toward his car. Only to stop dead in his tracks. Someone stood not five yards away, heavily cloaked arms folded.

She motioned to the broom in his hand. "If you were planning on flying out on that thing, I have to warn you, the guarantee expired last month." Her softly accented voice carried easily through the wind. It was strong, and if he wasn't mistaken, more than faintly amused. An intriguing combination that got his full male attention, despite the surreal nature of the situation.

"I think all flights have been grounded due to weather anyway," he responded. He gestured toward the truck. "Yours? Or are you just out for an evening stroll?"

She lifted a mittened hand. "That and trying to get a signal on my mobile."

He brightened. Maybe the evening wasn't going to end with him sleeping pretzel style in his compact after all. "Any luck?"

She brushed snow from her face and it made him wish she'd step closer so he could see her more clearly. She was tall, but that was about all he could tell, with her bundled head to toe. Whatever hair she had was tucked up beneath a tassled knit cap.

"I suppose the smart answer, given the circumstances, would be to say yes, absolutely," she told him. "Two burly men will be here shortly to tow me out."

"Don't kid a man who's lost all feeling in his toes."

He could have sworn she flashed a smile. It took a surprising amount of control to keep from stepping closer to find out for sure. But rather than follow up with a witty rejoinder, she shifted gears. "Was that my fault?" she asked, motioning to his car. "I didn't have anything to set out as a warning. I was hoping I was far enough off the road." She laughed a little, in what sounded like relief. "Though I was just thankful I was still on enough of it to get out in one piece."

"What happened?"

"Front tire blew coming around the bend. I almost—" She broke off as she looked past him at her truck, hanging so close to the edge. She hugged her arms closer and shook her head.

Tag was moving closer without even thinking about it.

She put up a hand, stopping him a few short feet away. "Sorry. Don't worry. I'm fine, really. I guess I've been operating on automatic pilot since it happened and looking at it now, it just kind of hit me how close . . ." She trailed off, looked at her truck, then smiled as she shook her head. "Guess it wasn't my turn. But I'm sorry I got you stuck."

Now that he could see her smile, he wanted to see her eyes. Mostly he just wanted her to keep talking. He wasn't typically seduced by an accent. Apparently there were exceptions. Or his mind could be going numb along with the rest of him.

"Not your fault," he said. "I should have taken the turns more slowly. I guess I was just anxious to get into the next town and find a bed for the night."

"Here visiting from the States?"

He nodded, locking his knees together as the shivers started to set in. He'd been okay when he'd been moving around, but standing in one place wasn't such a good idea.

She shook her head. "I'm afraid Durnish, which you probably passed through a ways back, is it."

"I was hoping Calyth—"

She was already shaking her head. "It's hardly more than a bump in the road, though there are a few little shops right there at the heart of it." She lifted a shoulder. "I've never really stopped there, so I could be wrong." She cocked her head. "First time out of the city?"

Now it was his turn to smile, even though he could no longer feel his lips. "Not hardly." He glanced back at his car. "But, since getting into town isn't an option, I was planning on clearing out the tailpipe so I could run the heat off and on during the night. You're welcome to join me. I don't think you should risk getting in your truck." He lifted his hands. "And you won't have to worry about me making any untoward advances. I have no feeling left in my extremities at this point."

She regarded him for a moment, then said, "Yes, that would slow things down a bit, wouldn't it?"

There it was again, that sly amusement. He knew she realized she was in a potentially dangerous situation for a young woman, but she was handling it with an almost insouciant disregard. He rather liked that. Made him wish he'd met her under other circumstances. And that he hadn't promised her he'd be on his best behavior. Despite being numb, she made him think about doing things that weren't entirely civilized.

"Why don't you wait in the car while I dig out a tunnel? You can have the backseat and I'll take the front, if it would make you feel more comfortable."

"Quite the gentleman Yank, aren't you?" she said. "But I'm numb enough myself to take you up on your offer. Besides, it's either trust you or freeze to death, isn't it?"

"Yes, well, it's gratifying to know I can get a woman to choose me over certain death."

She tucked her hands in her pockets and started toward his car. "Oh, I'm sure women choose you even when death isn't certain."

"Thanks," he said, falling into step behind her. "I think."

Her laugh trailed behind her through the wind and falling snow. It made him curl his hands against the desire to reach for her, tug that cap off and see for himself what lay beneath. A long fall of hair? Or something short and spiky? For a tall woman, she had something of the nymph about her. Probably her playful smile, amused tone. From her stride, long-legged and sure, he'd bet she wasn't slight of frame, no matter the bulk of the parka. Which likely played into her air of natural confidence, though it did next to nothing to decrease his interest in her. If anything . . .

She paused at the rear side door to his rental. "Are you sure there's nothing I can do to help? Or would I just be in your way?"

He stopped beside her, closer than he'd been as yet. Close enough to see the sprinkle of freckles across her nose and cheeks, the wide fullness of her mouth, the delightful tilt to the corner of her eyes when she smiled, though the color of them was still a mystery. One he was finding himself quite compelled to solve.

"I can handle it," he told her, hoping like hell she attributed the lower pitch in his voice to the weather . . . and not his reaction to being so close to her. Yet so impossibly far from being able to do anything about this sudden and quite intense feeling of attraction.

Her smile curved even more deeply. "You know what, Gentleman Yank?" she said, a bit more softly this time, though every bit as amused. "I believe you can."

He might have spent the better part of the past several years deep in the Yucatan jungle, but even he recognized a come-on when he heard it.

At least he was pretty damn sure it was a come-on. Maybe it was just wishful thinking that had taken on hallucinogenic proportions due to the cryogenic loss of brain cells. Which was entirely possible.

Her hand was on the door handle, only she didn't open it. He was holding the broom in a frozen death grip, only he made no move toward the wall of snow encasing the rear end of the car.

"You should get out of the cold," he said, after the silence had spun out far too long.

"So should you."

"If I don't clear the tailpipe, we won't have any heat."

Her smile curved in a way that could only be described as wicked. His body was more than responsive. In fact, he didn't so much mind the numb parts any longer. As long as that one part had life in it, that was all that apparently mattered.

"Something tells me we'd manage," she said, then opened the door.

For all that Tag rarely, if ever, felt dull-witted or slow, he felt very much of both at the moment. She had presented him with a perfect opportunity, and he'd squandered the moment with inane talk of snow removal. Serve him right to sleep cramped in the front seat. An adventure that would be even more uncomfortable in his current state.

She began to unfasten her jacket.

"What are you doing?"

"I thought it might be smart to brush all the snow off and stow it above the backseat. Didn't want to get your car any more damp than necessary." She quickly slid out of the jacket, shivering as she quickly smacked at the snow crystals coating the collar and shoulders.

"Here, let me do that. You go on and get in." He didn't let her argue, but took the coat and opened the door.

She smiled over her shoulder. "Used to giving orders are you?"

Now it was his turn to smile. "You might say that."

"Well then, there's something we have in common." She turned and propped an arm on the open door, as if the sun were shining and snow wasn't fast collecting on her shoulders. "Do people generally jump when you bark a command?"

He merely continued to smile, then said, "You're getting snow on your sweater."

"Well, then, I suppose I'll just have to take that off too, won't I?"

Yep, his body was definitely on board with wherever she wanted to steer it. "Are you always so stubborn?" He'd almost said stunning.

"Somehow I think that might be another shared character trait."

"Well, as much as I might enjoy seeing just how far you'd go with this, I only arrived in Scotland this morning. I really don't want to start my trip by explaining to local law officials why I have the frozen corpse of a half-naked woman laying next to my car."

Her eyebrow lifted. "Only half-naked? Hmm. I might have misjudged you after all."

It had already occurred to Tag that this was possibly the oddest conversation he'd ever had with a woman, or anyone for that matter. Which, considering he'd once talked himself out of being the dinner entrée for an aboriginal tribal chief, was saying something. He nodded to the backseat. "You're letting snow into my car."

"So I am," she said, then sighed and shook her head. "Alright then, since you're being such a Good Samaritan, and in the spirit of welcoming you to our bonny shores, I suppose I should play nice. It's just that it's been a simply dreadful day and for some reason, you're fun to play with."

Tag chuckled at that, and without thinking about possible repercussions, reached out and tugged her cap free. A coil of dark, springy hair uncoiled to her shoulders.

She arched a brow in reaction, but said nothing.

He slapped the tassled wool cap on his jeans. "Just getting the snow off your hat."

"Ah," she said with a brief smile. She took the hat from him but didn't get in the car right away.

"Now you're just getting snow in your hair."

She regarded him for another long minute, then said, "Maybe I'm hoping you'll brush it off." She glanced down, then back up. "You look like you have nice hands."

That choked a surprise laugh out of him. She'd gone from flirting innuendo to a no-nonsense invitation in less than five minutes. It should have turned him off. He wasn't much for pushy women. But there was something about her that made him think she wasn't quite the aggressor she was making herself out to be. Maybe something having to do with that bad day she'd mentioned. "Are you always so forward with men you meet on the side of the road?"

"Never," she stated, easily and quite unequivocally. She wrinkled her nose a little. "Interesting, isn't it?"

Interesting indeed, Tag thought. And interested. Because he was definitely interested.

She finally moved to duck inside the car. He reached out reflexively and brushed the snow from her hair, making her pause, then turn back again. His gloved hand drifted to her cheek, then her chin.

She looked him steadily in the eye as she leaned toward him. And he held that gaze as he slowly lowered his mouth to hers.

Her lips were cold, or maybe it was just that his own were frozen. And yet just one soft kiss managed to heat him up quite nicely.

"And that was for?" she managed, when he lifted his head and let his hand drop away.

He shrugged, smiled. "You looked like you had nice lips. Turns out I was right."

She just laughed as she finally slid into the car. "Let me

know if you want your engine started," she said as she pulled the door shut behind her.

"Oh, I think you've already taken care of that, thanks," he murmured under his breath as he moved to the rear end of the car.

He began the arduous task of clearing snow with a broom, and realized that despite the fact that he was stranded in the middle of God knew where, freezing his ass off in a Highland snowstorm . . . he was grinning like an idiot.

He even started to whistle. *A bonny welcome indeed.*

Chapter 6

As soon as he moved toward the back of the car, Maura slumped back in the seat and let out a surprised laugh. "And just what was that you were doing out there?" she asked herself, a disbelieving smile curving her lips. She sighed and let her head drop back, closing her eyes and daring herself not to replay the last ten minutes over in her mind.

That hadn't really been her out there. Maura Sinclair, independent woman, and all around smart girl. Smart girls didn't flirt with strange men, much less goad them into stealing a kiss. And they certainly didn't carry on while stranded in a snowstorm with no hope of escape. For all she knew he was a serial killer, come to Scotland to skip out on being executed back in the States.

She snorted at her flight of fancy. "You've definitely got to stop reading thrillers past midnight." She craned her neck and peered out of the rapidly fogging windows. She was unable to see him, but she could hear him digging and rooting about.

He'd seemed like a good sort. Of course she was inclined to believe so considering the liberties she'd all but encouraged him to take, wasn't she? Besides, what were the odds she'd have an accident and get stranded with an axe murderer anyway?

He had a nice voice. And kind eyes. A rationalization perhaps, but true enough. Even in the gloom, she'd been struck by that right off. And yet there'd been something more. Even when he'd smiled and his eyes had crinkled at the corners, there had been a certain intensity. Observant was the word that came to mind. And yet she'd felt no sense of threat. Maybe because it had been that very element that had attracted her to him in the first place.

Because she certainly hadn't come on to him just because he'd been there. It had been a bad day or two, no doubt, but that hadn't compelled her to suddenly throw herself at every man who strayed into her path. And men had stared intently at her before, but there was usually an element of tongue lolling to it that immediately left her cold. Not this man. He didn't stare so much as study. Yes, that was it. He'd been quite . . . aware. She shivered, and it wasn't entirely because the air inside the car was almost as cold as the air outside.

It really wasn't like her to shamelessly flirt like that, even with a bloke she'd had her eye on for some length of time. Of course, in the past forty-eight hours she'd certainly witnessed her share of out-of-the-ordinary behavior, hadn't she? Perhaps she just wanted to give it a go herself. No one could blame her.

She sighed again, but this time there was more an air of defeat in it. She didn't want to think about coming back from town yesterday morning to find . . . well, what she'd found. Much less dwell on what Jory and Priss might well be doing at this very moment. And her meeting with Wentworth had done little to lift her spirits. As it happened he hadn't been able to see her any earlier today, and she'd only caught Val in time to learn she was off spending the night out with her new boyfriend. At least she'd still offered up her couch so Maura hadn't had to pay for a room on top of it all. The whole trip had been a colossal waste of time. And for her trouble, her reward had been a blown tire and a near-death experience.

That last part alone might possibly explain her brief display of promiscuity out there. It wasn't every day she got to watch her entire life flash before her eyes. Complete with a few scenes from yesterday she could have definitely gone without reliving.

"So, in summary," she stated aloud, ticking off the list on her fingers, "you've lost both your lover, and your best friend; gotten dismal news from the land agent; come an inch or two away from dying; and stranded yourself in a snowstorm, with no hope of rescue." Honestly, put like that, it was amazing she hadn't jumped him, really.

Could anyone blame her if she indulged in some torrid, tawdry little one-night stand? She folded her arms more snugly around her, trying to ward off the bone-seeping chill inside the car. Hardly, she thought, starting to feel a bit righteous about the whole thing now. He was a tourist, passing through. The perfect man, really. And she could give him a little Highland fling that would have him fondly recalling his trip to Scotland for many years to come. An all around win-win situation. And Lord knows she could use one of those right about now.

The sudden rapping on the roof of the car made her jump and let out a squeal of surprise. She spun around to find her future partner in gratuitous sex motioning her to start the engine. Her cheeks warmed as she peered at him through the fogged window, wondering what he'd think if he knew the plans she'd been sitting here rationally making. Of course, she had given him several broad hints already.

He motioned again and she quickly turned her attention to the matter at hand. There'd be plenty of time for the other as soon as they got the heat working again. She'd been about to lean over the seat to reach the keys when she realized it wasn't an automatic. She'd have to get in the front seat so she could reach the clutch. She debated getting out and going around, but rather than face the cold wind and snow, she opted to just crawl over.

After a few minutes, much swearing, and an altercation with the stick shift that was definitely going to leave a mark, she managed to arrange herself in the driver's seat with a fair level of aplomb. When she finally dared look out the window, fully expecting to find him laughing, she was relieved to note he was already back by the rear of the car, apparently wanting to make sure the tunnel he'd dug around the pipe held up.

She depressed the clutch and turned the key, doubly relieved when the car started without so much as a hiccup. The air that belched out of the vents was cold, though, and she snatched her hands off the steering wheel and tucked them in her armpits.

Then he was there, tapping on her window, mouthing something she couldn't make out when the windows swiftly fogged over as the fans kept pumping out cold air. She started to lower the window, but the snow had edged up the glass and would likely cave in all over her if she did.

Which left her with the option of motioning him to get in the back—thereby giving up any chance she had of reclining with leg room—or moving across the stick shift to the passenger seat. Or attempting the ever-so-graceful crawling back over the seat maneuver. Thankfully he kept her from having to decide by rounding the front of the car and climbing in front next to her.

"God, I'm frozen through and through," he muttered as he quickly closed the door behind him. He'd already peeled out of his coat, which he stowed on the front dash, to the side of the vents, then he shifted so his back was to her. "Don't take this the wrong way." He gripped the back of his sweater and pulled it over his head, revealing a white T-shirt. Which came off immediately thereafter.

"Not that I'm minding the show," she said, which was most certainly the truth. He virtually filled the car. Or so it seemed to her. She hadn't remembered him as being so tall. Or wide. Perhaps it was the tight quarters making him appear more so. She'd certainly never have assumed his shoulders were so broad. Or that he was so deeply bronzed. Even in the dark she could tell his skin was a great deal darker than her own.

As he leaned forward to tug his T-shirt out of his pants, her gaze dipped downward, whereupon she learned another interesting fact. He was apparently tan all over. She swallowed hard. "What exactly are you doing?"

All too soon that fine expanse of muscled back was once again covered up as he quickly yanked his sweater back on. He turned around and shrugged back into his coat. "I figured we should tie something to the antenna. As a warning."

She nodded to the shirt in his hand. "I'm not sure white is the way to go." She smiled, unable, it seemed, to keep her mouth shut for more than five seconds when she was around him. "Although if you're wanting to discuss terms of surrender . . ."

Even in the dark she had no problem making out his broad grin. "Hold that thought," he told her, then bailed out of the car, quickly closing the door behind him.

Her heart tripped over itself. Had he really just said— "Och, what are you doing here, Maura girl?" But she was already leaning forward and rubbing a spot on the windshield, trying to clear the fog so she could watch him. But the fog was actually caused by the snow piling up on the outside of the glass. She fumbled a bit around the steering wheel until she found the knob she was looking for. Only to hear a yelp from outside before the blades had finished two complete swoops.

"What are you doing!" came his shout.

She immediately flipped the knob back off, then glanced through the now clear windshield. He'd been tying the shirt to the top of the antenna . . . which put his stomach in direct line of where the wiper blades had deposited most of the snow. "I'm sorry," she called out, not sure if he could hear her.

He said nothing, but when he got done tying the shirt, he turned and stalked off, quickly disappearing into the swirl of the night storm. "Where are you bloody going?" she called out, knowing he couldn't hear her. The whip of the wind tossed the T-shirt about, catching her eye. It was then she realized that it wasn't a whole T-shirt any longer. How the hell had he torn the thing? With his teeth?

She shivered a little again. And again it had nothing to do with the cold. Of course, she might have just blown any chance she had with the guy. Not that there was much they could do in the close confines of the tiny car anyway. Besides, she hadn't been much for backseat wrestling as a teenager, and no matter how bad the past few days had been, she sure as hell wasn't horny enough to cram her body—

Just then the door was yanked open and he climbed back in, bringing a swirl of snow inside the car with him, and all over her. Something she now realized he'd been careful not to do the first time around. She supposed she deserved it.

In the narrow pool of overhead light, she watched as he doffed his coat once again and hung it around the back of the seat. Only this time she didn't have to imagine what his body looked like beneath that worn sweater. The light blinked off as she was squeezing her thighs together at the mere thought of him stripping again. She couldn't help but wonder what the front of him looked like. Was he truly golden . . . all over?

Okay, so maybe she wasn't wanting to try full-out shagging in such a tiny space. But she might be up for a bit of snogging in one. He was a good kisser, that she already knew, even from that brief brush of lips.

His hair was a shaggy mop of dark curls, which had been one of the first things she'd noticed about him, and had found herself surprisingly attracted to. She typically went more for the well-groomed, which did limit her choices around home, what with most of the men being farm lads or construction workers of some sort. Still, there was a difference in being a bit moppish and the shag of curls this man sported.

Of course, the farm lads did have a boundless enthusiasm when it came to sex—likely being around all those barnyard animals and seeing nature take its course as a purely natural thing. But she noted that outside of bed, conversations didn't go much beyond the latest technique in sheep shearing. And though she wasn't much for long-term arrangements, she did want her relationships, however long, to engage both brain and body. Which of course didn't begin to explain Jory's presence in her life for the past six months. Apparently she wasn't immune to that baby-of-the-family charm of his either.

But Jory had been natty about his appearance. Something about this one's shaggy curls had struck her differently, though. Maybe it was that awareness in his gaze she'd noted earlier. The overhead light had stayed on long enough to illuminate other details she hadn't picked up the first time around. His hair wasn't nearly as dark as she'd thought. In fact, it was a heavily sun-bleached brown if she wasn't mistaken. Had she found herself the stereotypical California surfer boy, then?

He certainly fit the physical mold. Yet, that intensity of his, along with the educated pattern to his speech, said otherwise. There was a brain beneath that mop of curls, she'd bet on it. Lord knows her libido already had.

"Where's your coat?" he asked her, shifting so he faced her.

She would have answered him, but she was too busy staring at his neck. Even with the brief flash of light, her eyes had long since acclimated to the dark. Enough that, at this close range anyway, she could more than make out the shape, or she should say shapes, tightly circling his neck. Even the gloom couldn't disguise the long pointy teeth, interspersed with what looked like short, skinny bones, all woven into some kind of choker.

Not an axe murderer, she thought. *Just a cannibal.*

He smiled then, his own teeth a white beacon in the dark. A slash against his tanned skin, which sent a thrill coursing through her that was only partly fear.

"Sharks?" she asked, thinking it might be some kind of surfer thing. Praying.

He looked confused for a brief moment, then his smile widened as he realized the direction of her gaze. "Crocodile. This was made for me about five years ago, as a good-luck charm, at the request of a tribal shaman. It's supposed to ward off those with evil intent. Considering it kept me from being an appetizer later that evening, I figured he might be on to something."

She didn't quite know what to say to that. Had it come from just about anyone else, she'd have thought they were having a go with her. Something in the easy, comfortable way he related the story, yet so directly holding her gaze at the same time, had her believing he spoke the truth. "I don't suppose I'd take it off either, then," she finally managed, unable to pull her gaze away from it. Or him.

"It was actually woven around my neck as I sat there. By six of the tribe's prettiest women. All the chief's daughters." He grinned. "Virgins of course."

"Of course," she echoed, still trying to wrap her mind around his fantastical story.

"I wasn't quite sure of their intent at the time," he went on, quite casually. "I thought they were going to chain me to a leash or do something else with it. The whole process took hours."

"That would explain the fit." She could understand his trepidation. It was like a collar of sorts. And given as she had absolutely no taste for kink with her sex, that didn't remotely explain why she had to fight the urge to squirm. In a good way. Something about the way it served to make his neck look thicker, stronger. Daft, she was, of course, but she couldn't shake the image of him in some kind of tribal loincloth, paint streaking his face, as a circle of women bent around him, their slender fingers flying as they wove him into his choker. It made even less sense that the whole visual only served to stimulate her more.

"It's a long time to spend wondering about your fate," he said. "Especially given as the hut I was in directly faced the central fire pit. And they had a big enough one going to roast an ox. Or me."

"My God," she said, truly unable to imagine it. Of course, for all she knew, he'd bought the thing in some odd trinket shop. But she had to admit, if he was having a go, he was being awfully convincing about it. Must be the way those light eyes of his gleamed, shining out like twin beacons from his dark face. She caught herself rubbing her arms, and hoped he thought she was merely warding off a chill. And not nervous. Or trying to scrub away the twitchy tingly effect he was having on her. It was only serving to make that part worse anyway. It felt like her skin was screaming for contact. Preferably with him.

"It wasn't my best day, that's for sure."

"Five years ago," she said, scrambling to re-establish some kind of normalcy in this conversation. Which had started out pretty unusually earlier, so why this should come as a real surprise, she didn't know. From the moment her life had flashed in front of her, the whole night had taken on a rather surreal feeling anyway. "And yet you still wear it?"

"I'd have to cut it off. Which, according to tribal legend, would render my soul ripe for the plucking by any number of evil spirits. And trust me, if you'd seen the drawings of those spirits on the inside of their dwellings, you'd be in no hurry to get rid of it either." He shifted and leaned his weight back against the door, smiling easily. "Occupational hazard, I'd guess you'd say."

Welcome heat was now pumping from the vents and her toes and fingers tingled as they began to thaw. *Might as well join all of the other tingling body parts,* she thought. She'd worried earlier that they might not have enough petrol to see them through until morning, when someone was bound to come across them and hopefully ferry them into town.

Now? She wasn't so concerned. Somehow, as long as she was in close proximity to the man presently studying her, body heat was going to be the least of her worries. "So you're not so much Moondoggie, as Indiana Jones then, I take it."

He barked out a laugh. "Moondoggie?"

She was thankful for the dark, as it hid the blush she felt climb into her cheeks. Some women looked delicately abashed with flushed skin. With her fairness and freckles, she generally managed to look as if she'd just come running from a fire. "I suppose I must confess my addiction to your corny American beach movies. And your less-than-corny adventure flicks."

"Have you ever been?"

"To the beach? Or cutting a swath through the jungle?"

He shook his head and the shaggy curls rustled about his head. The abundance of snow outside created its own sort of night glow. But though she could make out his smile, or the gleam of his eyes, she couldn't make out the details, such as gauging his thoughts or reactions, in anything but a general body language sort of way. It disconcerted her. She was unabashedly curious about the man, but then who wouldn't be, given the few details he'd shared so far? And yet there was this sense she had about him that he didn't need any sort of light to be able to detect her thoughts or feelings. It had her feeling a bit edgy.

Well that and the fact that he'd just folded his arms across his chest. Shallow though it may be, the play of muscles in his forearms and the way this new pose showcased just how broad of chest and shoulder the man was again, admittedly affected her. Her mind jumped back to that kiss they'd shared, what seemed like eons ago now. A mere brushing of the lips, but the thought made her body hum all over again.

Her gaze was drawn to his hands, and her thoughts turned to what it would feel like to have them on her. All over her. He'd tucked them next to his body, precluding her from adding more detail to her little fantasy. She wasn't really that big a sucker for brawn, but she had to admit that a tall man with big hands could get her attention quite readily. Everyone had their own preferences after all.

She realized she was staring, but then, he'd been studying her, had he not? Of course, it had been more the way a scientist studied a specimen, or so she'd felt, than the lusty notions that were presently filling her apparently empty head. She shifted and settled her weight back against her door, letting her gaze drift in what she hoped was a casual manner, away from him and out the front windshield. Not that she could see anything. Snow had once again coated the glass. But if he'd noticed the direction of her gaze before, much less the direction of her thoughts, he mercifully didn't let on.

"Have you been to America?" he reiterated, as if there hadn't been an awkward gap in their conversation. His voice was deep, but there was a pure tone to it. No raspiness, no huskiness. If he sang, it would probably be a rich, full baritone, with pitch-perfect clarity.

The very idea of hearing that voice in her ear had her rubbing her palms up and down her arms again. It took damn little to send that quivery sensation rippling through her. The slightest provocation and she was all twitchy and damp. Just by existing in her personal space, he effortlessly plucked at every nerve ending she had.

And yes, she was aware that maybe this was all just a knee-jerk reaction to, well, everything. All she had to do was decide if that mattered. "No, I've never been to the States," she told him, pleased at her casual tone. "Nor have I surfed, or searched for treasure, for that matter." She hugged her knees to her and tried to find a comfortable position in the little bucket seat. *Would it be terribly rude of me to move to the backseat,* she wondered? With the stick shift between the seats, stretching out fully up front was going to be difficult at best. He was the larger of the two of them, and he had done the work clearing the space so they could run the heater. She supposed if anyone was due the back bench seat, it was him. Of course, they could stack themselves up back there, conserve body heat and be more comfortable . . .

She debated mentioning that, but for all her forward suggestiveness earlier, she felt oddly reticent to make that first move now. So she tried not to think about it as she shifted around once again. "So," she asked, thinking it best to keep her mind off the backseat altogether. "What is it you do that brings you into such close contact with cannibals?"

"I'm an anthropologist. Right now I'm working for a museum that is co-sponsoring a dig in conjunction with a university program out of New Mexico. My focus is mostly on Mayan history. They currently have digs in Mexico and Central America."

"Not the most stable place in the world. Sounds dangerous in all sorts of ways."

"Yes, though we generally have more to fear from the local political and drug factions than we do the aboriginal tribes."

"So what does an anthropologist do? I mean, I gather the archaeologist's job is to dig up the actual artifacts, right? What role do you play?"

"My job is to figure out what all the artifacts mean in terms of how that particular civilization worked. Both the layout of the ruins themselves, as well as whatever remains we find, and where we find them, can tell us a lot about how that particular segment of society lived. And died." He smiled. "You really don't want to get me started, trust me. I could bore you to tears for hours on end with Mayan history alone."

She smiled in return. She liked his easy confidence, the warmth of his voice, the ease that seemed to settle between them so naturally. He was pretty sexy. For a geeky sort. "It's not like we have anything else to do for the next eight to ten hours."

"Oh, we could probably think of something more entertaining."

He'd said it more casually than suggestively. Not that it mattered. Funny how quickly a spike of sexual tension could reinsert itself into their easy camaraderie. She found herself thinking about that backseat idea all over again. How easy would it be to push things back in the direction they'd been heading outside? She got the feeling he wouldn't need much encouragement. At the same time, she didn't sense any overt sort of threat from him either. Despite the tribal teeth circling his neck. Or maybe because of them. What with him worrying about spirits protecting his mortal soul and all.

"You're rather far afield then, aren't you?" she asked him, stalling. A little. It wasn't like her to be indecisive. But then, it wasn't exactly like her to plot a one-night stand with a tourist, either. "Or did the Mayans make a trip to the auld sod that I'm unaware of?"

"Actually, you might be surprised how far reaching their influence was. But no, I'm here on an unrelated matter."

He didn't elaborate, so she didn't pry. Not directly anyway. But she wanted to. She tucked her legs closer and propped her chin on her knees. "Your first time to Scotland, then?" she asked instead.

"I was on a dig in Wales while I was still in college. But that's the closest I've come." He shifted a little, then noticing her watching him, said, "The sweater is a bit itchy without the undershirt."

It was on the tip of her tongue to suggest he could take care of that little problem pretty easily. Somehow she managed to resist. Barely. She tried not to openly admire the play of muscles beneath the dark knit. But it was tough. "A shame you can't get another shirt," she said, which was a bald-faced lie. She wanted him in no shirt, not more clothes. "I guess your luggage is in the boot?"

He nodded. "I'll be all right. I'm just not used to wearing so many layers."

Maura had to all but bite off her tongue. Why, she wasn't sure. She wanted him. She was reasonably sure, given he hadn't exactly fended off her earlier advances, that he was like-minded. They were both adults. And heaven knew they weren't going anywhere. "A fair-weather sort, are you?"

"I wouldn't say there's anything fair about the weather in Chacchoben." He shrugged. "Still, I guess I prefer swatting mosquitoes to risking frostbite."

"Understandable, I suppose."

He cocked his head. "You don't look too convinced."

"Let's just say I don't mind working up a good sweat, but I'd rather there not be insects involved in the endeavor. Most especially the sort that like to take a piece of you home with them."

He grinned. "Understandable, I suppose."

They were both smiling, all convivial and the like, and then the moment shifted, the silence dragged on a wee bit too long. And that finely tuned sexual tension that so effortlessly arced between them, spiked up again.

"I should probably go out and make sure the pipe is staying clear," he said, but he didn't so much as hazard a glance out the window. Which were beyond fogged at this point, inside and out.

"We should crack the windows a bit," she agreed. "Safety and all that."

"I meant to do that when I got back in the car. I guess I was a bit sidetracked," he added, his tone somewhat acerbic.

"I'm so sorry for that, really. I just couldn't see and I didn't think. Honestly. Maybe I should get out and check. After all, you've barely begun to thaw out after being out there all that time." She uncurled her legs and was shifting back around when he leaned forward and touched her arm. She stilled instantly, glanced over at him, then down at his hands. A nice, wide hand, with long, strong fingers. It was all she could do not to sigh in catlike contentment. "It's only fair," she told him, though that was a joke if she'd ever heard one. Not that it wasn't her turn to go outside, but honestly, nothing about life had been fair of late.

However, she was thinking she could be persuaded to overlook a good deal of it, or at least put off dealing with the fallout from it, for another couple of hours. If he was so inclined to indulge her.

He squeezed her arm, smiled in a friendly way. "I'll take care of it. Why don't you go ahead and crawl in the back. It's getting late and we might as well try to stretch out as best we can."

"You're the tall one, you should take the backseat. It's your car, after all."

"It's the rental company's car," he corrected glibly. "I don't even own one."

"You do have a license though, right?"

"What, you're suddenly worried about my driving abilities?" He grinned. "I'd hazard to say neither of us should be pointing fingers there. Although in my defense, I haven't had to drive on the left, with a stick shift, no less, in a long time."

"All of which is to say you aren't going to answer my question, are you?"

He leaned forward so he could shrug into his jacket. The motion brought his face within inches of hers. "I might not be the one to preach about playing it safe. But I'm not reckless, if that's what you're worried about."

Why did she think they were no longer talking about his driving abilities? At least not where cars were concerned. "Well," she said, her lips curving of their own volition. Apparently she'd made her decision. "There's reckless . . . and then there's reckless."

Chapter 7

She was really something. If he'd been the type to spend any time imagining the perfect vacation fling, he couldn't have come up with a more unlikely scenario. But considering his life was generally made up of a string of unlikely scenarios, this trip and the reason behind it being a prime example, he wasn't going to complain about this latest detour.

Tag smiled. "In all the snowstorms in all the world, how is it you had to come walking into mine?"

She laughed. "So now I'm Ilsa to your Rick? Funny, I don't seem to recall dumping you in Paris."

"Well, this isn't exactly a gin joint in Morocco, either, so it's a stretch to begin with." He should get outside, check the snowfall around the tailpipe. But he couldn't seem to pull away from her. Up close like this, he could make out the freckles on her nose, and the way her eyes tilted up at the corners when she smiled.

"You know that bad day I was mentioning earlier," she said, covering the hand he'd laid on her arm with her own, "It was Top Ten kind of bad. I figured cheating death was just a cosmic joke, seeing as I'd managed not to launch myself off a cliff, only to end up facing freezing to death. Anyway, all this is to say, that, though I'm really sorry I'm inadvertently responsible for you having to spend the night in your car—"

"You're happy just to have a car to spend the night in?"

Her smile widened, and he thought he spied the hint of dimples. It was an odd juxtaposition. From their limited time together, she'd come off as assured, confident, and not a little determined. Dimples didn't seem to fit that character study. Funny then, how they only served to hike up his already growing interest in her.

"That," she agreed, her voice a shade smokier than before, "and that you happened to be the one driving it."

He managed a casual shrug. Which was admirable considering what he wanted to do was grab her and taste that smart mouth of hers again. "Hotels with stuffed down mattresses can be highly overrated," he said, trying like hell not to look at the backseat. Heated flirtation was one thing. Actually doing something constructive about it was another.

His work required thoughtful consideration, applied logic, and a great deal of deliberation before any conclusions were drawn. Much less action taken. Impulsive he was not. This recent trip notwithstanding. Of course, that same methodology applied to his personal life had resulted in a sex life that was sporadic at best. Perhaps it was time to continue just going for it, doing what he wanted, when he wanted.

Hell, he might as well have something to show for it besides a serious case of jet lag, and a pissed-off project director. He didn't want to think about the call he'd made to Manny Ortega before booking his flight to Glasgow. As it was, he'd already taken what had turned out to be an extended leave of absence when he'd come back to the States just before Christmas after getting word of his father's death. He'd been certain he'd be back on the flight by the new year and it was already close to the end of January. So asking his supervisor to extend his absence further hadn't been a joyful task. Worse was the fact that when Felix had asked him how long he'd be gone, he'd hedged. If he was going to dig around his own ancestral past, he might as well dig to his heart's content. Whether that meant a week, a month, or the rest of the damn winter, he didn't know.

Felix had given him two weeks. After that he'd be bumped from the dig. If he let that happen, it would be the first time he hadn't been either actively working a dig, or busting his ass to help find financing for the next one, since college. He wasn't too sure how he was going to feel about that, so he'd put it out of his mind for the time being. Right at this moment however, he was feeling pretty damn good. One man's sabbatical was another man's vacation, right?

"Considering what little you've told me about your work," she said, tracing little patterns on the back of his hand and up his arm with her fingertips. "I'm guessing sleeping in your car isn't the worst accommodations you've ever had."

"It might rank as the most cramped. And the coldest. Speaking of which, I should either go check the snowfall, or get out of this damp jacket."

"Do I get to vote?"

He laughed, which suddenly turned into a yawn. "Jet lag," he said, by way of apology. "I've been going since yesterday and I guess the heat in here is starting to zap me."

She reached up then, and stroked the side of his face. Her fingers were warm against his skin, and though fatigue might be claiming certain parts of his body, other parts were making it well known they weren't ready for sleep quite yet.

"You should get in the back," she told him, her eyes searching his. "Sleep while you can. I'll keep an eye on the snowfall." Her fingers drifted down the side of his face, but when he thought she'd let them drop away, she let them linger along his chin. "I'm a night bird anyway."

He instinctively covered her hand with his own, then turned his mouth into her palm, and kissed her there. He heard the soft intake of breath, knew how easy it would be to shift from the warm skin of her hand, to the soft fullness of her lips. He kept her hand to his face as he shifted his gaze just enough to catch hers. "I'll check the snow," he said, his voice hardly more than a murmur. "Then maybe we should both curl up in the back. Shared body and heat and all that."

Her lips curved and he literally ached to taste her. "So, chivalry isn't dead after all," she whispered.

"I wouldn't go that far," he said, then decided the hell with it and pulled her the rest of the way to him. "How is it we only just met, and yet I feel like I've been dying to do this for eons."

"That makes two of us," she said, just before his mouth closed on hers.

This was nothing like the kiss outside. Her skin was warm now, her lips soft and inviting. And it wasn't going to be over before it began. Any thoughts he had about keeping some shred of sanity regarding what he was doing here dissolved the instant she opened her mouth under his and welcomed him inside. It wasn't just that it had been a long time since he'd kissed a woman like this—well, okay, the instant hard-on he was sporting probably had a little to do with that—but there was more going on here somehow. It was like it wasn't enough to just kiss her, he wanted to consume her. It made no sense. But it didn't make him stop.

She wove her fingers through his hair and clutched his head, and he thought maybe he wasn't the only one losing his mind. She shifted her lips on his so she could take his mouth just as fully as he'd claimed hers. And it went quickly out of control from there. They dueled for possession, and he wasn't sure if he cared much who won. In fact, losing control altogether was feeling pretty damn imperative at the moment.

He needed to feel more of her on more of him, was all he could think. He leaned back and dragged her across the center console to sprawl awkwardly across his chest and thighs. It was the most uncomfortable position possible, and yet neither of them so much as came up for air. Her body was heavy on his, pressing the armrest into one kidney and digging a knee into his thigh. He didn't care about either. He wanted more. He wanted to feel her pressing against all of him, some parts more than others.

She was tugging at his coat, and he at her shirt. "Backseat," she mumbled, the words muffled against his jaw.

"I know," he panted. "We will. Just—" And then her mouth was on his again, and neither of them wanted to stop long enough to get comfortable. Maybe it was because if they allowed themselves so much as one tiny pause, they'd both realize just how insane this was getting, not to mention the further insanity of where it was heading.

He wrestled out of his coat and sweater, then helped her get her own sweater over her head. The air in the car was both warm and humid now from the heat of their bodies. Which meant her nipples were pressed like bullets through the silk of her bra because of him. Strict biological function from being aroused, he knew that. So why it made him feel such a strong sense of accomplishment, he had no idea.

"You're beautiful," he murmured, dropping kisses along her neck as he slid his hands down along the slope of her back.

"Och, I'm a freckled country lass," she said on a breathless laugh, then gasped as his fingers found the clasp of her bra.

He shifted her body higher as the straps slid from her milky white shoulders, revealing small, beautifully shaped breasts with dark nipples begging for attention. "I could spend the rest of the night kissing every freckle," he promised her. "And I'll get started on that, right after I take care of—" The rest of his sentence was lost on a deep groan of satisfaction as he took that dark bud between his lips.

She arched more fully into him, moaning softly. He was deeply gratified when she tugged his head back down the instant he tried to move away.

"Mmm, yes. I need—" was all he managed before capturing the other one. After all, there were two. It was only fair. He slid his hand up between them and cupped her free breast with his palm, rubbing the engorged nipple between his fingers.

"Jesus and Mary," she panted, her body writhing beneath his touch. "Do they teach you how to do this in the jungle?"

He laughed and shifted her back down so he could kiss her again. "The cultures there can be a lot . . . freer," he admitted, then sucked in his breath as her now damp nipples rubbed along his naked chest. "And there are a lot fewer clothes to get off," he said, wishing like hell he wasn't stuck in a goddamn compact car.

"Good point," she panted, then they both laughed when they reached for each other's belts at the same time.

She lifted her head just enough so he could see that sparkle in her eyes, eyes he wished he could see more clearly. He wanted to memorize every speckle of color and life in them, though he doubted he'd ever forget one second of this night. Or this woman.

"Maybe we should move to the spacious and roomy posterior of the vehicle," she said, her accent making the exaggeration even more amusing.

"Smashing idea," he said, making her snicker. "Ladies first."

He tried to help her over the seat, but as neither of them was exactly petite, it wasn't a simple maneuver. With only a few muffled *oofs* and epithets, she eventually landed in the back with her bra dangling off one shoulder and her sweater hanging crookedly off the driver's seat headrest.

"Well, that was ladylike," she said with a laugh, pushing her hair from her face as she shifted around so she could look at him. "About as graceful as a dancing elephant, I am."

"I don't believe I've ever seen an elephant dance," he said, leaning forward so he could dislodge his coat and sweater from where they'd become tangled around his waist.

"Well," she said, "now you won't feel as if you've missed anything."

Maybe it was her direct approach to, well, life in general,

and him specifically, but what should have been an awkward pause, ended up being easy and smooth. And despite the silly banter, just as sexually charged. He tossed his sweater and hers into the back. "Pillow," he told her, then quickly shrugged into his damp coat, shivering as it caressed his now quite heated skin.

"What are you doing?"

"A dancing elephant is one thing, though you should know I don't agree with your assessment. But a bull in a china shop would be better than me trying to wedge over those seats. I'm going the chilly route." He glanced in the back then, intent on telling her to use their sweaters as a temporary blanket, but the words got all hung up on his tongue when he got a good look at her.

She was leaning back with her legs sprawled, one along the seat, one propped on the floor. She clutched the sweaters to her belly, but otherwise she was all long trousers and luminescent bare skin. Her hair was a disheveled mass of curls, and if there were more light, he'd imagine her skin would be flushed where his cheeks had rubbed against it. She was relaxed and easy in her partial nudity, which for some reason made him all the more hyper-aware of his own. Every inch of his skin felt alive.

And it was about to feel more so, he thought, blindly reaching for the door handle behind him. Only an idiot or a fool would prolong their time apart. He was both often enough that he still couldn't figure out what he'd done to deserve this waking fantasy dream of a night. Well, if you didn't consider the freezing weather and the cramped quarters, anyway.

Her grin widened. "Not that I'm trying to dampen our spirits . . . but, um, just how long have you been in the jungle anyway?"

His own smile turned sheepish. "I'm sorry, do I have drool on my chin or something?"

"Maybe it's all that talk about cannibals, but you're looking at me like you want to devour me whole." She shuddered a little then, but he didn't think it was in dread as he was quick to note how she shifted and pressed her thighs together.

His body leapt in response. His mind leapt even farther. "Is that a bad thing?"

She laughed. "As long as it doesn't involve big black pots sitting over an open fire, I guess not."

"I think you can safely rule that out."

She cocked her head and said somewhat pointedly, "Well then, speaking of safety . . ."

It surprised Tag to know he could still blush. There were a number of women in his profession, and given the substandard living conditions and harsh realities they often faced, few of them were the shy or retiring sort. So why this woman's directness would catch him off guard the way it did, much less affect him so viscerally, was a mystery. Which was perfectly fine with him. He lived to solve mysteries.

"I might have been in the jungle a bit too long, but given that, I've been inoculated against just about everything a human being can be given shots for. And my employers are pretty demanding when it comes to medical screening. I'd like to say it's because they worry about our health, but it's really just an insurance issue."

She hugged the sweaters she still held and her smile spread into one that was both amused, and if he was seeing right in the dim light, affectionate. Imagine that.

"What?" he asked her, when she simply continued to study him, her expression unchanging.

"You're the most unusual man I've ever met. Which, given that I live in the back of beyond, possibly isn't saying much, but I've been to university, spent some time living in the big city, and well . . ." She lifted a bare shoulder, and he thought she was possibly the most lovely woman he'd ever seen. "You fascinate me," she said.

"The feeling is decidedly mutual."

Her face lit up, and though it probably wouldn't hold up under prolonged analysis, at that moment, he felt quite smitten. Beyond, even, the possibility that there might be actual sex in his near future.

"I appreciate the medical history," she told him, "and if it makes you feel any better, I'm my own employer and I care about my health for both personal and insurance reasons. But my safety query was actually of a more . . . immediate nature." At his perplexed look, she asked, "Were you ever a Boy Scout? You know, their motto? Always be prepared?" She leaned forward then and rested her elbows on the back of the front seat. "Has it been so long that you don't carry a spare in your wallet, is what I'm asking."

"I guess I really have been left in the wilds for too long," he admitted, heat again filling his cheeks. "I promise I'm not usually so slow on the uptake."

She folded her hands and rested her chin on them. Her dimples winked out at him as she smiled. "No, I definitely didn't get that impression earlier."

He leaned forward, so their faces were mere inches apart. "I'm usually a patient, methodical type, but I can move quickly when properly motivated."

"Don't sell patient and methodical short."

Now it was his turn to study her face with an amused smile of his own. "Does it strike you as completely bizarre, as it does me, that we're having a semi-rational discussion about having sex, and not only have we not known each longer than a few hours, but I have no idea what your name is?"

"I thought about that earlier, when you were still out digging tunnels. I couldn't decide which was more appealing. A mysterious and wildly romantic snowstorm fling with a nameless stranger. Or a far more fleshed-out fantasy—no pun intended there—where I give in to my insatiably curious nature and learn everything there is to know about you, so I can pine for you ever so romantically long after you're gone. Not because I'm expecting this to lead to something, mind you. Obviously you're just passing through. A plus, I might add, seeing as if I had an inkling this could actually go anywhere, I'd never do, well, what I'm doing. But we will part, never to cross paths again, so I'm far more free to be indulgent and act on whatever whim strikes me."

"So I'm an indulgence. I find that strangely flattering."

She beamed. "As you should. But, back to my original dilemma. An air of mystery is quite alluring, of course. But with details, I can fully embellish any future sexual scenarios I might need to dream up about you. You know, to . . . facilitate things during those lulls that so often happen in a single girl's life."

He laughed. "Are you always this direct?"

Her smile was one of self assurance, but not arrogance. He didn't think he'd ever seen anything so sexy.

"I've no real patience for subterfuge," she said. "Life is too short to spend any real amount of time being anything other than straightforward. I find it gets me where I need to be much more quickly." She lifted one hand, and ran her fingertips over his mouth. "Which leaves me more time to . . . indulge myself."

He caught her fingertips in his mouth, then slowly pulled them in. He wished there were more light. He wanted to see that punch of awareness, watch her pupils expand, witness the intoxicating effect his touch had on her. Intoxicating to him, that is. How had he forgotten the simple pleasure of turning a woman on, watching her respond to his touch, his voice, his kiss?

Of course, he couldn't recall ever having his senses quite so alert to every tiny thing, so hyperaware of something as small as her soft intake of breath, or the instinctive reflex of her pressing her thighs together against the need burgeoning between them. It wasn't that he bulldozed through sex without taking time to appreciate the finer points of intimacy . . . it was just that he hadn't been with anyone who elicited this kind of reaction in him to make him care enough to notice. Something about her called to every one of his senses . . . and not just the blatantly obvious one presently throbbing painfully inside his trousers.

He slid her fingers from his mouth, but held her gaze as he shifted his weight back and reached blindly behind him. First he cracked the window a tiny bit—because the need to check the tailpipe had ceased to be all that overwhelmingly important—then he dug out his wallet from the glove compartment and fished out the lonely condom that resided behind his social security card.

His smile was somewhat abashed when she reached out and took the travel-worn packet from his fingers. After examining it for a moment, she gave him a crooked smile that did funny things to his insides. "For a guy who gets around a lot . . . you need to get around a lot more."

He grinned, thinking he'd never laughed this much with anyone when sex was on the immediate agenda. He decided right then and there that humor would be a far greater prerequisite for him in all future couplings. "You might have a point. But I'm quite liking where I've gotten to right at the moment."

Then he shucked his coat and made her squeal quite delightfully as he slid his body over the seat and finally took her fully into his arms.

Chapter 8

How he'd maneuvered that big body of his into the back-seat of such a tiny car without serious injury, Maura had no idea. Nor, at the moment, did she care. He shifted around so he sat in the middle of the seat, and pulled her across him, so she straddled his lap. The sweaters she'd been clutching had fallen who cared where. All she knew was that a pair of big, warm hands currently gripped her waist, and she was facing an embarrassingly lush smorgasbord of broad, mus-cled chest and big shoulders. Her only dilemma was whether to attack first, or let him steer the course.

If only her other dilemmas in life presented her with such difficulty.

"You have the most amazing skin," he said, taking the de-cision from her hands, by moving his own so that his thumbs skated up the center of her torso.

"I'm glad you think so," she managed, gasping slightly when his hands came to rest just beneath the weight of her breasts. "Came with the package, so I really can't take any credit." Jesus and Mary, his hands were warm and wide, and his fingers so long and strong. Her nipples ached to the point of pain, already in dire need of his touch. Straddling him as she was, she had a pretty fair idea they were both in dire need. She was usually the direct stimulation sort, but she was pretty sure she was a brush of a fingertip away from climaxing. Still, she had to fight against shifting her hips that wee bit to find out.

She arched her back in silent invitation instead, gripping his knees with her hands for support. She was torn between wanting that sweet pressure between her thighs to shoot up and push her over the edge, and wanting to delay the inevitable for as long as deliciously possible. He slid one arm around her back, bracing her, as he slid one palm up and over her bare breast, sliding her painfully tight nipple ever so exquisitely down between his fingers.

She was already moaning, pressing the inside of her thighs tightly against the hard length of his, as he drew her closer and took her other, poor neglected nipple into the startling warmth and wetness of his mouth. Her moan turned into a much more vocal groan of satisfaction. "Jesus, you can just never stop that and I would die happy and complete."

She could feel him grin against her skin. A small moan of disappointment slipped out as he stopped swirling his tongue so expertly around her now very lucky nipple and lifted his head.

"You certainly don't leave a man guessing about how he's doing."

She gasped through a light laugh as he flicked the tip of her nipple with his tongue, all the while gently drawing his open palm over her other one, grazing it so lightly she thought she'd die from the sensations shooting through her. "I'm a firm believer in not leaving anything to chance if I don't have to," she managed.

"Well," he said softly, between teasing tongue flicks, "I'm quite appreciative of the response. It's . . . motivating."

She dropped her head back and gave herself up fully to his clever tongue and fingers. "Lucky me."

"We could debate who's luckier, but that would waste valuable time," he murmured against the now damp skin between her breasts. "I'm a firm believer in making the most of what's given me."

"Here, here," she sighed, as he kissed his way up to her neck, those perfectly perfect palms covering both aching breasts now.

"Yes," he murmured, "come here." He wove his fingers into her hair, and pulled her to him. Damp nipples met the warm, bare skin of his chest, and they both moaned their approval as he took her mouth in a very deliberate kiss. He didn't wait for her to open to him this time, penetrating her with his tongue in exactly the way she prayed he'd penetrate her with other, hopefully equally clever body parts later on.

She rested her hands only briefly on the seat back on either side of his head. Wanting—needing—to touch him as fully as possible, she slid her fingers into all those luxurious curly locks of his, surprised a bit at how softly textured they were. She'd never known just how decadent it could feel to have a man's hair fill her fists. She had an inkling now of why men so coveted long locks on their women. It would be a crime to shear off this glorious mane, especially when it felt so wonderful tangling around her fingers. And made yanking him to fit her mouth the way she wanted so much easier.

His groan of approval only served to encourage her further. She enjoyed being an equal partner in the bedroom—or the backseat, as the case may be. It thrilled her to realize he didn't mind a bit of a tussle himself. She dueled with his tongue, loving those big, strong hands skimming back down her waist, gripping her hips hard. She liked that he wasn't too gentle with her. It didn't alarm her, but rather aroused her even more, that he trusted her to guide him if she didn't like what he was doing. She didn't think that was going to be a problem. She was hardly fragile. And from the feel of him swelling rather magnificently between her legs . . . neither was he.

She left his mouth and trailed kisses across the long line of his jaw, around to the side of his neck. His cock leaped against her when she softly bit his earlobe. So she did it again, albeit just a little harder.

"Hungry are we?" he murmured against the side of her neck.

He was pushing his fingers inside the waistband of her pants. Just the feel of his fingertips brushing along the sensitive skin where the base of her spine ended and the swell of her buttocks began, then on down further, had her squirming against him. He pushed a bit farther, his breath warm and heavy against her neck. This had never been a part of foreplay for her before, and she wasn't entirely sure where he was going with it now. But it felt undeniably, wickedly wonderful.

"I'm feeling a bit famished myself," he whispered, then gently pressed his teeth along her shoulder.

Shaking now, she slid her hands between them and fumbled her pants open. As he slid his hands fully down, cupping her bottom, her zipper slid down, providing him even greater access . . . if she wanted him to have it. His fingertips traced lightly down the crease between her cheeks, so extraordinarily sensitive, making her shudder against him. She lifted up, which had the added benefit of putting her nipples in direct range of his mouth and tongue.

The combination of his fingertips drifting ever closer to where she so badly wanted him to touch her, and the wet warmth of his mouth closing first over one nipple, suckling, making her gasp, moan, before shifting to the other one . . . was driving her wild.

He palmed her cheeks fully now, so warm, so close, his fingers brushing along the back edge of her inner thighs. Her pants shifted down her hips and she found herself pushing against those questing fingers. So close . . . so close.

They both groaned when he finally found her. A quick brush over her clit had her shuddering, made her want to beg for more. "Yes," she breathed, wanting to tell him what she wanted, and at the same time, wanting him to do what he wanted without direction.

He'd been doing pretty bloody well so far.

Then he was lifting her up and forward. His mouth had left her breasts and was trailing downward. He slid his body down a bit, his knees coming up behind her, spreading her thighs and his wider. He kissed his way past her navel, then slid his hands free, making her whimper in protest. But then he was shoving her pants down as far as he could, and pulling her up, and closer, so he could—oh dear Lord.

She hadn't thought it possible, but his tongue was far more clever than she'd given him credit for thus far.

She arched, head thrown back as he flicked his tongue repeatedly across that most sensitive bud, drenching her, driving her to a frenzy, then backing off just when she thought she was going to splinter into a thousand pieces. Her thighs shook with need, her hands trembled as she dug her nails hard into his shoulders.

He slid down further still, pitching her forward until her bare breasts were pushed into the soft fabric of the seat back above his head. She groaned at the added stimulation, thinking she couldn't take much more. She was proven immediately wrong.

He moved his palms up the backs of her thighs as his tongue continued to flick over her. Fingers slid around . . . then up . . . then in. She gasped loudly, then groaned in exquisite, protracted pleasure as he finally let her climb all the way to the top, then pushed her over. She swore she saw stars as she climaxed. She shuddered so hard, it was a miracle he was able to continue perpetrating such wickedly delightful deeds. And yet he did. Pushing her up again. A first for her, and so soon after.

And she'd thought herself wanton in bed. Hah.

The second climax came quicker, wasn't as strong. More like riding the same wave only longer, and longer still. Stretching it out until she couldn't wring one more drop of pleasure out of the ride.

She wasn't sure how she managed to keep from collapsing

into a trembling, knobby heap as the final quivers smoothed out. He gripped her hips, steadying her as he shifted her back so he could slide up again.

She managed to push her hair from her face and smile at him, hoping it didn't look as loopy as it felt. "I'm not sure I quite believe you've been as alone as you claim," she said, her voice barely more than a raspy whisper.

His grin was wide and gleaming, and so confident it had her clenching all over again.

"As it happens, I'm quite good at finding buried treasure."

She laughed, then squealed as he dumped her gently to the seat beside him, her legs sprawled across his lap. He tugged at the laces to her boots, his expression questioning, clearly asking her if she wanted to continue.

Given what they'd just been doing, and where he'd taken her—twice—she was surprised he'd so willingly given her the benefit of calling a halt to things. Most men of her acquaintance would simply assume all was a go at this point, unless told otherwise. And even then would likely do whatever necessary to coerce her into changing her mind if she said no. Given the fact that she'd already had the pleasure and relief of coming, and still felt she'd only been served the appetizer to what promised to be a full gourmet meal . . . she could only imagine the range of needs he was feeling at the moment.

She held his gaze and nodded with a smile . . . and no hesitation.

He tugged her pants and panties the rest of the way down as she shifted her weight to facilitate the action. By the time they were around her ankles, he'd shifted to his own, now straining zipper. Their movements were severely hampered by the restricted space, causing them both to grunt and swear a bit as they tried to disentangle themselves from the last of their clothing. She had her jeans hooked on one heel and he was struggling to tug his pants down and not dump her on the floor at the same time, when a split white beam of light shot like arrows through the fogged windows.

"Shit," they both said in unison, then caught each other's gaze in one of those frozen moments in time. They had company. They remained unmoving for another agonizingly long moment, waiting to see if the truck—judging from the height and breadth of the beams—moved on, or stopped. The instant the arcing beams of light swung to a stop, they both burst into a frenzy of action, each of them struggling to put on the clothes they'd just fought to get off. Elbows and knees connected, hair tangled, both of them were panting and swearing.

"Wait, wait," he told her. "Don't hurt yourself. I'm closer to being dressed. I'll put my coat on and get out, see what's what. You take your time. I'll make sure no one looks in here until you give me a signal."

Normally she was the one who jumped to the fore when things went amiss. She liked calling the shots. Easier to place trust in the outcome of things that way. So it was a surprise to her that rather than argue with him, she felt an almost overwhelming wave of gratitude and affection. Of course, the fact that her panties were tangled around her knees and her jeans were half inside out might have played a small part in that. The sound of a heavy truck door slamming shut only served to underscore her appreciation. "Thank you," she said, never more sincere. "If necessary, I'll lower the window a wee bit, or toot the horn or something."

He was already jamming his arms into his coat, his jeans and sweater already back on. "Don't worry about it. I'll come right back."

"Everybody all right in there?" came a shout. From the tenor, it sounded like a man.

"Slide closer to that door," he instructed with amazing calm. He put his hand on the rear-door handle closest to him. "Snow's likely to blow in when I get out. Sorry. I'd climb back up front, but I'll be lucky if I can walk upright at the moment as it is."

She couldn't stop the sudden splutter of a laugh, then caught his responding grin and paused in her renewed grappling with her clothes long enough to reach out and briefly touch his face. "We can still take care of that, you know."

He just wiggled his eyebrows, making her laugh again, which quickly turned to a squeal as he swung the door open and ducked out as fast as he could. The door slammed shut immediately, but snow and bone-chillingly cold air managed to seep in anyway.

"Hi there," she heard him call out. "Thanks for stopping. Hope we didn't cause you any problems staying on the road."

With the extra room, it didn't take long for her to put her clothes back on. It wasn't until she'd pulled on her sweater, only to have it hang from her like a sack, that she realized he'd grabbed the wrong one. For all his calm assurance, hadn't he noticed the snug fit? She clamped a hand to her mouth and giggled, hoping he'd buttoned up his coat. The driver of the truck might wonder at the rows of flowers stitched about the neck and waistband of the sweater his rescuee was wearing.

She pulled her coat down from the seat ledge behind her and shrugged into the still-damp parka. Bracing herself, she pushed out of the backseat and into the snowstorm once again.

The truck was a big lorry with wheels half the size of the compact she'd just spent the better part of the last hour romping in. The driver was no small man himself. He was older though, judging by the furry white eyebrows, and the paunch that was noticeable even beneath his heavy coat spoke of few missed meals.

"I dinna have a hook with me, lad, so I canno' tow you out," the older man was saying. "But I can give ye a lift to the next village if you'd like. At least you and the missus," he nodded his head toward her as she stepped in closer, "can spend what's left o' the night in comfort. Helen Stewart runs a boardinghouse in Calyth and I'm sure she won't mind being rousted up to get you folks settled for the night."

Maura smiled at his assumption, wondering how he'd come to that conclusion given there were two vehicles stranded here. Only upon looking across the road to where her truck was stuck, she realized he likely hadn't noticed. It was nothing but a misshapen lump now with a white flag sticking out the back. She remembered how he had stalked off with the other half of his torn T-shirt and realized he'd tied it to something in her truck and stuck it in the snow as a marker.

Just then he slid his hand into hers and pulled her closer. "That would be fine." He glanced at her. "Okay with you, honey?"

Now what game were they playing? Whatever it was, she found herself smiling and nodding. "Aye." She turned to the truck driver and extended her free hand. "Thank you for yer help."

His eyes lit up. "Ah, a Scots lass." He glanced between them. "Are ye both from around here then?"

They looked at each other and she knew there was no reason to let the man think anything other than the truth. They were two strangers, stranded by happenstance and a run of bad luck. But pretending to be otherwise was more fun. And harmless, really. She smiled at him. "Just traveling through. Showing him a bit of my homeland, as it were."

"Ah," he said, apparently not curious enough to care for more details.

Maura was disappointed. She had no idea why the game appealed, but it had. She'd been prepared to embellish, to be fanciful. And she'd been a bit curious to hear her "significant other's" side of things as well. Oh well, at least they'd be out of the storm and removed from possible monoxide poisoning. The question was, by the time they got to Calyth, would her partner in adventure wish to continue their night of anonymous debauchery? She found she wasn't quite ready for it to be over yet. And not just because they'd stopped before the best part.

She was liking him, her nameless, rogue lover. It was all nothing more than a random fling, they both knew that, but there was nothing to say it couldn't last just a tad longer, was there? Sure she had to get back to Ballantrae and face the mountain of worries waiting for her there. Not to mention the memories of Jory and Priss in her bed.

It was that latter part that decided her on doing whatever was necessary to convince her shag mate to continue their romp, at least through morning. Any longer and it would likely get awkward anyway.

The driver had them both tucked up snug in the bench seat, with her in the middle. The cab smelled of coffee and stale pipe tobacco. It wasn't altogether an unpleasant smell. It reminded her of her Uncle Niall and the mornings she'd come downstairs and listen as he railed on about this parliament issue or that farming inequity. When she'd been younger, she hadn't cared so much about the topic of the day, she'd just enjoyed the flair with which he ranted on about them. She'd always thought he'd missed his calling. He should have sat in the House of Lords. Lord Niall Sinclair, fifteenth laird of clan Sinclair of Ballantrae, could have debated with the best of them in Parliament. Wouldn't he have fancied that?

The truck rumbled down the mountain and she let the pleasant memories wash through her and her eyes drift shut as the men chatted amiably. She must have fallen asleep, because it only seemed like moments later that she was being gently roused. She blinked and yawned, and pushed away from that wonderful chest she'd been nestled against.

"We're here." He nodded toward the front windshield.

She sat up, stifling another yawn. "I'm sorry I drifted off on you."

His smile was just for her. "It's been a hard night."

She managed to swallow a snicker as she caught the twinkle in his eye. "Aye, that it has. Happily," she said quietly, "it's not over yet."

He slid his hand into hers as the driver appeared on their side and opened the door. He stepped down first and levered her down beside him, those big, confident hands of his easily commanding her hips. She worked at keeping the images of those hands on her hips, and how confidently they'd steered her earlier. And how she hoped they'd be steering her again shortly.

"I've spoken to Helen," the driver was saying. "She's waitin' on you inside there."

Maura collected herself and turned to face him. She held out both hands and took his, warmly shaking it. "Thank you for your rescue, kind sir," she said with a smile and a little curtsy.

He might have blushed a little. "Och, 'twas nothing. Glad I could help." He looked past her and tipped his hat. "Enjoy yer stay in the Highlands, T.J." He grinned. "But next time, have her bring ye in the spring, aye?"

"T.J." smiled, nodded. "Will do, Angus. A pleasure making your company. If you're staying on tonight, I'd be happy to buy you breakfast in the morning."

"Thank you, but I'm no' so far from home. The wife is waiting on me." He tipped his hat again. "You'd best be getting inside before yer covered in snow again." Then he was around his truck and climbing up in the driver's seat.

They ducked under the narrow awning of the inn, but stayed there long enough to wave him off. She'd barely registered their surroundings. Angus had called him T.J. Apparently her rogue lover and their Good Samaritan had had quite a lovely chat on the drive down the mountain. Part of her was undeniably thrilled with this added tidbit of information. And yet another part of her wished she hadn't overheard it. The less she knew, the easier it was to maintain the fantasy . . . and discouraged her from forming any more than a fleeting affection for the man.

"Shall we?" he asked, holding the door into the narrow row house.

If he was aware she'd picked up on the driver's slip, he apparently wasn't going to mention it. She barely had time to glance about as they stepped inside the tiny foyer. She'd driven through Calyth before, but as she rarely had cause to head south into the Cairngorms, usually going up to Inverness instead when she needed something, she'd never stopped here before. It was hardly even a village proper, with only the scant row of buildings lining the main road. But as long as it boasted a spare room with a bed, she'd be more than happy.

"Come in, come in," came a gravelly voice from the dim recesses across the landing. Startled, both Maura and T.J. peered into the gloom behind the staircase that stretched upward in front of them, and took a tentative step forward.

"Didn't Angus say the owner's name was Helen?" Maura whispered, leaning closer to T.J. as they shuffled forward.

"Maybe she sent her husband out to meet us."

Just then a small, stooped woman scuffed her way into the narrow pools of light provided by the matching pair of sconces positioned on either side of the closed panel doors, set in the wall to their left. Probably leading to a little parlor, Maura thought.

The older woman—Helen, their hostess, she presumed—was rail thin and sported an amazing rat's nest of steel gray hair piled high on top of her head. It added at least another half foot to a frame that still only managed to come up to Maura's chin. She stopped in front of them, having to crane her neck up to look them in the face. Maura couldn't help but wonder how the old woman balanced such a thing on her skeletal neck, but was saved from further ruminations when their hostess spoke again.

"Angus said ye'd be needing a room." That rough-as-gravel voice coming from such a small frame was just as startling the second time.

Maura wondered just how many cartons of ciggies a person would have to smoke to create such a sound. She resisted a shudder at the thought. "Yes, ma'am, if you'd be so kind," she said.

Helen wore a housecoat patterned with faded roses and overlarge slippers on her feet. She peered first at Maura, then at T.J., through tiny eyeglasses that perched precariously on the end of her bony nose. If she found T.J.'s less-than-conventional appearance off putting, she didn't let on. Although how one could tell, given her generally pinched expression, Maura couldn't say.

"I've only one room left. Skiers, ye know," Helen announced flatly. "You'll have to share the W.C. with the other boarders."

"That's fine," T.J. said. "We really appreciate this." He pulled out his wallet, but the old woman waved it away.

"Settle up in the morning." She held out a room key, then motioned up the staircase. "Second landing, to your right. You'll have to carry your own bags as the mister is already snoring. Ye'd think he ran the place all himself for all he drops off like a stone at half past ten."

Maura felt a smile tug at her lips, and when T.J. bumped shoulders with her, she knew he'd been amused as well. She didn't dare look at him for fear of bursting into a snort of laughter.

He took the key and sketched a slight bow. "We appreciate your hospitality. We can see ourselves to the room. Sorry to intrude so late."

Helen merely jerked her chin in terse acceptance, then shuffled back beyond the gloomy recesses of the tiny foyer, down the hallway that stretched out behind the stairs. "There'll be tea and scones in the parlor come morning," she called back without pausing. "If you want more than that, there's a shop on the other side of town that serves breakfast."

"Other side of town?" Maura silently mouthed. "There's hardly a town to have a side of," she whispered.

Helen's exit was finalized by the creaky opening, and quite definitive closing of a door somewhere in the distance.

" 'Night, Helen," Maura murmured, then glanced at T.J. and gave in to the snicker she'd been repressing. "Quite the character, isn't she?"

"I happen to like odd ducks," he said, a bemused, yet fond expression on his face. "Probably a case of like being attracted to like."

Maura gave him a considering look. "I'm not sure how to take that."

He turned away from the dark hallway and looked at her squarely for the first time since entering the place. His eyes were still cast in shadows, but the wild curls and sharp curve of his jaw as his mouth spread into a knowing grin tugged at something inside her. Something that should be simple attraction, but was somehow more complex than that. Despite their physical interaction to date, he was still a stranger to her. And yet she had this sense of a communal spirit between them.

He held up the room key. "Why don't we head upstairs and I can clarify my feelings on the subject."

It was clear the kind of communing he had in mind. Apparently he had a much more direct take on the basis of their attraction to one another. One she'd be wise to adopt.

Morning would come soon enough and her grand adventure would be over. She might as well get the most from it that she could, right? Besides, given what she faced at home, it would likely have to hold her over for some time to come.

She slipped the key from his fingers and gave him what she hoped was a suitably saucy wink. "Why don't we, indeed?"

Chapter 9

With a wink and a very promising smile, Maura took off up the narrow staircase. Tag didn't need any further encouragement. The carpeting on the stairs was worn, but muffled their footsteps adequately. Or so he hoped. All he needed was Helen storming upstairs in her bed slippers, wielding a cane and that harsh voice. He wasn't sure which he'd fear more.

He caught her on the second-floor landing, snagging her sleeve and pulling her back around so she banged up against his chest. He let the weight of her push him into the corner and tugged her tightly into his arms. *Finally,* was all he could think. Like it had been eons instead of a measly few hours since he'd had his hands on her.

"Why is it we always have too many clothes on to suit my needs?" he murmured, enjoying the flash of her dimples. Did odd things to him. Made something in his chest shift. And a few not so odd. Like making him go hard instantaneously.

"I believe you're the one wasting time here," she noted, not trying in the least to wiggle free.

"Wasting time, am I?" He lowered his mouth until it hovered just over hers. "Is that what this is?" He took her in a slow, deep kiss. He'd been too impatient in the car, too aware of the cramped surroundings and the serendipitous nature of their rendezvous to settle down and appreciate every taste, every touch. Now they'd made the conscious decision to continue, and with all the room in the world at their immediate disposal. Just not all the time.

And he found he wanted to use what little they did have to imprint her on his every sense. He wanted to remember exactly how she tasted, the scent of her, the texture of her skin, the feel of her hair brushing his face and her fingertips skating across his back.

Mostly he wanted to remember how she kissed him back. Possibly one of the things he enjoyed most about her. She didn't wait for him to lead, but neither did she take over. What she did was engage herself fully, immersing herself in the moment with no hesitation, no censorship of emotions. It was a little intimidating, especially for a man who by nature tended to guard his emotions, control his actions. Yet it was also intoxicating, possibly for the same reasons. She made him want to act with abandon.

So far she'd been pretty damn successful.

The result though, was that merely kissing her took him places that actual sex with anyone else never had. It made him hunger, filled him with a voracious need that had him puzzling over how it was he'd gone so long without experiencing anything like this.

He knew the answer to that, in part anyway. He'd spent his life studying ancient civilizations . . . and largely avoiding contact with those in the current one. Even so, he wasn't a monk. And yet, he'd never felt anything remotely as powerful as this. Maybe it was because she so effortlessly drew him out of himself, that had him behaving in a manner he otherwise never would. Or maybe it was just her.

Or maybe he was simply delirious from lack of sleep.

She slipped her hands beneath his coat just then, and skimmed her palms beneath the snug knit of his sweater. Sleep was going to have to wait a bit longer.

"Nice flowers," she murmured against his lips, and he

could hear the smile in her voice. In fact, he couldn't imagine her without that thread of humor lacing her every phrase.

"Flowers?" he asked, the fog of arousal clouding his thoughts.

"Your sweater. I'm sure Helen wondered just what manner of a man I'd gotten myself tangled up with." She leaned back and he glanced down, spotting the row of lively blue and yellow flowers woven into the knit of his sweater that he was certain hadn't been there when he'd put the thing on this morning. He looked back into her dancing blue eyes. Blue, he thought. Of course they'd be blue. Suited her perfectly. "A slight mix-up, I'm guessing," he said sheepishly.

She moved her hands, slid them back down to his hips, tugging him more tightly against her. "And a bit snug, I'm guessing."

His knees might have buckled a little at the word "snug." Jesus, could he be any harder? "Care to trade back?" He let her go long enough to tug on the hem. She smacked his hands, laughing as he grabbed them and pulled them back around his waist, planting them on his ass.

"You have a thing for unconventional sex, do you?" she said, squeezing his cheeks.

It was a miracle he was able to stand upright, considering just how upright he was. He framed her face with his hands, wove his fingers into her curls. "I'm pretty sure 'unconventional' aptly describes our entire time together."

She smiled up into his face, eyes twinkling, dimples winking. "Well, I wouldn't have taken you for the kinky type, but now I realize what was I thinking? A man who's faced down tribes of cannibals has probably seen and done a few other things that would raise my eyebrows as well."

"The chief's daughters did have clever fingers."

"Hmm. I'm torn now."

"Between?"

"Finding out if those clever-fingered virgins did something

other than weave that necklace around your neck . . . or ripping both our sweaters off and getting back to what your clever fingers were doing to me earlier."

He grinned, feeling almost giddy with lust. His work was his whole life, but even so, he'd never really thought of himself as the overserious type. Yet he couldn't remember the last time he'd indulged in such lighthearted banter, when the last time was he'd just cut loose and played around, for playing's sake. Not often enough, gauging from his body's reaction to it. "And this decision is presenting you that difficult a dilemma?" he asked her with mock seriousness. "Because, you know I have a lot of stories, but we only have a little bit of time to—"

She pressed her fingers across his lips. "I know. Don't say it out loud, though."

He nodded his head in agreement, rubbing her fingers across his lips in the process, which only served to enflame his senses further. He turned them so her back was in the corner and pushed his hips into hers. Her pupils punched wide, and he shifted his lips enough to pull her fingertips between them, all the while keeping his gaze on hers. Her hips in the cradle of his.

"I . . . uh . . ." Her voice had gone a bit hoarse, which delighted him to no end. She had to clear her throat. "I guess we both know what your answer would be."

He nodded slowly, let his lips curve quite deliberately, and nibbled on the ends of her fingers.

"I still say you've a bit of the cannibal in you," she told him, somewhat breathlessly now.

His grin widened further. "I thought you'd have figured that out back in the car."

Her breath left her on a surprised laugh. "Yes, well, you have a point." Her lips quirked when he wiggled his eyebrows. "Such a naughty mind you have. One of the numerous things that attracts me to you, by the way."

"Funny, but I've never thought of myself as particularly naughty. Until I met you."

A door at the top of the stairs creaked open and a man said, "For God's sake, will you bloody well take her to bed, lad? I'm alone here and the two of you and all this sex talk is killing me." The door shut again.

They'd both frozen at the sound of his voice, then she'd grinned quite devilishly and whispered, "Yes, why don't you bloody well do that?"

"Come on," he murmured next to her ear, then took her hand and finished climbing the last short flight of stairs. They tiptoed with exaggerated silence past the room of their offended and apparently horny fellow boarder, then collapsed against the door to their room barely stifling their laughter. It took Tag three tries with the old-fashioned room key to finally get the door open. They both all but tumbled into the darkened room. He didn't bother looking for the light switch, though he planned on doing so later. He wanted to witness every moment of her. They'd had enough of shadows and stealth. But that could wait. Right now he needed to

She leaned back against the closed door and yanked him to her. "Great minds think alike," was all he managed to get out before she crushed her mouth to his. He willingly reciprocated.

In seconds they were tearing at each other's clothes like rabid animals. Which was an apt description of the state she'd driven him to. He wanted her with a ferocity that would have astounded him if he'd taken the time to think on it. At the moment, he had more . . . pressing concerns.

"Wait," he said, as she went to toss his jacket. He grabbed it and fished around in the pocket. "Ah," he said, closing his hand around their lone packet of protection with the fervor of a man who'd just unearthed the Holy Grail. "Okay, resume."

"Ye've only to ask," she said, her accent delightfully

stronger the more aroused she got. Coats and sweaters gone, their shoes kicked off, she spun him around this time, pushing his back up against the wall so she could slide her hands down his chest to his waistband.

His eyes had adjusted well enough to see her lower herself to her knees as she went to work on his zipper. He started to caution her, but she was taking her sweet, excruciatingly arousing time, lowering the damn thing one set of teeth at a time. It was all he could do not to tear her hands away and rip the zipper straight out. Much more of this and they wouldn't need the damn condom. "I don't think I can take— Jesus," he ended on a long groan, knees going weak as she finally freed him and took him easily into her mouth. He wanted to fist his hands in her hair. Wanted to watch her, dammit. Instead he squeezed his eyes shut and curled his fingers into fists, fighting the urge, hell, the primal need to buck against the back of her throat until he came shouting.

Even with restraint, it was a toss-up which way it was going to go.

When the first moan escaped her lips, he knew he was done. He tore the packet open with his teeth, pulled her to her feet. He was moving purely on instinct, driven now to do one thing and one thing only. He yanked her pants and panties down, taking her moan and the way she gripped his shoulders as acquiescence. His pants were still around his hips when he rolled the condom on with shaking hands, then spun her back to the wall, yanked her legs up over his hips and drove himself home with one grunting, groaning thrust.

"Oh God. Yes," she growled, her back up hard against the wall as he buried himself to the hilt inside her tight, welcoming body. She dug her nails into his back as he gripped onto her calves, wrapping them around his hips so he could stay locked deep inside of her for this long moment out of time.

Then she moved against him, and that was all it took.

He thrust into her as if he'd never been inside a woman before. He'd surely never been inside this woman, was all he

knew, all he cared. He'd never been taken like this. Which
made no sense since it was his body pinning hers to the goddamn wall. His hips slapping hers, his rock-hard cock ram-
ming inside her. Over. And over.

But she took him . . . and took him and took him. Meeting
every thrust, claiming ownership of him as surely as if she'd
been commanding his every thrust. So tightly she held him,
so deep, she controlled him, controlled this. Because, God
knew, he completely, and utterly had none.

He found her mouth then, crushing his lips to hers, thrusting his tongue inside her in the same driving rhythm as his
hips. She met him there, too. Insatiable as he was, her response only drove him higher. He couldn't be deep enough,
couldn't taste her enough, take her hard enough, fast enough,
long enough.

And then she tore her mouth from his and arched violently
against him, gouging her nails into his skin as she half panted,
half sobbed her way through a climax he thought might actually dismember him. The pleasure of knowing he'd taken
her to such an extreme fused with the pain of her nails on his
back, her body squeezing the life right out of him, and sent
him ripping over the edge so hard he shouted in shocked
gratification.

As the wracking shudders finally slowed and he slipped
from her body, he knew right off that standing was no longer
an option. But with his pants around his thighs, his options
were limited. "Hold on," he grunted, and wrapping his arms
around her for support, he rolled so his back was to the wall,
then slid them both slowly down to the floor.

Still breathing heavily, mind spinning too fast to form co-
herent thought, he closed his eyes and tipped his head back
against the wall. He instinctively pulled her close, tucking her
head beneath his chin, tangling his hands in her hair. *Just like
this,* was all he could think. *I could die happy, just like this.*

Later, when he was able to form objective thought, he
knew he'd understand that the fierce emotions rocketing

through him right now were nothing more than the exaggerated feelings any man would have after experiencing sex that ranked right up there with seeing God.

But until then, he wasn't letting her go.

"That was quite possibly the best use of a single condom ever," she murmured hoarsely, moments later.

He barked out a raspy laugh. "I don't suppose I could convince you to hang around for, I don't know, a week or two, until I've recovered enough to do that again?" He felt so incredibly replete, his body so heavy and satiated that the mere act of lifting his eyelids was a monumental accomplishment. But he did it. Because he had to look at her, had to see her face. He tipped her head back, barely making out the shine of her eyes, the glimmer of a dimple, in the glow cast by the street lamps below through their dormer window. "I want to watch you next time."

She reached up and traced her fingers along his face, his mouth, then down to his neck. His skin quivered at her touch, his heart tipped at the solemnity in the curve of her lips.

"I'm not sure I can take much more of you," she said softly. "You're a dangerous man."

Forever he'd remember the soft brush of her skin along the row of teeth that lined his neck. He'd done a lot, seen a lot, survived it all. Yet he'd never felt so powerless as he did against the power of her touch. "Not so dangerous," he said, rubbing his thumbs over the curls wrapped around his fingers. "Careful. Controlled. That's how I'd have described myself. Before tonight, anyway."

She curled her fingers around his neck, urged his mouth down to hers. "That's what makes you so dangerous," she whispered, right before she kissed him.

This time it was soft, and achingly tender. The wave of affection that swept through him nearly took his breath away. He'd have given almost anything to see into her eyes the moment after she ended the kiss. And thought maybe it just as wise that he couldn't. "I'm thinking careful and controlled are highly overrated," he managed to say, around the lump of heart lodged in his throat. He wanted to say more, so much more, which was the very reason he didn't.

The silence stretched out as she laid her head back on his chest. A thousand questions fought to be asked, but he knew if he asked the first one, he'd do whatever he had to, to keep her here until he asked the very last. That wasn't what this was about. This was about her mystery man fantasy and him simply getting incredibly, undeniably lucky for one long, stormy night.

So there was no reason for a sense of despondency to seep into him. Better to focus on the here and now. She was still in his arms, wasn't she? No point in wasting the now, lamenting the inevitable later. Then he felt her lips curve against his chest, and the corners of his own mouth tipped up as well. "What?" he asked.

"Am I the only one who finds it curious that even when presented with a nice, soft bed, we still managed to do this the hard way?"

He chuckled. Leave it to her to bring things back around. "Generally speaking, I find it goes better when it's hard."

"Oh, har har," she said, giving him a light tweak on the pec.

"Hey," he said, flinching, then sighed when she kissed the spot. Right over his heart.

"So," she said, quite conversationally as she toyed with the hair on his chest, "any reason we're freezing our bums off on the floor now?"

"Other than the fact that you've zapped every last ounce of energy out of me, no."

"Oh, so it's my fault is it? Funny, I don't remember being the one bucking like a wild man."

He couldn't help it, he was a man after all. He grinned in supreme self-satisfaction. "True."

She laughed, then kissed his cheek before carefully disentangling herself from his lap. He reluctantly let her go, leaning forward to steady her as she slowly stood up.

"Why don't you go ahead and use the W.C. while I find my clothes," she said. But first she groped her way to the nightstand and plucked a few tissues from the box there and handed them to him. "Here. I figure you'd want to . . ."

He took them from her. "Yeah, thanks." Condom disposed of, he scraped together the energy to stand up. He was well and purely exhausted, but he managed to pull his pants up and stumble down the hall to the bathroom. He washed up at the sink, deciding he'd save the shower for the morning. Maybe he could convince her to conserve some hot water with him. He smiled at the image of her, all damp and warm, tucked back into bed with him, sipping tea and nibbling on a muffin or biscuit or whatever they ate over here as the sun came up. Talking, laughing, loving the morning away.

"Dream on, Morgan," he told his reflection, once again fighting off the impending gloom he already knew he'd feel when she was gone.

He let himself back into their room, expecting she'd be waiting to use the bathroom. Instead, she was already curled up in the bed, the sheets and comforter tucked up under her chin. The dim light of the street lamp caressed her bare shoulder, played across the tangle of hair that splayed across the pillow.

The sight of her there had him pausing in the doorway. He so didn't want this night to end. There was no use pretending otherwise. And ignoring it wasn't going to make him want her less. He wanted more. A lot more. Not just more sex. More . . . everything. More her.

He quietly shucked his pants and slid into bed behind her. His instinct was to pull her back against him, nestle her in his arms. He was beyond exhausted by now, could barely keep his eyes open, and could think of nothing he'd rather do than sleep with her in his arms, enjoying the warmth of her, the life of her, for what time they had left.

And yet he propped his head up on one elbow and simply looked at her. Minutes ticked away, as he studied her, thinking up and discarding one plan after another, for extending their time together. He wasn't here to get emotionally tangled up with someone. He was likely to get his emotions tangled up quite enough when he got to Ballantrae tomorrow. And if he wanted to keep his job, he was on a flight back to Chacchoben in two weeks, no matter what. Even if he found a way to see her while he was here, it would only make it more difficult to leave her in the end. "No point in prolonging the torture," he muttered.

And yet, he reached out and traced his fingertips down the length of her bare arm resting above the covers. Lifting one long curling strand of hair, then another, he let them wrap around his fingers, before finally giving in and leaning down to bury his face in the soft, silky mass. "I don't even know your name," he whispered against the soft skin at the curve of her neck.

She shifted against him, reached blindly for his arm and pulled it around her. As if she were used to sleeping spooned against someone. *And well she might be,* he thought. After all, what did he really know about her? She'd claimed she was single, but that didn't mean much these days. He slid lower beneath the covers and tucked her up against his chest, burrowing his face into her hair. Wishing like hell he didn't care who she spent her other nights with. She was his tonight, wasn't she? That was all that mattered. All that could matter.

Fatigue, extreme jet lag, and the shocking resurrection of his sex life combined to pull him under almost instantly. He slipped an arm around her waist, tucked an ankle across hers, and let sleep claim him, knowing he'd still have the morning to figure things out.

Only when he opened his eyes hours later, weak winter light streaming in the quarter-paned dormer window, he was alone. He rubbed his palm over the empty bed next to him, already knowing he'd find it as cold as the air that filled the small bedroom. He scrubbed a hand over his face and tried to pretend he wasn't reeling with crushing disappointment.

The room was small, with the ceiling slanting toward the gabled window. The walls were papered with striped white and rose patterned paper. The carpet was a faded rose and green that matched the stuffed chair that was tucked between an old armoire and a tall lamp across the room from the bed. His clothes had been carefully folded and laid on the cedar chest beneath the window. She'd placed a partly used bottle of shampoo, an unwrapped bar of soap, and a toothbrush on top.

Otherwise, there wasn't anything left of her. He didn't tease himself with the hope that she was just down below in the parlor, sipping tea and chatting with Helen over scones. No, she was gone. He knew it. Felt it.

"Well, you had the night with her," he muttered. "No use being greedy." A headache was forming behind his eyes even before he swung his legs over the side of the bed. At least he'd have one glorious memory of his time here. Considering what he'd be facing later today, he supposed he should thank her for giving him that much.

One thing he did know, he'd need something a hell of a lot stronger than tea. His stomach took that as a cue and growled quite insistently. Reluctantly, he stood and stretched, rubbing his palms over his rumbling belly. He had a long day in front of him, so he'd best get on with it. No point in dwelling on what couldn't be.

He'd grab a shower and then find out where that café was that Helen had spoken about. While he was at it, he supposed he'd have to find out how he was going to go about getting his car out of that snowbank. Worst case was he'd buy a few shovels, and pay someone to drive him back and help him dig out. Maybe a few hours of hard physical labor would get his mind off of how he'd have preferred to spend his morning.

He pointedly didn't look at the bed, or the wall where he'd taken her so fiercely mere hours ago. Instead he pulled on his pants and scooped up the rest of his clothes and shoes before heading resolutely down the hall to the mercifully empty bathroom. It wasn't until he was standing under a mostly hot spray of water that he thought to wonder what she'd done about her truck. His heart gave a little start when he realized she could still be up there, digging out herself. If he hurried, he immediately thought, already rinsing himself off, then abruptly stopping. "Don't be an idiot," he counseled himself. "She left you with no note, no nothing." *Her fantasy is complete. Let her have it and be thankful she chose you to share it with.* "Yeah," he groused as he pulled a fresh towel out of the cabinet and scrubbed himself dry. "Be thankful." And he was. "Probably better you'll never see her again."

Believing that was going to take him a bit longer.

He pulled on his clothes, caught off guard by the lingering scent of her on his sweater as he pulled it over his head. "Great," he thought morosely, even as he was secretly delighted that he got to keep a hint of her about for a little while longer. He hoped that didn't make him too pathetic a figure. But what the hell did it matter if it did?

When he descended the stairs to the lobby, only pausing slightly on the second-floor landing, then shaking his head and going the rest of the way down, he found a tall, slender man hunched over the desk tucked beneath the stairs. He hadn't noticed it the night before, but it had been pretty dark. And he'd been a little distracted. "Morning," he said, by way of introduction.

"Afternoon, is more like," the man responded, scribbling something down before finally glancing up.

Tag hadn't even bothered to look at the clock this morning. "Really? Well, I guess I'm still on Virginia time."

The older gentleman, who Tag could only presume was Mr. Helen, smiled easily. "Best to let your body adjust on its own," he said, quite congenially. *A case of opposites attract-*

ing, was all Tag could think, trying and failing to picture a romance between this amiable gent and the crotchety woman who welcomed them last night.

He had a shock of white hair that sort of erupted all about his narrow head. But his face was a soft, smooth pink, belying his age. His eyes were a watery shade of blue, but sharp for all they were faded. "Checking out?"

Tag smiled and pulled his wallet out. "Yes, I am." He handed him the key. "Room four. How much do I owe you?"

The man's smile faded as he took the key and looked at the room number. "Thought ye was one of the skiers," he grumbled. He glanced back up, studying Tag as if seeing him in a new way.

Tag knew he wasn't the most conventional-looking man, but the innkeeper wasn't looking at his choker, tanned skin, or unruly hair. He was studying his face, as if sizing him up. Clearly, Tag had been found wanting.

Bemused, he allowed the man the less-than-polite silent inquiry.

"Ye owe nothing," the man said abruptly, before looking back down to what Tag now saw was a crossword puzzle.

"I beg your pardon?" Tag asked him, surprised.

He flicked him a glance, then put the tip of his pencil to his tongue before filling in another row of letters. "Bill's been paid. Early this morning. By the young lass."

Tag could have simply nodded, thanked the man and walked out. But it was obvious the innkeeper was upset about something. "Is there a problem?"

"No. What people do is their own business."

Tag's mouth quirked. Clearly the old man believed otherwise. "Very true. And we both very much appreciated your hospitality."

Still working on his puzzle, he said, "We Scots are a hospitable lot." He glanced up, caught his gaze from the corner of his eye. "But then I gather you've already discovered that."

Tag had wondered if one of the other boarders, the man on the second floor perhaps, had complained about them. But now he realized it was something else entirely. They'd let Angus believe they were a couple, married even, and apparently Angus had said as much to Helen when he'd found them a room. So when his "wife" had checked out without him this morning, and paid the tab, it had apparently raised a few eyebrows. And lowered their opinion of him. Fair enough, he supposed.

So, how to explain to the old man that no one had been taken advantage of? Tag knew she didn't live in Calyth from what she'd said about passing through the town, but she could live nearby. He had no idea if she knew people in this area or not, much less cared what they thought of her, but he didn't want to unintentionally leave her reputation in tatters if he could help it. He understood the mentality of small villages. No matter the progress of man, he knew at their core, the societal dynamics hadn't changed much in the last millennium.

Still, it surprised him that two adults, obviously well past the age of consent, who'd agreed to spend time together behind closed doors, could raise the eyebrows of anyone in this day and age. Not without due cause anyway. He frowned. "Did she say anything, or leave any message?"

Now the innkeeper abandoned any premise of working on his puzzle and straightened, holding his gaze directly. "She was pleasant enough. Charming lass, actually." He slid his glasses off and leaned against the desk. "I may need these to see beyond the end of my own nose," he said, waggling the eyeglasses, "but no matter her smiles, any fool could see she'd been crying."

Tag took that news like someone had poked him in the heart with a sharp stick. "Crying? Are you sure?"

The old man studied him for a moment, then relented a bit, apparently believing Tag's concern was sincere. "She wasn't sniffling or the like. But . . . well, a man doesn't raise five daughters without knowing when a woman's been shedding a few tears."

Shit. He'd only just made peace with losing her by telling himself he'd at least given her what she wanted, her anonymous fantasy fling But now? Now he didn't know what to think. "Did she say where she was headed?" he asked, before he could question the wisdom of the decision. "Our cars were stuck up on the mountain and—"

"She did say something about that. I directed her to Robey, down the end of the lane. I imagine they've long since dug the car out. It's been hours ago now."

Tag's spirits flagged again, but he smiled and stuck his hand out. "Thank you," he said, sincerely. "I appreciate your concern for her. And I'm sure she'd appreciate that you were looking out after her."

After a brief shake, the innkeeper slid his glasses back on, picked up his pencil and went back to his puzzle. "If you're interested in doing the same," he said, as Tag turned away, "I imagine Robey is back in his shop by now. Pearson's is the name of the place."

Tag flashed him a smile. "I was already on the way. But thanks for the additional information."

The older man's lips were still pursed, but his eyes were a bit more friendly now. "None of my business of course. But glad I could help."

Tag tipped an imaginary hat and let himself out the door, resolute now in this impulsive decision to track her down. He wanted to embrace the concept of playing more anyway, right? Well, why not start with a rousing game of Catch Me If You Can?

He didn't stop to ask himself if she wanted to be caught. Or what he'd do, or say, if he did catch up to her. But he couldn't shake the image of her leaving his bed with tear-stained cheeks. He had to at least make certain she was okay.

The snow had been cleared from the street, but the cobbled sidewalks had more snow than bare patches. It hadn't stormed as heavy here as it had further up the mountain. And with the wind whipping, it was likely both their vehicles had been completely buried.

Depending on what equipment this Robey had at his disposal, it wasn't entirely out of the question that they could still be at it. Regardless, the mechanic might know something more about her.

Her name would be a good starting-off point.

"And isn't that going to be an interesting conversation," he muttered.

Chapter 10

She had to stop thinking about him. At least until she could do so and not have her eyes well with tears at the thought of never ever seeing him again. Navigating the winding road down into the valley was difficult enough. The constant winds had drifted the snow across the peaks, making the remainder of her trip home a slow, tedious one. Giving her plenty of time to think. To remember.

Of course, it had only been seven hours or so since she'd crawled from their bed, from the toasty warm shelter of his deliciously perfect body. Seven hours since she'd watched him sleep, memorizing every last detail of him. The way his eyelashes fanned out darkly against his sun-burnished skin, the strong line of his jaw, the firm, deliberate curve to his lips, even in sleep. The way the muscles bunched in his arms, those wide palms, the long, clean line of his fingers. As if there was a chance she'd ever forget.

Seven hours since she'd discovered the pale brown tribal tattoo marking his bicep, and warred with herself over whether to wake him, and find out where else on his body he might have been branded. Seven hours since she'd debated the wisdom of allowing herself the luxury of feeling those hands on her again, that mouth, one last time . . . or if, for once, she'd do the smart thing and simply steal away.

If she had roused him, she knew she'd have told him anything he wanted to know about her. Would have begged him for every last detail of his life. Right before she pried his itinerary out of him, and worked out some way to spend more time with him. Any amount of time.

Somehow she'd found the strength to steal away instead, leaving her fantasy night intact. Any other path would have been beyond foolhardy. As if a wild night spent with a stranger hadn't been foolhardy enough. Besides, a few more days would not have been enough to work him through her system and back out again. She'd have only have gotten more attached, making their inevitable parting that much more difficult. And her heart had taken enough of a beating of late, hadn't it?

Okay, so maybe it had been more about pride and ego with Jory, rather than her heart. But forming an attachment to anyone new right now was probably not wise. She had a mountain of problems facing her at Ballantrae. Namely how she was going to keep it in Sinclair hands. She sighed as she drove along the low, crumbling walls that marked the property boundaries, not for the first time feeling as if every stone that had fallen from the stacked walls lay heavily on her shoulders, each one another mark of her failure to her ancestors, to her heritage.

She fought against giving in to the useless resentment of her fated position as the sole remaining Sinclair, burdening her with a responsibility more suited to a team of engineers and a raft of well-fed investors, than a thirty-year-old writer with no other prospects and nothing more to lean on than her rapidly dwindling resources.

Then she rounded that last mountain curve, where a clearing in the pine provided a stunning drop-away view of the valley below. Her valley. And she paused, as she always did, unable not to. No matter the season, whether it be the bleak and barren brown of winter, or the dazzling green and purple heather carpet of spring, the land that sprawled out before her was breathtakingly magnificent. And knowing that more often than not over the past seven hundred years, it had been a Sinclair standing on this very spot, looking out over that very dramatic landscape, intimately aware of how it had survived a long and oftentimes brutal history, yet still belonged to him . . . or her . . .

Her hands tightened on the steering wheel even as her heart tightened inside her chest. As it always did, with pride, with fear . . . and with determination.

Though it was true she'd oftentimes wished her parents had borne a son or six before bearing her, their only child and heir, she understood that the obligation she felt to Ballantrae went far deeper than a heritage handed down by the whims of birth order or chain of law. The responsibility was often daunting to the point of being crushing, and yes, on occasion she railed and ranted against the burden put upon her by the untimely deaths of both her parents just past her sixth birthday, and again, almost two decades later, when her adored Uncle Niall had passed.

But she always knew, deep down, that her heart would be here even if she had been able to stay in Inverness after graduating, pursue a career away from the castle, knowing a throng of family was still there to take up the financial and emotional slack. She loved Ballantrae with every fiber of her being. This land, the people who made their living from it, the castle, the crofts, and every last sheep that grazed here, were, together, the soul of who she was. Ballantrae wasn't just about her bloodlines, it was the very beat of her heart. And because it was, she'd never give up, never give in. And most definitely never walk away.

She drove on, her purpose renewed, and her faith, though still shaky in herself, was resolved in its purpose. She was going to have to write to Taggart's children in the States. It was the only angle left for her to pursue. As Mr. Wentworth had so gently pointed out, selling off a parcel, even a large one, of the property would only provide a temporary stopgap to the steady drain on the Ballantrae accounts. And that was

if he could find a buyer, which he hadn't seemed too enthusiastic about.

As it was, she was barely keeping the castle from crumbling to the ground, much less continuing the crucial restoration work on it, or even general property repair. She did
fairly well with her writing, as far as that went, but the lion's
share of the benefit there was the tax-free status it afforded
her. Which was huge, but didn't reduce the ongoing drain
that simply maintaining the building put on her reserves.

If she could only manage to lease out more land to
crofters, earning back a percentage of what they reaped, as
her forebears had done for centuries. But crofting wasn't the
ongoing concern it had once been in her valley. Her tenants'
offspring more often than not headed to university in Inverness
or Aberdeen, never to return. Or, if they did, it was with degree clutched in hand, ready to put a shingle out in the village, starting up their own business.

And then there was the village, which was suffering from
the same exodus of its young as the farming community.
Without the farmers coming into town, the need to provide
services for them dried up. She knew the villagers were a re-
sourceful lot, and that it had long since ceased to be the
Sinclairs' responsibility to see to their welfare. But she felt a
strong sense of it nonetheless. When the crofts were leased to
capacity and the renovations and work on the castle continu-
ally ongoing, the village benefited exponentially from their
labors.

And when she failed to maintain those things, she knew
they suffered exponentially as well. How could she not feel
responsible?

So, as her ancestors had done, in varying fashion and
under varying description, since shortly after the turn of the
fourteenth century, she'd team up with the laird of Clan
Morganach, sept to the mighty Clan MacKay, so that they
might join forces and once again prevail, keeping Ballantrae

safely in their clan's possession, as it had been, in one or the other's, for seven hundred years.

The trick would be finding out just how receptive the new Morgan clan chief was going to be to her proposition. Beginning with, she supposed, finding out if he was even aware of his clan status or his father's pledged support of her own.

She drove through the crumbling pillars that marked the gated entrance to what had been, centuries before, a proud fortress. Ballantrae had long enjoyed the protection of being bordered both north and south by the Cairngorm mountains, with Loch Ulish providing the eastern border and the river Tay to the west. The loch wasn't enough to support any kind of ongoing fishing concern, but it had provided enough bounty to keep the bellies of many crofters' families full when fields lay fallow after the spring floods, or disease struck down the flocks of sheep that produced Ballantrae's main crop, wool.

The vast, rock-strewn meadows extending to the west were dotted with sheep and crofts. The forest-lined road that wound to the north, leading over the mountains to Inverness-shire, passed through the village of Ballantrae. Once exclusively the concern of the Sinclair chieftain, now a township in its own right.

She often wondered how in the world her distant predecessors had not only managed to maintain the castle, grounds, and crofters, but run a village as well. It made her burden seem more reasonable by comparison. "Yeah," she muttered as she pulled around the wide expanse of gray stone and mortar that made up the impressive edifice of the main house, skipping the entrance into the central courtyard and heading instead along the north wing to the small gravel lot behind her tower. "A bloody piece of cake."

Lost in her thoughts and trying to stay there to keep her mind from wandering back to last night and the man she'd left behind, it wasn't until she'd climbed the winding stairs to her tower bedroom, that she remembered. Jory and Priss. In her bed.

Despite the work she had in front of her, the fires that had to be set to ward off the winter chill, her article deadlines, the mountain of paperwork that began with prioritizing what repair work could be put off and what had to be done before spring, and ended with her formulating one very important letter to the States, she tossed her purse and coat onto the fireside chair and turned to the bed that dominated the circular room. Her bed, the centerpiece of her haven, the place she'd created as her hideaway from the responsibilities that lay literally below her.

"First things first," she stated, and with one clean yank, she tore comforter, linens and pillows clear off the bed and onto the layered rug floor.

With half of the eleven bedrooms in the main house both furnished and sporting working fireplaces, she could have taken Jory to any one of them when he'd finally begun spending the night so many months ago. As she usually did when her current relationship ascended to that level. Why she'd allowed him access into her private aerie hideaway, she had no idea. Had she really fancied herself in love with him? On a deep-down level, she knew the answer to that was no. But on the surface? Well, she'd certainly tried to convince herself that it was time to look for something permanent.

Her mouth twisted in a wry smile. Clearly she was under more stress than she'd allowed herself to understand if she'd gone after Jory MacTavish as her best prospect. Yes, the man was good enough between the sheets, but he hadn't much in the way of anything else going for him. Certainly if she was going to make a marriage match, she could do as her ancestors had done and strike a merger that would benefit both clan and bride . . . usually in that order.

That was her problem. She was too selfish. And, frankly, too used to calling the shots to be in a big hurry to let someone else in. Sure, it would be great to have someone to lean on, both emotionally and financially, but the reality of that was that she also had to give up some control on how things were done around here. And while she had an often testy relationship with Ballantrae, it was hers to be testy with. She wasn't in a hurry to give someone else any control over it. Or her.

She slumped down on the bare bed, absently pulling one of the pillows from the floor to clutch against her chest, only to toss it aside as Priss's perfume wafted up to tickle her nose. She really was going to have to burn these sheets after all.

She stood and dug fresh linens from the wardrobe drawer, forcing her gaze away from the tangle of sheets on the floor as she swiftly made the bed. Also ignoring the fact that rather than conjuring up visions of Jory's fine bare ass pistoning against Priss's, she instead saw the tangle of sheets she'd left this morning. And the fine, bare man she'd left tangled in them.

Shaking on fresh pillowcases, her thoughts veered to Taggart, and her heart pinched again at the loss. It had been the perfect "marriage" for her. A clearly defined business contract that provided a steady income, wise counsel, friendly conversation and companionship . . . all cosseted in a very nonintrusive, long-distance relationship. He hadn't cared where she'd channeled his money, as long as it was spelled out in the bimonthly reports she sent to him. All that was missing from their arrangement was a warm body to curl up with and hot sex on a regular basis. A role Jory had been filling quite nicely, actually. Bastard.

Taggart dying had started everything unraveling. Jory's betrayal had just been the capper.

She fluffed out the clean duvet, rubbing the kink in her lower back. *Having a man take you up against a wall was thrilling, but it did have its drawbacks,* she thought. Of course, she'd have done it again without a blink. God, she missed him. It was ridiculous how much she missed him.

And though she was grateful for the bright spot he'd been, to a degree, she admitted he'd made things worse for her as well. The hot sex had been fabulous, but he'd brought so much more to her. In that short time they'd been together, he'd made her realize how wonderful it was to have such a rapport with someone. To laugh, to understand each other on a level that was both elemental and intellectual. Jory hadn't come close to fulfilling her needs in that way. Of course, until T.J. she hadn't even known how starved she was for that, so she could hardly blame Jory. But she knew now. And would forever feel the lack.

Forcibly blinking back the fresh threat of tears, she wadded up the offending linens inside the old duvet and briefly deliberated on following through with her initial plan to stuff them in the fireplace and toss a lit box of matches after them. Instead, she dragged the unwieldy sack down to the main floor of the tower, then out the door, where she stuffed them in the back of her truck. Her tiny washer/dryer unit was good enough for clothing and a bath towel or two, but for this load she needed the industrial-size unit below-stairs in the main house.

She backed up to the massive front doors, then managed to heave, haul and tug the load through the winding maze of halls and down short flights of odd-angled stairs that wound through the hodgepodge of construction that was Ballantrae castle. Hundreds of years of renovations, upgrades, and additions to the original structure had resulted in a rabbit warren of cobbled-together rooms and passages that more closely resembled an M.C. Escher rendering than the spare and simplistic fortress it had once been.

Sack of linens in tow, she descended to the bowels of the castle, and the stone room that centuries ago had been a reputed torture chamber. The perfect place to install a washer, as far as she was concerned. She hated doing laundry. After cramming as much in as she could, she tossed in soap, then slapped the lid down and dusted off her hands. Both a figurative and literal end to her relationship with Jory. And, she supposed, Priss. If only the rest of her life were so easily tidied up.

She leaned back on the washer, shoulders slumping a bit now. Normally she'd be ringing up Priss to tell her all about her wild and stormy night. Priss would have drawn every sordid detail out of her. They'd have sipped tea and inhaled a whole box of biscuits as they examined, analyzed and discussed every second of her snowbound tryst. By the time they were through, Priss would have gotten her over this ridiculous melancholy. Talking with her best friend would have helped her put it all into perspective. They'd have sighed at the romantic tragedy of it all, of course. Then they'd have moved on.

As it was, only Priss had moved on. Right on top of Maura's boyfriend. "Ex-boyfriend." She pushed off the washer as it started to whir and hum and slowly climbed the stone stairs to the main floor. She'd head back to her tower, make some tea, then tuck herself into her little makeshift office, which was actually just a rolltop desk situated between the kitchen and the lounge on the main floor, and settle down to work.

Priss was welcome to him, she thought as she entered her tower home and hung her coat on the rack next to the door. She headed directly to the stove and set the kettle on to boil. After what she'd done last night, it was hardly fair to pretend her heart was aching at the loss. But that didn't mean she couldn't hate him for using such monstrously bad judgment. Screwing her best friend in her own bed was terribly bad form, no matter what Maura had done last night.

But why couldn't he have exercised his incredibly bad judgment with someone else? Anyone else? She didn't want to lose Priss. She had other friends, but Priss was her closest, her dearest, her most trusted.

"Ha!" she spat out, indulging in a rise of temper. Obviously Priss didn't feel as committed to their friendship if she'd toss it over for a toss on her back. And, when you got down to it, she supposed that was what bothered her more than any-thing, except perhaps for the lingering visual of Jory's pelvis pistoning against Priss's bare ass. That one would take a while to recede. And it didn't matter that Priss had harbored some secret crush, or that perhaps Jory had as well, she stubbornly thought. Priss was her best friend. The one person on whom she'd placed her trust, and her heart, and felt secure that her faith would never be betrayed. She supposed the lesson to be learned in all this was to never trust anyone.

Her thoughts strayed to last night, and the impact a total stranger had made on her, the feelings he'd roused, the emo-tions she'd ended up all but wallowing in. She was forced to roll her eyes at herself. "Oh, that's right, Maura," she said, steeping the tea egg in the steaming water, "there's a lesson learned. Trusting a complete stranger."

She knew she could congratulate herself on being strong enough and wise enough to get the hell out of there this morn-ing before she did something even more phenomenally stu-pid. But somehow that self-satisfactory accolade didn't fill the emptiness in the pit of her stomach. The void that had started with Priss's defection had yawned ever deeper when she'd walked out of the inn this morning. Without even hav-ing said good-bye.

"Bollocks," she swore. She was getting downright maudlin, which wasn't her style at all. So she stacked another biscuit or two on her plate—sugar was always her antidepressant of choice—before heading to her desk.

She'd thought about leaving him a note, of course, but she couldn't think of anything to say that wasn't emotional and pathetic. She'd regretted it as soon as she'd left, feeling a coward for leaving him that way. Not wanting him to wake and his last impression of her be a bad one. All the way up the mountain in Robey's tow truck, she'd debated tucking a note somewhere on his car. But it had taken so long to un-earth her truck, in the end she hadn't waited around while Robey had set about digging the car out. She'd told herself at the time it was because she had to get back, had to get to work on her next solution to her problems. When it had really been fear that had driven her away. Fear she'd wait too long and he'd show up. What would she say to him then? Sorry to have wild, unbridled sex with you then leave you sleeping it off?

But that wasn't her worst fear. The real source of her trepidation was that he might show up . . . and everything would be even more wonderful than it had been the night before. Only this time she wouldn't be able to walk away. Which would only lead her to fall even more for him than she already had.

She rolled the desktop up and set her teacup and plate on the corner, searching through one of the cubby drawers for some aspirin. "It was one night with a stranger," she muttered beneath her breath. "One night does not a lifetime of happiness make. You don't even know him." And what she had learned hadn't exactly set him up as a potential prospect. She let out a hollow laugh. For God's sake, the man lived in a South American jungle! Just how much more impossible a match could she make?

"Put him out of your mind," she counseled herself as she crossed the room and went about laying the fire. She rubbed her arms as she waited for the peat to catch and smolder. She wrapped her sweater tighter about her middle and settled into the aged oak-and-leather padded chair. The Maura she knew, a hearty, independent lass, would have woken the bloke up for one more toss before setting out. But no, somewhere during the night she'd turned into pathetic, needy Maura. "Still should have taken that last toss," she grumbled defiantly, ignoring the burn of tears that threatened again.

Lonely, she thought, sipping her tea and pulling her account books from the side drawer. That's what had made her so maudlin. Loneliness. Of course, anyone would go a bit batty, rattling around in this place all alone. Normally there would be masons and carpenters banging about. But since

Taggart's death, she hadn't been able to pay the laborers. That, and the onset of a heavy winter, had combined to make her the stereotypical spinster, holed up in her tower with nothing more than her cat and the stories she made up for company. If she had a cat, that is.

"Oh, for God's sake, get a grip," she commanded. Grabbing a wad of tissues, she blew her nose, blinked back the tears that refused to stop hovering on the brink, and pulled out a red pencil and the rough draft of her article. She'd scoot through this, then get out the ledgers, tote up the columns, look at her spreadsheets . . . and figure out which parcel of land would have the best chance at finding a buyer. The letter to the States would come next. But even if Taggart's heir responded quickly, she needed ready capital a month ago. The bank wasn't going to hold off any longer on a maybe. If she was lucky, she'd only have to sell off one or two small parcels to make ends meet, before an arrangement was made. She raked her hands through her hair, the words on the page a blur. Problem was . . . which plot would be the first to go?

And what if Taggart's son turns you down? a little voice added in the back of her mind.

She shut out that nagging whisper, but ended up shoving her rough draft aside and dragging out her ledgers. She couldn't think straight until she had a plan in place. The barren crofts were to the immediate west, between the castle and the working crofts closer to the river. The soil was richer there, and less likely to brown over the winter, allowing wider-ranging grazing. Those tenants had signed leases, and had paid more for the advantageous location. Even if they were of a mind to help her out, she couldn't very well ask them to move to a plot closer to the castle in the middle of winter. Which left her with parcels to the north and south. North made the most sense; it was the property closest to the village. If she could somehow sell it as commercial property, that would net her more money, but she'd have to petition to have it rezoned. No funds for that. Or time. Of course, she could sell it off anyway and the new owner could apply, but then she'd have to take a pittance for it. At the moment it was heavily wooded and no good to anyone for anything except hunting pheasant.

Her gaze drifted to her laptop set up on a side table. She should have written the letter to the States sooner. Right after she'd gotten word of Taggart's death. But she hadn't had the heart to intrude on a grieving family with something as mercenary as a request for money. Not that she knew for certain they were grieving, given their estrangement . . . but, grieving herself, she still couldn't bring herself to do it. "And because of that, you're going to lose Sinclair land. A lot of it."

She sighed and slumped back in her chair, her forehead throbbing despite the aspirin. She was a disgrace to her clan. She should have had more backbone, greater ingenuity. She should have found a way to follow through on Taggart's promise to her and damn the emotions of the sons who couldn't even be bothered to reconcile with their only flesh and blood when he lay dying.

She tossed her pencil down in disgust, only she wasn't sure who it was directed at. Taggart's cold and distant offspring, or herself. She was massaging her temples when she heard a distant rumbling noise that sounded like a truck engine rattling into the central compound. She stood and crossed the room, looking out of the tower windows behind her, which provided a view of the entire courtyard.

She frowned, not recognizing the black lorry that pulled around the courtyard . . . twice, as if not sure where to park. Finally whoever it was pulled up to the rear delivery entrance of the main house, and cut the engine. She was about to turn away from the window and start the descent down to the underground passageway that ran from the tower, beneath the courtyard, to the main house. With both wings either closed off entirely or under heavy construction, it was the fastest way to get from here to the main house without driving around. But she stopped short when the truck door opened . . . and a mop of curly hair emerged.

Her breath caught and her hand came up to her throat. He was too far away for her to see his face, but that hair . . . that lanky body. It could only be—"Don't be ridiculous," she scolded herself, turning away and crossing the room to the door leading to the stairs going below ground. "You've obviously gone completely round the bend now." First off, he'd been driving a small, silver compact, not a rattletrap black truck. And second, she'd left hours ahead of him. He had no way of tracking her down. No one back in Calyth even knew who she was. Except—*Robey!*

No, no, that couldn't be it. Sure, she'd told him her name, but she'd paid the man with cash. She'd already tapped her credit card paying for the room. A foolish sop to her guilty conscience that she'd regret when her bill came, but it was done. Was that it? Had he gotten Helen's husband to give him her name from the credit receipt? Still, what would a name have gotten him? She realized she was hurrying down the stairs at a breakneck speed, barely grabbing the lantern off the hook and flicking it to life before descending into the dark, dank passageways she knew like the back of her hand. Once in the main house, she charged up the stairs to the service level, praying he hadn't given up and left. Careening around corners, clinging to the banisters and knocking books off the miles of cramp packed shelves that lined every staircase and winding hallway.

The truck, she thought, grasping onto that fact, any fact, that would squelch the hope blossoming in her chest. Why would he be driving a truck? It was probably one of the laborers come to find out if she was going to be hiring again soon. It had been the long hair, the curls. It wasn't him. Couldn't be him.

"Slow down," she whispered raggedly, damning her breathlessness as she skidded to a halt on the threadbare Persian runner that lined the back hall leading to the delivery entrance just off the cavernous formal kitchens. Though these rooms hadn't been used even during Uncle Niall's lifetime, a childhood spent playing hide-and-seek had committed every inch of Ballantrae to memory. She made her way easily through the gloom of the main kitchen and the twin fireplaces, each big enough to roast an entire ox, past the huge doors to the double pantries and the scullery and herb room, only to skid to a complete stop when a shadow crossed the partially shuttered window panes of the rear door.

She went to reach for the handle, but something held her frozen in place. The man on the other side of the door was tall. With broad shoulders, and judging from the height of the window, long legs. She couldn't make out his face through the clouded panes of glass, but she could tell he wore a dark coat. And there was that wild mop of curls.

He's come for you. The words were there in her mind before she could stop them. Her heart sped up, even as she tried desperately to quash it. "Be reasonable, Maura. It's no' him. It canno' be."

He rapped on the door again, and her pulse leapt forward like a startled jackrabbit. "You're being a fool," she mumbled beneath her trembling breath. *And ye've made quite enough of a spectacle of yourself in the past twenty-four hours, now haven't you?* She tossed her hair, straightened her shoulders, and blew out a long, steadying breath. "It's no' but a laborer standin' out there. Just open the bloody door and be done with this silly fantasy of yours."

But it took the shadow shifting back as the man turned away from the door to spur her into action. Even then, her hand shook hard as she reached to unlock the twin bolts that secured the entrance. He paused at the sound of the locks being withdrawn, turned back to face the door.

Her heart pounding so hard now she could scarce hear her own thoughts, she yanked the door open, unable to withstand a moment more of suspense. "Oh," she said, the word a gasp of delight she couldn't contain. Because unless she'd lost her mind completely, that was him. Standing not a foot away from her. Where she could reach right out and touch him. "It *is* you," she whispered. And a joy and happiness that was likely unwise to indulge in, but impossible to tamp down, filled her clear to bursting. *He had come for her!*

At that moment, that was all that mattered. Not that they'd have to part once more, or that parting again would be made even more difficult the more time they spent together. No, at the moment, all that mattered was that he was here, standing before her, where she could reach out and touch him. Fall into his arms once more, feel his lips on hers, his hands . . .

So full of her giddy reunion excitement, it took her a moment to notice that he wasn't looking at her with the same joyful glee that she knew was beaming out at him. In fact, his mouth hung open and his expression could only be described as one of complete and utter shock.

"Maura?"

"Aye," she said, confusion swiftly crowding out the joy.

His eyes closed as if some sort of truth had just dawned on him. "You're . . . ?" His chin dipped momentarily and he blew out a long breath. When he looked back to her, his face was blank, utterly devoid of any emotion and completely unreadable.

Without knowing exactly why, Maura felt a chill creep over her that had nothing to do with the cold air whistling in through the open doorway. She folded her arms tightly in front of her, tucking her hands against her body for warmth. Hands she'd just moments ago thought about using to tug him through that door and up against her body.

If she didn't know better, she could only guess he had no idea she would be the one opening that door. But . . . what other purpose could he have for being here?

He was shaking his head, letting out a bitter laugh that was so unlike the man she'd been with the night before. "Jesus, he couldn't have planned this little set-down any better if he'd been alive and standing in front of me."

"I'm sorry?" she asked, wondering now if perhaps something had happened to him between Calyth and Ballantrae. He sounded a wee bit . . . well, daft.

He looked at her squarely then, and those bright gold eyes of his pierced her, and not in that sensual, electric way they had last night. He had an almost fatalistic look on his face now as he asked, "You're Maura Sinclair?"

She nodded, still quite confused. "Aye, I've already said as much." She shifted back a step. "You . . . you look as if you've seen a ghost or something. Did you no' come looking for me?"

He was still studying her, as if she were some specimen, or artifact he'd dug up, but couldn't quite figure out how it had gotten there. "Are you telling me you don't know who I am?"

"I believe you're the man whose bed I climbed out of this morning, if that's what you mean." Frowning now, she let her arms fall to her side. "What's going on here? Why are you behaving so oddly?"

Now he frowned. "So you're telling me you don't know, then? Who I really am?"

She folded her arms, temper beginning to rise. "Beyond my carnal knowledge of you, you mean? No. The only thing I know is what the truck driver, Angus, called you. T.J." She studied him. He appeared downright suspicious of something, but for the life of her, she couldn't imagine what. After all, he'd chased her across the mountains, not the other way around. "Am I supposed to know something more?"

"Did you know a man by the name of Taggart Morgan?"

The question caught her so off guard, she couldn't answer him right off. Now it was she who regarded him suspiciously, realizing quite too belatedly that despite their activities of the night before, and the foolish emotions he'd roused inside of her, he was still an absolute stranger to her. She took a slow step back, reaching for the door, debating if she could get it closed and at least one lock thrown before he stormed the castle. Which, judging from his expression, he was quite close to doing. "Why do you ask?" she said finally.

He swore beneath his breath. "The 'T' in those initials stands for Tag. Taggart by birth." He folded his arms now, regarding her closely. "The 'J' is for James."

Now it was her turn to stare in open-mouthed shock. "Taggart . . . James. Morgan? You're his son?"

Perhaps it was the row of teeth lining his neck, but the smile that spread across his tanned, handsome face made her shiver . . . and only part in dread. "At your doorstep," he responded. Then the smile turned downright lethal. "And . . . apparently at your service."

Chapter 11

Tag didn't know what to think, much less how to feel. His mind was still reeling. Foremost was the belief that, no matter what she pretended to know or not know, their meeting yesterday could not have been coincidental. Because, honestly, what were the chances of that?

Which meant what? But he couldn't follow that track, because, as the reality of the situation sank in, he realized that this woman in front of him, the one he'd taken like a man possessed not twelve hours ago, was the woman who'd written those letters to his father. Long passages of which he'd all but committed to memory. The woman who'd both captivated him with her wit and humor . . . and disconcerted him with her ability to develop a close relationship with his father.

Had he been so blind? Had last night just been the latest scheme of an accomplished mercenary? Of course, if she'd played on an old man's loneliness and terminal illness to secure the roof over her head, then why he wouldn't put it past her to seduce him to get the same, he had no idea.

He'd recalled how he'd braked the rattletrap truck he'd bummed off of Robey as he'd rounded that last bend coming off the mountain, just before descending into the valley. The entirety of the crumbling glory that was Ballantrae had sprawled before him, as he supposed it had for many a chieftain in past centuries.

Chieftain. He would have laughed at the folly of it, the absolute ridiculousness of it. Somehow it hadn't been laughter that had risen in his throat. Something else had, something he hadn't been able to name, but had choked him nonetheless. Ballantrae. It was hardly Camelot, but there was no denying the enormity of it, or the burden it had to impose on the owner. He'd swallowed hard then, realizing that that owner was him.

Which brought him back to the woman standing before him, hands now propped on her hips, looking at him as if she couldn't quite figure out his game. Well, that made two of them.

How could she have found out he was headed here? Had she finally given up ever hearing from Taggart's heirs and contacted Jace after he'd left? She had the roof over her head, so maybe she'd run out of ready cash. Of course, from first glance, it didn't appear the money was being used for its supposed intended purpose. No matter what those reports had said. And really, other than those pieces of paper, which she'd generated, and her say so, what proof had his father really had that she wasn't just blowing the money and enjoying free rent?

There were no work trucks, no obvious signs of labor, but plenty indication of the need for it. A few of the distant farmhouses he'd spied on his way in had smoke spiraling from their chimneys, but most plots appeared to be long-abandoned concerns. So just what in the hell had she been doing with his father's money?

And what in the hell had she been doing with him? Talk about a total mind fuck. Caught up in his train of thought, he didn't bother to stop and question the extremity of the measures she'd gone to in hopes of ensnaring him. Nor did he bother to consider that not only couldn't she have predicted he'd lose control of his car, she hadn't even been in close proximity of the accident site when he'd become part of it.

All he knew at the moment was that, while his father might have been taken in by her—his actions last night notwithstanding—he wasn't going to be her next sucker bet.

"At my ... service?" she spluttered. "What the bloody hell is that supposed to mean? I'm just as surprised by this as you are!"

Tag just snorted and pushed his way past her. Best for her to understand right off the bat just who was going to be calling the shots from now on. "Just what the hell kind of game are you playing here?"

She spun around and stormed in behind him. "Excuse me, but I don't recall inviting you in."

"Oh, I think you've invited me about as far in as a man can get." He tossed a very uncivilized smile over his shoulder. "Perhaps you should have thought about the possible consequences before you so readily straddled my hips last night."

Her mouth opened, but all that came out was a string of indignant, spluttering sounds. "Wait," she finally commanded as he strode down the dimly lit hallway. "I don't care if we shagged ourselves bloody unconscious, it doesn't give you the right to come storming in here and—"

He spun around so quickly she smacked right up against his chest. He gripped her arms before she could back away, unsure of just where his explosion of temper was coming from—he wasn't supposed to give two damns about Maura Sinclair or Ballantrae, right? But whatever the source, be it the humiliation of being used, or the destruction of his own personal fantasy about Maura Sinclair, letter writer—one he hadn't realized had taken such deep root inside him until the loss of it so thoroughly disappointed him—the sheer force of it overrode any ability on his part to control it.

His grip tightened. "From what little I've learned about our common ancestors, a Morgan has breached Sinclair walls more than once over the centuries. And only some of those boundaries were made of stone." He leaned closer. "I'm just continuing the family tradition."

He'd intended to insult her, to lash out in righteous indignation. And she flinched as if he'd struck her physically. But there had been a split second there . . . right before that flinch . . . where her pupils had shot wide. And not in fear. Much the way they had when he'd run his fingertips over her—

No! He shoved that thought and her away at the same time. He was hardly an adolescent in the throes of his first sexual experience. No matter that his experience with her had been unparalleled in the annals of his personal sexual history. Just another part of her planned arsenal, he was certain. She liked living here, on his father's dime, and who the hell wouldn't? She would do whatever was necessary to keep her cushy little overseer position.

Well, she would no longer be doing it with him. No matter that his body had gone hard as the stone beneath his feet the instant he'd put his hands on her.

"Listen," she said, obviously furious, and just as obviously trying to rein it in. "It's apparent that neither one of us knows what the hell is going on here."

"Oh, one of us knows quite a bit more than the other."

She gave him a patently false smile, as her blue eyes were still blazing. "Fine, then why don't we go settle ourselves down somewhere so you can fill in all the blanks. Because, I can tell you that I have a number of them. All of them starting with what the hell last night was all about."

She went to march around him, but he instinctively blocked her escape. To look at her, you'd think she was the one being wronged here, the one being duped in some way. She was damn good, he'd give her that. But then, he'd learned that firsthand last night, hadn't he?

"Just to make things perfectly clear, there will be no repeat of last night," he stated evenly. "Fool me once, shame on me."

"Fool you?" She laughed harshly. "Oh, that's rich. Let me ask you one thing. If I was out to ensnare you, then why would I leave your bed? Why not stay and continue weaving this supposed web of mine? And further, how on earth was I to know who you were in the first place? Much less that you were coming to visit? It wasn't like I received advance notice."

"A simple call to the States could have provided a wealth of information, including my travel itinerary."

Now she snorted. "I don't exactly have the financial wherewithal to ring up the States whenever the whim strikes me."

"Yes, I imagine things have gotten a bit tight without my father's handout."

"Handou—" She broke off, indignant once again. Color rose in her cheeks, that in any other circumstances would have been quite captivating. "Your father and I had a solid business arrangement."

"Yes, and I imagine his death put quite a hitch in your lifestyle."

"*Lifestyle?*" She choked on something that sounded like a cross between a burst of outrage and a laugh.

"I'm surprised you haven't hit the remaining Morgans up for money already."

If he wasn't mistaken, that indignant flush took on an air of mortification.

"So," he said, "you were planning on contacting us. Another of your charming letters perhaps?"

Her gaze sharpened instantly. "What do you know of my letters?"

He chose not to answer that. Anger and arousal, as it turned out, were a lot more closely linked than he was absolutely comfortable with at the moment. No sense treading into territory that was still raw and confusing to him. "I know you wrote my father chatty little letters, and in return he sent you large sums of money. As far as I can tell, you had the easy end of the deal. You didn't even have to spend time on your back. I suppose I should count myself fortunate for having shown up in person."

He caught her open palm slap an instant before it connected with his cheek. Her face was more than flushed now, her eyes had gone dark and stormy, her chest rising and falling in anger. He couldn't stop the thought that she was almost as arousing in full temper as she was on the brink of climax.

Her wrist still clasped in his grip, she spoke with exaggerated calm. "I think this little conversation has come to an end." She yanked her arm free and stepped back so she could pull open the courtyard door. "I'll thank you to take your leave. I don't know what you think I've done to you, or your father, but I do not have to stand in my home and be insulted by the likes of you. I begin to see where the estrangement stemmed from."

"What?"

"You and your brothers, abandoning your only living parent. Taking for granted how lucky ye are to have one a'tall. Alone and dying he was, with not so much as a postcard from any of you."

Tag's mouth dropped open briefly, then he barked out a laugh. "You can't be serious." But he saw she was, and whatever cold humor he found in her misguided statement disappeared as swiftly as it had come, until all that was left was the chill. "You have no idea what you're talking about, or should I say whom you're talking about."

"You know what? You're absolutely right. Your father never spoke of you. Or your brothers. Not once, beyond acknowledging your existence."

"Which should have told you something."

She studied him coolly. "In fact, it did. Meeting you further illuminates the matter."

"My, how nice it must be to fill in the blanks with your own overactive imagination."

She arched a brow. "Hello Pot," she said, sketching a mock-
ing bow. "Meet Kettle." She swung the door wide. "Now
please take your equally black heart and leave my property.
And don't worry, I won't darken your doorstep or your mail-
box. In fact, I'd rather be the Sinclair that fails Ballantrae altogether than take another cent from your Morgan coffers."

Tag had been all set to deliver a stinging comeback when
her words sunk in. Either she was taking her overseer position way too seriously . . . or she was under the impression
that she had a bigger stake here than she did. Either way, it
was clear she had no idea what his stake was here. Perhaps
she thought his father had left her the property upon his
death. For all Tag knew, his father had promised her
exactly that. Of course, if he had, he'd never followed
through with it.

Whatever the case, she was in for a rude awakening.

He stepped further away from the door. He had no inten-
tions of leaving before they got everything out in the open.
And he might not have any intention of leaving then either.
After all, for the time being anyway, he owned this place.

"I understand," he began, "the closeness with which the
current generation here cleaves itself to its own history. I
admit I've not read much about my ancestors beyond the
ones who settled on my side of the ocean, but seeing as I was
raised surrounded by Sinclairs and Ramsays, I am familiar to
some degree with our joint, albeit distantly joint, past."

"You mean to say you've made the study of past civilizations your life's work, and yet you've never delved into your
own?" She'd said it somewhat mockingly, but there was sincere perplexity in her tone as well. As if she simply couldn't
fathom a lack of interest in one's own roots.

"Which only goes to prove my point," he added. "Yes, I
am in the business of studying the past. My reasons for
avoiding my own are not up for grabs at the moment. Suffice
it to say, I'm here, delving as you put it, now."

She folded her arms. "Yes, having been part of said 'delving' I can attest to that. But what specifically do you want here? Beyond tormenting me with your narrow-minded and highly uninformed views, that is."

He sighed, growing weary of this. "I never set out to torment you. I think we can both agree last night was hardly torture for either one of us. I didn't even know Maura Sinclair *was* you, until you opened the door."

"So you admit you did come here with some negative intent toward me? The me you didn't think you'd met yet."

"No! If you must know the truth, meeting you was pretty much the only part of this trip I was looking forward to," he blurted out in frustration, then immediately wished he hadn't.

She frowned. "Well, you've certainly taken care of that bit of business, now haven't you?"

Teeth clenched, he spoke slowly, evenly. "I didn't know it was you, okay? Any more than you claim to know it was me. But you'd have to agree it seems a phenomenal case of serendipity if what you say is true and we just happened to come across each other on the road here."

"Seems a stretch. But, if what you say is true," she said, pointedly parroting him, "that's exactly what happened." She shrugged. "No different really than being half a world away and running into an old school chum in some airport. Odd, but it happens."

She held his gaze steadily, and he might be the biggest fool in the world, but he believed she was telling the truth. The more he thought on it, the particulars of it, the thing she'd said about leaving his bed this morning . . . and that look of absolute happiness on her face when she'd opened the door to him just now . . . *Christ.* He was an idiot.

Arms still folded, doorknob still within reach, she regarded him silently for a long moment. "You said you wanted to meet me. The Sinclair of Ballantrae me. Why? Did you talk with your father before he died? Did Taggart speak of me to you?"

Tag shook his head. "We hadn't spoken in a very long

time. I didn't even know he was ill until word got to me while on a dig, several months ago, that he'd passed on."

She cocked her head. "You don't sound particularly regretful."

He tightened his jaw, worked to keep his temper in check. He knew from her letters that she'd had an entirely different relationship with his father than he ever had. It was entirely understandable that she'd take his father's side in this. But it didn't make it any easier to swallow. And he'd be damned if he'd explain or apologize for living his life the only way he'd been able to, and survive with his sanity intact. "You don't know anything about what went on between my father and me and my brothers, so don't pass judgment."

"You could always enlighten me."

He could feel his pulse tic in his temple. "I could. But I won't. What happened between us is none of your business."

She didn't prod him further, for which he was intensely grateful. He'd known coming here would be fraught with unforeseen emotional snares, but he could never have predicted just how tangled he was going to make it, albeit unwittingly.

"Fine. So why don't we begin with what I know. I had a letter from Taggart's associate, Mick Templeton, notifying me of his passing, and saying he'd follow through with your father's wishes. I know what he'd told me he wanted, but not what he'd actually done about it. That was three months ago. It was the last I heard from anyone." She nodded toward him. "Your turn. What do you know about our arrangement? Why come all the way over here if you have no interest in your heritage? And why did you say you were looking forward to meeting me?"

Tag debated on how to answer her. He wasn't ready to reveal his unusual emotional connection to the letters she'd written. Or the confusion warring inside him now that he realized the woman he'd spent a once-in-a-lifetime night with, was the same woman whose words had somehow managed to captivate him as well. He wanted to trust that this was nothing more than a simple misunderstanding, that they would look back and laugh about this confrontation, and how suspicious they'd both been of each other's motives. But he wasn't quite there yet. Certainly not with the amusement, but more importantly not with the trust.

Which could get a great deal more complicated when he revealed why he was really here. He saw no point in putting that off any longer.

"I became aware of your existence at the same time I became aware of my father's overseas assets." He didn't see the need to mention that this was his father's only overseas holding. Nor did he see fit to tell her that his father had kept this particular purchase a secret, even from his own accountant. He regarded her closely as he finished. "Your name came up while I was going over the business papers dealing with his purchase of Ballantrae."

"Purchase? You mean the investment papers," she corrected.

Light began to shine on the situation. "You think my father was merely an investor in the property? As what? A tax write-off for him?"

"Of course that's what I think. That's what he was, what his investment was. In spare business terms anyway. It was far more than that personally. To him. And to me."

Tag scrubbed a hand over his face. Despite his previous anger and his continued distrust, he was finding no pleasure in this. "As the overseer, perhaps you aren't intimately familiar with the terms of his agreement, but—"

"Overseer?" She laughed. "Obviously whoever explained his 'overseas assets' to you hadn't read over the documentation."

She might be many things he was unaware of, but one thing he knew for certain was that Maura Sinclair was no fool. He hadn't read over the fine print of the contracts, taking Mick at his word that his father was the owner. He'd pieced the rest together, yes, but from what little he'd skimmed, the contracts had appeared to back up that claim. Could Mick have been misinformed? Had his father merely been an investor in the property? Which, he supposed, would make him part owner. Mick had been pretty clear about it, though, very certain. To the point of making sure Tag understood his responsibilities regarding the property he now "owned." Responsibilities, which, come to think of it, might be the same as that of an investor.

He'd shoved aside the folder of paperwork when he'd opened the cherrywood box and began reading Maura's letters. And had, admittedly, never gone back to them.

In lieu of revealing that to her, he said, "Why don't you explain to me exactly what your arrangement with my father was?"

She eyed him guardedly. "Why is it I feel there is an underlying tone to that question? If you think there was something untoward about my relationship with your father, be man enough to simply come out with it."

He was confused, frustrated and still disconcerted about discovering he'd slept with the woman who'd written those letters, but he had to admit he admired her control. But then, at the moment, without the paperwork in front of him, she held all the cards, didn't she? Well, they'd see about that.

"No, I don't think there was anything untoward," he told her truthfully. Her letters, after all, had been that of companionship, not some sordid May–September love affair. "Not in the way you mean, that is. But if in fact you own Ballantrae, or owned it at one time, I can't help but wonder what was in it for him? He funneled a great deal of money your way, and didn't appear to be getting much of a return for his investment, tax write-off notwithstanding. I assumed he'd expected his money was being used to increase the worth of his investment. Money that, from the rather dormant looks of things, hasn't exactly been spent spiffing up the place. Although, come to think of it, maybe that was a wise calculation on your part. If you don't make the improvements, then he can't sell your childhood home out from under you. Which means you might have known my father better than I thought. Because that would be exactly something he would do. In fact, the more I think about it, the more I'm sure that was probably exactly why he did this." Tag could only wonder why he hadn't put it together sooner. "That way he can screw over his entire heritage and all his ancestors in one fell swoop."

She merely looked at him as if he'd lost his mind. But he wasn't exactly tossing out wild speculations here. In fact, that was the only rational explanation he could come up with.

"He would never have sold me out, even if he could have, which by the way, he couldn't." She waved that away with a brisk flip of her hand, as if that weren't the part that was bothering her. "But how is it you do what you do for a living, and have absolutely no understanding of the worth of heritage?"

"You're telling me my father handed over tens of thousands of dollars as an investment in his ancestry?" He laughed. "My father may have changed in his final years, but no man changes that much. He loathed his ancestry, his heritage."

She sighed, then raked her hands through her hair in weary frustration. "Do you have the paperwork you were given with you?"

He had a great deal more than that, but he was still unprepared to tell her that. About the letters his father had kept, carefully preserved in that cherrywood box. Maybe she knew his father had kept them, tucked away like cherished mementos. Tag had no idea what had been in his father's letters, after all. But he did know that the man who'd raised him had not one sentimental bone in his body. Yes, he cared deeply about their heritage, but only in the way of a man ashamed of his ancestors' past actions, a man determined to change the way in which his family name would be remembered. To listen to his father's lectures on the subject, it was clear he'd have been thrilled to discover a way to wipe clean from the slate of history every mention of any Morgan before him.

"Yes," he said at length. "Out in the truck."

She stared at him through the gloom of the small service vestibule. "Well, since we've spent almost the entire duration of our relationship fumbling about in the dark, I say it's time to bring everything into the light. Figuratively and literally. So why don't you retrieve whatever files you brought with you, then we'll ascend to a higher level—" she sent him a pointed look, "and get to the bottom of this matter once and for all."

She pulled the door open once again, and he stepped past her, back into the chill wind that whipped about the courtyard. He sent her a pointed look of his own, all but daring her to try and lock him out, which given how this meeting had gone so far, he couldn't exactly blame her if she did. But he wasn't leaving until he had some answers. And he had more questions now than when he'd arrived. To that end, when he opened the back of the small work truck, he pulled out both his duffel and the backpack he'd stowed his carry-on items in.

"Why the lorry?" she asked from right behind him.

He hadn't known she'd followed him out, so her voice, so close behind him, stilled his actions for a moment. Then he went ahead and slung the duffel over his shoulder and turned to face her. "Apparently someone else came up the mountain in the storm last night and missed the warning flags. The front right panel of the rental car was smashed in and the tire was toast. I'm surprised you didn't notice when you had your truck removed."

"It was fine when I was up there. At least I thought it was. In truth, I was more concerned about my truck not going over the edge while we hooked it up to his lorry. Robey put my spare on and he was planning on digging you out when I left. Didn't he mention that to you?"

"Robey wasn't exactly big on talking." Much to Tag's frustration, as he recalled. Not exactly the wealth of information he'd been hoping for. He hadn't even given up Maura's name, claiming he hadn't caught it. Tag's little Catch Me game had come to a swift and unfortunate end before it had even begun. "He loaned me this truck. I'm due back in Calyth at the end of the week to pick it back up."

"I'm sorry. Honest. I had no idea."

He slung his backpack over his other shoulder and kicked the rear panel door shut. He had wondered when he'd arrived at Robey's only to find his car all dinged up, for a split second anyway, if she'd been somehow responsible. She'd been upset according to the innkeeper, but he hadn't given the impression they'd been angry tears. Besides, he hadn't done anything to hurt her. Jesus what a tangled mess this all had become.

She stood in front of him when he turned toward the house. "Why are you bringing in all that?" she asked, motioning to his baggage.

"It's already getting dark and I'm not about to go driving through the mountains again."

"There is a lovely inn right in the village. I can ring Molly up and—"

Now he smiled. She had the upper hand at the moment, but he held a few cards in his own. "I might be unclear about the specifics, but I'm pretty sure I own at least a chunk of this crumbling edifice. I'm sure you can find someplace to put me up for the night."

She folded her arms, her gaze turning to steel.

"No need to look at me like that. Last night was last night. I have no expectations in that direction, trust me."

Now she had the nerve to look offended.

He pushed past her. "And don't worry about the accommodations. I'm used to sleeping in pretty rustic conditions. I don't require anything fancy."

"Good," she said, storming past him, through the court-yard door. "I believe we have some free space in the dungeons that would suit you fine." She tossed what could only be described as an icy smile over her shoulder. "It won't be the first time a Morgan has spent a night in there."

Chapter 12

Maura led him on the winding path up several short, twisted flights of stairs, then down the wide, bookshelf lined hallway to the main parlor. She only used it for company, which was rare. But she wasn't ready to invite Tag into her private quarters. An hour ago, she'd been fantasizing about dragging him there and picking up where they'd left off last night.

How quickly things change.

Taggart's son. Taggart's estranged son. She still couldn't quite grasp it, though she knew she'd better, and quickly. She couldn't believe he thought he'd inherited the whole of Ballantrae. That's not how she and Taggart had set up their agreement. In fact, he was a few short weeks away from having no claim on it whatsoever.

She paused inside the door of the cavernous parlor. The room itself wasn't that large by the standards of some of the other rooms in the castle, but the high ceilings, tall, narrow windows, and oversized fireplace gave a person the sensation that if you spoke loudly in here, your voice would echo for ages. "How are you at getting a fire started?" she asked.

For a brief second, the wry humor she'd so quickly come to associate with him flickered around his mouth and eyes. "As long as I've got the proper materials, I'm generally pretty proficient."

She wondered if there was some sort of hidden message there, but was still too flustered by this whole turn of events to take time to ferret it out. "Well, it's already laid," she began, then winced inwardly at the unintended pun. For all the frustration and tension arcing between the two of them since his surprising arrival, she was forced to admit that a large percentage of it—for her, anyway—was still sexual.

She really must work on that.

"All you have to do is strike the tinder there," she went on, refusing to let his imposing presence or her overactive libido get the best of her. "I'll go get my documentation. It'll take me a few moments. Make yourself at home." She'd said it automatically, as a good hostess would.

Only he looked over his shoulder, glancing at her from where he'd crouched in front of the massive grate, and his expression made it clear what his thoughts were. *Of course. I am home.*

Yes, well, she thought as she hurried out to the hallway, ducking behind the mammoth main hall staircase and through the door leading back down to the underground passages, *we'll see about that.* It was clear he had completely misunderstood, well, pretty much everything. From the nature of her relationship with his father to the nature of their agreement.

Breathless from rushing, she still took the final steps up to the main floor of the north tower two at a time. She didn't want to leave him alone back there for any longer than necessary. Stooping in front of a metal file cabinet next to her desk, she yanked out the bottom drawer, tugging free the appropriate accordion file. It not only contained the original papers they'd both signed, but also held the deposit tickets reflecting his monthly payments and the notes from the bank regarding the loans she'd secured based on that monthly stipend. And in the rearmost dividers, she'd kept all the letters Taggart had sent her over the duration of their relationship.

She sat back on her haunches, debating on whether to pull

them all out, or if she should show these to Taggart's son. As proof, if necessary, of their agreement and their relationship. It was clear the two hadn't reconciled and she was protective enough about the man she'd become so fond of, that she wasn't going to toss his words, feelings, and thoughts, which had been intended for her eyes only, in the lap of his ungrateful son. But she left them in there all the same. He didn't have to see them.

File tucked under her arm, she debated driving back around or taking the passage, but opted for the passage. She didn't want to explain how she'd come to drive up to the front door. Grabbing the lantern from its post, she hurried back down the stairs.

She still could not reconcile the handsome, funny, fascinating man she'd met and become so wildly enamored of that she'd actually gone to bed with him hours after meeting him . . . with the moody, suspicious man currently prowling about her parlor. How was it a family came to be torn apart as his had been? Taggart had spoken only once of his wife and the tragedy of her early demise, leaving Maura to draw her own conclusions about his grief and that of his young sons. Had that been the beginning of the rift between them? But to last for so many years, to the point that even his terminal illness hadn't been enough of an impetus to encourage a reconciliation?

Of course, Tag had alluded to the fact that she had no idea what his relationship with his father had been like, and Maura was adult enough to know that just because she'd gotten along with the man, did not mean his sons didn't have valid reasons for removing themselves from their own father's life. And yet, what could have been that awful? The man she knew was opinionated and gruff on occasion, and he wasn't the most open of men emotionally speaking—but then what man was?

Still, he'd been a great observer of those around him and had great command of the written word. His letters had been shorter than hers, and as a whole, he hadn't been too keen on responding to her requests for more information about the American side of her roots, but he had spoken of his life's work, the cases he'd tried, both as a lawyer, and those he'd sat on as a judge. He'd been impassioned about the importance of law and his devotion to upholding his part in the—as he called it—best judicial system in the world. It wasn't something she'd ever followed, though he made it fascinating. Uncle Niall, of course, would have been enraptured. She'd wished more than once that the two of them could have met.

He had granted her request for more detail about the Hollow itself, and on occasion she was fortunate enough to get a story or two about the neighboring Ramsays or Sinclairs. He was quite proud of Mack Ramsay, who she'd gathered was the same age as his sons, and was now the town sheriff. Of course she'd noted the absence of Morgan stories. His sons were the last in the Rogues Hollow line and she supposed it was simply too painful a topic for him.

She'd only asked him once, and though his reply had been brief bordering on curt, she'd sensed a deep well of sadness there. Perhaps that was her own fanciful imagination. She supposed she'd never know. Tag's side of the story was bound to be different from his father's.

She climbed the stairs back up to the main hall. So she was curious. Insatiably curious, as it turned out. She wanted to know the whole story, or whatever parts of the story there were to know. The man she'd romped in the backseat with last night did not strike her as the kind of man to be so cutting and cold. She also couldn't reconcile his obvious devotion to his work, with his absolute disinterest in his own heritage. But neither could she reconcile his version of his father's motives with what she knew to be the truth.

"Of course, he did just come all the way to Scotland," she murmured. But why? To see his supposed inheritance before ditching it? Or . . . She stopped dead in her tracks. What if he'd come to do what he'd claimed his father had wanted all along? To try and sell it. She shook that thought off and hurried the rest of the way down the stairs. It didn't matter what he'd planned. After all, he didn't, in fact, truly own so much as a stone of Ballantrae. At least none that he could sell off. Which he'd soon learn.

She took a deep breath, squared her shoulders before entering the parlor once more. She'd be gracious, patient, understanding even, as she gently explained he had no lasting claim here. He could either agree to continue the lease agreement she had with his father, or walk away. Those were his options. She'd even be magnanimous and let him stay the night, if he still desired to do so.

And try like hell not to lay in her own bed all night long, knowing he was under her roof, and dwell on how things might have been. Of course, this also meant she could cross off writing that letter to the States. And, very likely, her last source of outside income with it. No matter how smoothly this little meeting went, she didn't dare fool herself into believing he'd want anything to do with Ballantrae . . . or her, when it was over.

"So," she said brightly, maybe too brightly, as she entered the room. "I think I have everything in order here." She broke off and came to a stop when she realized she was talking to an empty room. "T.J.?" she called out. She stepped back into the hallway. "Tag?" Nothing.

But then, for all the cavernous appearance of it from the outside, the web of cobbled hallways, rooms and stairs that made up the interior didn't lend itself to sound doing much more than echoing in the spot it originated in. Had he forgotten something in his car? She wondered if he'd remember the way back out, especially as it was mostly in shadows this late in the day. Working electricity didn't extend to all parts of the castle, as she'd long since shut down the areas that were kept closed off. That included the original kitchens and rear scullery they'd passed through from the rear courtyard.

The sun had set to the point that she was forced to take the lantern off the wall hook before heading toward the rear of the main castle floor. "T.J.?" she called out, holding it out in front of her as she hurried down the hallway. She paused at each turn, calling for him again, in case he'd taken the wrong route.

She finally reached the back door, which was still bolted. She peered through the panes anyway. Robey's truck was still out there, but no sign of Tag. "Bollocks!" Where the bloody hell had he gone? She retraced her steps, hoping he'd found his way back to the front parlor from wherever it was he'd gone. She was climbing the last short set of stairs, the length of one hallway away from putting the lantern back on the hook, when someone stepped out of the corner niche on the last landing.

"Hey, there you are."

She jumped at least a foot, letting out a small squeal of surprise and bobbling the lantern badly.

He grabbed her arms, steadying her so she wouldn't stumble backward off the riser. "Sorry," he said, still holding her arms as she steadied herself. "I was looking for a bathroom. A working bathroom," he amended.

"We have twenty of them, but none of the ones in this part of the castle are functioning."

"I believe I've managed to stumble onto most of those."

There was strained humor in his tone, and she wasn't sure if it was because of the awkward direction their relationship had taken . . . or because he was still looking for a working loo. "A bit of advice. Where the electricity isn't working? Nothing is working."

"Ah."

"Speaking of which," she nodded at the other passageway that branched off from the top of the stairs. "How have you been managing navigating the south wing without a lantern?"

"I have good night vision." She swore his lips curved slightly. "I thought you'd have figured that out by now."

She swallowed hard as the tension arcing between them took a decided turn back in time. She realized then how much better it would be if they could somehow find their way back to being the people they'd been with each other last night. She wasn't sure that was possible, but at the moment, it didn't feel quite so improbable. "Yes, well, you'd think so, wouldn't you?" she said, trying for light and unaffected. She realized then that he was still holding her arms, and that they were standing exceedingly close on the small landing.

"It's quite a conglomeration of construction, this place," he said, very conversationally. And apparently not in any hurry to let her go.

Of course, she knew he'd release her if she wanted him to. Or the Tag from last night would have. Which brought up the question of why she hadn't pulled away from him already. Why she wasn't pulling away from him now. "Most of the lowest floor, the part that's underground, is original, dating back almost seven hundred years. A large part of the entry floor of the main house and the base of the north tower have stood since the sixteenth century. They were built by the first Sinclair of Ballantrae. Every Sinclair chief since has rebuilt or added something to it." She could hear the hint of breathlessness in her voice, wondering if he could. Hopefully he'd attribute it to her being startled.

And not the real reason. He affected her. Irritating, enigmatic, cocky and occasionally arrogant . . . all things that weren't exactly libidinal enhancements in her book. And yet her body had its own set of standards, and was clearly in charge of deciding exactly what was a turn-on and what wasn't at the moment. "The, uh, result is a complete hodgepodge of architectural styles. A lot of uneven staircases that lead to nowhere, nooks and crannies at every turn, and—"

"Would this be considered a nook . . . or a cranny?"

He was flirting with her. She'd wondered for a moment if it had been wishful thinking on her part, or on the part of her libido anyway. But now she was certain. Ten hours ago her heart would have gone pitty-pat. And other body parts would have danced right along with the beat. Now? She could only be suspicious. "Why are you doing this?"

"This?"

"Flirting with me. Back in the parlor you were all but calling me an opportunistic slut who'd do anything she had to in order to take advantage of an old guy with money to burn."

"Is that what I said?" He slid his hands up her arms. "I guess my mind works differently when I'm touching you."

Despite the fact that his touch had her involuntarily shivering in pleasure—or maybe specifically because it did—she laughed in his face. "For a guy who's been lost in the jungle for years, you certainly are a smooth one." She slipped her arms from his grasp. She would have stepped down one riser as well, despite the height advantage it would give him, but he had her rather cornered against the wall. "So, if insults and an overbearing manner don't work, you turn on the charm instead? Is that your plan?"

"Would it work?"

She couldn't help it, she laughed, only this time it wasn't so harsh. "You really are a piece of work, you know that?"

His lips quirked, but the smile didn't light up his eyes. "I could say the same of you."

"It certainly would have been much nicer than the things you did say."

His smile faded, and the intensity in his gaze elevated a few hundred ticks. The scarcity of space between his body and hers became a point of excruciating awareness for her in the silent moments that followed. Leaving right now would be the smartest course of action. *Take control of the situation, make him follow you, be leader in both manner and deed.* Great advice, all of which fell on deaf ears. Or a deaf something, anyway.

"I honestly don't know what's going on here," he told her quietly. "I admit maybe I didn't read the contracts clearly. I was dealing with . . . quite a few other things. This—" he gestured beyond her with his hand, "—came as a shock to me, to all of us."

She wished she was better at reading his expression. Wished she knew more about the dynamics of the relationship between Taggart and his sons. Because, despite the things he'd said to her in that service vestibule, she wanted to believe he wasn't the cold, heartless bastard she'd believed all Taggart's sons must be. Apparently her good nature could be bought for the price of a few orgasms. "So, are you saying you've realized you have no permanent claim here?" she asked, forging ahead. Too much longer tucked away in the shadows like this, with him looking at her the way he was, and whatever good judgment she might have left to call on would likely be woefully inadequate.

"I'm not saying anything of the sort. Mick was quite clear in his explanations. My father places his trust in very few people. Those he does have generally well earned the spot."

He might not know it, but that comment suffused her with warmth. Taggart had trusted her, and she felt closer to him for knowing she was one of few that he had. She supposed she owed it to him to make sure she handled this the best way possible. "I'm sure we can sort this all out."

"Yes," he said quietly, "I'm sure we can."

Neither of them made a move to leave their little nook. "You were right before," she said, her tone also hushed. "I don't know what went on between you and your father. I only know that he helped me at a time in my life when I thought everything that mattered to me most was lost. So perhaps we're both biased in our opinions about him, for our own reasons." She paused, waiting for his rebuttal. When he said nothing, she took it as a positive sign. Ever the optimist. "Maybe we should leave him out of this, as much as we can, and focus on the legal issues at hand that are now between us."

"Maybe." His hand drifted up along her arm again, making her whole body tingle in awareness.

She couldn't figure him out. One minute prickly and reserved, the next minute looking at her like he could lap her up, one inch at a time. She immediately abandoned that imagery. She was having a hard enough time holding on to logic and rational thought as it was. "You confuse me," she said, before she could think better of it.

His hand drifted to her shoulder, then to her neck, where he toyed with several strands there. His expression intense as always, and just as unreadable. He said nothing. The mere brush of his fingers along her skin said enough.

"What are you doing?" she asked, a bit huskily. "Seduction won't change the terms of the contract."

"I suppose I deserved that."

"You deserved a lot worse."

"Probably." The corner of his mouth quirked. "And to answer your question, I have no idea what in the hell I'm doing. I just don't seem to be able to keep my hands off of you while I figure it out."

"Standing—" She broke off on a swift intake of breath as his fingers skimmed across her lips. She moved back, but only the fraction required to end his stroking touch. "Standing here is probably not wise then," she finished in one rushed breath.

"No," he said, moving closer, hanging the lantern on a hook in the window niche beside her head. "I don't suppose it is." Her back hit the wall just as his hands wove into the hair on either side of her neck. He tilted her head back so he could gain access to her mouth, but didn't push his body into hers, as she'd expected—hoped?—he would.

It was exquisite torture, the slow descent of his mouth to hers. The way he kept his gaze locked on her own, until the last moment when his eyes closed and his long lashes brushed his tanned, taut cheeks. "Stop me," he whispered against her lips. Whether it was plea or command, she couldn't be sure.

Nor, apparently, did she care. An instant later his mouth was on hers. No mere brush of lips upon lips, his fingers immediately tightened along the back of her head and neck and he pulled her into him, kissed her mouth open, and took her. Not with forceful thrusts, but with sure, confident strokes that had her moaning and reaching for him before she could comprehend what had just happened.

He was consuming her, taking her, breeching—easily—any and every defense. As if she'd ever had any against him. What was it about him that made her lose all sense? It was the last structured thought she was able to manufacture. Because he'd finally pushed his body up against hers. His hips found the cradle of hers and he dipped down before thrusting forward, so she could feel the full extent of his arousal.

Her knees went soft and she gripped his shoulders, digging in her nails as she opened for him. Mouth, hips, and legs. She'd be angry later, at him as well as herself. Where was her self-respect? Where was any sense of self-preservation?

But those were distant concerns at the moment, vague threads of doubt too ephemeral to cling to. When all she wanted to cling to was the vibrant, hard, very alive man who was taking her as if she were the last woman he'd ever kiss before being dragged away to his death. The urgency in the way he held her, the way his mouth plundered hers, the way his hips ground into hers now, should have set off claxon bells of warning.

Oh, it set off bells all right.

"Jesus," he swore against her mouth as he tore his lips from hers. "I just—" He broke off, breathing heavily. He slid his hands to her shoulders, made sure she was steady, then turned his back to her, his chin down, hands braced against the opposite wall of the stairwell landing. "I'm sorry," he said at length.

"For, specifically?"

A brief snort of laughter got out before he got it under control. "I have no fucking idea." He turned so his back rolled against the wall, his legs braced wide, hands by his side. "For swearing just then," he said, a helpless smile ghosting about his mouth. "Beyond that, I honestly can't say." He shook his head, then tilted it back and let his eyes close. "I should never have come here."

"Why do you say that?" She sounded quite calm and in control. Bravo, her. Because she felt anything but at the moment.

"Because you were right. I have no business here. I'm disrupting your life, and God knows I'm disrupting mine. I need to get back to work, not traipse halfway around the world on a wild goose chase that my father—" He broke off, his eyes still shut. She hadn't been sure if he was talking to her, or to himself. Not that it mattered, she supposed.

She folded her arms, still leaning against the wall, regarding him. "I don't know about that. Some of the disruption was quite . . . nice."

He opened one eye to a slit. "Nice?"

Her lips curved. "Men and their egos. I suppose it's the same the world round."

"I suppose it is." He closed his eyes again. "And don't answer that." His lips spread in a true smile this time. "But I know it was better than nice."

"Ballsy son of a bitch, aren't you?" she said with a laugh.

"A great deal of the time, yes. Only generally it has nothing to do with beautiful women and deep, soul kisses."

And just like that he took her breath, and whatever smart-ass remark she had, away. Deep, soul kisses indeed. "I, well . . . thank you." He merely opened his eyes and stared at her, and the tension spiked once again. How was it that it was like this between them? If it were mere animal attraction, she could deal with that. But he pulled at something in her that went well beyond sexual need.

"We're making this quite the habit," she said, at length. When he merely arched a tawny brow, she motioned to the narrow niche they'd tucked themselves into. "Tight places," she explained.

His lips curved slowly, into a smile broad enough to flex

the cords in his neck, tightening the choker that circled it. Her palms seemed to itch constantly with the need to touch him. The least little thing triggered it.

"I rather like some of the tight places I've been into of late."

She blushed even as she smiled. "I don't suppose I can fault you for speaking so directly, since I make a habit of it myself. In fact, it's one of the things I admire about you."

"One of the things?" He folded his arms. "You mean I've more than one admirable trait?"

She let her gaze drift slowly down his body, pausing a bit about midway down, then slowly shifted her gaze back up to his. "One or two."

"Touché," he said with a nod.

He is such a primal specimen, she thought, taking in his rangy body, his native good looks, that wild tangle of hair. And yet for all the earthiness of him, he had this almost overeducated, bookish air about him, the way he spoke, the way that, most of the time anyway, he kept silent and merely observed the goings-on around him.

The vestibule display notwithstanding, he didn't seem the sort who needed to command a room, or be the center of attention. And yet he so easily managed to command all of hers.

She realized, looking at him now, that even if she peeled away the overt physicality of him, and that professorial air, there was still an aura of mystery about him. Perhaps it was because he was so hard to read that she felt certain the thoughts ran deep behind those enigmatic eyes of his. Or maybe it was that hint of desolation when he'd spoken of his father just now that pointed to something more beneath his admittedly fine exterior.

"I'm starting to feel like I should be on a glass slide beneath a microscope," he said, but not unkindly.

"Sorry." She smiled. "I guess I'm just having a hard time figuring you out. I'm an unabashedly curious type, and I admit you've raised a number of questions I'm dying to have answered. So I'm trying to show some self-restraint and not poke my nose in where it doesn't belong."

"We don't seem to do real well with restraint," he commented.

"No," she said with a smile, "I don't suppose we do."

"So why start now?"

It might have been a rhetorical question, but she chose to answer it honestly. "Because now that I've changed my mind and want you to stay . . . I'm very much afraid you'll leave. And I'm torn between wanting to pry as much information out of you before you go . . . and not doing anything that might hasten your departure."

If he was surprised by her blunt honesty, he didn't show it. "What do you want to know?" His body posture remained relaxed, but she wasn't fooled. Never had she met anyone so intent, so focused.

She tilted her head, debating on the wisdom of asking him anything too personal at this moment. They'd reached a truce, of sorts, and she didn't want to blow it. "Whatever your reasons, you've come a long way. Can you honestly say that now that you're here, you're not at least a little curious? About your ancestors, your heritage?" She waved her hand to encompass the castle they stood in. "The whole tapestry that weaves their stories together?"

He didn't say anything for a few moments, then he finally pushed away from the wall and loomed in front of her. "I'm insatiably curious," he murmured. "But at the moment, and in a distinct departure from my normal nature, my curiosity has nothing whatsoever to do with the past. Much less those who have long since ceased to populate it."

"What—" She broke off when he moved closer still, fought to moisten her suddenly parched throat. "What are you curious about?"

He leaned down and brushed his lips across hers. It was more a caress, a tease, than a kiss. Then he braced his arms on the wall on either side of her and leaned in. He kept his body so close . . . so close, yet didn't touch hers. Instead, their only contact was when he pressed his cheek to hers and whispered in her ear. "I'm curious to know about my future. My immediate future. With one person in particular who is still very much alive."

Her breathing had gone all funny and she thought for certain her heart was about to pound out of her chest. "Like what?" she managed.

He lifted his head enough to look her directly in the eyes. "I propose we make a pact to be completely honest with each other. And, in the spirit of that pact, I will tell you that I don't know how long I'll be staying. In this castle, or in this country. But I do know I have no intentions of going anywhere tonight. And at the moment I could care less about our tangled past history, recent or distant. And I can't say I'm all that willing to worry about what's likely to be our just-as-tangled future." He slid his hands down the wall, then cupped her face, tilting her mouth to his. "All I know is that I'm insatiably curious about you. When I left our bed this morning, I had to talk myself out of going after you, told myself it was better to give you what you wanted, one anonymous night. But . . ."

Her heart tripped. "But?" The word was hardly more than a rasp.

He brushed a whisper of a kiss across her cheek. "Why were you crying?"

And just like that, she tensed. Was he still suspicious? Did he still think—

He tipped her chin up so he could look into her eyes. "I was going to leave you alone, leave this alone. But I couldn't stand the thought of you leaving with tears. So I came after you. In fact, I was going to do whatever it took to catch you."

She sniffed, unaware until that moment that her eyes were brimming. "You were?"

He nodded, brushing at a stray tear with the pad of his thumb. "Only you'd left me without a trail to follow. I figured it wasn't destined to be, but I hated having to give up before I even began." He tilted his head, his fingers tangling in her hair. "But now here you are." He slanted his mouth just above hers. "And I was thinking I don't care about much of anything else." He brushed his lips across hers. "I don't care whether it's one day or ten, whether it complicates matters or not." A smile teased his beautiful mouth. "I caught you after all. And I just can't bring myself to let you go twice in one day."

"What about what I want," she miraculously managed, every last ounce of her quivering in need.

"Now you get to decide if you want to catch me back. So . . . tag," he said, lips curving, "you're it."

He'd come after her, before he'd known about . . . any of this. Sure, it could be a big story, a ruse to get her in a vulnerable position. But Christ, wasn't she already? Because, the truth of it was, foolish or no', she wanted exactly what he claimed to want, and then some. Dangerous, yes. Not to her heritage. Ballantrae wasn't at stake here. But her heart might well be. And, at the moment, it seemed just as big a thing to risk.

"I . . . I don't know what to think anymore. I want . . ." She trailed off, warring with herself over whether to take what she wanted, or call it all off right now.

He nudged her chin up when she broke eye contact. "Honesty," he reminded her.

So she held his gaze, quite directly, and said, "Okay. I want you. Here. Tonight. And I don't want either of us to be alone. But that's all I'll commit to wanting. We have things to work out, you and I. And there'll be emotions involved and it'll get messy. Messier still the more tangled up we become. I—"

He pressed his thumb across her lips. "I want to spend tonight with you, too. Preferably in a bed, though I'm not all that choosy. There aren't too many walls in the places I inhabit. So I'm rather enjoying this novel habit we're rapidly adopting."

He kissed her again, sliding the palm of his hands down her sides, letting his thumbs brush along the swell of her breasts, before settling the full weight of him between her thighs. She moaned in almost desperate appreciation. It was as if this was how their bodies were meant to be, so perfectly fitted. Always. And anything less was torture. "Yes," she breathed, aching now for him to brush those clever fingers of his over her nipples, to push harder, higher between her thighs. Aching to feel his hands on her again, his body thrusting inside hers.

"Yes, you're enjoying the novel habit?" he asked, so close his lips brushed hers ever so lightly as he spoke. "Or yes, you want me to stay the night. In your bed." He kissed her then, flicked his thumbs over the tips of her nipples. "In you."

Chapter 13

Somewhere between leaving that cavernous monstrosity of a room she called a parlor, and finding her in a dark stairwell, he'd completely lost his mind.

He'd set the fire, then paced the room, waiting for her return. It had given him just enough time to ask himself what in the hell he was doing. And why. He was arguing with her for the sake of arguing. Did he really want the responsibility for this heaping pile of stone? Of course not. Hell, he hadn't even wanted to be responsible for the property he'd grown up on. And while Morgans may have factored into the history of Ballantrae, this castle and the land surrounding it was Sinclair-held. And had been for centuries. He had only to look at the massive framed portraits that lined the walls of the parlor, and any other wall space not taken up by soaring bookshelves, to observe the proof of that claim.

And those bookshelves . . . Now they had drawn his interest. He was an avid reader, but by necessity most of his material pertained to research. Still, the idea of shelf after shelf, crammed with all manner of reading matter, had lured him in like no amount of ancestral history could have. He'd glanced through a few and been bemused to find leather-bound histories of Scotland with copyrights dating back over a century, privately published treatises on fox hunting, complete with painstaking hand-painted illustrations, along with thick tomes dedicated to the vagaries of sheep breeding. All shelved side by side and in between current paperback pulp-fiction mysteries and romances. And that was just on the shelf or two he'd skimmed.

When she hadn't returned, he'd turned his attention to those imposing portraits. He supposed he shouldn't have been surprised to note a Morgan or Ramsay in a few of the group sittings, mostly hunting or regimental portraits. He might not know vast amounts of Morgan clan lore on this side of the ocean, but he did know the story of how Rogues Hollow came to be, and he knew that history was strong enough to tangle the Morgans, Ramsays, and Sinclairs together on his side of the ocean for another three hundred years.

But that didn't explain why his father had decided to financially obligate himself to this particular piece of Sinclair, and to a lesser extent, Morgan history. Tag had dismissed his earlier idea that it was some twisted revenge plot. If anything, his father was all about blazing new trails into the future. Certainly not dwelling on the Morgan clan's turbulent past. Recent or distant.

No, Morgans didn't dwell on past unpleasantness. They moved on.

By the time he'd gone off in search of a bathroom, his mind had been made up. He'd go through the paperwork with her, clarify all the facts, and if any part of this place actually was his, as Mick had claimed, then he'd just sign it over to her. This was her legacy, not his. As for the money, well, that was also her burden. He had his own legacy to take care of in Rogues Hollow.

This trip had been an ill-advised impulse that he should never have given in to. So, he'd do the right thing, restore Sinclair property to the rightful Sinclair . . . then find an airport and book passage back to Chacchoben, where he should have been all along. He'd spent the past few months since his father died feeling off-balance and out of sync. More so since coming here. He wanted to go back to a world he understood.

At least, that had been his thinking half an hour ago.

Now he had her up against a cold stone wall, his tongue down her throat, praying she'd beg him to stay.

She trembled beneath his touch. "Is this some new strategy?"

He could feel her heart pound through her shirt, wanted—badly—to remove that shirt and every other barrier between them.

"Strategy?" He trailed kisses to her ear. "No, no diversionary tactics. You're the Sinclair, the castle is yours. I have no claim on it, no matter what those papers say."

She struggled against him, pushed him back enough to look into his eyes. Her cheeks were flushed, her eyes glittering with desire, and he wondered how they'd gone from being a breath away from fucking each other senseless again, to talking about the damn castle.

"What are you saying?"

With barely restrained patience, he told her, "I'm saying that this place is your legacy, not mine. We'll go over the papers. If I have to, I'll sign whatever I have to so the property reverts back to you."

"But—"

"Jesus," he said on a half-laugh, "what more do you want from me?"

"I—" She looked like she'd been fully prepared to shoot back a retort, only she caught herself. "I don't know," she said sincerely. She blew out a breath, sounding both disconcerted and a bit overwhelmed.

The tension still screamed between them, but some small part of him gentled in the face of her revealing a more vulnerable side. Without questioning the wisdom of it, he followed his instincts and pulled her against him, wrapping his arms around her. She didn't push him away. Instead her arms came around his waist and she clung to him as he buried his face in her hair. "I just want to do what's right," he murmured.

She snorted softly, but her grip on him tightened. "You just want to get in my pants."

He smiled against her hair, slid his mouth down to her ear. "Not to put too fine a point on it, but I think I could probably do that without giving away an entire castle."

Her mouth opened, then closed again without retort. She shook her head and let out a small, rueful sigh. "What are we doing here, Tag? Dancing about each other like dogs in heat, with all this unfinished business we've yet to deal with still between us."

"Trying to figure out how to have each other without compromising our position," he answered. "Only I've just surrendered from the field of battle. So, as far as I can tell, the only thing keeping us from finding something soft and horizontal is my lack of knowledge of the floor plan."

She laughed and shook her head. "We're both too direct for our own good. You know that." Then her amusement faded slowly, though a certain tenderness lingered in her eyes. "I will probably regret saying this. And my Sinclair forebears are surely rolling in their graves at the moment, but . . ." She lifted a hand to his face, pushed back the tangle of hair at his temples. "This is Sinclair land, make no mistake. But their hold here has been entwined with Clan Morganach for centuries. This is partly your legacy, too."

"Maura—"

She pressed her fingers across his lips. "You can believe what you want, but I'm not saying that to try and lure you into feeling responsible, or to get at your bank account. If I want to strike a business deal with you, I'll come right out and ask." She let her hand drop to his shoulder. "I don't pretend to understand the undercurrent that ran so deeply in your family that it severed you all from your father. Or why you felt compelled to travel this far to track down a heritage you don't seem to care about." He started to speak again and she shook her head, talking over him. "But you *are* here. And the money aside, our personal situation aside, everything else aside, I think you should at least take the time to learn something of those Morgans who came here before you." She tangled her fingers in the edges of his curls and tugged gently. "You're already here. What can it hurt?" she asked softly. "What are you afraid of?"

"I'm not afraid of anything," he said without hesitation. Only as soon as he spoke the words, doubt assailed him. *Was* he afraid? Afraid he might learn something about his ancestry that would make him want to involve himself here in a more permanent way?

Or afraid it might lead him to some new understanding of his father, one that would require him to rethink everything he thought he knew about the man? He was quite comfortable with the situation as it stood. On both counts. He had no regrets. And all these years later, and months too late to confront his father personally, he really didn't want to do anything that would cause him to have regrets now.

She slid her hands down his arms and wove her fingers through his. It made absolutely no sense, but when she curled them inward and wedded her palms to his, he felt the threat of an intimacy that was far more dangerous than any they'd shared up to now. Which, considering the way he'd claimed her not twenty-four hours earlier, was saying something.

But being deep inside her body was a far cry from delving deep into her mind, or her heart. And, even more of a threat, was opening that same path inside himself to her.

"You know," he said, conversationally, wanting to slide his hands free before she sucked him in any further, but not wanting to reveal the root of his fear. "There's a reason I live in the jungle with a bunch of bones and broken crockery to keep me company."

She tilted her head, dimples winking. "Because you communicate better with the dead than the living?"

She was teasing, but he nodded, quite serious. "Discovery

isn't mutual in my line of work. You can ferret out their secrets, without risking exposing your own."

"A very guarded existence."

"It's worked well for me."

"I imagine it has." She lifted up, kissed him quite softly on the lips. "You asked for honesty. So at the risk of losing at least one last night of amazing sex, I'm going to give it to you." She squeezed his hands and looked him directly in the eyes. "I want to know your secrets, Tag Morgan. I've wanted to know all about them since you kissed me in a snowstorm minutes after meeting me. Knowing what I do now, that curiosity has only compounded. I want to know what happened between you and your father. I want to know why you've removed yourself from civilization as we know it. And I want to know why you came here. What, deep down in your heart, you'd hope to find." She tugged him closer. "Maybe this wasn't as much an impulse trip as you think. Maybe this was just giving in to something you've wanted for a very long time, but were, for whatever reason, too afraid to reach out and take."

He realized then it was too late to barricade himself in emotionally. She'd already breached that barrier as if it were nothing more than a flimsy shield. And perhaps, to the right woman, it would always have been that easy. "I don't know," he said, striving in vain to sound casually amused. "I think I've proven I have no problem taking what I want."

She smiled at that. "You're more like your ancestors than you want to believe," she told him. "You're not the first Morgan man to fall into the clutches of a Sinclair woman, you know. Along these very halls, in fact."

He found his fingers tightening on hers of their own volition. He was getting pulled under her spell. The cadence of her Highland burr, the throaty tone of her voice, the feel of her against him, her touch, her scent. "Is that what I'm in? Your clutches?"

"Evade and parry," she said. "You're quite good at deflection, aren't you? But then I'm sure you're well aware of that." She leaned back on the wall again, pulling him against her. "There's one more thing I want to know about you."

He was already lowering his mouth to hers. "Which is?"

"I want to know if I can engage the curiosity that must be inherent in a man who does what you do for a living."

"Trust me, I'm curious about you."

"I meant about your clan, about this place, your history."

"Why don't we work with my curiosity for one Sinclair woman." He took her face in his hands, tilted her mouth to his. "And go from there."

"It's a start," she murmured, and then took his kiss, took him into her mouth, into her arms and, he was very much afraid, into her heart.

His own was pounding all out of proportion to the moment at hand. His emotions were all over the chart and no longer easily categorized and maintained. "I'm in trouble here, aren't I?" he asked, meaning to tease, needing to lighten the moment. But somehow the words came out sounding a bit shaky and bewildered.

"You're just now figuring that out?" With a smile he was sure she meant to be reassuring, but was just knowing enough to up the terror quotient by about a hundred percent, she squeezed his hand and led him back down the stairs. He managed to grab the lantern, though she apparently didn't need it.

He had choices here, he thought wildly, as they retraced their steps back to the parlor. He didn't *have* to follow.

She scooped up the file she'd put on the massive granite-topped table by the parlor door and motioned to his knapsack and duffel bag. "Grab those."

"Where are we going?"

She just smiled. "Where's your sense of adventure?"

At the moment he hesitated to answer that one.

"Do you need any help with that?" she asked, motioning to his bags.

He held her gaze for one long moment, then shook his head as he slung the backpack on one shoulder and the duffel across his back. *I'm well and truly in it now, aren't I,* he thought, as she grabbed the lantern on her way back into the hall.

She moved back down the wide hallway, past the grand staircase, but bypassed the stairs they'd been on, and the hall leading down the labyrinthine corridors to the rear entry he'd come in through earlier. Instead she angled them along another, less obvious hall, ending at another, wider staircase that was likely at the rear of the main house. He'd thought for a moment they were heading up them, presumably to her room or rooms, but instead she ducked around behind them, then stopped in front of a narrow oak door, angled back in a skinny little niche in such a way that it would go completely unnoticed if you didn't know to look for it.

"Shortcut," she told him. "You might have to duck." She opened the door and stepped into a low passage. After rearranging the weight on his back, he hunched a bit and followed behind her. "Where are we?"

"Servants' passage." She held the lantern up in front of her, illuminating a narrow corridor that stretched out before them, angling downward and continuing on into the darkness. They passed two offshoots before she turned down the third. "Most of the castle is no longer accessible by these tunnels," she told him. "The Sinclair who oversaw the first major reconstruction of the castle had the foresight to include a series of passageways, connecting the house to the towers and outer wings, both for security and ease of service by his attendants. They were maintained until Finlay Sinclair took over in the late eighteenth century. He undertook the second major renovation, but the castle was in pretty bad shape by then, having taken the brunt of several battles during the rebellion.

"The towers and battlements had taken the most abuse, but the central structure and the wings connecting it to the north and south towers had suffered some severe damage as well. He did his best to restore what he could, but the southern passages are largely impenetrable now, as is the south wing, but that's due to other problems that came later on. Some of these offshoots lead to nowhere now. The western wing leading to the loch was added at the turn of the following century, and has no access to this network at all. Which was a problem for a few of my ancestors who were in need of another means of escape." She flashed him a smile. "Usually in the dead of the night."

Tag took in the information, but said nothing. He knew what she was trying to do. She'd played Scheherazade for his father, weaving her tales of times past, in exchange for stories of her clan's American counterparts no doubt. And a lot of money.

He'd had a pretty good look at the overall structure of the castle as he descended into the valley and drove into the courtyard. It was no small stronghold, with an impressive gray stone edifice of a main structure, flanked by two wings which fanned out in triangular fashion, connecting a matched set of towers stationed at either end like sentries. Crenellated battlements topped the central building and ran the length of both wings, circling the top of each tower as well. But that was where the standard fortress structure ended.

Windows of different sizes and styles had been installed, apparently as needed or desired over the years, in various locations throughout. The battlements atop the towers differed significantly in style from that of the main building. And the western wing she'd mentioned was of an altogether different architectural style, and jutted out at an odd angle from the section that connected the two towers, pointing toward the lake. It was a hodgepodge really, one which he imagined could give future anthropologists quite a headache if they didn't have the written history at hand. But even keeping all that in mind, he doubted quite seriously that this was any kind of a shortcut.

He had an excellent sense of direction. It had long since become second nature for him to peg due north in whatever territory he was inhabiting. Even with all the twists and turns they'd taken, he knew they were heading toward the north wing tower. With the courtyard central to the structure, that would have meant a hike around the perimeter wings. But even with the winding maze of construction that likely made such a trip somewhat convoluted, this winding maze of underground passageways, or the ones she was taking him on anyway, wasn't any more a direct route. She just hoped to seduce him, and not in the way he'd intended her to.

But despite her stories, it still wasn't personal with him yet. Not in the way that struck a chord deep inside him, where an undeniable connection was felt. He did admit that he found the history interesting. Maybe a little more personally than a tourist would, but not much.

She tossed another look over her shoulder as she tugged him down yet another dark passageway. "We're here." She stopped in front of another oak door, this one smaller and more rough hewn than the first.

"The north tower?"

Her eyes widened fractionally in surprise. "Remind me to take you along if I ever plan on getting lost." Then she smiled and opened the door. "*My* tower."

She entered first, then held the lantern up so he could wedge his backpack and duffel through in front of him. They were in a circular vestibule of sorts that was all stone and just as cold and damp as the passageways had been. "Cozy," he commented, as he shuffled in far enough for her to close the door behind him.

She turned and lifted the lantern so that it illuminated a set of stone stairs that appeared to be built right into the stone walls of the tower. Stretching up beyond the circle of lantern light, they were just wide enough for one person . . . and had no railings or other means of support.

"Let me put my file in your pack and I'll tote that up so

you can manage the duffel." She was already slipping the pack from his shoulder.

He was still looking at the spiraling stone staircase.

She tucked the thick accordion file in a rear pocket and muscled the pack onto her back. "What have you got in here anyway?" she asked, then noting the direction of his gaze, she smiled. "You're not afraid of heights or anything, right?"

"No. I was thinking more of balance."

"Don't worry, the steps are slightly slanted toward the wall, so you lean away from the edge. Really, you get quite used to it. One or two trips and you'd be skipping up and down without even a lantern. Trust me."

He shifted his gaze to hers. "I think I've done a pretty fair job of that."

She just shot him a wink that could only be described as saucy, then literally danced up the first half dozen steps, taking the light with her. "Well then, no reason to slow down forward progress, is there?"

He shifted the duffel so it was centered on his back, and began the climb. Heights didn't bother him, but he was careful not to look down anyway. No sense in borrowing equilibrium trouble.

"It's not far to the main landing. We've electricity from there." She tossed a smile back at him. "And wider stairs."

He found if he focused on the swing of her hips and the way her tightly curved backside tucked into the taut muscles of her thighs, it made the trip up far more enjoyable. He barely noticed the iron fittings hammered into the stone at regular intervals, intended to support lighting and weaponry. In fact, by the time they got to the trapdoor that led to the main landing, he was a wholehearted supporter of stone stair climbing as an excellent form of physical fitness. Her ass wasn't the only thing rock hard by the time they squeezed through the narrow door.

"You can leave your bag here for now," she said, turning him as he entered the doorway and helping him slide his duffel down his back to the floor. She'd already taken off the backpack, which he scooped back up. Her paperwork was still tucked in the front, but his own files were zipped inside. Along with the cherrywood box and all its personal contents. Better to keep that close at hand, he figured. They'd get to it eventually. At the moment, his mind was on other matters. Namely finishing what they'd begun back in that earlier stairwell.

"Welcome to my home," she said, flipping on a light switch after she closed the door. "My castle within a castle, as it were."

The soft glow of wall sconces and a heavy wheel-shaped chandelier overhead lit up the circular room. It was significantly warmer in here than in the passageways or the subterranean stairwell leading up here. But there was still a damp chill in the air. He supposed that was castle living in winter. It was one open room, the full circumference of the tower, with easily a fifteen-foot ceiling. The floor was layered with several carpets, all antique and faded, but providing a nice barrier to the cold stone beneath. It was part kitchen, part living room, with a big rolltop desk wedged between the tiny kitchen table and the stone fireplace.

There were three doors leading from the room. Two of them were paneled, painted cream, and from their position, he imagined led to the wings that connected her tower with its twin in one direction, and the main house in the other. The last door was heavier, painted a deep green, sporting a row of tiny, thick panes of diamond-shaped glass across the top, and obviously led outside. A small antique table was positioned by that door, on which was a small glass dish that held a handful of coins, a pack of gum and a set of keys. The staircase leading to the next floor was in fact broader, and not carved from stone. It sported a beautifully carved filigreed balustrade that all but begged to be stroked. And from the looks of the polished worn pattern, many hands had done just that.

He tried not to imagine who those hands had belonged to, if any of them had been Morgan hands, perhaps gripping the banister as they ascended the stairs toward another Sinclair in some earlier era. He tried not to, but it was against his nature not to. Visualizing the past and the people who'd populated it was too much a part of who he was, of why he'd gone into the field of anthropology, to easily switch it off.

That it was his own ancestors he was visualizing this time and not some forgotten Mayan subsect didn't mean . . . well, anything. His interest could merely be of professional significance, not personal.

And it was getting harder and harder to deny what a crock of shit that was. He'd said on the way in he was just going to go for it, immerse himself if he felt like it. His father was gone, so what difference did it make? Why was he still so intent on fighting any notion that it might be personal? He didn't want to think about the fear Maura had mentioned, or analyze, well, anything at the moment. What he needed to do was just calm down, stop overthinking every little thing, and go with the flow for a goddamn change. He was with a fascinating woman who seemed as intent as he was on spending some naked time together. Just focus on that, for Christ's sake. It wasn't like the rest of it was going anywhere.

"The Sinclairs were big on portraits, I see," he commented, nodding to the oversized, gilt-framed canvases that filled most of the available wall space, stacked up in a hodgepodge manner, almost to the ceiling. There were a few scenic pieces, but most were of stoic-faced, heavily sideburned Scots. The main house had been decorated much the same way. Whatever space hadn't been consumed by bookshelves anyway.

"Imagine what they'd have done if cameras had been around back then," she said, in her typical dry tone. "Didn't the Morgans on your side of the pond detail their history this way?"

"If they did, I wouldn't know about it. As you probably

know, my father wasn't much on celebrating his immediate forebears. If any paintings existed, it's quite possible he destroyed them."

She didn't look particularly shocked. If anything, she looked sad, and maybe a bit resigned. "If he did, I'm sure he came to regret it," she said, ever the stalwart defender in all matters pertaining to his father.

Tag swallowed a cynical snort. She'd had a different relationship with the man; he had to get past letting that bother him. No sense in tainting her memories with his personal views on the subject. One had nothing to do with the other, after all.

"What about the Sinclairs or Ramsays?" she asked. "Growing up with them, you've been in their homes."

He shrugged, thankful enough to sidestep the topic of his father that he expanded more than he normally might. Talking about his childhood wasn't high on his list of enjoyable ways to pass the time. "Sure. But as a child, I don't know that I paid much attention to artwork. I was more interested in digging up arrowheads and old fossils."

Her lips curved, her dimples flashed. "So, that's where your life's passion started, eh?"

His lips quirked a little. It was hard to be moody around Maura. For all her passion for the past, she seemed to have little patience for getting maudlin about any of it. "Yes. I used to dig around old man Ramsay's pond. I had dreams of discovering a dinosaur and becoming famous like Indiana Jones."

"Ah, we share a childhood idol, then."

"Indiana Jones?"

Her lips curved more deeply. "Harrison Ford."

"Ah," he said, smiling himself when she sighed in deep appreciation.

"Ah, indeed," she said. "So, dinosaurs. You must have spent a lot of time digging."

"I probably could have tunneled to China and back several times over." He shrugged, but sharing didn't feel as uncomfortable with her. "It became a more serious pursuit in high school. Before that it was mostly just a way to stay away from the house." *And away from my father,* he thought, but didn't add. From the look on her face, he didn't have to.

"What happened in high school to make it a serious pursuit?"

"My history and sociology teachers were married to each other and had both been on digs when they were in college. Between the two of them, they showed me a whole world of adventure just waiting for me to reach out and go for it. I think they were mostly interested in getting their students to look ahead to college. Most kids in my county didn't go past high school back then."

Her gaze flicked to the outside door, then away. "That used to be the case here, as well."

"Did you go to college?"

She nodded. "I went to university in Inverness. I am the only Sinclair in my generation, so I've known from birth that this would be my legacy, my responsibility. My degree is in business management, but I minored in literature. I, um, I write articles and short stories."

Why it surprised him to discover she had a career outside of running this place, he didn't know. It wasn't because he still had notions of her lazing about, sponging off his father. But she'd never once mentioned it in her letters. Which he almost blurted out. He caught himself in time, and asked, "Published, I presume?"

She nodded. "Most of them in a monthly put out by an Edinburgh company, but I pick up some freelance work for some smaller publications."

"That's a lot to manage, along with this place."

She smiled briefly, and he thought it was odd how direct she could be about everything else, but about this she was almost rather shy. Which made him realize that it was important to her, and that perhaps she didn't share that part of herself readily. She hadn't shared it with his father, at least not in any ongoing fashion.

"Unfortunately," she went on, rather briskly, "most of our children, both crofters and villagers alike, who manage to make it to university, don't come back. Some move on anyway, when they become of age. So there's no' much crofting business to manage of late. And the village is struggling because of that, as well."

He noticed that her burr was more pronounced when her emotions were in play. He rather liked it . . . although he'd rather the cause of it be something less oppressive.

"I'm sorry," she said, sincerely. "I'm no' advertisin' for a, what was it you called it? A handout?"

He felt the shame rise to his cheeks. She'd said it without edge or condescension, which was better than he deserved. "I know you aren't," he said quietly. "Did you ever resent it?" he asked, admittedly curious. "Being saddled with this, I mean?"

"Aye. Who wouldn't? But we had completely different upbringings, you and me. You say your father spent his time trying to blot out the past. Of course, he eventually realized the folly of that pursuit, I suppose, or he wouldn't have agreed to join his hand in this monstrosity." She paused when he looked away. "But in support of your side of it, I'll admit he wasna fond of talking about his own direct ancestors. In fact, it was a rare time I could pull a Morgan tale from him."

When Tag glanced back, he found her expression had turned tender again. He wanted to resent it, resent her intrusion into his past. He didn't want her to know his demons.

"But I suppose his interests here came far too late for the two of you?"

And it was the very understanding he saw in her eyes that provoked him to spill the real truth of it. "The time spent under his roof, from birth through my eighteenth birthday, was dedicated to one thing, and one thing only. Proving we were better than our past. Rogues Hollow was founded in part by a Morgan who was a thief and a scoundrel, and that was putting it mildly. I can't say much about the intervening Morgans, but my father's father, and the Morgan before him, were not men who led the kind of lives you boasted of, in public or private. Thieving continued to be a running theme in the Morgan line, as it happens. And somewhere along the way you can add in drinking and abuse."

Maura's mouth dropped open, but he was on a roll and wasn't about to let her try and step in with some understanding bullshit. "My father's way of dealing with his personal history was to make a mark so big that the Morgans before him would be forgotten beside the glow of all he and his sons had accomplished." Tag shot her a look. "He did it, too. He was the first Morgan to go to college, the first to go to law school and pass the bar. The first to become a judge, and most definitely the first to become an upstanding citizen in the community. He was a peer among peers with the most elite our county had to offer, and he could hold his own at the state capital as well. And he managed to do it all without the thievery and alcohol, so he definitely improved the stock for future generations as well." It was clear on her face that she'd noted the absence of that last part.

"I guess two out of three wasn't so bad, right?" he added with mock civility. "And he was determined that his four sons would not only match his shining example, but outdo it. In the manner in which he best saw fit, of course. Trust me when I say that that path didn't include any of the ones taken by any Morgan before him. And it certainly didn't include any of us making a career out of digging up the past. Ours or anyone else's.

"So you'll have to forgive me if I have a hard time believing he ever came around to embracing our Rogues Hollow heritage, or for that matter, our heritage on this side of the pond either. And even if the miracle did happen, and he realized just how hardheaded and hard-hearted a man he'd become in his single-minded pursuit to rewrite history, it was certainly too late to go back and undo the damage of a lifetime spent delivering pure, torturous hell upon his sons."

Chapter 14

Maura was both stunned and mortified by his outburst. Mortified, not for herself, but for him, because she could see he was already regretting losing his control, letting go of what he'd surely kept well buried for so many years.

At a later time, when she could think properly instead of merely reacting to the moment, she'd think about what he'd revealed of his father's character, and that of the Morgan men who'd preceded them both. And ponder over how difficult it must have been, for Tag to prevent those traits from manifesting themselves in himself, living in places where adopting the barest veneer of civility was all that was necessary to get by. Where he could be whatever sort of man he wanted to be, and never be challenged by what others knew about his family or their turbulent past. Which, come to think of it, might be why he'd gone to such a distant land in the first place.

At the moment, however, she was too busy trying to blend her mental portrait of the man she'd come to know and care for, with the alternate and quite vivid portrayal his oldest son had just painted for her.

"I'm sorry," she whispered, knowing it was too vague a sentiment for what he'd made her feel with his outburst. And yet they were the only words she had. "I . . . I had no idea." Which was absolutely the truth. Taggart could be somewhat curmudgeonly, but imagining him as physically abusive—to his own children, no less—was beyond her ken. Yet she had only to look at the man before her, the haunted look in his eyes, the shame that so infuriated him, for being weak enough, in his eyes, to feel it . . . No, she had no doubt that his claims were true. It explained a great deal regarding his behavior toward her when he'd first arrived.

And yet, now she had even more questions . . . with fewer answers.

He turned away then, looking back up to the portraits that lined the staircase wall. "How could you have?" he said wearily. "That's the benefit of having a pen-pal relationship, I suppose. You only know what the other person chooses to reveal. And even then it's a one-dimensional revelation at best."

"What do you know of my relationship with your father?" She didn't ask it defensively, but sincerely. She knew he'd seen the contracts, and spoken with Taggart's solicitor, but beyond that she didn't know much else. "How do you know we exchanged letters?"

He didn't say anything at first, then finally he sighed and turned back to her again. "He kept them," he said, somewhat grudgingly. "All of them, as far as I can tell."

It shouldn't have caught her so badly off guard. But that's when it truly struck her, that he literally owned all the remnants of his father's past. Including her part in it. She wasn't sure how she felt about that. It certainly hadn't been on her mind when she'd composed her monthly letters, not even when she knew Taggart was dying. She wasn't one to censor herself anyway, but never once had she thought anyone would see those letters but him.

Her mind spun out over the myriad things they'd discussed in three long years of correspondence, but it was too unwieldy a task to encapsulate so swiftly, and under duress to boot. Which was exactly what she was feeling at the moment, though it might not be fair. He'd legally come into possession of the letters, but that didn't negate the vulnerability she felt. Part of her didn't want to ask, didn't want to know, even as she knew she had to. "Did you . . . ?" She trailed off, unable to ask without revealing just how exposed she felt.

"Read them?" he finished for her. Holding her gaze, he nodded. "I'm sorry if that bothers you," he said, quite sincerely. "It wasn't something I had an intention of doing. What my father did with his time, and with whom, couldn't have interested me less. I came home to handle the details of his funeral and to put his estate in order. That was . . . difficult enough for me. For all of us."

"All four of you came back, then?"

He nodded. "Took awhile to track us all down, but yes, we eventually all made it in. It was hard for each of us in our own way, but none of us would have willingly placed more of a burden on the other."

"You've stayed close to your brothers, then?"

"As close as our livelihoods allow."

She wanted to ask more, wanted to know, to understand Taggart's children and what they'd done with themselves. But she knew it wasn't her place. He was obviously uncomfortable with what he'd revealed already. Still, her curiosity was such that she couldn't stifle all her questions. "How long had it been for you? Since you'd been home, I mean."

"Home." He snorted softly. "Each of us left 'home' as soon as we were legally able to. Actually, Burke left even before that. All of us went a different way, none of us looked back. We knew we had each other, that if we ever truly needed anything, we could turn to each other. And that was enough. That bond was our home. Not the house in Rogues Hollow."

She didn't know if he was aware of just how haunted he looked when he mentioned the mere word of the place of his birth. She rubbed her arms. "I'm no' certain I could be awa' from here for long, much less abandon it," she said honestly.

"We all have our burdens to bear," he told her evenly, but not unkindly. "Yours were very different from mine."

"Yes, but ye see the difference is I was brought up to treasure and revere what the circumstances of my birth brought to me. I may chafe under the responsibility now and again, but I have no desire to leave here, to run away." She held up her hand when he would have retorted. "But then, I had no reason to."

He visibly tamped down his temper, though she'd never seen his jaw so tight, the throb of the vein at his temple. It cost him, and she felt badly she'd put him in that position. "So it was a reunion for you and your brothers then," she said, turning the topic to one that was more uplifting and pleasant. "Despite the circumstances, that must have been a powerful thing for you. Or do you see each other often?"

He shook his head. And the emotion she saw in his eyes as he spoke of his brothers, or even thought of them, was palpable. For a man who'd so cut himself off from others, he had such passion in him. She couldn't help but think what a waste that was, to lock away something that powerful rather than embrace it.

"No, we hadn't been under one roof since—" He stopped, pinched the bridge of his nose, then blew out a deep breath. "In a very long time," he said finally, lifting his gaze to hers again. "It made it all bearable. The memories . . ." He trailed off, then looked away.

"Couldn't have been easy," she finished for him, her heart going to him for the suffering he'd been dealt. Though she knew he'd shun it if she offered him compassion any more directly.

"Actually, the part I'd been dreading the most, being under that roof, reliving all those years . . ." He shook his head, his expression softening a bit, becoming more bemused. "We sat around the table and shared stories from our childhood. Memories that had nothing to do with our father, as those were best left unspoken. But it surprised me that we all had so many recollections that were good, funny, heartwarming in their own way."

She wanted to go to him, hold him, soothe the ache she saw still in his eyes. "That must have been healing," she said.

His gaze and his focus turned outward then, and he shifted that focus to her. The impact to her senses was tangible. "You're quite a good listener," he said by way of response. "And I have to take back something else that I said earlier."

Surprised, her eyebrows lifted in response. "Oh?"

"When I said that communication by letters was one dimensional in what it revealed of a person. I was wrong. Written words can convey the meaning of one's thoughts, but without seeing the expression, hearing the tone in which those words are spoken, the reader is at a distinct disadvantage when it comes to truly deciphering the real meaning beneath the words, learning with any real truth about the person wielding the pen. It's easy to hide behind words, disguise the truth of who you really are. But not so easy face-to-face. One dimensional, instead of three."

"I think you have a point." *Obviously,* she thought, seeing as what she knew of Taggart and what his son knew of him were so vastly different. "But I also think that that very anonymity allows the penman to open up in a way that they may never have were they required to look the person in the eye. It can be very freeing, having that veil in place. Perhaps in some ways, what's written reveals more about the character of the person than any face-to-face meeting ever would. Somewhat like a confessional."

He nodded. "Which is why I said I was wrong." He clearly intended to elaborate, but instead he fell silent, holding her gaze, but shifting his weight as if suddenly self-conscious.

It was an interesting revelation, this sudden vulnerability, and wholly endearing. "What brought about that realization?" she asked, allowing a small hint of a smile to tease the corners of her mouth. He was a complex man, and she was becoming more and more fascinated with the idea of peeling away the layers of him by the moment.

"Your letters," he said, facing her squarely, almost rigidly, as if tensing against whatever retort she would volley back at him for his revelation. "As I said, I hadn't intended to read them."

"But?" She still felt vulnerable, as she had moments before, but now she also felt . . . a bit excited by it. People read her words every day, in her articles and stories. And there was a vulnerability there, and an excitement, too. But this was vastly different. He'd read her letters, her private feelings and thoughts, and they had obviously moved him.

"First, you have to understand the situation," he said, with a bit more intensity than she'd expected. "We'd already adjudicated the will. I was grappling with the reality that my father had left the house and our share of Rogues Hollow to me. I felt trapped, even though it hadn't been unexpected. I was angry, and restless. All I wanted to do was get the hell out of there. Again. Never look back. Again. But, despite what you believe of me, and my father notwithstanding, I do understand the importance of my heritage. For three hundred years, a Morgan has always owned that piece of land, and I knew it was important to continue that, to leave the chain of ownership unbroken. And yet there was a part of me that was undeniably interested in thwarting everything my father had done in his lifetime to change the course of Morgan history by handing it away, ending the Morgan legacy once and for all."

"Did your brothers feel the same?"

He lifted one shoulder. "Yes. And no. They understood my dilemma, just as they felt remorse for being relieved it hadn't been left to them. But in the end, they all pledged they'd support whatever I decided."

"Which was?"

He blew out a deep breath, turned once again to the paintings on the wall, began to pace the perimeter of the tower. "I wasn't sure. I was still undecided on what to do. That's when I got a visit from Mick Templeton. I didn't know about this . . ." He waved his hand about. "Until that visit. Burke and Austin had already taken off. It was just Jace and me. Jace was moving back to Highland Springs, he'd taken on a teaching position in town. But he was looking to build a new life, not return to his old one." His lips quirked a little. "Maybe it was his own way of besting the old man. Be a fine upstanding Morgan, but on his own terms. And not burdened by the past." He shoved his fingers through his hair. "I couldn't saddle him with the Rogues Hollow legacy, not our particular legacy anyway. He needed to make his own mark, free and clear from our dear, departed dad. Frankly, I didn't know what in the hell I was going to do."

"How did learning about Ballantrae change anything?" She thought back to how she'd felt about contacting Taggart's supposedly heartless sons, and contrasted that to what she knew now. Listening to him, knowing just from looking at him now what a difficult time these past months had truly been for him, for reasons she could empathize with, even if she couldn't truly comprehend. She couldn't imagine going through what he had, becoming the man he had, with such a passion for his work . . . coming back to face such a huge and painful dilemma.

"Finding out about Ballantrae would seem to have been the least of your worries," she added.

"Did you know that my father had kept this—" he waved his hand, "—a complete secret from everyone back at home, trusting the information only to Mick?"

"No. I didn't. I—considering what you've told me about him, I guess I can understand why he didn't make the news public. But . . ." She shook her head. "This must have come as a real shock to you."

"That would be putting it mildly, yes. For my father to want to have anything to do with a history he'd dedicated his life to wiping out, much less dump a ton of his own money after it, was so out of character, I wondered if he'd become addled from his illness."

"No," she murmured automatically. "He was quite sharp, to the very end." She glanced at him then, and hastily added, "I'm sorry. I'm no' defending or condemning here. It's a lot for me to take in as well, ye ken."

"Yes. And no offense taken. Mick told me as much himself when we went over the papers together, though I admit my mind was racing so far ahead, the details were all a bit fuzzy to me. But, to be fair, Mick wasn't the first to try and tell me my father had changed as he'd gotten older. I'd heard it from some of the people in town, as they stopped by to give their condolences. I—" He stopped, shrugged, but without apology. "I didn't really want to hear about it. But, as further proof that those people might have been right, Mick gave me this." He swung the pack from his shoulders and slid it to the floor, so he could loosen the ties and open it.

She gasped as he withdrew a beautiful carved cherrywood box. "I sent that to him," she said softly, touched that he'd passed it on to his son. "It belonged to Lillith Sinclair's first-born daughter, over a century ago. It held her family's Bible, and . . . well, you probably haven't read it, but it held some fairly important Morgan history. I thought he should have it."

"I didn't want to look in it, didn't want to care," he said flatly. "Mick told me my father had very specifically requested I look at the contents, that I'd understand everything then. It was Pandora's box to me. I wanted nothing to do with it."

"But you did eventually."

His lips quirked then and he nodded. "My father might not have approved of my chosen profession, but he certainly understood the nature that had led me to it. Yes, my curiosity got the better of me. I brought it with me because I thought you might want it back, seeing as what's in it would mean more to you than anyone else."

"Even after what I just told you about it?"

He didn't say anything. But he didn't hand her the box either. She thought it was a step, small though it may be, and let the matter drop. For now. "What was in the box?" she asked.

"I haven't looked through all of it. Your letters were on top. That was as far as I got."

She said nothing, merely held his gaze, compelling him to elaborate.

"I was still trying to come to terms with why my father had made such a complete turnaround on his feelings about Morgan heritage. And I wasn't sure of what to do with this property. Of course, there was a note from him as well, issuing a challenge to me." He looked away, blew out a short, harsh breath. "I don't know why I didn't slam the box shut then, or burn it. I was certainly in no mood to be dictated to from beyond the grave. I'd had enough of that when he was alive." He glanced over at her. "But I thought maybe the letters would help explain things. For all I knew he'd gone senile."

"Life has a way of changing people," was all she said. "Not necessarily for better or worse, just different. I don't claim to know why he was who he was to you as a father. Or why he was so very different with me. I can't apologize for him, but I won't defend him to you, either. I will, however, always tell you the truth. Whatever you want to know—"

"I didn't come here to learn more about my father."

She took a step forward. "Then why did you come?"

"Do you want to know the truth?" he asked softly, but with an intensity that had her pausing in her advance.

"Always. Even when it hurts."

He lifted an eyebrow in question.

She thought about Priss and Jory. "I'll take hurt and aware

over blissful ignorance any day." Now that the tables were turning, she suddenly wished they weren't delving into such emotion-filled territory. She wanted the Tag from yesterday. The guy who managed to be both geeky and incredibly primal at the same time. The guy who had her laughing one minute, and moaning the next. She wanted mindless, noncommittal, burning hot rebound sex. Which she could get in spades from the Tag of yesterday. The Tag of today came with too many complications.

He opened the box and lifted out a carefully bound stack of letters. "This is why I'm here."

She carefully took the bundle, immediately recognizing her handwriting on the top envelope. Her first reaction was a palpable sadness over this physical reminder of the meaningful friendship she'd forged from what had begun as an emotionless business liaison. She'd had months to prepare for his passing, months more to adjust to his death . . . and it was still hard to imagine never finding a missive from him tucked in her mail. Her grip on them tightened as she looked up at Tag. "What do my letters have to do with your decision?"

He lifted a hand toward her face, but let it drop away before he brushed her cheek. "I was only going to skim one or two. Just to try and figure out what his relationship was to this place, and to you. Mick had no idea why he'd become involved here, much less poured so much of his money into it. I just wanted to understand. Not because I cared what my father did or why, but because I had to make a decision on what to do with the place.

"I pulled a letter out at random and found myself reading more than skimming. It wasn't a business note from property manager to owner, it was a chatty letter, filled with anecdotal information about Ballantrae and the townspeople. So . . . I pulled out another one, then another." His lips twisted a little. "I can only imagine you're very successful at your chosen profession. You write with amazing clarity and perception. I was up half the night reading every damn one of your letters. I felt like I knew you, and yet I knew nothing about you.

"I gleaned little bits and pieces, but you never talked about yourself really. Still, your character came through. Your observations about people, your insights, your opinions. I didn't know if you were young or old, married, divorced, widowed. I thought before I'd read the first one that maybe this was some sort of long-distance romance, but though the tone of your letters made it clear you held my father in great esteem and affection, I knew this was no love affair. So . . . I didn't know what to make of you. A total stranger, and one I wasn't predisposed to like just based on your affection for my father alone. And yet . . . I couldn't stop reading.

"By the time the sun came up, the pile had dwindled down to the last one or two. And I found myself hating that. That I was going to lose that connection to you." His smile was self-deprecating as he glanced away. "That probably sounds a bit unbalanced, but then that pretty much describes the last few months for me anyway."

She lifted her hand to his cheek, turned his gaze to hers. "It sounds . . . amazing really. I had . . . well, I mean, I do put words together for a living but you're not there when someone reads them. And so you don't know how they affect people." She broke off, surprised to find herself fighting back a few tears. "I write for myself really. And . . . I guess I had no idea that anything I had to say could move someone like that. I—" Now it was her turn to break off, unsure of how to respond. "I don't know what else to say."

He tipped her chin up to his when she looked down. "I didn't either. I just knew that I couldn't sign anything until I'd met you."

"Well," she said, for once at a complete loss for words to explain the way he was making her feel, "you certainly did accomplish that."

His smile was slow . . . and deep. "You know, the Picts, an

interesting bunch of Celts with blue tattoos and great carving skills, were a highly superstitious bunch," he said, caressing her face now, then snaking his fingers around the back of her head, into her hair. He tugged her closer, shifting her so her mouth angled up toward his.

"So I've heard," she said breathlessly, her heart hitching just a wee bit, hearing him talk about her home, his heritage, with such warmth.

"Well, early on in my studies, I learned quite a lot about karma and fate from studying what is known of their beliefs. I always marveled at what I considered their blind faith in something so intangible, something that was impossible to prove."

"Ever the scientist," she murmured, sliding her hand up his arm, reveling in the taut feel of his muscles, the flex and play of his body. She'd never thought to have the pleasure again. And now, with everything they'd revealed, it was so much more personal, more meaningful, than she had ever expected.

"Generally, yes," he said. "Except now . . . well, now I find I have more ephemeral questions. Fewer concrete answers. And I don't usually care for situations where there are no answers."

"Join the club."

He smiled. "Something tells me you're the type to be far more at ease with intangibles than I am." He crowded his body closer to hers.

She let him shuffle her back until her spine met up with the wall beside the base of the stairs. "Well, there is the ghost that haunts the south tower. Although I suppose there is a bit of concrete evidence there."

He merely raised his eyebrows as he took the letters from her and set them on the table.

What was it about having his hands on her that affected her so? Her heart rate doubled and he made her knees go all shoogly.

"Proof?" he prodded her, when she lost track of the conversation thread.

"Oh. Aye. It's kind of hard to ignore the presence of a spirit when every time I enter the tower chamber I find he's tossed everything about." She shuddered with pleasure as he tucked her hair behind her ears, then cupped her face in his palms. "And I know I'm the only one who's been up there."

"He? You've seen him then?"

She managed to shake her head, but that only served to cause friction between her skin and his. Friction that led to heat. And she was already half on fire as it was. "No. He's choosy who he reveals himself to. It's Sir John, though. He's been like a member of the family for ages."

Tag's lips quirked, but the intensity in his eyes doubled when she sighed as he wove his fingers through her hair. "You know, before we met, only one woman had ever fascinated me like this. So swiftly and so thoroughly, with seemingly no effort at all." He brushed his thumbs across her lips. "I should have known from that first moment, standing in the middle of a snowstorm, that she was you," he murmured.

Then he took her with the complete confidence of a man who knew the woman he desired wanted to be taken, to be pulled into his arms, to have her mouth ravished by his, her body brought to a fever pitch by the feel of his hands roaming wherever they wanted. All of which was true. All of which he accomplished. Easily.

She lost all track of any plans she'd made, abandoned any hope of exerting control over the swift expansion of the situation between them. And she didn't hesitate in doing so, either. She'd ached for this since leaving his side. And she was still rational enough to know that it would only take a slight hesitation between them to allow the specter of his father, or the contracts, or the letters, the castle, any of it, to rise again between them.

They would take care of all of that. In due time. But for the moment, she wanted what she wanted. And what she wanted was exactly what he was about to give her.

Hallelujah.

Chapter 15

"Bed," he murmured against her mouth, his heart pounding and his body already aching from her soft moans and even softer lips. Taking her in a car, or up against the wall, had their distinct, memorable qualities. But now he wanted her on something soft, a place where they could sprawl their bodies in a languid tangle, where he had all the time and space in the world to explore her. She was intoxicating to him, and he no longer cared at the moment why that was. Why fate, if indeed there was such a thing, had put her in his path, and made her so irresistible to him.

Because, Christ, but he didn't think he'd ever get enough of her.

She flung a hand in the general direction of the stairs, right before she grabbed his hair and directed his mouth lower, to her chin, then her neck.

He nipped along the tender skin exposed there, pulling at her shirt. He slid his hands slowly down her arms, then linked his fingers with hers, dragging them up the wall until they were over her head. Pressing her hands in a silent plea to leave them there, he slid down her body until he crouched in front of her bared midriff, his thighs spread wide and braced on either side of her. She bowed away from the wall, back arching when he dipped his tongue in her navel. He was torn between wanting to nudge the hem of her shirt higher, and higher still, pulling it up and off her extended arms, her bra to follow, allowing him access to the soft weight of her breasts, the delectable enticement of her hardened nipples . . .

Or pulling her pants open, ripping the zipper down and burying his tongue deep inside her. She'd arch violently against him, this he knew. She'd be sweet, and hot, and oh-so-tight a man could die that very moment and feel cheated out of nothing.

It was only his determination to be in a bed when he tasted her again, felt her squeeze tightly around any part of him, that he directed his attention upward. Pushing her shirt up as he went, he drew the tip of his tongue along the center line of her body. His knees remained spread wide as he balanced on the balls of his feet. Slowly he uncurled his own body, drawing his thighs along the outer contours of her legs, her hips as he straightened. The shirt slid up her arms and off as his hips cradled hers. She fit neatly into him, perfectly against him. Her body molded to his such that every hard inch of him was wedged snug between the apex of her thighs.

He ached to free himself, to take her right here. Goddamn but he was like a starving mongrel. One whiff of her and he was salivating, intent on feasting until sated. It amazed him how hard he had to work for control. He'd had carnal knowledge of women from many different cultures, some of whom were intensely sexual and not afraid to indulge it. But while that had been exciting, heady even, it didn't come close to the firestorm of emotions that she stirred up with merely a brush of a hand, or a hint of a smile.

At no time in his life had he ever felt such twin needs fight within him for control. On the one hand, she called to some primal impulse inside him, driving him to take, dominate, and possess. And on the other, she made him want to give up control altogether, give in to the tender, more complicated emotions whipping through him, just to see where they'd take him. Take them.

Every time he was near her, it was as if something in her

called to him. As if his body, or some part of his soul, had known hers for centuries. Had lost her and only now found her again. Like he'd come home, and couldn't make up for lost time fast enough. Which would explain this . . . this anxiety that flooded him. As if he had to get his fill while he could, for that time when he'd lose her again.

Of course, the truth was, he would lose her at some point. Or leave her, anyway. But that was a conscious decision on his part, on both their parts. They both knew what this was . . . and what it wasn't. Her life was here, his was half a world away. At no time would it even be a consideration that it could be otherwise. A fling, a hot affair, an ill-advised liaison. Call it any of those things and it would be at least partly the truth.

But what it wasn't was a start of something more. Much less the taking up of something that had started so long ago it was merely an ephemeral strand in his psyche or hers. He'd witnessed many cultural beliefs, studied many religions . . . and had never once considered himself a spiritual man. Logic, proof, rationale. Those were the tools he worked with, that was the way his mind worked.

Which is why he was helpless to understand, much less interpret or analyze, the depth of the desperation he felt when he let himself think about the time he would no longer be able to reach for her.

He was pulling her bra off, his face buried in the curve of her neck, as if he could inhale her essence into him, make it a permanent part of him, when she gripped his shoulders, then his head, and yanked it back. Her eyes were huge and dark. He recognized the need and desire, but surprisingly he also recognized the swamping confusion. It wasn't possible that she was feeling the same disconcerting range of emotions that he was. That was too much to contemplate. At the moment there were more urgent concerns.

Like just how many flights up he was going to carry her. "Hold on," he told her, yanking her legs up around his hips.

"I'm too heav—"

He cut her off with a soul-deep kiss, gripping her to him with an arm banded around her back, and another fisted in her hair. He stumbled them halfway up the flight of stairs before coming up for air.

Her ankles were locked around his back. Her arms locked around his neck. "Really, Tag, let me down, I can—"

"Where?" he asked, nibbling on her lower lip as he stubbed and banged his way up the circular stairs, eventually emerging through a hole in the ceiling, leading to the next floor landing.

He rolled her back against the wall for support. Her hair was a wild tangle, her cheeks were flushed, her eyes were slightly unfocused and glittering with desire. He imagined his looked much the same. Perhaps a bit wilder. "I'm not letting you go until we fall onto a bed somewhere. And fair warning," he said against the side of her neck, "I plan to be buried deep inside you about a minute later."

She moaned deep in her throat when he pushed his hips tight between hers. "Sounds like a plan."

"So . . . where?"

She managed to motion with her head. "Right behind you."

Now he smiled, tugged the length of her hair. "I suppose I'm yet another marauding Morgan, storming Castle Sinclair after all," he said, in fair imitation of her accent.

Her eyes twinkled, dimples flashed. "So does that make me another innocent Sinclair lass, about to be ravished by a heathenish Scot?"

"Well, I don't know about innocent." He laughed when she dug her heels into his back. "But I am a heathen. And the ravishing part? Most definitely." He wanted to look around, to see this room, what it said about her. What was important to her, what she was frivolous about. Was she neat and tidy, or did everything lay where it dropped? Were her furnishings modern, or did she cling to the past in every part of her life?

But right now he couldn't seem to expand his focus beyond the bright blue eyes blazing into his. And he recognized then that the emotion washing through him was joy. Unmitigated, unquestioning joy. The kind of exultation that he usually only came close to experiencing when a historic discovery was made on a dig. It was like she was the most important discovery he'd ever made. Made more powerful by the fact that she was a living, breathing artifact of his life, his history. Everything that had come before . . . and all the possibilities of what could lay ahead.

He was obviously delirious. And yet, here in this stone tower, in the very spot where Morgans before him had once stood, perhaps gazing down into eyes just as blue, just as desirous . . . his fanciful imaginings seemed not only possible, but downright probable.

And could it be possible she was feeling the same? Because they didn't end up in a whirl on her bed as he'd planned. Instead her legs slipped from around his waist as he held her tightly against him. They stood there in her private tower, staring deeply into one another's eyes. Her fingers burrowed beneath his hair, and a shiver of pleasure snaked down his spine as she raked her nails gently over the nape of his neck. Her gaze searched his, and he wished he knew what she hoped to find there.

"Tag," she whispered, the dark of her eyes expanding, swallowing him whole, pulling him deeper under her Sinclair spell.

He shook with need, yet he only brushed his lips across hers, sighing at the softness, the pure fit of her mouth under his. "Would it alarm you if I told you I'd never wanted . . ." He paused as he discovered there were no words right enough to quantify it. "The way I want," he began again, only to find the words still wouldn't form. "There is something here, something between us that I don't claim to understand, but that I—"

She pressed a finger across his lips, softly shushing him. "I know," she said, looking into his eyes. "I know."

He wouldn't have thought it possible, because he didn't understand it himself. And yet he found it there, in her eyes. The truth of it. They were well and truly in this together. Bound in some way that defied description. Bound in a way that would surely only become more complicated if he were to take her again, here.

"Some things are better left unexplained," she whispered, then lifted up to take his mouth in a kiss that both enflamed him and left him reeling with the sweet tenderness of it.

"I want you with a force that's pure insanity," he told her when she lifted her mouth from his, the words tumbling out of their own volition. As if only by sharing them with her could they begin to make any sense to him. "I want you hard and fast. Right here, right now. No finesse, no tenderness, and without even the pretense of patience." He brushed her hair back from her face, surprised to find his fingers were shaking now. "And I want every second to last an eternity. I want to spend a lifetime learning every curve of your body, the texture of your skin, the scent of you, the taste of you. I want to savor you."

She was trembling now as well, and he knew he shouldn't have said those things. It was beyond ridiculous to feel what he was feeling, much less put words to it. He knew that. But he couldn't seem to help himself. It was like once he'd opened himself to this, there was no turning back, no room for moderation. And there had been the way she'd looked at him. Into him. Like she of all people would understand this. And he didn't want to experience this alone.

"It's terrifying," he told her. "I know that, but it's—"

"It's the truth of it," she finished for him, pulling him back down to her. "I told you, I know." She kissed his mouth, his chin, his jaw, his temple. "I know," she whispered again. "Because I feel it, too."

And it felt like everything clicked into place in that moment. Like everything was aligned as it should be, and he could finally stop searching. He would have laughed at that if he hadn't been petrified. It was as if he were standing on the edge of a very deep precipice. One step either way could be the difference between keeping his world secure and definable ... or launching himself into a place where nothing made sense and there were no hard, fast answers.

"You don't need to prove everything to believe in it," she whispered. "You only have to let yourself experience it to know it's true."

It should have shaken him that she seemed to so clearly read his thoughts, understand his fears. But, in fact, it was a relief.

Then he felt her teeth sink into the flesh of his shoulder, not enough to hurt, but enough to send a surge of lust through him that was almost paralyzing.

"Go with instinct." She looked up at him then, her eyes fierce with desire now, her gaze clear and true. "Or forever regret not knowing what might have been."

He framed her face with his hands, looked deep into those wise, timeless eyes of hers. "Who are you, Maura Sinclair?" he whispered.

She surprised him with an immediate broad smile, both eyes and dimples winking. "That's simple. I'm yours." She whirled him around and sent them both crashing to the bed. "Now for God's sake, would ye claim me already?"

He heard a bark of laughter, recognized that it was his, and finally, blessedly, let everything else go. Instinct and need would be his only guide. The moment he took her mouth he knew that would be more than enough.

She was reaching for his shirt, but he grabbed her hands. Rolling her to her back, he straddled her, pinning those questing hands above her head. Her eyes widened in surprise, but there was no fear there. Only anticipation.

"I believe I'm the one who's supposed to do the ravishing," he said.

"Aye, but ye can't fault a lass for trying to do a bit o' claiming of her own, now can ye?"

There must have been something of the marauder in his responding grin, because her eyes darkened with need, and her breath came in short puffs. " 'Tis a claiming you want," he said softly, " 'tis a claiming you'll receive." He leaned down and nipped first her chin, then her shoulder. "But ye'll be doing it my way." Still pinning her hands, he tugged one bra strap down with his teeth. She bucked and twisted beneath him, which only served to make him more determined. His pants were restricting and uncomfortable. But he was too intent on her at the moment to free himself just yet.

Growling now, he held both wrists with one hand so he could peel the soft fabric of the cups down, bunching it beneath her breasts so that it plumped them up fuller for him, pushed her tight nipples toward his waiting mouth. Sweet, taut, and begging for his tongue, he thought, as he took one, then the other into his mouth. She squirmed against him, moaning and arching . . . but no longer struggling for freedom.

It wasn't that he wanted her held captive, he merely wanted to have what he wanted, without any undue influence from her. If he were to release her, she'd be intent on taking what she wanted. Which would be perfectly fine with him. But later. For now, he wanted to feast and savor, none of which he'd have the opportunity to do if she so much as laid one of her pale, slender fingers on just about any part of him.

He flicked and tongued and teased her, pinning her more tightly to the bed with his weight so she couldn't arch so violently. Her moans had turned to throaty groans, but her wrists remained still in his grip. He took that as an invitation to run his free hand down the length of her torso. He shifted his weight off her, leaning forward enough so he could flip open the button of her pants and ease her zipper down. She writhed between his thighs, her eyes closed, her head arched back, as he toyed with the elastic band of her panties.

Leaning over her, he put his lips next to her ear, making

her gasp in surprise. "I'm in something of a quandary here," he murmured, then lightly bit her earlobe.

Panting heavily, she trembled against the palm he flattened on her stomach. "Regarding?" she managed.

He smiled against the tender skin at the crook of her neck. "I rather like keeping your hands from making mischief," he said, rubbing his thumb along her joined wrists. "And yet, I'm dying to yank your pants off and do whatever I please between your thighs."

She trembled harder, letting out a soft "Oh," at his words, ending in a little groan as he slowly slid his fingers beneath that elastic band.

"Unfortunately, I can't do both."

She shook her head, though it was more of a thrashing movement as just then his fingertip slid across the slick wetness he'd discovered waiting for him. "Maura," he said, twitching hard himself when she whimpered at the removal of his finger.

She turned her head, treating him to a heavily hooded gaze of desire. He almost came himself at the wealth of want and need he found there. Slowly, he slid his finger into his own mouth. The sweet taste of her only served to enrage his senses further. He bent lower, so his face was just above hers. "Of course, you could promise me your hands will stay like this," he pressed them against the bed. "Until I say otherwise."

She groaned long and low when he settled himself against her open zipper. "I think I can do that," she choked out.

He chuckled. "Do ye now."

She managed a slight grin, fighting to keep her hips from grinding against him, only partly succeeding. "Aye. But fair warning, my turn will come."

"Oh, I certainly hope so," he said, grinning now. Slowly, he released his grip on her wrist, then slid his palm down along the tender underside of one arm. He tucked his hand beneath her, making her arch just enough so he could release the clasp of her bra. Straddling her hips, he freed her completely and tossed the silky garment aside. "Beautiful," he said, amazed to find himself even more aroused just by the sight of her, so bared to him.

"Freckled," she commented. "And no' too bountiful."

He covered her with his palms, making her gasp and arch reflexively. "A perfect fit," he said, teasing her nipples between his fingers. "Like they were made for my hands." He shifted his weight back so he could lower his mouth to them again, only he found one freckle dotting the valley between them and kissed it gently. And then he was kissing another, and at her soft sigh, another, and yet another still. Until he'd found them all, branded them all, cherished them all.

When he finally lifted his head, it was to find her eyes swimming. Alarmed, he stopped immediately.

Her hands came down then, and she took his head between them. "No," she choked out, "don't stop. It's just that . . ." She sniffed. "That was perhaps the loveliest thing anyone has ever done." She slid her hands to his face, then tugged him up to her and kissed him. "Ye make me feel beautiful."

He lifted his head. "You are beautiful."

She laughed a little, even as she sniffled again. "Ye say that like I'm a raving beauty that has men falling at her feet daily. I assure you it's no' true." Her grin broadened, a bit cheeky now. "Weekly, maybe. But then we don't get too many blokes around here under the age of fifty. And I do have my standards."

She was making light of it, too light, and he realized he'd embarrassed her somehow. "I'm sure if there were more blokes, they would be laying at your feet, hearts shattered," he told her, wondering how the hot lust arcing between them had so suddenly shifted back into that unbalanced emotional territory. "I'm sorry if I made you feel self-conscious, it wasn't my intent. I just . . ." He wasn't sure how to explain why she moved him to want to do the things he did. He didn't yet understand it himself.

She turned his face to hers again. "Now I've done it to you, haven't I? You didn't make me feel self-conscious. At least, not in a bad way. I'm aware men find me passing attractive, okay? I dinna believe in game playing and the like. But generally speaking, when a man gets to, well the point you'd gotten us to, he's no' thinking about the sweet gesture." She smiled dryly. "Actually, he's never thinking about the sweet gesture unless he's still trying to get my pants off. So you . . . you caught me off guard there is all." She tried a brush-it-off laugh, but missed the mark. By a fair mile if he was any judge.

He pulled her hands from his face, and clasped them between his own, pinning them between his body and hers. "I can't say that I'm a sweet-gesture kind of man. All I know is I look at you and I want. Period. Big things, little things, everything in between. It's like I've been cut loose in a place filled with treasures, and I alone get to uncover them. I'm not big on rushing. I like to take my time. Make sure I miss nothing. Savor my finds. Catalogue them carefully, so there will be no doubts encountered later."

Her gaze searched his. "It's an interesting way to approach sex, I'll grant you. But it certainly makes a woman feel treasured."

Now he smiled. "Honestly, I'm usually pretty much like you described earlier. There aren't too many 'lassies' about in my line of work. So I don't generally have extended patience when it comes to physical gratification, other than to make sure we both end up with a smile." He winced a little. "I do know I've never once compared sex with a dig. Sorry for that."

"It was actually quite lovely. Unique, but lovely."

Now his smile faded. "I don't know why I'm like this with you. I just—you're just—" He broke off this time, staring helplessly into her eyes.

"We're just," she said softly. Then she tugged her hands from his and slowly lifted them over her head, crossing them symbolically at the wrist. "Now, I believe you were mapping out a very interesting course there a bit ago." She arched her back, a perfectly wicked smile curving her lips, so at odds with the splash of freckles, those two tiny dimples. And yet so perfectly . . . her. "And I'm quite interested in finding out if it pans out for you."

Chapter 16

Maura would pay a great deal to know what was going on behind those enigmatic golden eyes of his. He was like this giant jungle feline, all tawny and sleek and powerful, intent on his prey and knowing exactly how to go about ensnaring it. And Lord but she was willing to be the big cat's supper. But then he'd do something so disconcertingly tender, so . . . for lack of a better word, romantic, that he quite literally took her breath away. And perhaps a piece of her heart along with it.

She couldn't reconcile him, couldn't neatly label or categorize him. He was both self-assured and a bit gawky. A highly intellectual man, definitely a physical one . . . and just out of step enough with civilized society to be awkwardly endearing. He could be incredibly genuine and open one moment, then unreadable and downright inscrutable the next. All of which combined to make him absolutely enthralling to her.

At least, that was her rudimentary attempt at an analysis. It didn't take into account the intangibles. Like the way he said things that should have been laughably ridiculous, things intimating there was some connection between them that surpassed the physical plane. And yet she found herself nodding in complete understanding. A part of her knew it was imperative that she keep a level head, and the right perspective about all this.

But his hands were on her again, and her body was clamoring for release. She didn't want to waste time quantifying it, dammit, she just wanted him to get the bloody hell on with finishing his claiming of her.

He was trailing the softest kisses down the center of her body, his hands following the damp trail. His fingertips lingered on her breasts, her nipples, as his tongue dipped once again into her navel. Then he was sliding the rest of her clothing down her hips, baring her to him in a way far more blatant than before. She'd thought them intimate in both the car and in the room at the inn. This was somehow different.

No dark, no candlelight, no storm. A weak winter sun lit the room just enough to create a soft gray glow, made somehow more romantic than gloomy when she glanced down to find him looking up at her, his chin resting on her belly.

Oh yes, far more intimate this was.

Don't think about it. Just feel. She tipped her head back, her crossed wrists pressing into the bed when she felt his warm mouth move once again. She arched slowly, languidly, as his tongue found her, teased her. He toyed almost absently with her nipples, and yet so expertly that she was writhing beneath him a mere moment later.

Just feel.

He brought her slowly to the edge of reason, sinking his tongue into her, flicking it over her, then drawing it over and around, before sinking into her again, until she was whimpering, panting for that one last touch that would send her screaming over the edge. But he left her balancing precariously on the brink. She felt his weight shifting off the bed completely and forced her heavy eyelids open.

He stood next to her bed, and she realized she was stretched before him, supine, with wrists crossed overhead, presented like some sort of willingly submissive gift. He'd already peeled off his shirt, but he'd paused in shucking his trousers, caught up in simply looking at her. Their gazes met, and as he shoved his pants down over his hips, springing free, so full and hard for her to see, she felt anything but submissive. She felt infused with an incredible power. She lay before him, yes, open to him, to whatever he wanted to do to her . . . and yet she controlled him just as surely. The idea of it made her moan deep in her throat and fight against the need to close her legs, press her thighs together. But she left them spread, just the way he'd had them, filled with the absolute knowledge that he was being just as tortured as she was. And oh, what a delicious torment it was.

He straightened after stepping out of his clothes, and she arched her back very slightly, thrusting the rigid nipples he'd so expertly manipulated upward. His eyes flared and his thick, fully erect cock twitched hard. He was beautiful to look at, all of him. Never had she felt so female, like sex incarnate. She wanted to wrap herself around that turgid length. Hands, mouth, body. All of her, around all of him. She wanted to feel the velvety length of him brush against her palm as she wrapped him in her hand. She wanted to taste the warmth of him, the salty sweetness. And she wanted to feel every hard, throbbing inch of him sink slowly inside of her.

She groaned at the thought of it, unable to stop her hips from shifting, lifting as her need for him grew. "I want you," she demanded hoarsely.

He held her gaze, neither smiling or frowning. Just need meeting need. "How do you want me?"

The question surprised her. And provoked a fresh onslaught of possibilities that left her squirming. She let her gaze drift over him, down the full, twitching length of him, then back up to his eyes, which were now dark with want, hooded as he fought for control. Something wicked inside her wanted to test that control. Only because if he lost it, she'd still win, wouldn't she?

Slowly, she drew her tongue across her bottom lip. He twitched so hard his body jerked with it. He moved to the side of the bed and leaned over her, so close, yet not close enough. She could move, but she didn't want to. There was something deeply erotic about the tableau they'd set, and she wanted to see it through. Or at least until she couldn't take it anymore. She thought he'd move close enough so she could put her lips around him, take him into her mouth.

Instead he reached for two pillows above her head. One he put aside, the other he bunched up and slid beneath her head. His hands were gentle, sliding beneath her hair, lifting her neck. When he was done, her chin almost touched her chest. The position, with her arms still stretched long over her head, extended her in such a way as to make her somehow even more open to him. Her mouth now as much a sexual orifice as any part of her could be.

Then he straddled her body, and again she was taken with the sleek musculature of him, the easy way he moved, the control he exerted with seeming effortlessness. So dark in contrast to her pale skin, tanned as he was, everywhere, so sinewy, naked but for the teeth gleaming about his neck and the tribal tattoos marking his skin. *Primal,* she thought with a deep shudder of pleasure, as he moved higher on her torso. And all for her.

Then he was sliding himself between her breasts. She gasped at the sensation, arching as much as his weight would allow. He shifted forward still, until he brushed across her chin, then her lips, easing back slightly when she parted them. She wanted, badly, to lower her hands, to take him, guide him. Control this.

Which was precisely why she didn't.

She'd always known she was an aggressor in bed, and rarely if ever did her partners complain. She liked having the upper hand, as it were. It resolved things for her, like issues of trust and control. She could steer the course, literally. And that suited her just fine.

Only now, she was undeniably, insatiably curious to find out what it was like to give up that precious control. To find out just how far he could take her. It occurred to her then that any issues of trust had obviously already been resolved by her subconscious. Or she'd never have let him take the liberties he already had. Much less the ones he was about to direct her into sharing with him.

It should have worried her, but it didn't. He wouldn't do anything that they both wouldn't find supremely pleasurable. Of this she was somehow certain. But danger to herself wasn't the only issue that trust revolved around. She was handing over a great deal more than her well-being into his care. She understood that. But even that momentous realization wasn't going to stop her. Stop this.

He leaned just forward enough that she could flick out her tongue and brush across the tip of him. So she did. He gasped, jerked hard against her lips. And she grinned. Oh no, there would be no stopping this. She'd never once felt this way, and she might well never again. Whatever regrets might await her after this was over, wouldn't compare with the regrets she'd certainly have if she backed away from this now.

He was close enough for her to flick her tongue over that velvety tip again. He sucked in his breath, and his thighs tightened against her ribs as he fought for control. She wanted him to struggle with that battle just as she was. The ache between her legs was a sharp, insistent need, but she didn't move anything other than her tongue and mouth. The control cost her, but also made the need climb higher, the ache sink deeper.

He finally shifted forward again, enough for her to swirl her tongue fully around him. His growl was low, guttural, as he eased himself forward, letting her finally take him into her mouth. His thighs tightened further against the need to pump, to thrust himself against the length of her tongue, the wetness of her mouth.

She moaned herself as she held him, so rigidly taut between her lips, her tongue wrapped around the warm head of him. Her fingers curled into her palms against the need to touch him, hold him, stroke him. His hips shifted forward once, so that her lips slid down the shaft, then again. And again. Until he finally, with a groan of regret, pulled free. He shifted his weight back and off of her, though still straddling her hips.

Veins stood out rigidly along the length of his cock, the soft tip darker now, and twitching with the need for continued attention. He noted the direction of her gaze, then took himself in hand, stroking slowly. It was far more intensely erotic, watching those strong, tanned fingers slide up and down that taut, velvety length. She tore her gaze away, lifted her eyes to his, thinking he'd have his squeezed shut, only to find his gaze hot and steady on hers.

"Please." The word was torn from her before she realized she'd been brought to the point of begging.

"What would please you?" he asked roughly, his hand stilling, then dropping away.

"You," she said, her gaze flicking down and back up. "All of you."

He reached for the second pillow then. Moving down her legs, he bent over her and swiftly slid an arm beneath her, lifting her hips so he could slide the pillow beneath. She moaned as her body arched more fully. With her arms extended, her hips elevated, she was now, more than ever, an altar to him. It was intensely arousing, the ache so strong now she was certain the merest brush of air between her legs would make her climax, wrenching her hard over the edge. She wanted to tip her head back, squeeze her eyes shut and just sink into the sensation of it, without having to think about why this was such a powerful turn-on for her. But her head was propped in such a way as to make that impossible.

No, instead she'd been arranged in a way that gave her the perfect angle to watch him as he slowly smoothed a condom on, then with torturous patience, bend to kiss a spot on the inside of one knee, then the other. She gasped, bucked despite wanting to control herself, her nails now digging into palms to keep from reaching for him. She wanted nothing more than to sink her hands into those streaked blond curls and drag him up and inside her body. One long moan after another was wrenched from her as he kissed his way up the inside of one thigh, then the other, always stopping just short of what had been so perfectly presented for him. She wanted to scream with frustration, muscles so tight now she was almost to the point of pain.

A moment later she did scream, but it was in indelible pleasure when he shifted suddenly and speared her fully with his tongue. Even then she couldn't tear her gaze away from watching him, watching what he was doing to her. It was the most erotic, intimate thing she'd ever witnessed. She whimpered repeatedly as he continued to alternately tease her, then fill her. She twitched, she panted, she begged him, until finally, blessedly, he moved that spare inch up . . . and slid his fingers inside her at the same time. She shouted in stunned shock as her climax ripped through her with such intensity, stars winked in front of her eyes. It was a miracle she didn't buck them both off the bed, she came so violently.

And then he was on her.

"Maura," he rasped.

She opened her eyes, only then aware she'd finally closed them. The room was spinning, or maybe it was just her mind, and she had to force herself to focus on him as her body was still wracked with the shuddering aftermath of her orgasm. He took her hips, pulled her up and rather than watch himself enter her, he watched her as he pushed inside of her. Fully, inch by inch, claiming her as fully as he'd declared he would.

Her throat closed over, even as she began climbing the peak again, more swiftly this time, every nerve ending still engorged and ready to be set off. Her heart was pounding, but only partly because she could barely draw a breath. Deeper he pushed, pulling her legs up over his hips, moving up until her back was the only thing on the bed, until his hips met the insides of her thighs and he was fully buried inside of her.

He didn't move. He just . . . watched her. A vein in his

temple throbbed. His cock throbbed. His entire body was taut, shaking with the strain of maintaining even this thin veneer of control.

"Maura," he said again, only there was this thread running through it this time. Not a command. More a plea. His fingers dug into her hips.

Instinctively, she unlocked her wrists. Reached for him.

His expression opened then, his eyes so fierce and dark and filled with . . . She couldn't put a name to it. He met her reaching grasp, and all but yanked her up into his arms, spearing her more fully down onto him, making them both gasp deeply as he wrapped her tightly against him.

Her mouth found his as she gave in to her most visceral needs and began to ride him. They grunted, groaned and all but sobbed with relief as they thrust and pumped and bucked against each other with wild, almost animalistic abandon. He had one arm tight around her back, his other hand tangled in her hair. Her nails raked his back, dug into his shoulders.

And then he reached behind her, yanked the pillows away, flinging them unseen across the room before pushing her onto her back, settling his weight between her hips. Settling himself inside her. So perfectly inside her. And, shockingly, something calmed between them, if you could call it that. Instead of driving himself and her over the edge, he slowed, pushed up onto his elbows and brushed the tangled hair from her face as he framed her cheeks with his palms. He continued to move inside her, slower, steadier now, as if the bloodlust of their need for one another had been sated somewhat. Allowing them both to savor each stroke, instead of wasting what they'd built up in a mindless frenzy of thrusting body parts.

He kept his warm palms against her face, looking deeply into her eyes as he moved deeply inside of her. She didn't know what he was feeling, or perhaps was too afraid to assign anything so powerful as what she swore she saw in his eyes, to what he could be feeling. Not yet. Surely not yet. They were strangers.

And yet, when he slowly lowered his mouth to hers, joined his tongue with hers as he took her harder, faster, and finally, blessedly over . . . she couldn't shake the feeling that they'd been like this before. Right here in this tower. Again. And again. When he came, the words that echoed through her, resonated within her, as incredulous and unexplainable as it was, were, "Finally. Finally, you're back where you belong."

And when they'd both finally spent themselves in a rocking, shuddering release, when they couldn't wring one more wracking thrust of pleasure from it, he rolled to his side, pulling her with him, tucking her against his chest, tangling his legs with hers, his chin nestled in her hair, as they both allowed their hearts to slow, their breathing to even out. Her mind was racing even faster than her heart, and yet she willed the tumble of thoughts and emotions away. She simply wanted to feel. To let the waves of pleasure continue to ripple through her, spreading farther and farther out, calming her, settling her, as she came back down to earth.

She didn't want to think about that instant when he'd come inside her, here in her bed, in this centuries-old tower chamber. She didn't want to think about the talks they were going to have about his involvement in the property, and the inevitable effect it was going to have on them. And most of all, she didn't want to think about him leaving.

Because whatever it was they had just shared was a finite, once-in-a-lifetime thing. No matter how amicably they settled the rest, he would go when they were through. There was no altering that. No altering that his place was half a world away. And that her place was irrevocably here.

Their destinies were different. And she couldn't stop that fleeting thought from returning, that irrevocable sense that once again, they were going to allow themselves to be torn apart by circumstance. That once again they were going to ruin their chance to unite for all eternity.

He pressed a kiss against her temple just then, blessedly taking her mind off her obviously orgasm-induced delusional thoughts. But nonetheless making her eyes burn at the sweetness of the gesture. How did a man who'd just taken her like some jungle god, turn around and touch her in a way that made her feel so special and revered?

Oh Maura, you puir foolish lass. Ye've gone and let him into yer heart.

Aye, she thought, nestling against his warmth, his strength, that she most shockingly had. Sure, she was fascinated with tales of the past, of her family history, that of the land of her birth. There was a romance to those tales, certainly, but she did not consider herself personally to be a romantic woman. She was a pragmatist, a realist. God knows she'd had to be. The intelligent, modern woman who knew what she wanted and did her best to get it. Whether it be funding for renovating her family's ancestral home, or a slaking of her more base needs. She went about achieving both the same way. With careful planning and conscious decision-making.

Neither of those things came close to describing how she'd handled this affair with Tag. Affair. Even the word was somehow an affront to her. To that unnamed part of her that wanted to suddenly believe in fanciful fairy tales. The heretofore unknown romantic that had apparently resided within her all along, just waiting for the right moment . . . or the right man, to set it free.

Her eyelids grew heavy as he toyed with her hair. A languid sort of bliss stole into her body and she let herself fall under its sway. Surely after a restful, restorative spot of sleep, she'd awaken clear-minded and focused once again. Not to mention sane.

When she did wake, hours later, the room was dark except for the glow from the embers in the fireplace. She wasn't sure how clear-minded she was, but she knew one thing: she was alone. Yet, she didn't feel any sense of alarm or abandonment. Mostly because Tag's pants were still draped haphazardly over the chair by her wardrobe.

She smiled then, and indulged in a very long, self-satisfied stretch. Another woman would probably have awakened feeling at least a shred of shame. After all, she'd taken two men to her bed in the past three days. But she was feeling too much like a tabby with a belly full of fresh cream, one who'd just found a big, fat ray of sunshine in which to doze away the afternoon, to allow herself to wallow in self-loathing. Besides, she had no doubt that would come back into play at some point.

She rolled over to her side and stared at the flickering embers of the fire Tag must have started at some point while she slept. She wasn't one to forge long-term relationships, but she also wasn't one to dally about with more than one man at a time. Nor was she one to hop from one man to the next, discarding lovers like day-old bread. But it wasn't like she'd gone looking for this, for him, now was it?

And she could hardly be blamed, considering the reason she'd discarded her last lover, if she'd taken advantage of a rather serendipitous situation to indulge herself. It was hardly her fault that that occasion had come so soon after Jory had been booted out of both her bed, and her life. It wasn't like she lived in the land of opportunity, after all, that she could so cavalierly dismiss one when it presented itself, now could she?

She snorted and rolled to her back to stare at the domed ceiling. "Such dedicated rationalization," she murmured, but she still refused to let guilt creep in. She was an adult. An unattached adult. Who could take as many men to her bed as she pleased. Whenever she pleased. So there.

She tossed the covers aside and drew her legs over the side of the bed with a sigh. Who was she kidding? *Och, yer a slut, Maura, that ye are.* Which did nothing to explain the impish grin that lit up her face a moment later. "But a very happy, satisfied one."

Well, so much for self-flagellation.

But the truth of it is, she thought as she quickly tippy-toed her way across the chill flooring that was bared between the thrown rugs, *my only regret about Jory was trying to make him into someone he was most definitely not.* And that was a man she could have a future with. She snagged her bathrobe off the bathroom door, then as an afterthought, shut it behind her. She wasn't used to having guests up here.

Which had been her other critical mistake. Not bringing Tag into this place she'd kept so sacred, her tower chamber. But bringing Jory there. It was surprising how right she felt about Tag's presence in her private rooms, in her bed. Of course, the sacrosanct feeling she'd always extended to her most personal space here, her one haven in the vastness that was Ballantrae, had been shattered when she'd found Priss and Jory desecrating it.

In fact, she'd wondered how she'd recover from that violation, much less how she'd ever sleep in her own bed again. A smile curved her lips. "Well, it no longer appears that's going to be an issue." In fact, she couldn't have imagined a more perfect way of reclaiming it.

She'd often been asked how she could stand living in such a huge, empty place. But Ballantrae, the castle and the grounds, from the loch to the tenant farms, were so steeped in family history, she hardly felt alone here. In fact, at times, she felt downright crowded.

As a child, she'd had this fanciful idea that the inhabitants of the portraits that lined every nook and cranny of the place were watching over her, making sure she lived up to Sinclair standards, didn't disappoint all they had done to keep Ballantrae steady and strong for so many centuries. She'd been made aware at a very young age, as soon as she was able to understand in fact, the mantle under which she'd been born. The responsibility she'd be groomed to take over.

Of course, she'd assumed her Uncle Niall would live a far longer life, and that her inherited burden wouldn't become a direct responsibility until she was much older. As it turned out, she'd been only a little over a year out of university, living in a tiny flat in Inverness, when Niall had taken so ill. A pneumonia that he couldn't seem to shake had eventually claimed him the winter before her twenty-fifth birthday.

She stared into the narrow mirror above the sink. That had been such a bleak time, so overwhelming. To go from the excitement of getting her own place, starting her own career, separate from the demands of her heritage, to just live a normal life for a bit.

She brushed her teeth, splashed water on her face and made a meager attempt to unsnarl her hair. It was full of tangles and knots. A glimmer of her smile returned. Sex with Tag was like a full-contact sport. Next time she'd do well to wear a helmet and pads for protection.

Her smile flickered, then dimmed. Next time. Would there be a next time? Would she be even more a fool to allow him more access to her head, to her heart, than she already had?

She sighed and leaned in to turn on the shower. To think she'd ever thought she'd truly let Jory into her heart. He was fun, he made few if any demands on her, and he was just smitten enough with her that she could sway him to see things her way on just about every occasion. The perfect boyfriend, so she'd thought at the time. Perhaps the right mate. He wasn't a serious person, no, and seemingly had no real ambition in life, but he didn't add stress to hers, easygoing as he was. She slid out of her bathrobe and stepped under the stinging spray of the shower.

And then there was Tag, who was nothing if not a giant complication in every way. There was nothing remotely easy about him. And yet he'd claimed more of her in the short time they'd been together, broken past more barriers, touched her more deeply, than she'd ever realized was possible. And despite the fear and trepidation that struck into the very soul of her, she couldn't help but think back and wonder, *had I really been ready to settle for anything less?*

She let the hot needles of water pound at the muscles of her shoulders and back. She'd met a man now who made her think even when he made her laugh, who was thoughtful and witty, sharp-minded and intelligent. Who also happened to make her knees go all shoogly with little more than a glance from those hooded eyes of his. He wasn't the least bit malleable, nor did she have any illusions about controlling him in any way.

Nor, truthfully, would she want to. Most of what intrigued her about him was wondering what he'd say, how he'd react, what he'd do next. It was exhilarating, actually, even as it was disconcerting. She didn't like feeling so unbalanced, so removed from being completely in control. And yet she could hardly wait to get done here and go find him.

She massaged shampoo into her hair. *Which,* she thought as she winced through snagging a few more snarls in her fingers, *begged the question of what was she going to do with him when she did find him?*

She closed her eyes and stepped under the spray. She knew what she wanted to do with him. In fact, if he were to join her right now, she could all but ensure the two of them could spend a very delightful time conserving hot water together. Sighing, forcing the accompanying visuals of slick tanned skin and clever soapy fingers out of her mind, she shifted out of the spray and reached for the conditioner. She'd have to use half the damn bottle, most likely.

She was doing her best to ignore the other part of what had happened while she and Tag had been deep in the throes of lovemaking. She paused in the act of working conditioner into her tangles. *Lovemaking.* It had certainly been hot and sweaty and intense. Sex at its finest. But—and here was where her heart squeezed a bit—there had been those moments . . . those amazingly tender and sweet moments, where sex didn't begin to describe what they'd been sharing. She sighed again, this time with no small amount of angst. "Bollocks."

And then there was all that business about past lives and deeper connections. Surely she'd simply been half out of her mind with need. He'd had her aching to the point of insanity for want of release. She hadn't been thinking clearly was all. All that talk beforehand, about their ancestors and the entwined threads of their clans' histories. That's all it had been. Fanciful notions planted in her mind, whimsy no doubt.

And yet . . .

"No," she shook her head, then swore when conditioner flew into her eye. Swearing beneath her breath, she turned and rinsed her eyes. What in the bloody hell was she to do about this? About him? She turned her face to the spray, wincing as the piercing needles of water stung the tender skin of her cheeks. *Razor burn,* she thought, though she hadn't felt it at the time. He'd been nothing but gentle with her; even when he'd been thrusting furiously inside of her, he'd taken great care with her.

Jesus and Mary, how could she want a man so badly? But she did. Only a handful of hours spent together, a scatter of time . . . and yet she already couldn't bear to think of him gone forever. It was stupid of her. And weak. She knew that, knew she'd already become the fool she'd worked so hard never to be. And yet it didn't seem to matter. She could ignore that intangible bond they'd forged, deny all she wanted that such a thing, one soul reconnecting throughout time with another, was possible, but it didn't change what she knew in her heart to be true.

She was about to let him walk away. Today, tomorrow, a week or month from now. But walk away he would. And there was no doubt in her mind that it wouldn't be the first time. Or, perhaps, the last.

But it was the only time she would be the one able to do something about it.

Chapter 17

Tag let the stack of papers drop to his lap, and stared into the crackling fire. He'd heard the squeal of water run through the pipes some minutes ago. She was awake. And in the shower from all indications. He tried not to imagine her there, skin all slick, head tipped back, eyes closed. He tried not to. Failed miserably.

He shifted in the worn leather armchair as his body tightened in response. How was it he could want her again? So ferociously, as if he'd been waiting ages to have her, an eternity of excruciating foreplay between them. When he'd only crawled from her bed mere hours before? He'd thought that taking his time, having her as thoroughly and completely as his body had screamed for, would finally take the edge off this . . . whatever the hell it was driving him to have her. He'd had her now, dammit.

And instead of dimming his need, it had only stoked it. Like the fire he'd laid in the fireplace of her bedroom, and down here on the main floor of her tower, the more it burned, the more source material it needed to keep going. She was source material alright. Much in the manner air was necessary for him to keep on breathing.

He slapped the file shut abruptly and slid it to the floor beside his feet. He stood, stretched. It was this place, the whole of the castle, that was provoking such irrational thoughts and feelings. Sitting here, in this tower that still stood, still functioned, centuries after the hands that had painstakingly constructed it had passed away . . . leaving its care to those who followed. Entrusting their hard work, dedication, and fortitude to their progeny, their progeny's progeny. It was nothing short of a miracle that the chain hadn't been broken.

Broken by someone like myself, he thought, his mind heading once again down the disturbing path he could no longer seem to avoid. A son like himself, who, for his own reasons, no matter how valid, had turned his back on centuries of his forebears simply to thwart his immediate forebear: his own father. Short-changing himself? Yes. Perhaps. But he'd never thought past his father, never allowed himself to. Was he short-changing his ancestors? Most definitely. But it was only now that he was beginning to really see that. Or let himself see it.

Only now was he beginning to realize that by turning his back on his own heritage, focusing his intense curiosity most purposefully to another lineage, another heritage, so far removed from his own . . . that he was simply feeding directly into his father's purpose, his goal. Which had been to wipe out the past, their past.

He'd abandoned studying his own ancestry when he'd thought he was doing it to prove something, to force his father to accept its importance. But he'd started, and stopped, for all the wrong reasons. He should have done it for his own sense of satisfaction, his own fulfillment, and to hell with the rest. It seemed so painfully clear now, but then hindsight usually was. He'd been too emotional, too close to it, too affected by his father's views to see it, or think clearly about what his heritage meant to him, and only to him.

He thought about how much more meaningful his life's work could have been, if he'd married that innate interest to his natural desire to dig in the past. And wondered if perhaps that's where the desire had sprung from all along. Not that his years of dedicated research and discoveries hadn't fulfilled him in part. What he'd discovered and pieced together on the Mayan culture was now part of their known history, to be studied and examined and interpreted by those who came after him, those looking for answers to the "what-ifs" that had driven them to make their own discoveries. He was proud of that, proud of the mark he'd made, of his place in that history.

But what about his place in his own? What mark would he make on Morgan history? What mark *could* he be making?

He rubbed his eyes, blew out a long breath. "And why does it suddenly bloody matter so much?"

So his father's death was affecting him in ways he'd never anticipated, making him question every important decision he'd ever made. But how any of that had anything to do with his growing obsession with one Maura Sinclair was beyond him.

Except he wasn't the only Morgan who'd fallen under her sway.

He glanced down again, at the thick file filled with letters. Letters he'd given up ignoring some hours ago. Like his father, apparently Maura was also a pack rat when it came to clinging to their correspondence. He still didn't know what to think, how to feel. The man in those letters, the man who'd written them, was not the man he'd grown up with. The man whose carefully penned words he'd just spent the past two hours reading over was a total stranger to him. And always would be.

Certainly the foundation of his father was there, some of his ideals, his opinions. But in place of the rigid inability to accept anyone else's point of view, much less question his own, was a man who, at some point had begun to question all of it. Had it been his diminishing health that had caused such a dire shift in his personal thinking? Had he suspected his own mortality long before the tests he'd mentioned in one of his letters, well into their pen-pal relationship? Was that why he'd given Maura the financial aid she'd requested?

Or had the change happened after meeting her? As it would seem to have from reading his letters. At least in part. Maybe it hadn't been his health, but merely his advancing age, causing him to reflect. Not that his father had ever been the reflective type. For a man who'd had such strong convictions of right and wrong that he'd become a judge, making a life out of adjudicating the right and wrong of everyone who came before him, one would think he'd have long since learned to appreciate the vast gray area that inhabited the space between the two. The man he'd known, the man who had been judge and jury to his sons, presiding over the seemingly never-ending trial that had been their childhood, had been intensely black and white.

Somehow that had changed. Tag didn't know why. Would never know. Had Maura somehow managed to trigger in the father, the same element of theretofore untapped desire she'd triggered in the son?

Not the kind of desire that had had him taking her like a rutting beast mere hours after they met. The desire for knowledge, to become not just familiar with the Morgan past, but intimately connected to it. Was that how she'd pulled him—and his financial backing—into it? Which begged the question that had come to him at some point during his foray into her files: why approach a Morgan at all when there were Sinclairs—certainly more direct descendants to Ballantrae—still living in Rogues Hollow?

Maybe she had tried them first, though he'd seen no documentation of it. Of course, Tag was forced to admit he didn't know what was going on in the Sinclair branch of the Hollow these days. He kept up with his brothers, but not with anything or anyone else from his childhood. When he'd left, he'd needed to sever himself from all of it. And there hadn't been anyone close enough to him that he'd felt the need to keep in touch with. He'd been a very guarded person with his emotions, and his heart, and he supposed that had definitely shaped a pattern to which he still adhered. At least until he'd met the woman presently showering overhead.

He was pacing, thoughts and questions echoing over and over in his mind, with very few answers forthcoming. The only thing he knew was that at the core of all this confusion, was one person. Maybe the only person who could help him make sense of any of it. He was staring up at the portraits one minute, and the next he was climbing the stairs, continuing through the bedroom and let himself without so much as a knock into the small bathroom that had been carved out of her bedchamber a generation or two earlier.

She was still in the shower. Standing in the clawfoot tub under a meager spray, a flowery circular curtain drawn around her. Steam filled the room, as did the heady scent of body soap and shampoo. None of which compared to the heady scent of her, which he'd be able to pinpoint, blindfolded, fifty years from now. On one whiff.

And if there was any doubt that while he'd been sitting down in her living room, reading through the papers, the letters, trying to make some kind of rational sense out of her effect on him, that it was some kind of postcoital glow that had him exaggerating just how swiftly and deeply her mere presence affected him, that entire argument was instantly dashed when just the shadow of her body behind that curtain sent blood surging through him.

His hunger for her was a leveling, humbling force, which should be just terrifying enough to send him directly back out of the room, down those tower stairs and out into the cold dark night. Maybe the bracing wind off the moors would clear this fucking irrational obsession out of his mind. Out of his body. Allow him to think straight, to put all of this together in a way that made some semblance of sense.

Surely then he'd be able to sort through it, handle it, and ultimately walk away from it. From her. Rational in mind, body, and spirit.

Should have.

Instead it was what drove him, like the rutting beast he'd compared himself to just moments ago, to rip open the curtain, making her give a short scream of startled surprise. "Tag, Jesus! What's wrong?"

She was perfect. Shiny wet and perfect. And he'd never wanted anyone so badly. "What in the hell am I doing here, Maura?" he demanded roughly.

She tried to smile through her obvious disconcertment. "Giving me a dead chill?"

Heedless of the water going everywhere, of the fact that he was still in sweats and a T-shirt, he stepped into the narrow tub, grabbing her arms when she wobbled backward in surprise.

"Your clothes!" she sputtered. "What are you doing?"

"What I can't seem to stop doing, ever since I laid eyes on you." And he hauled her delicious, wet body up against his and took her mouth with his own. She clung to him, though he wasn't sure if it was for balance or because she needed him with the same unwavering intensity he seemed to need her. All he knew was that an instant into the kiss, she was returning it with all she had. And that was all that mattered.

Hot needles of water drilled the back of his head and neck as he continued to plunder her mouth. He slid his hands down the slippery curve of her spine and cupped her bottom with his palms, pulling her tight against him, groaning as she pressed into him. What he wouldn't give for a nice, hard, tile wall at the moment.

"Are you okay?" she murmured against his cheek when he finally broke the kiss. Both of them were breathing hard, both still clinging to the other.

"I've long since given up trying to figure out what 'okay' is," he said. He slid his hands up her arms, framed her face. "I thought I knew why I was coming here. I just wanted to finish things. Tie up the last loose end. Maybe get a few answers while I was at it. Only now . . ." He trailed off, not knowing how to finish.

She moved her hands over his shoulders, down the sodden T-shirt covering the front of his chest, until her palm was flat over his heart. "Only you have more questions than ye knew, right?" She trailed a damp finger along his lower lip. "It's to be expected, don't you think? You were parted from him for a long time."

"What makes you think the questions were about my father?"

She simply arched a brow. "Were they no'?"

He dipped his chin, rested his forehead on hers. "I'm not even sure of that much." He glanced up through wet, clumpy lashes. "I read his letters to you. They were written by a man I never knew."

She didn't frown, didn't chastise him for invading her privacy. Instead she stroked his face. "Puir man," she said softly. "I'm so sorry."

"For?"

"That the two of ye didna get the chance to make things right between ye."

"I'm not sure that was possible. Or, to be brutally honest, something I felt he deserved."

She held his gaze steadily. "That might be a fair thing to say. As I said, I'll make no excuses for him. I can only know what was said between us." She slid her hands into his hair. "But that doesn't make me less sorry. For the both of you." She leaned in, kissed him so gently it made his heart squeeze, painfully hard, inside his chest. "If it makes you feel any better," she whispered, "you've gone a good way toward shaking me up, too."

"I don't think I've ever been this confused."

"About?"

"Everything. You, this castle, my father, my past." His lips curved very slightly. "You."

She responded with a small smile of her own. "Aye, I ken that. I also think the water is finally running cold." She maneuvered an arm around him and shifted enough to shut the water off. "Grab me that towel, will you?"

He lifted a folded towel from the stack of shelves built into the wall over the commode. "Let me," he said, but she took it from him and, using him as leverage, stepped from the tub onto the mat.

"Peel out of those wet things," she instructed, wrapping the towel around her shivering body. She snagged another one and wrapped it around her head. "Here," she said, grabbing the last towel and handing it to him as he tossed his wet T-shirt and sweats into the sink.

He wrapped it around his waist as he stepped out. He tugged the towel from her hair. "Come here." He stepped between her and the small fogged oval mirror. "Turn around." He shifted her so her back was to him, then he began drying her hair, gently folding the curly mass inside the towel and squeezing the water out. She sighed as he continued working, and his body leapt in response. He managed, barely, to keep focused on the task at hand. "I'm sorry," he said, at length.

"For?" she said, her voice a little vague and drowsy.

"The letters. I only meant to compare contracts, but when I saw them . . ."

"It's okay," she said quietly. "I would have done the same thing if the situation had been reversed."

He leaned down, impulsively kissed the side of her neck. Her breath shuddered beneath his touch, and she moaned a little. He tossed the towel toward the sink, then ran his hands down her arms, shifting her weight back against him, so he could nuzzle her neck again. "I want to be clear-minded. Sure. Certain of what to do," he murmured against her damp, warm skin. "But it's impossible when I'm around you. Everything just becomes this blur of need and want and I can't separate out anything else. I can't seem to shove this aside, to deal with what needs to be dealt with first. I—" He tugged the towel from her, making her gasp as he let it drop to the floor. He held her arms to her side, kept her nestled back against him. "I can only think of this," he whispered, running his fingertips lightly up her arms, then skating them down along the front of her body, teasing her nipples into stiff buds, then trailing downward. He took her hips, snugged her back between his. "I'm like this all the time," he growled, knowing she could feel him pressing between her cheeks. "And when I'm not, I want to be." He slid his hands down her belly, let his fingers dip between her legs.

She shuddered then, moaned, but made no move to shift away from him, or move his hands away.

"Open for me, Maura. Maybe we just need to do this until the want goes away. Until clear thinking returns."

She let her head tip back and rest against his shoulder, her body jerking as he slid his fingers deeper between her thighs. "Clear thinking," she said hoarsely. "I'm no' sure it's possible for us." She parted her thighs just enough so he could slip a finger inside her. "Jesus," she said on a long groan. "I'm no' certain I want clear thought."

He ran his free hand up her body, toyed with her nipples as he slid his finger more deeply inside her, slid his thumb over that swollen, slick nub.

She moaned, pressing down on his fingers as he gently twisted one nipple then the other. Moans became groans, pleading sounds of a woman on the brink. He could feel her grow wetter as his own body throbbed to replace finger with cock. "Come for me," he whispered in her ear. He bit her earlobe, making her cry out, but not in pain. "I want to feel you come to my touch."

"Tag, I—"

He drove his finger deeper, let his thumb nestle just a bit higher, and simultaneously skimmed his palm lightly over her nipple.

She gasped, clenched tightly around his finger.

"Yes, that's it. For me, Maura." It was all he could do to stand upright. "Come for me."

She convulsed once, then pitched forward, gripping the sink with her hands. He bent over her, holding her back against him, the pad of his thumb still where she needed it most. But as she shook and shuddered against him, control abandoned him completely. He yanked his towel off and shifted her so she sank onto him. With one long, gliding thrust, he was inside her, his thumb still against her, his other arm around her waist, bracing her against him.

She made a low, growling noise as he withdrew, then slid home again.

"Yes," he groaned, fighting like mad to stave off the climax that was already upon him. But she was still convulsing, her muscles still in the throes of her orgasm. Any hope of slowing it down was beyond him. She was still braced against the porcelain sink. He shifted back and gripped her hips, plunging fully into her. Again. And again. Hips slapping against her as he repeatedly buried himself as fully as a man could. She pushed back against him, meeting him thrust for thrust, crying out each time he filled her.

Pulse thundering, heart pounding, he took her wildly. Hard, deep, and fast, no longer able to do anything but let his body take what it wanted. He came growling, teeth clenched, jaw tight. His fingertips sank into the soft flesh of her hips as he let it rush up and over him, swamping him, his growl turning to a choked shout as he poured himself into her.

Her knees buckled and he immediately pulled her weight back against him, stumbling backward himself. He slid out of her as his back hit the wall. He grabbed the towel rack for support, his arm still clinging around her waist. She turned into him, her arms going around him as she fell against him, her breath coming in hard, fast pants.

The realization hit him then. He hadn't used anything. No condom, nothing. "Fuck," he bit out.

"We most definitely did," she managed on a breathless gurgle of laughter. "And quite brilliantly, I might add."

Despite the shock of realizing what he'd just done, he barked out a short laugh himself. It was that very spontaneity in her that drew him in so easily, so swiftly. No matter what came at her, she didn't dodge it, she didn't take immediate offense, or demand explanations. She assumed the best, then parried with wit and panache. In his experience, that was a rare trait, man or woman.

Their bodies slick from the steam and the exertion, he nudged her back slightly, then tilted her chin up. "We didn't use protection," he said, straight out. She didn't dodge, so neither would he. "I—I'm—I—"

She laughed, then kissed him. Hard and fast. "You're a special man, Taggart Morgan, that's what you are." She smiled into his bemused expression. "Ye needn't worry I'll show up in the jungles of the Amazon a year from now with a wee bairn on my hip, okay? I'm on the pill."

"I wasn't worried for me," he said, realizing that he hadn't once thought about what it could have meant for him. Further rocked by the realization that he just might not have been all that upset about such an outcome. Not because he fancied himself a father. In fact, he'd never fancied himself being a parent. Ever. But the vision of Maura, her belly swelling with a child—his child—did things to that primal part of himself he was just coming to realize played such a strong part of his makeup. At least where she was concerned.

But mostly it was the thought that if he had made her pregnant, then she'd be forever connected to him.

"No," she said, her voice holding a note of wonder, "I don't believe you were." She slid from his arms, scooped up the towels and tossed one to him. "As I said, you're a special man, Taggart Morgan."

He caught the towel to his chest, watched her as she busily wrapped one about her, then closed the shower curtain and pushed the floor mat about with her foot to soak up the water from the floor. She seemed casual and relaxed, but he knew her well enough now, whether it was from instinct or observation, to know she was anything but.

There was something hanging in the air between them, and they both knew it, though neither was apparently in any hurry to confront it. Well, he could change that. "So, would you?" he asked.

"Would I what?" she asked, still busying herself with mop-up duty.

"Travel halfway around the world to tie up loose ends."

She glanced up, the corner of her mouth curving. "You consider an infant a 'loose end'?"

"Okay. Bad example."

She stopped, straightened. "You're asking if I'd do what you did?" She leaned against the sink. "Maybe. If I thought it was the only way to resolve things." She looked around the room. "This place is a pretty demanding master. I'm not as free to move about the globe as you are."

"You always handle all this alone?"

"You read my letters, you should know that."

He shook his head. "Not necessarily. You discuss in vague terms the ongoing work being done, but you don't talk much about yourself. About the burden you're under, anyway. I saw in your paperwork the reports you filed. I hadn't seen those before."

"Surely your father kept—"

"I'm sure he did. I looked over the paperwork in general, but I admit that wasn't what pulled me in." He held her gaze. "I never made it past your letters."

She didn't have an answer to that.

"Who you are shines through in the way you talk about the people here, the land, the goings-on in the village. I feel like I know half the people in Ballantrae. Gavin, Molly, your friend

Priss." There was a flash of . . . something across her face. "What? Have I gotten that wrong? I thought she was—"

"Was." Maura waved her hand. "Long story. Definitely not the moment to tell it."

"Hmm," he said, knowing he had no right to delve into any aspect of her personal life, despite the intimacy they'd shared. Sex, no matter how explosive and emotional, was just sex after all, at least until someone said or did something to make it more than that. Which, of course, neither of them could. "I'm sorry," he said at length.

She lifted a shoulder, but couldn't keep the disappointment from her eyes. "Me, too."

He pushed off the wall, reached out his hand. "Come on."

She shot him a dry smile, dimples winking out. "Sex is not the answer to everything, you know."

"A few days ago, I'd have agreed. But that wasn't my intent just now."

She took his hand. "Then what is?"

He pulled her close, then elicited a squeal of surprise when he bent and scooped her up in his arms.

"Tag—"

"Shh." Both their towels fell as he carried her back to the bedroom. He lowered her to the bed. "Climb in while I build the fire back up."

Watching him, she did as he asked without comment.

He could hear the rustle of the bed linens as he crouched in front of the fireplace, feel her gaze caressing him. *Isn't this a cozy little nest you've built for yourself here, Morgan.* The fire snapped as it burned brighter. A woman, warm and willing, tucked into bed, fire roaring against the cold of the winter night. He couldn't ask for much more now, could he?

He stood, turned, only to find her tossing back the covers, her pale skin burnished gold in the glow of the fire. "I've changed my mind," she said softly. Her gaze burned over him as he crossed the room toward her.

He'd never been so self-aware. Of his nakedness. Of how

it affected her. Of how badly he wanted it to affect her. Wondering if he could ever match in her the desire she stoked inside him. Because minutes ago, in the bathroom, he had only had thoughts of climbing in bed, pulling her close to him and burrowing under the covers for the night. Surely when the sun rose in the morning, they'd be able to sit across from one another like the lucid, rational adults that they were. But for now, for what was left of the night, he just wanted to forget everything else and feel her heart beat next to his as he drifted off to sleep, knowing she'd still be there, warm and his, when he awoke.

For now, that would be enough. More than enough.

Or it would have been, if she wasn't looking at him like she could eat him alive. And damn if his body wasn't stirring in response. "Changed your mind about what?" he asked, though he knew without a doubt exactly what she wanted. Just as he knew he wouldn't deny her. In fact, he wasn't all that certain he'd ever be able to deny her anything. Bewitched, that's what he was. She'd lured him to her tower and despite the fact that he'd done the taking, they both knew who the prisoner was here.

"I believe I was told earlier that if I were patient, I could have my turn." She patted the bed next to her. He hadn't known a woman with dimples could smile so wickedly. "My patience has run out. I want my turn. And, as it happens, I want it now."

His lips curved. His cock twitched. She noticed both. "Be gentle with me?"

She laughed. "Why? You weren't with me."

He climbed in the bed. If he ever were to find the strength to deny her, it was definitely not going to be right now. "True," he said, as she rolled him to his back and pinned his arms over his head. "Very true."

Chapter 18

Maura sat gingerly on the hardwood chair at her small, round kitchen table. *Day Four of living with Tag,* she thought, wincing a wee bit as she tried to find a comfortable position for sore muscles. She'd had athletic, energetic lovers before. But with them sex had been something of a sporting event, where she'd half expected to look up after finishing to find a row of people holding up scorecards.

It wasn't like that with Tag. By turns rough and demanding, then gentle and achingly tender. Hard and fast, slow and thoughtful. He was all those things and more. He'd wrung orgasms from her that could only be described as vicious, then turned around and played her body like a fine-tuned instrument, bringing her up and over the edge slowly, like a wave lapping at the shore. Relentless, timeless. She'd come growling and she'd come with a lump in her throat, barely able to contain the sob of emotion fighting to get out.

She had no idea how to categorize him. In her head or her heart. All she knew was that she had never been so well and thoroughly made love to by anyone. And rough or tender, somewhere during the past several days, they had crossed that indefinable boundary from sex to lovemaking.

He was inexhaustible, she thought, steeping her tea egg. A smile curved her lips. But where he was concerned, so, apparently, was she. Another storm had moved in two days ago, keeping them penned inside the castle. Most of that time had been spent in her tower, in her bed. She shifted again, this time in remembered pleasure, thinking of the ways he'd taken her, the times he'd taken her. Last night, yesterday afternoon, first thing in the morning. The night before that.

She sighed. A girl could get spoiled.

Which is why she had absolutely no cause to pout this morning. Yes, she'd woken up to find the sun finally shining and the other side of her bed empty, but it was just as well really. Because a girl could also get confused. And she was that, in spades. He'd swept into her life like that first snowstorm, and thoroughly staked his claim on her. Just like that. And she had no earthly idea how he'd managed it. Or what to do about it.

Since his arrival at Ballantrae, they'd spent hardly a moment apart. As much as she'd like to be outside wandering along the loch with him right now, showing him her favorite spots, she knew it was good to finally have some time alone with her thoughts. When he was near, she couldn't seem to think at all. About anything other than him, anyway.

She bobbed at her tea egg with her spoon, staring into the brew as the water swirled about, growing darker and darker. He'd left her a note. She smiled a little, remembering how she'd found it, tucked into the scrollwork of her wrought-iron headboard. His handwriting had been a neat and tidy slash of words. He'd wanted to assure her that he wasn't off snooping about the castle without her, so she didn't go off on a wild goose chase hunting him down.

She'd looked out from her balcony and hadn't spotted him, but a glance out the other side had shown his lorry still parked in the same spot. She'd had a moment's panic when she'd thought he might have gone wandering down to the village, and that gave her pause. She leaned back with a sigh, abandoning the tea she didn't want anyway. She'd hoped for a clearer head this morning, to go with the clearing skies. Or, perhaps, she'd hoped that he'd wake her up with more of what they'd been at all night. Leaving her to wonder how long she would have continued to let him preoccupy her like that.

She snorted. She *was* human.

She'd met her deadlines, e-mailed her article off, but that had been pretty much the extent of what she'd accomplished, outside of making love with Tag. She smiled again as she recalled his surprise when he'd woken the other morning to find her tucked into the chair in her bedroom, madly typing away on her little notebook computer. She'd reminded him that while this was a remote area, she was hardly as removed from civilization as he typically was, and that they had computers and mobile phones and fax machines and everything.

And he'd smiled and told her that he used a laptop, too, even in the jungle. Indiana Jones of the new millennium. His surprise, he explained, with that patient, so sexy glint in his eyes, was because of the handwritten letters she'd sent his father. He'd assumed she'd use the easier method of e-mail if it were available. And she'd explained that there was something more fulfilling in drafting a personal letter by hand. And that receiving a handwritten note, tangible evidence of the person who'd sent it, was always more cherished and personal than seeing words pop up on her computer screen.

And then she'd woken today to find that handwritten note from him. Her smile softened as she fingered the folded piece of paper she'd brought downstairs with her this morning. As if, finally parted, she still needed to keep a little, tangible piece of him within reach.

She tucked it in her shirt pocket, then propped her chin in her hands and stared through the narrow window, past the woods, to where the village lay beyond. She still wasn't sure how she felt about the idea of him traipsing down there. About letting him loose on the villagers.

Her villagers. Her tenants. Her whole life.

It was one thing to have him here, locked up in her tower like some kind of personal pleasure escapade, meant for her and her alone. Quite another to allow him access to the rest of her world. To impact other people with his presence here. And impact them he would. If only for the shaggy locks, tanned skin, and reptilian necklace. Like Crocodile Dundee had stuck out in the big city, Tag would stand out here in Ballantrae. And when they found out he was a Morgan? She blew out a long sigh and dipped her chin. Oh, he would create quite the stir, he would.

And later, when he was gone? That was where the panic had risen from, she realized. Because she'd never be able to just tuck him away then, in her own way, a private memory that was hers and hers alone. Her marauding jungle Scot. The Morgan who'd come to claim what was rightfully his, and had claimed her right along with it, before heading back out to do battle once again, far far away.

She shoved away from the table with a snort. "Apparently a few hours sleeping like the dead wasn't enough to set your foolish head to rights," she muttered, clearing away her tea. There was another cup, rinsed and sitting on the drain rack. It gave her pause, too, though she couldn't have said why. They'd shared tea together before, although admittedly it had usually been in bed.

It was more something about the casualness of it. And perhaps the separateness of it. That he'd padded about her kitchen, helping himself to what he needed, as if he belonged here in some way. Jory had done the same on the few occasions he'd spent the night. But she'd never picked up the cup to run her finger around the rim, thinking that his mouth had been pressed right there, then shuddered as she'd thought of other, far more intimate places he'd pressed those lips.

She tucked the mug in an overhead cupboard and shut the door on a sigh. "Jesus and Mary, you're like a schoolgirl with a hopeless crush." Only, given the carnal knowledge she had of him, it was a very, very adult crush, indeed. But the root of it was, Tag was imprinting himself on more than just her heart. He was becoming part of her life. And she was liking it. Far too much for her own good.

She headed to the stairs, intent on taking a shower and changing the bed linens. Again. "It's getting to be like a regular brothel here," she stated as she stamped up the stairs, unsure why exactly she was suddenly in such a stroppy mood, but there it was. "Hell, Maura, perhaps that's how you can save the place. Just hire on a few girls and give it a go." She strode into her bedroom and yanked the sheets from the bed.

Once the bed was stripped, she stomped into the bathroom, then had to force away the tightness in her throat on first glance at the sink. The sink she'd clung to as he'd plunged every hard inch he had and then some into her quite willing body. She caught her reflection in the mirror over the sink, found herself wishing it hadn't been fogged that night so she could have watched his face as he'd taken her.

Her cheeks flushed and she spun away. Christ, she couldn't even look at her bloody, goddamn sink again without thinking about him. She yanked the towels from the floor and the rack and tossed them on top of the linens in the bedroom. The whole of the castle was already indelibly imprinted with the man. She'd never get him out of her head.

She didn't even want to think about the lasting impact on her heart.

All the more reason not to share him with the rest of Ballantrae. Or Ballantrae with him, as the case may be. It was one thing to give in to the romantic folly that was their little escapade here, with silly thoughts of souls lost in another time, reunited once again. Quite another to invite him to expose her ridiculous little folly to the world. Her world, anyway.

She was balling up the linens when she heard the sound of a car engine. Not a truck engine. So it wasn't Tag rumbling off in his borrowed lorry. Which meant it was someone else come to pay a call. Well. She let her chin clunk down on her chest. *Too late to hide him now.*

"Bollocks," she muttered, kicking the linen pile to the side as she marched to the turret door and stepped out onto the battlement to see who'd come to visit. Maybe Tag would stay out on his hike and no one would be the wiser. She could make up some story about the banged-up lorry parked in the courtyard.

No one need ever know a Morgan had once again invaded Castle Ballantrae.

The cold wind snatched her breath away and she wrapped her arms tight around her waist as she stepped outside. She cast a quick glance toward the loch, but there was no immediate sign of a dark figure wandering along the edge. A rapping came at the door below and she leaned out and looked down. And swore. "Just what I don't need at the moment," she muttered as she stepped back inside and closed the turret door. *Isn't she content with the destruction she's already wrought?* Maura thought as she descended the stairs to open the outside door.

Sending up a little prayer for Tag to stay out of her line of sight, Maura flung the door open and confronted Priss.

"I come bearing peace offerings." Priss thrust a white bakery bag between them. "Cinnamon scones. Still warm." She lifted the thermos she carried in her other hand. "And Beanie's hot cocoa." She gave Maura her best sorrowful pout. Which, on Priss, was pretty damn effective. "I can't stand this any longer. Can we please talk things out?"

Maura's heart tugged and she realized how desperately she wanted to talk to her best friend about all that had happened to her since they'd last seen each other. Not that she had any intentions of doing so, but it didn't stop the longing. They'd been each other's sounding boards for so long, it was hard to imagine not sharing the startling turn her life had taken. But she wasn't ready to confide in anyone just yet. Not only because of Priss's betrayal. There were going to be trust issues between them, that was for certain, but that wasn't entirely the reason.

It was more of the same concerns she was having earlier, thinking about Tag going into the village. The moment she shared him, in any way, with anyone, things would change. She hadn't come to terms with the changes that had already taken place, much less invite more past her doorstep.

She looked behind Priss, doing a quick scan. She'd like to start down the path to putting things right with Priss, if that were possible. But right now was not the time for an extended visit.

Priss misunderstood the glance and quickly said, "I'm alone. I know you're mad at me and Jory. And I don't blame you. I—he doesn't know I'm here."

That brought Maura's attention back around. "You need his permission now? You say that like you're sneaking about."

Priss's cheeks colored slightly.

Maura rolled her eyes. "For Christ's sake, ye left him in your bed to come here?"

She firmed her shoulders, even as the glow remained bright in her cheeks. "We have to talk this out. Please, I need to explain. I wouldn't have done . . . what I did, if I'd been in my right mind. But when I'm around Jory . . ." She looked helplessly at Maura. "I can't explain what comes over me. I've never been like this before. You know that better than anyone. It's like there's some kind of connection between us. I took one look at him and it was like some kind of spiritual thing, like we were—" She broke off, swore to herself. "Christ Jesus, it sounds more ridiculous saying it out loud than it did thinking it in my head. And let me tell you, it sounded pretty far-fetched then."

Maura's hand tightened on the frame of the door. Any other time in her life, she'd have thought her friend had gone round the bend. Priss was the least spiritual woman she knew. But then, Maura's bottom wasn't exactly warming a pew every Sunday either. Still, they had morals, standards . . . and they were definitely two of the most pragmatic women she knew when it came to men. But she could hardly tell her old friend that she understood exactly what she was feeling, now could she? Not without explaining how it was she understood. She darted a glance over Priss's shoulder once more, but there was no sign of Tag anywhere.

Priss shivered and shifted her weight back and forth. "Please, Maura. Cocoa's getting cold. And so am I."

Maura sighed and stepped back. "Well, maybe you should have reconsidered stockings and a miniskirt in the dead of winter."

Priss scurried past her, pausing on the foyer rug to stamp the snow from her knee-high, black leather boots. "Aye, well, that's quite true, that it is, but—"

"Wait a minute." Maura closed the door then leaned back on it with a brief snort of disgust. "Isn't that the same outfit you were wearing when I booted you and Jory out of my bed—how many days ago has it been?"

Priss flushed beet red this time. "So, I havena been home as yet. But it's no' like I've been in them much since then." She waved a hand. "Yer thinking me a slut, but then ye already thought as much when ye caught me upstairs. And I can hardly make that right, now can I?"

For reasons beyond comprehension, Maura laughed. Something about Priss standing there, all defiant and fiery-eyed . . . wearing rumpled, five-day-old clothes. She couldn't help it. "Nay, ye hardly can." She pushed off the door, snagged the bag and thermos from Priss's hands and marched across the lounge to the kitchen. "God only knows if Jory put as much effort into a career as he does in bedding women, he'd have made his fortune ten times over by now."

"Och, ye don't know him at all, do ye?" Priss said, toeing her boots off and setting them on the kitchen hearth to warm.

Maura tossed her a wry look. "Oh, I'd say I know him pretty well."

Priss made a face. "Ha ha. I don't mean in *that* way. I

meant . . . when you were together, didn't the two of ye ever talk about your dreams? Your plans?"

Maura pulled out her chair, plopped down, then worked hard to conceal the wince that followed. "Yes, we talked. Of course we did."

Priss tugged out the other chair and curled her foot beneath her before sitting down. She poured the cocoa in the cups Maura had set on the table. "You forget, I'm the one you talked to after you talked to Jory. I don't seem to recall the two of you getting very deep into conversation."

Maura bit into the scone, allowed herself a sigh as the decadence of it melted on her tongue. "So you're telling me you spent the last five days in deep . . . conversation?"

Priss rolled her eyes at the innuendo. "Not all of it." Her cheeks pinked again. "But even Jory can only go at it for so long."

Maura snorted, bit into her scone again, unable to keep from thinking she hadn't found Tag's limit as yet. She shoved that out of her mind. It should bother her more, talking like this about a man they'd both bedded in less than a week's time. She could say the reason it didn't feel awkward was because she'd already moved on. But that wasn't it. Not entirely. Priss had hit closer to home than she knew with her comment about her knowledge of Jory.

Thinking back, when they had talked, it had mostly been about Ballantrae, about her worries and problems. Jory didn't talk about his own aspirations. But then, beyond working in his parents' pub, she hadn't thought he really had any. Of course, he'd hardly proven otherwise in action or deed, but still . . . it was difficult realizing just how shallow their connection had been. And that perhaps she'd been mostly at fault for that. She dipped her chin, poked a piece of scone into her cocoa. Given proof of her abominable ability to relate to men, that was hardly a heartening endorsement for what she was currently feeling for Tag. "It's not Jory," she said quietly, desperate to change the track of her thoughts. She glanced up at Priss. "That's not what needs fixing between us."

Now it was Priss's turn to lower her chin, stare into her cocoa. "I know," she said softly. "I don't even know where to begin." She looked up. "I value your friendship above all else. You know that. And I know I betrayed it on the most basic of levels. I—" She stopped, lifted a shoulder, then blew out a deep sigh. "I screwed up. Royally. I can't even say I didn't realize what I was doing. I knew it was wrong, what we were doing."

"And where," Maura said pointedly.

Priss's skin couldn't get any darker. "Yes," she said in a choked whisper, putting her scone down, pushing her cup away. "Yes."

"Was there some sort of thrill in it?" Maura asked, more seriously than she'd intended.

"No," Priss said immediately, then stopped. "I don't know." She swore. "I don't know what I was thinking. I *wasn't* thinking. Other than there he was, the man I'd been privately lusting after ever since, well, forever."

"Why didn't you tell me?"

"I did! Every time you talked about him, didn't I agree how hot he was? And how I completely understood your infatuation with him?"

"That's not exactly the same thing."

Priss lifted her hands in a gesture of helplessness. "What was I supposed to say? I wanted him first, please let him go?"

Maura opened her mouth, then shut it again when she realized Priss was right.

"It didn't give me the right to do what I did. Especially where I did it. But you were actually talking about him like you were serious, when I knew he was all wrong for you. Then opportunity stepped right up and I had to take what was probably going to be my only chance. You know?"

"So now you're telling me you slept with my boyfriend, in

my own bed, as a favor to me? To prove we weren't meant for each other?"

"Of course not, but the fact that he took advantage of the opportunity does prove my point. Kind of." She slumped back in her chair. "There's no defense for what I did, what we did, okay? And I don't know if this will make things better or worse between us, but I meant what I said. About it not being just sex. There is something special between Jory and me. And now that we've been together, it's only gotten stronger. Shockingly stronger."

Maura snorted. "Yeah, until the next 'opportunity' knocks."

"I suppose I deserved that, but I mean it, Maura, he's . . . I know you don't want to hear this, but he could be the one."

"Okay," she said. "But I wasn't talking about you. I meant Jory. If he screwed around on me, 'the one' or not, what makes you so sure he won't screw around on you?"

"He wouldn't," she said, and not defiantly. She said it as if, well, as if she simply knew. "I don't want to hurt you. But it's different between us, between Jory and me, than it was between the two of you." Priss fell silent, then picked up her cup and slowly stirred her cocoa, seemingly contemplating what she wanted to say. "Did you two ever talk about your future? Together, I mean? Not about Ballantrae, or your problems with keeping it from crumbling to dust, but about things like family and wanting to travel and dreaming of running your own shop. You know, life things?"

Now it was Maura's turn to fall silent. She'd thought of all those things, she'd even thought about the possibility of having them with Jory. But she'd never gotten around to actually discussing it with him. "He's just so easygoing. You kind of assume he'll just go with the flow." She hadn't realized she'd spoken out loud until Priss responded.

"I know. I think everyone assumes easygoing equals lazy. He's not lazy, Mo. It's just that his hopes don't match those of his family. And he hasn't found the heart to tell them otherwise. So he plods along working for his father, and no one thinks he has ambition, because his ambitions are else-where." Priss leaned forward, propping her elbows on the table, her eyes lighting up as she talked about him. "He wants to open his own film shop. Develop pictures, have a small gallery of framed prints for sale of local points of inter-est. Fantastic, isn't it?"

There was no way to hide her surprise except to duck her chin. Jory did like taking pictures, that much she knew. He'd even turned the guest room of his flat into a darkroom. But she'd thought it nothing more than a hobby. "I—I didn't know."

Priss didn't have to press that point, and mercifully, she didn't. It was painfully obvious to them both that what Maura thought she had with Jory wasn't remotely the kind of relationship that he and Priss had. Nor was it remotely the kind of relationship it needed to be, the platform to build something solid on. For that to happen, both parties had to actually communicate. Rather than one party doing all the plotting and planning, assuming the other party would just be swept along in her wake. She sighed, disgusted with her-self.

Had she done the same thing with Tag? Not that they had a relationship, really, but there she was, all starry-eyed and dreamy about this amazing connection they shared, and yet since the talks they'd had that first night here, any time they'd come close to a topic of importance since then, she'd backed away, shifted gears. To be fair, so had he.

But it wasn't like they'd spent their entire time together naked and going at it. They did talk, a lot, in fact. And they did share with each other, more than she had with anyone else. They talked about her writing, her desire to write a novel someday. He told her about digs he'd worked on, some of the historic finds he'd been part of. But they danced around the rest. Partly because once they'd confronted it, there would be nothing left to say afterward. Once things were resolved, he'd have no reason to stay. So, what point was there in forging a strong foundation if there was never going to be anything lasting built on it?

And yet, in her heart of hearts, didn't she know the foundation was already there? Just waiting for her to do something to make it permanent so they could keep building on it? And didn't the fact that he was stalling, too, mean he felt the very same thing?

She picked at her scone. But on the other hand, what the hell did she really know about it? Hadn't Priss just pointed out, complete with clearly defined examples, just how tragically inept she was at deciphering men and relationships?

"It's not that he doesn't have the backbone to stand up to them, you know," Priss was saying. "It's just that he doesn't want to hurt them. He's got a huge heart, Maura. Most people don't see that about him."

"Maybe because most women are sidetracked by his other huge . . . attribute," Maura muttered, her mind still on Tag.

To her surprise, Priss snickered. "You have to admit, the man is blessed."

Maura knew she shouldn't smile. There was something inherently wrong with two women sitting around a kitchen table discussing their carnal knowledge of the same man over cocoa and scones. But then she wasn't one to tout propriety, was she? "He is that," she agreed. She broke the remainder of her scone into little pieces as she thought about everything Priss had said. "So, you've talked about these things, your dreams and the like, you and Jory?"

Priss nodded as she took a sip.

"And you've only been together a few days," she murmured, more to herself than to Priss.

"It's been longer than that," she said, then lifted a palm when Maura shot her a shocked look. "Not the sex part. What I meant is, well, you've been dating him for a while. I see him in the village, and out with you. We've . . . chatted." She frowned. "Stop looking at me like that. I wasn't flirting with the man or anything. I was just being nice to him because you were going out with him. Only—" She broke off, then didn't finish.

"Only you developed your own crush on him in the meantime."

Priss lifted a shoulder, her gaze darting away. "I couldn't help it. It's just this inexplicable thing with us." She sighed, perhaps unknowingly. "I had no idea he was feeling the same thing. It's amazing really." Her tone was that of wonder and awe.

And Maura knew *exactly* how she felt.

Priss looked up, her expression earnest. "I'm not sorry we're together," she told Maura. "I can't give you that. But I will forever regret how it started. I didn't ever want you hurt." She reached across the table, putting her hand over Maura's wrist. "I know this probably doesn't make any sense to you, but you have to believe me. It was the wrong thing to do to you, but it's the rightest thing I've ever done for me. It was like I had no choice, it was my one and only chance. Maybe it's greedy of me, and I probably don't deserve it, but I honestly don't want to lose our friendship over this."

"I don't want to, either," Maura said, quite truthfully. She covered Priss's hand with her own. "And I do understand." She paused briefly, taking a courage-building breath. She was still torn over what she was about to share, but it had taken a great deal of courage for Priss to come here today and both apologize and try to explain the choices she'd made. It seemed only right that Maura come clean as well. Keeping more secrets was not the way to start things over.

Priss seemed sincerely remorseful for her actions, and beyond that, Maura could hardly hold the rest against her. Especially in light of what she'd been doing almost since the moment the door had hit them on the way out of her bedroom.

Besides, she was confused and troubled by her feelings for Tag, which had only been complicated further by the things Priss had made her think about. She needed outside perspective. And, surprisingly, it seemed that Priss might actually be the person to give it to her.

"I . . . uh, I have something of my own to tell you."

Priss's face split into a wide grin and she squeezed Maura's arm. Hard. "Then you're forgiving me?" She pushed out of her chair and leaned over the table, dragging Maura up as well as she pulled her into an awkward hug. The table wobbled dangerously as she clung to Maura's shoulders. "You won't regret giving me another chance," she whispered fiercely. "I swear it." Still beaming, she released her and plopped back down in her seat. "Now, what's this you have to tell me about?" She picked up her mug and cradled it in her hands, her eyes dancing with avid curiosity, mouth pursed in a ready smile.

As if nothing had changed. When, in fact, everything had. Only, at the moment, Maura couldn't help but look in her friend's so familiar face and feel like maybe, just maybe, it might have been a change for the better.

Only Priss could have pulled that off.

Maura couldn't help it, she laughed and shook her head as she eased back into her own seat. "I don't really know where to begin."

Priss's expression shifted to one of concern. "Is it about the loan? You had the meeting with Danders, right?" Her expression fell. "Oh, Maura, they turned you down, didn't they?" She swore. "And on top of what Jory and I did . . . Jesus, it's a—"

"It's not about the loan, though, yes, they did turn me down. I haven't gotten the leases to support it, but we both knew that was likely to be the case. Maybe come late spring, but even then it would take time to prove the tenants have an ongoing concern. You and I both know I haven't the finances to make it that long."

"I know you don't want to hear this," Priss said, "but I think you should contact Taggart's heirs."

"Actually, on my way back from meeting the land agent, I'd decided to do that very thing."

Priss smacked the table. "Well, good for you! When do you think you'll hear back?"

"I—I didn't write the letter."

"Maura," Priss began with a long-suffering sigh. "What's the worst that could happen? The bastards turn you down, right? But ye'll never know if you don't try, now will you?"

"I didn't change my mind. You see, I got stuck in a snow-storm on the way back. I hitched a ride into Calyth with a truck driver and stayed the night in a boardinghouse there."

Priss waved her hand. "What has this got to do with the letter?" Something must have shown on Maura's face, be-cause Priss's eyes grew round. "You didn't spend the night alone, did you?" She hooted and lifted her cup in a toast. "No wonder you were so quick to forgive me." She put the cup back down and pressed her palms on the table, leaning forward, curiosity blazing from her eyes. "So, tell me all about him!"

When Maura didn't immediately launch into the tale, Priss added, "Now you know I'm hardly going to say anything about your jumping in the sack with a stranger. I mean, first after what I did, it would be a bit of the pot and kettle. But any woman would understand why you took advantage." She gasped. "The old lorry in the courtyard! The Good Samaritan truck driver's, I presume?" Then her eyes grew rounder, if that were possible. "Oh Lord, he's here then, isn't he?" She swung her gaze toward the stairs leading up to the bedroom. "Bollocks!" She looked back to Maura. "I've gone and interrupted something, haven't I? Jesus, Mo, why didn't you send me on my way?"

"It wasn't the truck driver," she said, then sighed, wonder-ing if this had been such a wise idea after all. But, in a way, it felt good to tell someone about it. "I wasn't the only one who got stuck atop Ben Avel, Priss. My truck was all but hanging from the edge of the road, and another driver came along and swerved to miss it. Unfortunately, he half buried his rental car in the doing."

Priss leaned back, her expression considering now. "Hmm, the two of you, stuck in a storm, then. I supposed you decided to ride it out in his car." She snorted then. "And I'm guessing that's an appropriate phrase in more ways than one, then, aye?"

Maura felt her cheeks heat. It sounded so . . . bawdy when Priss recounted it. And, well, it had been quite bawdy. Deliciously so, as she recalled. "So maybe I did enjoy the idea of a little adventure," she said.

"Spill it, tell me about him. You said rental car. Is he just a visitor then? No' a Scot?"

"He's Scot by descent, but no, he's here from America." She smiled. "By way of the Yucatan rain forest."

Priss had already opened her mouth to retort, but that shut it right back up. "Did you say rain forest?"

Maura nodded. It was a shame really. She wished she could simply share the details of what happened in the backseat of that car. And in the stairwell at the inn, and up against the bedroom wall. She shifted a bit on her seat, just thinking on it herself. That alone would make the story legend. Had it ended that night, in Calyth, it would have remained just that. A wild tale about the sort of erotic interlude most women could only fantasize about. But it hadn't ended there. It hadn't ended still.

"There's more to it than ye know," Maura told her.

"Well, I should hope so. Ye brought him home with you, so I'm guessing it was one hell of a night in that inn." She grinned. "You havena even told me the good parts yet. Come on, details."

"I didn't bring him home from the inn. In fact, I left him there, sleeping."

"So, what, he tracked you down?" Priss smiled. "Why that's rather romantic, isn't it?" She leaned forward again. "Come on now, tell me the whole of it."

"He didn't track me down, per se. We met up again by coincidence."

"Coincidence? Calyth is a good hour from here. What were the chances? Did you bump into each other in the village then?"

Maura shook her head, then she closed her eyes and let out a deep sigh. When she opened them again, Priss was frowning at her.

"What's going on here, Maura?" she asked, still curious, but far more serious. She lowered her voice. "Won't he leave then? Is that it?" She drew in a short breath. "Are ye in trouble?" she whispered. "Is that why ye asked me in? Is that why—"

Maura lifted her hand, cutting off her friend's rapidly escalating imagination. "No, no, it's nothing like that. He's here because . . . well, because he belongs here. In a manner of speaking."

Priss rolled her eyes. "You are the most confounding woman, I swear it, Maura Sinclair. For Christ's sake, will you just spill the story? Who is he? Why did he come here?"

"He came to Scotland for Ballantrae. And, in a way, for me. Only I didn't know that at the time we—at the time we were—" She broke off, having no idea how to explain it so it would make any sense at all.

"You say he came here for you, and yet you just said he didn't come tracking you down. You're talking in circles."

"I know, I know. It's . . . complicated. You see, we didn't confide our names to each other that night. We'd kept it as some sort of, I don't know, anonymous moment out of time. We both had our reasons, as it turned out. I didn't know what his were until he showed up here. When I first saw him, I thought he'd tracked me down, too. As it turns out, he was tracking down Ballantrae, and me. Only he didn't know I was Maura Sinclair." She looked at Priss directly, and just blurted it out. "And I didn't know he was Taggart's oldest son."

Priss looked like she was going to pop a vein. She slammed

her palms on the table. "Taggart's *son?* Taggart Morgan's *son* is here?"

Maura could only nod.

"Ye mean the very bastard who couldn't be bothered to show up by his own father's deathbed?"

"Aye," came a deep voice from the door leading to the underground tunnel stairs.

Maura and Priss both whipped their heads around. Tag filled the doorway. In his arms were a stack of dusty, oversized leather-bound books. The heft of them made the muscles in his arms bulge, and showed off the breadth and width of his shoulders. He wore jeans and an old sweater, with her thick, ragwool scarf wrapped around his neck, but she almost didn't recognize him otherwise. He'd bound his hair back tight, which set off the stark planes of his face and the sculpted lines of his mouth so differently than when his mop of hair was springing wildly about his face. The cold winds off the loch had pinked even his deeply tanned face, making the white of his teeth an even stronger contrast when he bared them.

"That very bastard would be me." He stepped inside and closed the stairwell door behind him.

Chapter 19

What had begun as an outdoor exploration, had ended as an indoor scavenger hunt this morning, and Tag piled the stack of books he'd brought up with him on the table beside the door. He'd been surprised—and disappointed—to hear voices as he'd climbed the stairs from the tunnels. He'd made some pretty big decisions since leaving their bed this morning and he was chomping at the bit to share them with her.

He'd done a lot of thinking about . . . well, everything. And during his walk along the lake he'd decided it was time to stop running. Leaving his father out of it, and even Maura, as much as he could anyway, the bottom line was that he was still interested in being here. For himself. He wanted to know more. About his history, his ancestors. And, because she was part of the decision, too, about Maura Sinclair.

They would finally talk about Ballantrae today, and his claim to it. He'd known for some time now that he wouldn't—couldn't—abandon her to the burden this place had put on her. They hadn't spoken much of it, but she'd taken him around inside and anyone could see what she was up against. He'd signed the papers this morning, continuing the payments. All he had to do now was place a call to Rogues Hollow and see that the money, including the back payments as well, were issued.

He had to talk to Jace, too, but he knew Jace wouldn't blink over his decision to funnel some of the trust to Ballantrae. They would work that out some way. He'd make sure of it. Harder would be explaining why he was doing it, but he'd muddle through that, too.

And that hadn't been the most momentous decision made this day. No, that one had been forming over the past several days. Beginning with his nosing about the bookshelves in her tower the past day or two, while she tapped away on her laptop, and ending with him stumbling across a crumbling text that referenced the Pictish religious relics that had once existed here at Ballantrae. Complete with ancient, hand-drawn maps pointing to the revered rowan oak and standing stones they'd once worshipped.

He'd intended to talk to her about it, find out what else she might know of it, but they'd sort of gotten sidetracked. For about thirty-six hours. This morning when he'd gotten up, the sun was just rising and the sky had cleared. He'd set out to walk the loch, do some thinking, make sure he was wanting to do the right things for the right reasons.

On his way out, he'd grabbed the legal pad on which he'd sketched his own copies of the maps. And, once he'd realized he was at peace with his decision to stay here, to pursue his interest in his past . . . and his interest in Maura, he'd left the loch and set off toward the forests to see if he could find the stones. Even then he hadn't had a plan in mind much beyond fulfilling his curiosity. Only what he'd discovered that morning had turned out to do far more than that.

The thrill of discovery had taken over him then, eventually driving him back inside, but into the main house this time. He'd already been through all the books in her tower, so he was hoping that somewhere in the miles of bookshelves lining every hallway and crooked staircase, he'd find further documentation of some kind.

The kind of documentation he would need if he was going to get funding for a dig.

It had taken a couple of hours, focused determination, and a good lantern, but finally he'd hit pay dirt. Excited, nervous, and completely unsure how to approach her with this or what her reaction would be when he told her his plans, he'd been unable to wait another minute to find out. He'd grabbed what he'd found and headed down into the tunnels, his brain racing even further ahead as he tried to find the words he was going to use to explain to her what he wanted to do. And why it was so important for him to do it. With her by his side.

In all of the variety of scenarios he'd expected to encounter, none of them had included her not being alone when he finally got to her.

He unwound the scarf he'd borrowed, having enjoyed the scent of her tickling his chin and lips as he'd wandered about. He'd thought to take it off when he'd come inside, but he'd quickly learned that without fires going, the temperature inside of the castle was pretty much the same as outside, just sans the everblowing wind. That part was going to take some getting used to.

"Tag," Maura said, coming around the table to take the scarf from him. "This is my friend, Priss. I'm sorry, she didn't mean—"

Priss shoved back her chair. "I can speak for myself," she said, proving the point when she turned to face him and added, "And I did mean it. I just didn't mean for you to overhear it."

"Fair enough," Tag said. Of course he knew who Priss was from Maura's letters. But he hadn't known what she looked like. Somehow, given the larger-than-life picture Maura had painted of her, he'd been expecting someone more . . . imposing. As it turned out, she was petite, with dark hair, fair skin, and the kind of cute, turned-up nose that probably made men trip over themselves to open doors and throw coats over puddles. At the moment, he wasn't feeling so inclined.

He skimmed his gaze over her interesting choice of outfit, which did fit his mental image of her to a tee, then allowed his lips to curve slightly as he met her gaze once again. "I suppose I could make a similarly uninformed observation about you, but I'll refrain until you're out of earshot."

To his surprise, she merely arched a brow and sent Maura a reassessing glance. "Well, well, you've finally managed to land one with a bit of an attitude, haven't you?" But before Maura could respond, Priss's mouth dropped open. "My God." She took an inadvertent step closer, her eyes narrowing as she peered at his neck. "What are those—are those . . . *teeth?*" Her eyes darted from Tag to Maura, back to Tag. "When you said he arrived via the jungle, I thought you were joking. You never said anything about the man being a barbarian."

"No, I didn't," Maura said, shooting him a smile from her position behind Priss's back. A smile that contained a wealth of private meaning, shared only between them. "Because I'd never joke about something like that."

It was interesting, he thought, that in the face of being confronted by the two women, who'd known each other far longer and far better than he did either one, that he didn't feel like the odd man out. In fact, it was just further proof of this sense he had, that their connection ran deeper than logic could possibly define. "Yes," he responded, holding Maura's gaze a moment longer before shifting his attention back to Priss. "They are teeth. Maura can fill you in on the whole sordid tale. I didn't mean to interrupt. I can just, ah, make myself scarce."

It was killing him that he couldn't tell her everything right this very minute. Once decided on the course of action, he was chomping at the bit to put it in motion. But maybe it was for the best. He could head upstairs for a nice, long shower, to steam the chill from his bones. Maybe look over the books he'd brought with him, and formalize exactly how to approach Maura after Priss took her leave.

And he started to do just that, but stopped, suddenly unsure if traipsing up to Maura's bedroom in front of her friend was an appropriate thing to do. It was a bit surprising, he supposed, how at home he'd come to feel here, in her tower. And though it was cold and damp, he did have to admit her bed was wonderfully soft and big . . . and he didn't miss the mosquito netting and privacy of his hammock quite as much as he'd thought he would.

"What have you got there?" Maura asked, motioning to the stack of books. "Some light reading material?"

If only she knew. "A bit more than that," he told her. "If you don't mind, maybe I'll poke around the west wing a bit." He hadn't made it that far earlier, as the only way presently available to access it was from Maura's tower.

Priss frowned. "You can't," she answered for Maura. "It's not open." She looked from him to Maura. "Doesn't he know anything about this place?" She sent him an arched look. "Or couldn't you be bothered to do that either?"

"Priss, please."

Tag waved her off. "No, that's okay. She's just being a protective friend." And despite her prickly attitude, he liked knowing Maura had her staunch supporters. God knows, faced with the obstacles she confronted every day here, she needed all of them she could get.

"Yes, well, Priss likes to make a habit of saving me from my apparent poor taste in men," Maura said dryly.

Priss's mouth dropped open with a gasp of indignation, but surprisingly she didn't retort in kind. Instead she surprised Tag by smiling impishly. "True, true, but I'm rather full up this week, darling, if you know what I mean. So you're on your own with this one."

Maura spluttered a short laugh, then shook her head. "God, and to think I forgave you. And so easily, too. You're incorrigible."

"I know, it's one of the reasons you keep me around." She stepped over to Maura and gave her a tight hug. "And thank God you do," she said, with surprising emotion.

Surprising to Tag, anyway. Maura hugged her back just as

fiercely. Making him wonder what Maura had had to forgive her friend for.

"We'll talk more later, okay?" Maura said.

Priss shot a look at Tag, then smiled at Maura. "Oh, you'd best believe we will." She gathered her things and turned to Tag. "I don't know what you're up to, but be warned. She may be smart and funny and great in bed—" She tossed a grin to Maura. "It's hell coming after you, you have no idea," she added, then shot her attention back to a now completely nonplussed Tag. "But you cross her and you cross me. And half the damn village. You have no idea what you're up against. There isn't a jungle far enough away that will save you from a band of Scots intent on righting a wrong."

Now it was Tag's turn to surprise Priss by smiling and extending his hand. "You know, I believe it's more of a pleasure meeting you than I initially thought. As for the villagers, I'll take my chances. But with Maura, you have my word I will always tread with the greatest of care."

Priss paused then, and gave a considering look. "I believe you mean that." She shook his hand, then turned it over front and back, before glancing back to Maura with a wicked grin. "I believe he passes another test, as well."

Maura's eyes widened and her cheeks grew pink. "Well. Thank you so much for your input." Her gaze shot to Tag, who was grinning now, and, as always, that instant *wham!* thing happened. Where the rest of the world sort of fell away, leaving the two of them gazing at one another, thoughts and needs being communicated with one wordless glance.

"Well, well," Priss commented. "I suppose, I'll leave ye to having at each other, then. Which, from the looks of things," she went on, though neither of them so much as blinked in her direction, "I can see is going to happen whether I leave or no'." She grabbed her purse. "And though you've watched me, I believe I'll pass on the return engagement."

That got his attention. Tag lifted a brow, dragging his gaze to Priss, then back to Maura.

"Oh thanks, Priss," Maura said with a sigh.

Priss grinned and sketched a brief curtsy before heading to the door. "Don't thank me. Pleasure's all mine."

Maura followed her to the door, her dry smile surfacing finally. "Oh, I wouldn't bet on that."

Priss's laughter trailed behind her as she sailed out. After she was gone, Maura closed the door, then leaned back against it and turned her attention to Tag. "She takes some getting used to."

Tag's mouth curved slightly. "The same has been said of me on more than one occasion."

"I'm sorry if she offended you."

"Don't be." Unable to wait another second, he crossed the room and took her in his arms. His mouth found hers for a slow kiss. He never got tired of how well they fit together.

"Are you hungry?" she asked, sighing as he trailed kisses along her chin, to her neck. "Priss brought scones."

"It's not scones I have a hunger for." He continued his assault on the soft curve of her shoulder.

"No?" she said, dropping her head back on a sigh and allowing him full access.

"But first I was thinking maybe a nice hot shower would steam the chill out of my bones. I'm afraid I've adapted too well to life on the equator."

"Yes, I can see you're terribly distressed by the weather." She moaned softly as his hands slid down her back and cupped her to him.

"Terribly," he murmured, shifting her away from the door and backwalking her toward the stairs leading up to her bedroom. "In fact, I should probably have help in the shower."

"Should you?"

"Just to make sure there are no aftereffects from prolonged exposure to the elements."

She laughed. "Oh, you've been exposed all right, but I don't believe the elements affecting you were out there about the loch."

"You have no idea," he said, grinning and scooping her up against him when her heels banged into the first riser. "There were some sheep giving me a few sideways looks out there. I could have nightmares."

"Well, it is cold and they have been awfully lonely," she said earnestly, earning a bark of laughter from him.

To think he'd once thought he was the one doing the catching. Christ, but he was hopelessly ensnared. He'd rushed here earlier, all wound up with excitement over his discovery, dying to share his plans with her. But now they were finally alone, and she was in his arms again. And suddenly there was no rush to do anything but just savor the absolute pleasure it gave him to hold her like this. Nothing seemed so important as making her sigh, making her laugh, making her want him the way he wanted her.

Would it always be like this? he wondered. And when she chose that moment to pull his mouth to hers and kiss him, so softly, so perfectly, that last edgy, unsettled, disconnected part of him finally clicked into place. Because now he'd have all the time in the world to find out, wouldn't he? Here he'd raced to share with her his excitement over his latest adventure, only now he realized he'd already embarked on the grandest adventure of them all.

"I see they lent you some reading material from their extensive library," she commented, nodding over his shoulder at the stack of books.

Filled with a whole new kind of energy and excitement, he set her down on the second step and pressed his lips against the advantageous opening provided by the vee in the front of her shirt. He didn't want to talk about the books now. Or the dig. Or financial arrangements. Or his ancestry, castle restoration, or whether it was this blasted cold all year round. There would be plenty of time for all that. All the time they needed. And where she was concerned, he had a deep, unending well of need.

"Actually," he murmured, nudging aside her shirt so he

could kiss the freckles dotting the swell of her breasts, "they wouldn't part with so much as a pamphlet." To think he could chart every freckle on her body. Every day. For the rest of his life. He was truly a very lucky man. "I came in through the main house. I hope you don't mind, but I pilfered a few to look through later." He started opening the row of buttons. "At the moment I'm hopelessly sidetracked by something else entirely."

She gasped when his cold hands circled the warm, bare skin at her waist. "I'm sensing a pattern developing here."

He lifted her up to the next riser, so he could lean in and kiss the spot right above her navel. "Is this a problem?"

"I—I'm sure it will be. At some point." She was sounding distracted. He intended to keep her that way. For at least the next hour or so. "I have work to do," she managed to choke out, as he tugged the knot free on her sweats. "A proposal. And some paperwork that needs filling out." She sucked in her breath as he nudged the front of her sweatpants down, exposing the elastic band of her panties. "Tenants' calls to return. Oh!"

He'd tugged the skinny band of elastic down with his teeth, as he braced her hips with his palms, then slowly began sliding down both her panties and sweats. "Could you make those calls after our shower?" he murmured as he drew his mouth lower, then lower still.

One hand flailed out for the stair railing, while the other grabbed the top of his head. "It's possible I could—dear God," she said, her knees buckling as his tongue found her. "See—see my way clear to—Jesus." Her nails raked his scalp as she clutched at him for support. Whatever else she'd been about to say was lost on a long moan of pleasure.

He was already so hard he ached, but he'd noticed how carefully she'd stood up earlier, when he'd first come in the room. She was sore. Hell, so was he. But at the moment, that didn't seem to matter. Not that he intended to do anything to her that would make it worse. Giving her pleasure was too intensely satisfying to him. But there were ways to please and soothe. In fact, that deep tub in her bathroom would be a nice place to start.

But first things first. Gently, softly, with a tenderness he'd only ever possessed with her, he used his tongue, his lips, and brought her slowly up. He wrapped an arm around her thighs for support, and sunk his tongue deeper, flicked softly, then on a long, slow groan of satisfaction—both his and hers—he took her over. She was still shuddering when he straightened and scooped her up into his arms.

She was limp and soft against him, her arms immediately coming up to circle his neck as she buried her face in his chest. "How is it you do that to me?"

He slowly climbed the stairs, brushing his lips across the top of her head, fighting the ache of his own raging hard-on as her hips brushed repeatedly against it. Fighting against the need to tell her everything he was feeling, afraid he'd overwhelm her if he did. "I could ask the same thing," he said quietly.

He pushed the door to the bedroom open with his foot, and carried her directly into the bathroom before letting her slide to her feet. She stayed in the circle of his arms, pressed up against him in a way that left no doubt about his current state of arousal. "I'm thinking bath instead of shower," he told her. "Scrub my back?"

She slid her hand down his chest, then made him both jerk and groan as she cupped him in her hand. "Are you sure it's your back that needs attention?"

"You're sore," he said.

"But—"

"Run the bathwater. If you've got anything soft and scented to dump in with it, that would be fine, too." He tugged her hand away, put it back up on his shoulder. "I just want to lay in the warm water and soak, with you leaning back against me." He brushed his lips against hers. "Just for a little while."

"Sounds like a very nice way to spend the morning."

"That was my thought," he said, then kissed her again, deeply, slowly, until they both sighed. "I'll even fix lunch later, while you work. Although I have to warn you, my cooking skills are best described as rustic."

"I'm okay with rustic," she said, her dimples winking as she smiled at him.

Yes, a man could get used to this. To bartering a bath for lunch, seducing her away from her work, or anything else if it would make her smile at him like that.

"Only I don't have anything in my kitchen at the moment. I have to make a run into the village to—damn," she said, breaking off, frowning all of a sudden.

"What?"

"The village. I didn't say anything to Priss about not talking about you, so she's probably down at the Fox and Pheasant right now blabbing all about you."

Now Tag was frowning. He wasn't sure he felt anything one way or the other about being fodder for village gossip. They'd get to know him eventually. But it was clear that Maura did. "Is it because you have a man staying with you, or because the man happens to be a Morgan that's the problem?"

She looked at him then. "Neither, it's—" She broke off, chewed on the corner of her lip. "We're progressive enough that a single woman entertaining a man is hardly going to raise eyebrows. That you're a Morgan might, but even that I don't so much mind. It was just—" She stopped again, sighed, then shook her head.

He tipped her chin up. "What?"

She looked at him, then with a little eye roll, said, "This is going to sound silly, but . . . well, I guess I just don't want to share you. This. I'm still sorting it all out and I don't really want any input from anyone else."

"You told Priss."

"Yes, but I had to. You see, she—God, but that's another long story."

His lips quirked. "Yes, so I gathered."

She gave him a little nudge in the ribs. "It wasn't so sordid as all that. It's no' like I planned on watching. I walked in on her in bed with another man." She chewed on her lip again, then swore under her breath. "Okay, I may as well just tell you the rest. The bed they were in was mine."

Tag's eyebrows lifted. He didn't know which question to ask first.

"Remember the night we met, and I told you I'd had a really bad day?" she said.

"That was the day you found them?"

She nodded, but looked away again.

"There's more?" She nodded again and he had to nudge her chin back again. "Just tell me. It can't be as bad as all that."

She touched his cheek. "It's just that, I don't want to ruin . . . anything."

He smiled. "You've intrigued me, no doubt. But honestly, I can't imagine anything you could say that would—"

"The man she was in bed with was the guy I'd been dating for the past six months," she blurted out in one breath. "That's what she was apologizing for today. I—" She broke off, shook her head.

The news did take him aback. More than a little. Inappropriate though it may be, somewhere along the line he'd come to feel proprietary where she was concerned. He didn't want to think about her with anyone else. In the past, or in the future. Then the rest of it hit him. The night in the car in the storm. The same day as—

"I know what you're thinking and yes, that was likely why I was so forward with you. Initially, anyway."

He reeled the rest through his mind, but while it didn't make him feel wonderful to know she'd had someone else in her bed so recently, she'd done nothing he could truly fault her for. But there was one thing he did have to know. "Do you love him?"

"Once upon a time I wanted to think so. But no. I realized that day I was in love with being in love, with being in a relationship. But I wasn't in love with Jory." Now she cupped his cheek, turned his gaze back to hers. "I know this doesn't say a lot about me, but honestly, I don't just jump from one man to the next."

"It's okay, you don't have to say anything. You're an adult, free to do what you want. With whom you want."

She continued to look into his eyes. "Priss told me some things today that made me realize I haven't been all that open with people. That I've never really opened myself up to anyone in a relationship. She and Jory have been together less than a week and she already knows more about him than I knew in six months. For that matter, in all the years we've both lived in Ballantrae."

She brushed her fingers across his cheekbones, along the side of his face. "You know, I wouldn't have believed it was possible to form that kind of connection with anyone in so short a time. Or in any amount of time. But maybe it just takes meeting that right person. Then you don't have to think about whether to be open, you just are. Because you can't be anything else." She let out a short laugh. "Of course now you're going to think I don't know my own mind, and God knows I've thought that about myself a lot lately, but I need you to believe me that with you it *is* different. *I'm* different. Entirely different."

I know, he thought, thinking how he was not the same man when he was with her, *once in a lifetime different.*

"And maybe I'm making a bigger fool of myself by assuming this matters to you at all, but—"

He stopped her with a kiss. "It matters to me," he told her intently when he lifted his head, then kissed her again. "It matters."

She looked into his eyes, searching. "Tag, I—"

"What matters to me now is that it's over. It *is* over for you, isn't it?"

She nodded so solemnly, but that didn't stop her lips from quirking ever so slightly. "I think you can safely say that, yes. Even before you and I met, it was definitely over." She held his gaze. "If it hadn't been, if my heart had truly been engaged, I could have never done . . . well, what we did. Have been doing ever since." Her dry smile faded. "I think that was the hardest part. Realizing just how little I did feel. I was more hurt by Priss's betrayal than I was by Jory's."

He wanted to ask her how she felt now, about him, about what was developing between them. If it would be as easy for her to put this aside as it was for her to put her last relationship aside. From what she'd said, and that she was so worried about how he'd take this news, made him believe otherwise.

"I wish the timing had been different," she told him. "But you don't get to choose when you meet someone. And had I the chance to go back, I wouldn't change anything I did that night." She brushed his cheek. "I just hope this doesn't change things between us now."

"It's okay," he told her, turning his head so he could kiss her fingertips. "We're okay."

And for a man who'd spent his life thinking in terms of "I" and "me," it surprised him to discover that thinking in terms of "we" and "us" wasn't as difficult an adjustment as he'd have thought it would be. Perhaps she was right. Maybe you just had to meet the right person.

"Thank God," she said, looking so relieved it made him feel even better. "I wasn't prepared for this. I don't mean Priss's visit, or telling you what happened." She looked at him, a true smile edging out now. "I wasn't prepared for you. And what I said before, about the village, about you meeting everyone, that wasn't because I don't want you to know them or vice versa. It was just me being selfish. I'm still getting used to . . . all of this. To us. It's a small village and they'll talk about you, about us, for years. I—"

He quieted her again, this time with a long, deep kiss, until she relaxed against him and kissed him back. They were okay. More than okay. Then he pulled her into his arms, tucked her against his chest, and let out a long sigh of his own. "You're not the only one who's feeling selfish."

She wove her arms around his waist, and once again he was struck by how just the feel of her against him soothed something inside of him. Everything else ceased to matter, and it was so much easier to believe things would all work out, when they just held on to each other.

He debated for a moment on whether to try and put how he was feeling into words. But if not now, then when? "I've never felt any particular connection to my past," he began. "Not in the intimate, personal way you do. And yet . . . I can't help but feel I have a very particular connection to you. One that feels like it goes beyond the short time we've been together." He pressed a kiss against her hair. "Does that sound crazy to you?"

She lifted her head. "No," she said, the word barely more than a whisper. "Not at all."

Now it was his turn to sigh in relief. He should have known she'd understand. "In rational terms," he went on, "this all seems very fast and overwhelming. But then I think about it and I don't see how it could have been any other way between us. What you do to me, what you make me feel, simply . . . is." He cupped her cheek, wove his fingers into her hair. His heart was pounding and his knees felt all funny. But he'd come this far, so he came out with the rest. "And I don't want to walk away from that. I don't want to walk away from you."

Chapter 20

Maura's heart was pounding so hard she was certain she hadn't heard him right. But the way he was looking at her, the way he was touching her . . . Surely he didn't mean— "I don't want you to walk away, either," she said, returning his honesty. "But—"

"I signed the papers," he said quietly. "I'll need to make a call to get the ball rolling, but you'll have your funding. Including what's owed you since my father died."

It was what she wanted, hoped for, lost sleep over, and worried about for months on end. And she was undeniably thrilled to finally have it done with, and in her favor. The relief that flooded her was so strong it left her week in the knees.

But it was no longer all that she wanted. The moment he'd put it out there, that there was even a remote possibility that he wasn't going to leave soon, her heart had taken wing. Maybe it was greedy, maybe it was selfish, but dammit, didn't she deserve to want something just for herself? Not for Ballantrae, not for the good of the clan . . . just for the good of her heart. And her soul.

And she was terrified that she'd misunderstood him, that she'd let hope fly too soon. "How—how long—" She stopped herself. Maybe she shouldn't ask. Maybe it was better to take it as they had been, one day at a time. One amazing day at a time.

He smiled then. "As long as you'll have me."

And there was no quashing the joy, or the hope. Her face split in a wide smile and she tightened her hold on him, partly to assure herself she wasn't imagining this entire conversation. "I don't understand. You have a dig, in Mexico. You said you only had a week—"

"Until they replace me. And they will. Felix has a good crew. That's another call I have to make."

"So, what will you do?" That had probably come out sounding wrong, but he wasn't the sort to just bum about. And the look in his eyes told her there was more to this. Much more. He had the look of a man with a purpose.

"I want to learn more about my own ancestry." He stroked her hair, held her gaze. "I was sort of hoping you could help me with that."

"You know I will. I would love to. Are you . . . are you sure? I mean, after everything with your father—"

He nodded. "It's taken me a while to get to where I can set all that aside and get down to the root of what I want. Maybe what I've always wanted, but was too blinded by my anger toward my father to see clearly. I started my studies here because I had an honest interest in the history of this land. Remember I told you about my high school teachers? They were responsible for turning me on to the Druids, the Picts, the Celts and the Gaels. And that interest, that curiosity to know more, has nothing to do with Morgans or Sinclairs, or Rogues Hollow, or my father. My interest in that is all my own. It's a culture and society we know so little about, with such opposing theories, that I was fascinated by the potential for discovery. I still am."

She had only to look in his eyes, to know the absolute truth of what he was saying. It was as if those eyes were lit with an inner purpose. When he spoke about discovery and possibilities, it made her own blood thrum. And to think she was going to be part of this with him, brought an excitement and anticipation to life inside her that was impossible to deny.

"I let my interests get all tangled up in my personal past, my own ancestry, my father's warped sense of right and wrong," he told her. "And by the time I got to that first dig in Wales, I wasn't sure if I was there because I wanted to be, for my own fulfillment, or because I was trying to prove something to my father. Or, worse, seeking his approval."

"And now?"

He smiled. "Now I have no doubt what I want to pursue." He tugged her closer. "Professionally. And personally."

Her body tightened, she wanted badly to just take the leap of faith he had. The very idea of just reaching out and taking what she wanted was as exhilarating as it was terrifying. "You're certain of this? It's so . . . sudden."

"Maybe. I don't know. It feels like it's taken me forever to finally figure this out." He stroked her cheek, pushed her hair from her face. "I know my father's death caused you sadness," he told her solemnly. "And, I suppose, I'm even a bit sorry that I didn't know the man that you did. But it took his death to shake me up, to make me step back enough to examine the choices I've made, why I made them. And I realize that, despite being happy with my work, I've been basically hiding out all these years." He kissed the corner of her eyebrow, his fingers sinking in as his hold on her tightened further. "And it took meeting you to make me realize that I don't want to spend any more time doing that. I want to dig, to discover, but I know now it can mean so much more to me. Be so much more fulfilling. This is where I want to be. This is where I want to start my life again."

Her throat was tight with emotion, and she framed his face with her hands. "I just don't want you to regret this decision."

"I already know it's the right one."

She smiled a little then. "So confident."

He covered her hands. "I know in my heart this is right."
His eyes lit up again, and she could feel a kind of energy
shoot through him. "And any lingering doubts I might have
had were definitely put to rest later this morning with my
other discovery."

It filled her with immense pleasure to see him like this, so
excited, wound up. About life. And she realized then what
was so different about him. The shadows were gone. He
looked . . . open. Ready. "What other discovery?" she asked.

He took her hands, all but squeezing the life out of them.
"I know I promised you a long soak, but would you mind
taking a walk with me? I want to show you something." He
stopped, smiled a bit sheepishly, as if realizing how he must
be sounding. "Or we could go after, I guess."

She laughed, her heart feeling like it just might burst. And
that was okay with her. "My God, you can hardly stand still.
Does this have something to do with that other discovery?"

"Yes, but you'll have to dress more warmly. It's outside. In
the north woods."

"Well, there's a new twist on our relationship, you wanting me wearing *more* clothes."

He grinned. "It will just make it more fun to unwrap you
later."

"Promise?"

He surprised a squeal out of her by lifting her off her feet
and swirling her around. "Anything you want. Just come see
this with me." He all but dragged her into the bedroom.

Laughing, she let him. "I've never seen you like this."

He yanked her against his chest, kissed the daylights out of
her, then said, "That's because I've never been like this."
With a sigh he let her go. "But if we stay in here much longer,
it'll be dark before we get outside." His grin made her insides
go all shoogly. "Or tomorrow."

"I think that might fall under that 'anything I want' heading," she told him. "Just a fair warning."

"Done. As soon as we get back, you may do with me as

you will." He grabbed a sweater and some jeans and tossed them to her. "Meet me downstairs."

She felt almost giddy with excitement the entire time it took her to get dressed. This was a whole new side of the man she'd spent the past week falling in love with. It would take some getting used to. She'd known he could be intense. Boy did she know. But to see him like this over something else . . . well, she was grinning so stupidly, just picturing the look in his eyes, how excited he was, apparently she wasn't going to mind very much. She supposed she should have known he'd bring the same intensity to his work, to whatever interested him, as he did to making love to her. A complex man, her marauding Scot.

She wanted to hug herself, and she did give in to the urge to do a little victory shuffle. Because he was just that. *Her* marauding Scot.

"So," she said as she came down the stairs, only to find him waiting with her coat and hat in hand. "What's this discovery you made about?"

She turned and let him slide her coat on. Then sighed when he kissed the side of her neck as he tugged on her hat.

"Come on," he said, grabbing her hand. "I'll show you."

The cold wind took her breath away. And so did Taggart Morgan. The sun was shining down on them, Ballantrae was safe for a while longer, and he wasn't going to leave. What more could she ask for?

"So," he said, making her skip a bit to catch up to his long strides. "What do you know about the Pictish relics over in the north forest?"

The question caught her completely off guard and she paused, only to be tugged along as he kept walking. "What Pictish relics?" She frowned. "I don't think there are any relics or ruins in the north forest. I've wandered those woods my whole life. There are the remains of an abbey, over along the ridge to the south." She pulled on his hand to slow him down. "Are you saying you found something?"

He shot her a grin.

"But . . . how? I mean, how would you have even known where to look?" She finally tugged him to a complete stop. "What did you find?"

He turned then, took her other hand. "Remember when I was snooping through your books, while you were writing the other day? Well, I found an old text in there, having to do with Celtic history in this area. There was a folded page, with notes in the margins. It took some deciphering, but I realized that section of the book dealt with land that is now part of Ballantrae." He was all but bouncing on the balls of his feet, so she let him pull her ahead. "There was a hand-drawn map, which I copied." He grinned. "And this morning, I decided to go on a treasure hunt."

"You're very cute, you know that?"

He looked momentarily nonplussed. "This isn't a joke."

He'd said it so seriously, looked so affronted by the notion, that she squeezed his hand, tugged him close so she could kiss him noisily on the cheek. "I know, that's what makes you so cute."

He just looked at her. "It's history. History isn't cute."

She laughed. "Well, it is when you're telling it. Would you feel better if I said it was sexy? Because it's that, too."

He smiled then, and that other intent came back into his eyes. "Well, that might be a handy thing to know. Come spring anyway."

"Oh, I'll make sure to remind you."

He swung her close, and put his arm around her. "You won't have to. If it has to do with you naked in an outdoor setting, I won't forget. Trust me."

"So," she said, tucking herself under his arm and shamelessly using his body to block the wind. "What is it you found?"

"A stone circle."

"In the north forest?" she said, honestly confused. "I've wandered every inch of them, I played in those woods growing up. I'd know if there was a circle there. Besides, they're usually out in the open, aren't they? Not in the woods."

"I'm sure they were out in the open originally. According to the map, there was no forest there at all. Just several very old oaks." He smiled. "From little acorns grow, I guess."

"You do know stone circles aren't all that rare here."

His grin was a hint smug. "This one is."

"Wait a minute." She stopped again. "What is this all about? I mean, this is about more than you finding a stone circle, isn't it?"

"Maybe," he told her. "At least, I'm hoping it might be. You asked what I was going to do here. I know that even with my father's investment, you're having a hard time just maintaining here, much less making any real progress. I know you'll pick up more crofters in the spring, but with the village having problems as well," he paused, shrugged, "I was thinking maybe you could use the economic boost of having a few scientists move in. Maybe do a little digging."

Stunned by the suggestion, she pulled from his arms, pushed her hair from her face. "If you mean that I should let the government come in and take over restoration, I won't have that." Surely, despite his disconnect from his own heritage, even he understood she'd never agree to something like that.

"That's not what I meant at all." He took her hand, grew serious. "If you wanted that, you would have done it by now." He pulled her closer. "And frankly, I'm feeling a bit proprietary myself about that big pile of rocks. I just found it; I'm not about to help you hand it over to someone else."

"Okay," she said, relieved and feeling a little foolish for doubting him. "So what is this grand scheme then?"

"I want to explore the possibility of getting funding for a small-scale excavation in the north woods. And only in the woods."

"Why would anyone pay to dig up another stone circle?"

"I don't have the proper equipment with me, but my guess

is they are at least fifth century, possibly even earlier. Once I'd realized what I'd found, I didn't want to disturb it any more than I had." He squeezed her hands. "The altar stone is there, and the carvings are magnificent, Maura. So little is known about them really, the religion they practiced early on is much like the Druid religion, definitely pagan, but there is little definitive proof. They died out in the ninth century. Their carvings set them apart, though. So to find something like this, so well preserved by the elements because of the forest growth? It's truly amazing."

"Where are they? Why haven't I ever seen them?"

"You'd have to know where to look. They're all but buried beneath the overgrowth."

"The map led you to them?"

He nodded. "Hand-drawn, exquisite. A find in and of its own right, really. The text it was in was well over a hundred years old itself."

She took a moment to try and digest all of this. "Why didn't you tell me before?"

He smiled easily. "I was going to mention finding the book, ask if you knew anything about it. We seem to get sidetracked. A lot."

She grinned, and her body hummed just at the reminder. "But your specialty is Mayan history. If you really think it's worth pursuing, how can you make it happen?"

"That's why I went into the main house, to look for additional documentation."

"The books you brought up with you earlier." Her eyes widened. "So you found more information on it?"

"Some. Maybe not enough, but I only had a few hours of searching and you have a lot of books in that place. I wanted to be more sure before I told you, but—" He smiled sheepishly. "I couldn't stand it. I had to share the news with you."

Then the pieces fell into place. And her heart stuttered. "So, you're staying then because of the potential dig?"

He squeezed her hands, tugged her close, his gaze so intent

on hers, she couldn't look away. "I know I'm doing the right thing, by pursuing a career here. This find was just further proof, but I already knew. I began here, and I should have stayed here." He lowered his mouth to hers, kissed her. And it was both tender and filled with such promise. "But then if I had, I wouldn't have met you. Things happen as they do for a reason. Something I'm more convinced of now more than ever. I'm staying because I belong here, Maura. Because I don't want to be anywhere else."

"What would you have done if you hadn't discovered them?" She believed what he was telling her—it was hard not to when he looked at her with his whole heart in his eyes—but it had to be asked.

"There are digs on this continent, too, you know," he said, his smile teasing and confident. But then the amusement fled, and she could see that he was intent on making her understand, that it was important to him that she believe this. "But I did find the relics. And I truly believe I'm on to something. It won't be a huge excavation, and it may only last a couple of years, but   "

"Years?"

He nodded. "It won't be a huge boon to the local economy, but it will bring something to the castle coffers, and the village, too. The crew will probably want to lease the crofts closest to the woods, to set up quarters and an analysis center. And depending on the number of students that are brought on, we might even consider opening up part of the main house to them."

She didn't know where it came from, but the laugh just rolled out of her. It was one of shock really. "My God, you've really thought this all through, haven't you?"

"I can't help it," he said, cute all over again when he shrugged. "It's what I do. We don't have to do any of this if you don't want to."

But she could tell from the look on his face that it would nigh kill him if she said no. And, to be honest, now that she'd had all of ten minutes to think on it, she had to admit it was rather an exciting proposition. "It sounds wonderful, really, it's just that it's all so sudden."

"It will take a few months minimum before I know if I can put the funding together. It will be spring by then, which is the earliest they could start anyway." He squeezed her hands. "I want to contribute here. I want to take some of the burden from you. You shouldn't have to bear that weight alone. I don't know what we'll do when all is said and done on the excavation, but we have years to work on that."

"Years," she said again, only this time there was a tremor of trepidation, as it truly began to sink in. Years. With this man. At her side. In her bed. She should have laughed like a loon at the very idea of agreeing. Maura Sinclair, the woman who couldn't keep a relationship going much past a month, contemplating jumping into a full-time living arrangement with a man. For years.

And yet the hot thrill that very notion sent through her was so powerful and so strong it took her breath away.

His hold on her gentled then, and he pulled their joined hands up between them and brushed a kiss over her knuckles. "I'm overwhelming you."

"You are," she said, then did laugh in disbelief. "But if my heart's to be any judge, it's the best kind of overwhelmed to be."

His eyes glittered with a fierce joy. "I don't need any promise from you," he said, "other than you'll give this— give me—a try."

From somewhere, her old self surfaced, but it was almost a relief to know she was still in there. "I believe I've tried you out every way a woman possibly can."

He cocked his head, his lips curving in that way he had that made her toes curl. "So you have no more use for me then?"

She grinned, even as her bottom lip trembled. "Oh, I've a use or two for ye."

And she felt him tremble. "Maura—"

She pressed her fingers to his lips. "This—all of this—is so unexpected. I don't know what to say." Her smile, at first so tremulous, grew wider, and something settled inside her as she took that leap of faith. "But then you were so unexpected, and look how well that's turning out."

His smile was slow, and filled with such emotion, it made her throat tight. "So . . . that's a yes?"

"Aye." Then she wrapped her arms around his neck. "It only took three hundred years, but the Morgan finally came back to claim what was his. And you had the right of it. All this time lost, and all they had to do was be willing to try." She kissed him. "I can't believe we were the first ones to finally figure that out. But lucky for me, we were." Grinning, she slid from his arms. "Now come on, let's go look at our stone circle."

Chapter 21

Tag felt like he'd just had the entire world handed to him. And maybe, just maybe, he had. All he knew was that the most important part of it was standing right in front of him. "Maura—"

"Uh uh," she said, dancing out of his reach. "Because the way you're looking at me right now, we'll be back in the tower or naked right here on the ground." She took off on an easy run, shouting over her shoulder. "Last one to the woods has to be bath slave later."

He grinned. "Well, when you put it like that." And he took off at a dead run.

She was faster than she looked. And crafty, dodging and weaving. He scooped her off the ground about fifty yards from the edge of the woods, making her whoop with laughter as he spun her around. "Come on," he said, breathless and happier than he could ever remember being.

"This way." Most discoveries were shared with the dig crew, but this was his first time sharing this with someone he cared about. It was silly, but he was as nervous about it as he was excited.

She hopped in front of him and touched the first tree they came to, then smiled devilishly back at him. "Anything you say. Bath slave boy."

His grin spread. "We'll see who the real loser of this little contest is later."

Her eyes darkened, just at the suggestion, and the next thing he knew, he had her up against the closest tree, his mouth on hers. Relief, joy, excitement, anticipation all pounded through him and he couldn't go another moment without showing her, touching her, telling her. His hands were in her hair. Hers were fisted in his jacket. And they suddenly couldn't get enough of each other.

Lifting his head, his eyes blazed into hers. "It's always going to be like this, isn't it?" he said, his breath coming in short gasps. "Why do I know I will never have enough of you?"

"You've had me for centuries," she said, her smile sure and knowing. "And if that wasn't enough, then no, it never will be."

There was a story there, in her eyes. And he would hear it. But first . . . "This way," he told her, taking her hand, leading her into the woods, around trees that had stood here for centuries. Deeper into the forest they went, and he helped her over fallen trunks and through heavier undergrowth.

"How on earth do you know where you're going?" she asked.

"You don't forget something like this." A few minutes later, they climbed down a short, rocky embankment, and stopped in front of a mound of overgrowth. "There," he said, more breathless with anticipation than exertion. "See that tree?" He pointed to a massive trunk about fifteen yards away.

"The oak?" she said, pushing her hair from her face.

"The Picts were reputed to be very superstitious about trees. Especially oak trees."

"And you think they actually worshipped under that one?"

He nodded. "I know they did. The altar stone is there. They believed old, wise spirits resided in oak trees. They made sacrifices to them on altars built beneath them." He turned her around, then reached out to the overgrown mound, and very, very carefully, pushed away a small section of the leaf and shrub covering. "And then there is this."

Maura leaned forward, peering through the gloom of the forest, to see what he was so carefully exposing. "All I see is what looks like rock." She straightened. "This area isn't much more than a tumble of rocks. Why do you think this is a standing stone?"

He could have shown her the markings, but it took a trained eye to see past what looked like nothing more than weather marks. There was a more direct way to prove his find to her. He let the tangle of leaves and barbs shift back to cover the spot, then turned her and pointed to similar mounds dotted amongst the trees. "Look. See? There," he pointed. "And there, and there."

She gasped.

The circle wasn't that wide, and no one was likely to notice the pattern of the mounds, as the whole area was rocky strewn and overgrown. But once you noted the pattern, it was impossible not to see it for what it was.

"My God. To think I've walked through here so many times." She looked at him. "How did you ever find this?"

He pulled a folded piece of yellow paper from his jacket pocket. "This map."

She looked at the series of lines, squiggles and compass notations, then glanced up at him in disbelief. "You took this? And found this?" She swept an arm out before her.

He pulled her back against him, circling his arms around her waist, so they both stared out at the mounds before them. "What can I say? I'm good with directions."

"I'm beginning to think you're good at a whole lot of things."

He tucked her closer to his body. "You want to race me, double or nothing, back to the tower and test that theory out?"

She covered his hands with her own. He'd expected some smart remark, but instead she sighed and leaned back against him. "This is really something, isn't it?"

"Yes," he said, looking down at her, for once in his life, having something to look forward to, as well as back. "Yes, it is."

"There's an old man, in the village," she said, serious and intent. He could hear the wheels all but turning now and his grin was fierce with satisfaction. She understood. This would mean something to her.

"His name is Kester," she went on. "He's something of the village historian. If anyone knows anything of this, it would be him. Maybe we should pop down, have lunch, chat him up."

His arms tightened around her. "Thank you," he whispered against her hair, hoping she understood the depths of his gratitude. "For sharing this with me. For sharing all of this with me. And I'd very much like to meet this Kester." He kissed the side of her neck. "Tomorrow." When she arched her neck around to give him a surprised look, he smiled. "I don't want to share you quite yet." His smile grew. "In fact, I think someone has a bath promised to them."

"And a slave to go with it, if I'm no' mistaken." She turned in his arms, and the desire in her eyes was banked with a quiet intensity. "I want to make another deal with you."

"Does it involve racing?" he asked, smiling. "Because I'm afraid I'm somewhat hampered at the moment." She was tight up against him enough to know what he meant.

Her lips curved. "No racing. Ye've lost that one fair and square, there'll be no getting it back."

"Okay then, what's the deal?"

She cupped his cheek, pushed his hair from his face. "You tell me everything you know about these people, this place. I want to understand the power and pull of it, as you do." She searched his eyes. "And I'll tell you tales of the Morgans and Sinclairs that came after them. Ramsays, too."

He turned his head and pressed a kiss into the palm of her hand. "That's a deal," he said, looking back in her eyes, moved beyond words.

She pulled his mouth down to hers, and the kiss she gave him was a promise. A promise to try. And just as he knew they were standing in the middle of something very special, here in the north woods of Ballantrae, something possibly historic. He knew he was standing in the circle of something even more powerful as long as her arms were around him.

"Now," she said, when she finally lifted her head, her eyes lit with desire and need, "I believe I'd like that bath now."

"Does the slave get to be in the bath with you?" he asked.

She smiled then. "Only if he's very, very good."

He let his hands drift down between them, let his thumbs trace over the nipples he knew were hard beneath her coat. Still, her breath stuttered, and her throat worked as she swallowed. Hard. Settling his hands on her hips, he tugged her closer, then slid his palms around to cup her tight against him. "Why don't I let you be the judge of that?"

"Yes," she managed. "Why don't you."

He wouldn't exactly say they raced back to the tower, but they definitely didn't waste any time. He had his hands on her the moment the tower door shut behind them.

"Wait, wait," she said, breathless and laughing as she smacked at his hands. "We're going to do this properly."

He raised his eyebrows. "You have proper rules for bath slaves, do you?"

"Well, now that you mention it . . ." She pushed him toward the stairs as she dragged his coat off his arms. "I'm thinking naked bath slave has a really nice ring to it."

He was halfway up the stairs, and paused to look down at her, mouth curving into a lethal grin. "I think I can handle that."

She let her gaze drift slowly over him. "We'll see who handles what."

He started shucking his clothes right then and there.

She laughed. "My, you are impressionable."

"Just following your command, oh mistress of the bath," he said, a decidedly wicked note in his voice.

She climbed the stairs until she stood a riser or two below him and motioned for him to turn around. "Stop," she said, when his back was to her.

The next thing he felt was her hands skimming over his calves and up the outer flanks of his thighs. His body hardened and twitched as her hands slipped so close, but moved upward, over his stomach to his chest, as she stepped up behind him. "Just making sure you're up for the job," she whispered behind his neck.

"I only have one question," he asked, enjoying her brand of torture quite a bit.

"Ask it."

He dared to dart a quick glance over his shoulder. "Do you get to play bath slave next time? Because you're giving me some really interesting ideas here."

Her pupils shot wide and her lips parted at the mere suggestion of it, and it was all he could do not to haul her upstairs to bed right then and the hell with the damn bath. But he was definitely winning the next bet.

"I don't know," she said at last, but there was a rough undernote to her voice now. "I suppose you'll find out if you win the next bet."

Then she shocked him by smacking him right on the ass. And damn if that didn't make him twitch even harder.

"Upstairs."

"Yes, ma'am," he said with an amused smile. Oh, there was going to be another bet, and soon. Or maybe he'd just talk her into it. Either way, his turn was going to be a hell of a lot of fun.

He went right to the bathroom and turned on the taps,

then when the water was adjusted and steam began to rise, he put in the plug and reached across for the bath salts sitting on the wicker side stool. The fragrance was spicy rather than floral, which he thought suited her perfectly.

He rose to find her standing behind him, still fully dressed. Without being asked, he approached her, and slowly, perhaps even a bit deferentially, he began to undress her. He'd never been much for bedroom games—sex was difficult enough a maneuver in a hammock—so this was a new thing for him. And perhaps all the more fascinating because of it.

He drew her sweater off, then began unbuttoning the blouse she wore beneath it. After each button was released, he parted the fabric wider, and placed one kiss on the newly bared patch of skin. Her swift intake of breath told him he was on the right path. When she started to reach for her waistband, he caught her hands and put them down by her sides. "Allow me," he offered, his voice having gone deeper as well.

She kept her hands by her sides, but said nothing.

He walked around behind her, and skimmed the blouse down her arms slowly, letting the soft cotton drift along her skin before finally letting it drop to the floor. He kept his lips close to the nape of her neck, inhaling the scent of her mixed with the steamy fragrance of the bath. Fingering the thin straps of her bra, he dropped a kiss to a spot between her neck and the curve of each shoulder, as he slowly tugged the straps over her shoulders to let them dangle there.

Stepping closer, his body almost, but not quite, brushing up against her bare back, he skimmed his fingertips across her collarbone.

She sighed and her body swayed a little. He glanced up to see her eyes had drifted shut. His fingertips dipped down to trace the edge of her bra, then with as much patience as he could find, he slowly, so slowly, peeled the soft fabric back. She gasped as he let it scrape ever so lightly across her nipples, before freeing her breasts fully to his view. She sighed in disappointment when his hands left her, but gave no order otherwise.

He flicked open the hooks and her bra fell to the floor. Standing close once again, he sunk his teeth into one earlobe, making her gasp again, then moan softly when he took it into his mouth. "Tell me what you'd like me to do next," he whispered.

She shook her head slowly from side to side.

So he reached around her waist, careful to barely brush her skin with his, and freed the button on her pants. Again she swayed slightly, letting her back rest against his chest with a long sigh as he lowered the zipper, then pushed them down over her hips, taking her panties with them.

He slid his body down along hers, steadying her hips with hands when she swayed again. Now it was his palms skimming along her thighs, down to her calves. "Step free," he told her, holding her as she stepped out of her pants. He shoved them out of the way, then, still kneeling, gently turned her to face him. Slowly, so slowly he thought it might kill him, he skimmed his hands up the front of her body, dipping between her thighs, but not touching her where he knew she'd be wet and aching for it. He stood as his palms rode upward, barely testing the slight weight of her breasts, whispering over her nipples, making her jerk and moan, as he straightened completely and pushed his fingers through her hair and dropped one achingly tender kiss on her unsuspecting mouth.

She groaned deep in her throat, but just as she opened to him, he stepped back and scooped her into his arms. Her eyes flashed open in surprise and she quickly threw her arms around his neck for support.

"What are you—"

"Shh," he soothed. "Let me take care of you." His cock was so rigid by now it was painful, but he was enjoying every minute of attending to her. It was worth a little discomfort. He carefully lowered her into the steaming, silky water, making her groan as her body unfolded and stretched out the length of the tub.

"Lay back," he told her, dropping a folded towel over the higher curved end, then reaching for a washcloth from the pile on the wicker stand. "Close your eyes."

He turned off the taps, then knelt next to the tub, wanting to squeeze his eyes shut, too, against the absolutely stunning picture she presented. He wanted nothing more than to slide in that warm water with her, lift her over him, so he could sink into her until he filled her so fully, so tightly—

He had to shut that track down, and momentarily closed his eyes to find some thread of control. Then he dipped the cloth in the water and began at her ankles, slowly, gently working his way up her legs. She was writhing ever so slightly by the time he reached the top of her thighs, and he drew the towel slowly between them, making them both groan when she arched.

Before either of them could lose control, he slid the towel upward, trailing one corner around her breasts, then letting it barely drift across her nipples. Her groan was so deep, it was more growl than moan. She arched her head back, thrusting forward, seeking out the feel of the towel across her nipples again. Once, twice, he gave her what she wanted. Then he dropped the towel and ran his fingers over them instead, rolling them gently, making her hips jerk, the water slosh. Her hands came up to grip the sides of the tub as he rescued the cloth and once again drew it down to the vee of her thighs, only this time he let it lay more heavily, drew it across her more slowly, until her knuckles whitened and her legs trembled from the restraint it took for her not to take hold of the rag and finish herself off.

"Tell me if you want something more," he told her. "Perhaps you'd prefer this." He dropped the towel and slid his finger between her slick, heated folds. "Or this." And he entered her, sending her immediately over the edge. She bucked, water edged over the tub, cascading over his thighs and his rigid, dancing cock. And her eyes opened then and she looked directly into his, her climax still ripping over her.

And his control snapped.

He slid his arms beneath her, pulling her from the tub in a cascade of water, still shuddering and moaning, so soft and pliant, wet and slippery. Heedless of the mess he was making, he carried her to the bed and her back had barely come into contact with the sheets when he was on top of her, and in her with one long growling thrust.

She arched instantly, clutching at his shoulders and back, her legs wrapping tightly around his waist as he drove into her, again and again. And his own climax was upon him before he could master any semblance of control over it, so he buried himself to the hilt and let it take him over, shouting through the deep, shuddering spasms that rocked him, and her, right to the edge of the bed.

He managed to catch her before they both slid to the floor, and rolled so she was sprawled across him, wet and damp, the sheets clinging to them both.

They were both breathing so hard, it took long minutes before either of them could lift their heads, much less for speech. Maura's hand finally slid up and over his still-thundering heart.

"Remind me," she rasped, "to win every bet from now on."

He laughed hoarsely. "Shouldn't be too hard since I plan on throwing every single one."

He finally found the strength to pull her up next to him, and rolled so they faced each other. He pushed the wet tangle of hair from her face and looked into those eyes he'd already come to cherish. Again he was assailed with the sense, so much stronger now that they'd admitted their feelings to one another, that he'd looked into these eyes for eons. "You said, earlier, that I've had you for centuries. What did you mean?"

She looked a bit surprised by the question, but smiled and

settled herself a bit more comfortably in his arms. "How much do you know of the history of Rogues Hollow?"

Now he was surprised. "I know the three men who founded it left Scotland to escape the hangman's noose for their crimes."

"That much is true," she said. "Your ancestor, Teague Morgan, was quite the scoundrel, as were his cohorts Iain Sinclair and Dougal Ramsay. He and Dougal's sister, Lillith, were lovers. In fact, when he left, she was pregnant with his child."

Tag's eyebrows lifted. "Did he know?"

She nodded. "Oh yes. It's said the two were fated, that it was quite the love match. Unfortunately they were from opposite sides of warring clans. And more unfortunate still, Teague lost Ballantrae to Dougal and Lillith's brother."

"In battle?"

She smiled. "In a game of cards."

"What?"

"His father and brother had been killed fighting a battle alongside the MacKays, taking Ballantrae from the Sinclairs. The Ramsay chief then won it from Teague before the blood had dried on the fields, and promptly made it a dowry for his sister, Lillith, who he quickly betrothed to Calum Sinclair as a way to bind their clans together against further attacks from the MacKays and Morgans."

"So why didn't she leave with Teague?"

"An ocean crossing was no place for a pregnant woman. But Teague was facing the noose, as were her brother Dougal and Calum's younger brother Iain."

"What of Calum? And Lillith's brother? They were clan chiefs, they couldn't protect their own flesh and blood from the hangman?"

"I don't think they wanted to. They didn't trust Teague and it was well known the three were quite in cahoots, despite the battles raging amongst their clans. Lillith herself urged them to flee. She swore she'd follow when she was able, and bring Teague's child to him."

"Did she?"

Maura shook her head. "Calum got wind of the plan and kept her on a very short leash. Basically by keeping her pregnant with his own bairns."

Tag's eyes widened then as another realization struck him. "The Bible, the one in the cherrywood box."

"Yes, that was hers. The son she bore to Teague didn't survive his fifth year, according to the notes written in the Bible. So it went to her daughter, a daughter she had with Calum. The story goes that she passed it down to Carys, in the hopes that one day she'd carry it to Teague herself, or his own offspring, had he any."

"Only Carys never made it to America."

"No," Maura said. "But it stayed in Sinclair hands, handed down in a tangled chain, from daughter to son, son to brother, sister to sister, generation to generation." She met his gaze as she wove her fingers through his and held them to his heart. "Until it ended up with me."

"Three centuries," he said quietly and reached up to stroke her cheek. "A history forever entwined. Forever apart."

"Until now." Her smile was filled with contentment, her eyes glassy with emotion. "We finally brought them back together."

Tag pulled her close, rolled so she was beneath him. And when he kissed her this time, he finally understood the promise he felt, the promise he was making. And he reveled in the rightness of it. "Together," he vowed. "Right where we belong."

Please turn the page for an advance look

at Diane Whiteside's

THE IRISH DEVIL,

coming next month from Brava . . .

Donovan & Sons was busier than usual, with men working hard to load a series of wagons. Viola's eyes passed over them quickly, seeking one particular fellow clad in a well-tailored suit. He could be found occasionally in a teamster's rough garb but only when driving a wagon. His clean-shaven face was always a strong contrast to every other man's abundant whiskers.

Her eyes lingered on a midnight head above broad shoulders, tugging hard on a wagonload's embracing ropes. The right height and build but red flannel? Then the man turned and Donovan's brilliant blue eyes locked with hers.

Viola gulped and nodded at him.

His eyebrows lifted for a moment then he returned her silent greeting. He strode toward her, still gentlemanly despite his dust. She was barely aware of his men's curiosity.

"Mrs. Ross. It is an honor to see you here." Her grandmother would have approved of his handshake but not his appearance. His black hair was disheveled, his clothing was streaked with dust, his scent reeked of horses and sweat.

And his shoulders looked so much more masculine under the thin red flannel than they ever had in English broadcloth.

She swallowed and tried to think logically. She was here to gain his protection, no matter what distractions his appearance offered.

William smiled down at Viola, curious why she'd come to the depot. Probably for money to return back East.

"May I have a word with you in private, Mr. Donovan?"

Poor lady, she sounded so awkward and embarrassed. "Certainly. We can use the office," he soothed and led the way across the yard. "Would you care for some fresh tea or coffee?"

"No, thank you. What I have to say should not take long."

She must want a seat on the next stagecoach out of town, if the conversation must be fast. Buy her that ticket and she'd be gone in a day. Bloody hell.

William ushered her into the small room, bare except for the minimum of furniture, all solid, scarred, and littered with paperwork.

She accepted the indicated seat but was wretchedly nervous, almost fidgeting in her chair. He wanted to snatch her up and swear the world would never hurt her again, then hunt down Charlie Jones and his fool wife. William closed the wooden shutters on the single window, filtering out much of the light and noise from the bustling corrals, then settled into his big oak swivel chair.

"What can I do for you, Mrs. Ross?" He kept his voice gentle, his California drawl soft against the muffled noises from outside.

She took a deep breath, drew herself up straight and tall, and launched into speech. "May I become your mistress, Mr. Donovan?"

"What?! What the devil are you talking about?" he choked, too stunned to watch his language. He knew his mouth was hanging open. "Are you making a joke, Mrs. Ross?"

"Hardly, Mr. Donovan." She met his eyes directly, pulse pounding in her throat. "You may not have heard but my business partner sold everything to Mr. Lennox."

He nodded curtly. He must have been right before: she needed money. "I met Mr. and Mrs. Jones on their way out of town. I won't be doing business with them again," he added harshly.

"Quite so. But my only choices now are to marry Mr. Lennox or find another man to protect me. I'd rather be yours than an Apache's."

"Jesus, Mary and Joseph," William muttered as he stood and began to pace. Think, boyo, think. She deserves better than being your woman. Heat lanced from his heart down his spine at the thought of her in his arms every night. Marriage? No, she'd never agree to a Catholic ceremony. "There are other men, men who'd marry you," he pointed out hoarsely.

"I will not remarry. Besides, Mr. Lennox blocked all offers other than his."

"Son of a bitch." The bastard should be shot. "What about your family?"

"They disinherited me when I married Edward. Both families refused my letters informing them of his death."

How the devil could a parent abandon their child, no matter what the quarrel? His father had given everything to protect his children.

William's gut tightened at the thought. Condoms were helpful but not a guarantee. If she stayed in his bed long enough, the odds were good . . .

"You could become pregnant," he warned, his eyes returning to her face. Blessed Virgin, what he wouldn't do to see Viola proud and happy, holding his babe in her arms.

"I can't have children."

"The fault could be in the stallion, not the mare," William suggested, his drawl more pronounced. And this stallion would dearly love to prove his potency where another had failed.

And here's a sizzling sneak peek

at our new Brava anthology

HOW TO BE A WICKED WOMAN,

and Susanna Carr's "Wicked Ways."

What am I doing here? Peyton wondered as the man's groin invaded her personal space. It took all her willpower not to flinch, even as the musky scent of arousal and masculine sweat assailed her flared nostrils. She tried to maintain a casual pose, but every muscle in her body hummed with tension. Her hands clenched underneath her chair. Her rigid fingertips brushed against something gooey.

It's gum. She assured herself. *Please let it be gum.*

"Hey, I know you," the blond god said as he placed his hands behind his head and displayed his magnificent shaven chest. He rotated his hips to the restless beat. "You're my boss at Lovejoy's Unmentionables."

Peyton flashed him a tight smile. "That's right," she admitted. *Is there no end to this night? Why did she think she would have gone unnoticed? Nothing else was going her way.*

But who was he? She hadn't really been looking at his face. She squinted as the disco ball spun crazily, swirling white dots of light over everyone. "Bubba Joe from shipping?" she ventured a guess. "I'm sorry, I didn't recognize you . . ."

"Yeah, that's because I'm incognito," he said and punctuated each syllable of the last word with short pelvic thrusts.

Okay. . . .

"You know this is my alter ego." He gripped the back of

her chair. She felt like she was caged in testosterone. "But call me by my stage name, Hubba Bubba."

"Did you come up with that all by yourself?" Peyton willed her arms to stay at her sides, although her elbows started creeping in.

"Nah. I ain't that creative. It was the nickname girls gave me in high school." He got off her and Peyton slowly let out a relieved sigh. It lodged in her throat as he turned around and straddled her again, this time clenching and unclenching his buttocks. His bare buttocks. To the beat of the music. In her face.

"So whatcha doing here, Miz Lovejoy?" he asked as he turned around again. "This ain't no place for someone like you."

Tell me about it. "Entertaining some business clients." Why wasn't this song over? She didn't remember it lasting this long. Wagner's operas were shorter than this.

"All these women wearing black?" He nodded his head to the women sitting at the table, flexing their fingers wildly as they hollered about what they wanted to do with his butt. "I thought you guys just came back from a funeral or something."

No. it just felt that way. "They're here to relax." And to see if she was one of them. If she was willing to be a team player. She wasn't sure if she was succeeding.

"They could save Lovejoy's?" He did a cat stretch before dipping his spine. Peyton was momentarily entranced by the play of muscles until she realized he was rubbing his full erection against her black straight skirt.

Her knees knocked together. "We might reach an agreement that could bring us a lot of money," she replied hoarsely. Did everyone know about the company's financial troubles? "Nothing's definite yet."

Bubba Joe leaned in close until all she could see was his tight nipple. If she spoke, her lips would press against his slick skin. Peyton felt her cheeks turn a vivid red. "You want me to be real nice to them?" he whispered into her ear. His hot breath stirred the tendrils of her hair that escaped from her French twist. "Give them a private showing?"

Peyton winced. Oh, yeah. That's what she needs to do; make her employees studs for the night. "Thanks for the offer," she said graciously. "It's very generous, but I want you to come out alive."

He flicked a look at the group of women. His smile kicked up a notch, overflowing with confidence. "Don't worry, Miz Lovejoy, I can handle it."

It seemed like everyone could handle the evening but her. "I think it would be best if you didn't treat them differently. Why don't you go over there now?" She hoped the ah-ah-ahs from the speakers drowned out the desperation leaking in her voice.

He glanced down. Pointedly. Peyton reluctantly followed his gaze. Were the strobe lights doing something to her eyes or did those leopard spots seem bigger?

"You need to tip me."

"Oh, Oh!" She forgot about the dollar bill that was scrunched into her fist and probably stuck to the gum. Peyton tore it from under her chair and offered it to him.

Bubba Joe dipped his head next to hers. "No, Miz Lovejoy, I can't take the money. It's against the rules. You have to put it on me."

On him? He was her employee! Peyton's polite smile wavered. She cleared her throat nervously. "Of course." The heat emanating from his snug G-string scorched her hovering hand. She changed her mind and crammed the mangled dollar over the minuscule string on his hip, the furthest place away from any private parts. "I don't want to injure you."

"You couldn't. This is designed for protection from over-eager hands." His splayed fingers framed the leopard skin.

Peyton was at a loss. "Love the fabric," she finally said.

Bubba Joe smiled proudly. "Thanks. My mom made it for me."

An image of his quiet mother hunched over an industrial sewing machine popped in her mind. "She always does excellent work."

"I'll be sure to tell her you think so," he said as he strutted away. "See ya, Miz Lovejoy."

Peyton closed her eyes. Oh, God. She didn't want his mother to know she was anywhere around Bubba Joe's G-string! Her stress headache threatened to erupt into a full-blown migraine. Peyton shot up from her seat. She needed a break. She almost wished she smoked so she could have the excuse of escaping outside.

She sure couldn't get excited about this place. What was wrong with her? Why couldn't she be as enthusiastic as the other women in the crowd? They acted like they'd been trapped in a convent since puberty and were just recently released. She felt like if you've seen one half-naked man show off his package, you've seen them all.

As she waited in line for the bathroom, Peyton noticed the empty men's room. If she really wanted a moment's peace, that would be the place to go. She decided to take the risk of entering. Chances were she'd seen what was in there already displayed on the stage. The moment she stepped across the threshold, Peyton gagged from the stench. She clasped her hand over her mouth and nose and tiptoed her way through the debris to the row of sinks.

She pinched the edges of a coarse paper towel dangling from the chrome dispenser and blotted the sweat from her face. The humid June night managed to sneak its way into the strip joint despite the air conditioners chugging continuously.

Peyton looked at the row of sinks and tried to decide which one looked the least infectious. Turning the faucet knob with her elbow, she ran tepid water over the paper towel and pressed the damp wad onto the back of her neck.

She closed her eyes and sighed with relief before blowing the wisps of hair that tickled her forehead. Peyton opened her eyes and looked at her reflection. She looked—boring.

No, that wasn't true. She wouldn't let it be true. Peyton straightened in front of the mirror. There was nothing boring about her. Her job wasn't boring. It was challenging and demanding. Her social life wasn't dull. She had a group of wonderful, interesting friends.

No boyfriend right now, but not because she was boring! Peyton straightened her shoulders and tossed the wet towel in the vicinity of the stuffed trash can. None of her ex-boyfriends ever had complaints in that area. She knew how to have fun.

Even in bed. Peyton snapped her jacket collar into its perfect position. She'd had plenty of amazing sex in her life. Fantastic. Unreal. Okay, she hadn't quite accomplished multiple orgasms, but she was beginning to think that was an urban legend.

And so what if she hadn't had any sex recently? She'd been busy. Peyton briskly tugged the edge of her suit jacket. Everyone thought she was so lucky to have inherited the family business. They didn't see the struggle behind the scenes. They didn't understand the fear of being the Lovejoy who lost it all.

Peyton watched her left eyebrow arch. Her mouth set into a determined line as she hiked her chin up a notch.

I'll show them. I'll show them all. Peyton Lovejoy has what it takes to turn around the company.

She ripped open her jacket like a first-time flasher. What she didn't have in content, her enthusiasm should have made up for it with extra bonus points. She shrugged off her jacket and clenched it in one hand, her eyes intent on her reflection.

Peyton Lovejoy is not a dork or a loser. She is a wild, wicked woman who gets what she wants.

Her hair was next. The French twist had to go. She clawed out the pins with determined fingers and gave her straight brown hair a good toss. It didn't billow like the hair color commercials, but fell and landed onto her bare shoulders.

Peyton Lovejoy . . .

She made a face.

. . . has got to stop referring herself in third person because it's really annoying.

She gave her appearance another once-over. With a sharp nod of approval, she swung her jacket over her shoulders with two fingers and strutted to the door, pausing only to kick a fragment of paper off her heel.

Watch out world, here I come.

She exhaled sharply and—stood still.

Who was she kidding? Peyton dipped her chin. She needed those women execs more than they needed her. "If I have to walk across town stark naked, I will do whatever it takes to save my family's company."

She blinked and looked around the skuzzy stall. Not exactly Scarlett O'Hara shaking her fist with the sun setting behind her in blazing red.

It didn't matter, Peyton decided. She was going to be a sexy young thing if it killed her. She was going to walk the walk, talk the talk. But how was she going to convince those women out there? They were the real things and could spot a pretender.

Peyton paced the floor in front of the urinals, dodging sodden paper towels. She mulled over the problem before she opened her purse and grabbed her cell phone. She needed information and quickly. Peyton hit the speed dial. Accurate info because she didn't have the luxury to make any mistakes.

"Main Library Answer Hotline," the low masculine voice rumbled in her ear. "This is Mike. How can I help you?"